Lovin' 2 Leading Ladies

Deborah Holness

This book is dedicated to:

You! Thank you for choosing this book to read. I hope you enjoy it, and it raises a smile as was its intention.
Also, every parent that has ever endured the never-ending battle against glitter: may your vacuum cleaner stay strong and your patience intact.
And finally, to Maxine, whose kind words and encouragement over some misdelivered toilet rolls gave me the boost I needed to press on and finish what I'd started.

Contents

Chapter One

✦

I get back to my apartment and head straight to the ice box, retrieving a bag of frozen peas and holding it to my throbbing jaw. Jeez, that jerk Mitchel Dalton can pack one hell of a punch. He's lucky I'm trying to avoid any unnecessary attention, or he could have found himself on the receiving end of a right hook. As it is, it was better for me to fade into the background after his little display of aggression. That way, the focus remained on his unruly behaviour, and it didn't escalate to include me too much.

Up until four years ago, I wouldn't have been so complaisant. I'd been in more than my fair share of brawls growing up. My parents had pulled out all the stops to give my sister and me a decent education on a limited budget, working all the hours under the sun and ferrying us back and forth miles on daily basis to the school we hated with a passion. Being the kids from the wrong zip code in Beverly Hills all but made us outcasts with a target on our backs all through high school. I showed everyone I was a force to be reckoned with early on, challenging any snide comments and toxic behaviour at every opportunity. I took down the boys that picked on us one fist fight at a time, garnering me a certain level of respect amongst our peers, one that made them think twice before trying to take me on. For the most part it pretty much guaranteed I was left alone by anyone who didn't want their good looks marred with a few battle scars.

My sister, Ava, was the sensitive type, quiet and shy, she suffered mercilessly at the hands of the mean girls when I wasn't around to ward off any unwelcome attention. Girls were cruel, I should have learnt this from the way they treated my sister and the tears that she shed on a daily basis. I couldn't hit them like I had the boys, I wasn't raised that way. I had to find a different approach to bring them down. I had been blessed in the looks department, girls were drawn to me, so I seduced every one that had hurt my sister, playing them all off against each other before walking away unrepentant and unyielding, leaving them alone, miserable and in tears, just as they had her. Did I feel guilty? Not one bit.

Ava was in the year below me, so when I graduated, I was pleased that she found an ally in a guy that transferred in a few months before I left. He was tall, good-looking, and could have had the pick of any of the girls at the school, (after I'd finished with them of course). He chose Ava, saw in her what others refused to, her natural good looks, sweetness and generosity. He fought for her attention on a daily basis, chasing her relentlessly until she finally succumbed to his charm and agreed to let him take her out on a date.

Their relationship got off to a rocky start thanks to yours truly. She was my baby sister and I had to look out for her. I warned him off more than once, believing his intentions to be less than honourable. Thankfully, he wasn't easily deterred, ignoring me and continuing his pursuit, finally persuading her to sneak out of the house to meet him in secret one evening. I was furious when I realised that she was missing and ended up searching for them for hours. I never discovered where they went or what they did in the time they were together, Ava would never say, but I do know at some point during her absence a magical transformation occurred. She returned deliriously happy, and looking very dishevelled. The tears I was used to seeing on a daily basis dried up never to return. Despite my initial concerns, the pair of them became inseparable. Ava started to relax and enjoy life again. They married at twenty-one, and welcomed their twin sons at twenty-three. Even now, eight years on, they couldn't have been happier and more in love.

Although I was happy for Ava, my own experiences with the opposite sex had skewed my objectivity as far as love was concerned. As Ava started her new life with her husband, I preferred to concentrate on my dream of becoming a lawyer. I guess high school taught me that I wanted to find a way to help protect the 'little guy' from the rich assholes who always seemed intent on tearing them down.

However, when I found out how much my studies were going to cost, I had no option but to defer university while I tried to find a way of raising some cash. I started taking any and every job I could find to raise a few bucks. I worked through the alphabet of employment opportunities, doing everything from tending bars to washing cars. I didn't care where the money came from. One ad I answered was to become a runner at Universal Studios in Hollywood. I never thought I'd get hired, let alone end up working for some of the most influential people in the movie-making industry. The day I applied they were obviously desperate, I was in the right place at the right time, and that was that.

It didn't take me long to get hooked on the whole movie scene and for my dreams to evolve. It wasn't just the promise of a huge payday and lavish lifestyle if I could make it big. It was more than that. It was the ability to escape my own reality and try things I would never normally be able to do. I worked damn hard and learnt from some of the best in the business. I made sure I became friends with all the right people, and eventually I started getting pulled into scenes as an extra. Initially, they were only small non-speaking roles, then one day, I was asked to deliver a line. It was like all my Christmases had come at once. To sit in a faux diner and have to murmur, "Pass the salt," in a 'brisk unassuming manner' to the main character, wasn't exactly living the dream, but we all had to start somewhere. When I made my debut in a fleeting appearance on the big screen, my family and I went so crazy in the movie theatre, we almost got asked to leave.

I was still so excited the following day I made it my mission to get myself an agent, the cheapest I could find. My search led me to a guy called Jerimiah, Jerry if he liked you, whose card I found lying on a beer-stained table in a sleazy club one night when I was out to get laid. It turned out Jerry worked from a trailer on a piece of wasteland, and being an agent wasn't his sole profession. I didn't like to ask what other income streams he had, especially when he agreed to work solely on commission for the first year. I don't think either of us were expecting much from the other, and both thought after the year was up, we could walk away from the deal and each other with no hard feelings.

I should have had a little more faith. Jerry hooked me up with a few auditions before I got the opportunity of modelling some underwear for a famous designer brand. The money was good and I was behind on my rent, so I agreed, thinking my picture would be used in a small thumbnail in some advertising campaign I'd probably never see. I certainly didn't expect to find myself half naked and plastered on billboards all over the city.

In the space of a day my life changed exponentially. Much to my surprise more modelling offers came flooding in, but I turned them all down much to Jerry's chagrin. I wanted to be a big movie star and didn't want to go down that path. With a few thousand in the bank, I decided to bide my time and wait for the next call to audition in the field I wanted to pursue. Jerry helped me secure a small role in my first major movie soon after, ironically being cast as an attorney with a chip on his shoulder. The film wasn't a huge success, but it was great experience, and showcased my talents for being more than just a pretty face. After that, and despite being called to auditions frequently, it was a while before I got my next big break. When it came, none of us were prepared for the aftermath that followed.

My second movie turned out to be an unprecedented success. A victory made even sweeter by the fact Mitchel Dalton had originally turned down the role I ended up accepting. He'd demanded his full fee in advance, the production company couldn't afford the price tag he'd set, so reluctantly started looking for a more cost-effective solution. Compared to Mitchel, who was already a solidified A-lister, I was a relative unknown at the time, still struggling to make ends meet while trying to establish myself in the fickle acting industry. Jerry fought my corner with a passion I'll never forget, and will always be grateful for. He changed both our lives. The month he started his negotiations for me to get the job, turned out to be one of the best, and worst, of my life. Jerry made sure I attended any and every event he could get me in to, increasing my profile and spectacularly catapulting me back into the public eye. As people began to recognise me from my past successes, I started to become more of a household name, and I was finally offered the part in the movie for a fraction of the fee that had been budgeted for Mitchel.

As it turns out, Jerry was extremely good at his job. To help seal the deal, he negotiated a small percentage of the profits in lieu of an even larger pay reduction at the start. I balked when he told me what he had done, but it was clearly the best decision he had ever made even if I couldn't see it at the time. The salary that I lost at the outset was reinvested into the production to create a polished feature that attracted cinemagoers in droves. Jerry made us both very rich when the film became an overnight success. Our share of the profits was greater than we could have ever imagined. Neither of us were expecting the movie to take off the way it did. Jerry told me after, he just believed it would be another stepping stone along my path to success, another credit to expand my filmography, and a further platform to showcase my skills for future employment.

It definitely helped that I had the specific look the director wanted. Mitchel and I weren't that dissimilar, we were around the same age and both a little over six foot tall. He was a few pounds heavier than me, all of it muscle, but my regular trips to the gym were rapidly closing that gap between us. We both had brown hair and eyes, although my hair was a couple of shades darker. He had been voted

Sexiest Man Alive in some celebrity magazine whose title escapes me. Remarkably, I had come in a close second, thanks to the underwear campaign I had modelled for. It also earned me the title of Nicest Ass in the same issue. I would have loved to have been a fly on the wall when Mitchel discovered he had lost that accolade when reading further down the page.

Things just got better and better after that. Job offers came flooding in, I upgraded my dingy studio apartment to a plush new condo in West Hollywood, I was able to buy my sister her dream home on the outskirts of Morro Bay, and I made sure my parents were able to give up work and go on the world cruise they had always dreamed of, but could never afford. After my family was taken care of, I partied hard until the universe decided I needed a new challenge, delivering a shocking surprise that forced me to change my priorities yet again. I suddenly found myself shouldering a huge secret that I was willing to protect at all cost.

I honestly didn't know when the feud between Mitchel Dalton and me started, or why he hated me so much. Maybe he was pissed he lost out on the role that had shot me to fame, or more likely, he was just another entitled asshole intent on throwing his weight around. Sure, my popularity was rising steadily, and I was giving him a run for his money at the box office these days, but surely there was enough room at the top for both of us.

With hindsight, when his date at the charity gala we had both been attending asked me to dance,

I probably should have declined. Ever since they had arrived together, Mitchel had gone out of his way to make it abundantly clear he didn't want me anywhere near her. Mitchel's father was a well-renowned plastic surgeon. I started to wonder if his skills had been utilized in attaching Mitchel's arm to his date, given how tightly he clung to her for most of the night. I'd never seen him so gaga over one woman. He had a reputation for playing the field, but I could tell by the way he looked at her that this one was different from his usual conquests. I must admit the devil on my shoulder prompted me to ask to cut in when they were dancing. I knew it would piss him off and the likelihood of him agreeing would be slim to none. Even so, I had to let the cocky SOB know that I was no pushover. Especially after he spent the evening crowing to his friends about how he raised significantly more than I did at the bachelor auction we both got tricked into signing up for. His date, Jen, looked at me apologetically when he not so politely told me to move along. I did, the incredulous look on his face that I even had the gall to suggest I steal her away for a few minutes, was enough to appease the masochist within me.

Imagine my surprise when an hour later I saw her standing alone after having evidently shaken off her limpet for a few moments. It was obvious she wasn't used to attending these sorts of events. She looked like a fish out of water as she nervously scanned the room looking for her date. I could remember how intimidating these lavish functions could be when you weren't used to them. How daunting it was to suddenly find yourself alone and abandoned amongst a room full of the wealthy social elite, some of whom believed manners were something that could be bought if they didn't deem them to be a waste of money. I only wandered in her direction to check she was alright and to appease my guilt for making her feel uncomfortable when I had riled Mitchel up. I never expected her to apologise to me for Mitchel's attitude, and for her to go on to ask me to dance. We got chatting, and I was surprised to find as well as being gorgeous on the outside, she was beautiful on the inside too. She was sweet, funny and kind, nothing like the usual narcissists that I often rubbed shoulders with at these functions. I wasn't surprised Mitchel had snapped her up, and even after she made it abundantly clear that she would always favour Dalton over me in the romance stakes, how could I refuse the offer of taking her for a spin around the dance floor? I was just gearing up to ask if she had any like-minded single friends she might want to introduce me to, when we were unceremoniously interrupted. I could tell by her change in demeanour trouble was headed my way. I only got the chance to murmur his name before Mitchel laid one on me and then dragged the poor girl from the room like a caveman. I hope she gave him hell after.

Thankfully, security at the event had been tight. I was lucky to escape with minimal backlash from our altercation. That served me well, as I had to get on the road and needed to make sure I wasn't being followed.

I scrub my hand down my face, wincing as it drags across my swollen jaw. I'm so damn tired, but my sister is waiting for me, and there is no way I am going to let her down after all she has done for me over the last few years. It would be easier to leave now and make the drive tonight. There would be less traffic on the road; not only would it cut down my travel time, it would also make it easier to spot anyone tailing me. These days, I have to be sneaky. My desire to keep my personal and professional life separate is becoming more challenging as my fan base rapidly increases. Privacy is getting harder and harder to maintain, and I didn't set out to shroud myself in a mystery that the press and public became determined to decode; it happened gradually through circumstance.

I couldn't have been more shocked by the knock on my door that changed the trajectory of my life a few years back. I believed my dreams of continuing to forge a successful acting career were suddenly over. The thought of losing my fast-flowing income and the never-ending stream of women willing to cater to my darkest desires was a bitter pill to swallow. I was suddenly forced to make some unwelcome lifestyle adjustments. It was Ava's turn to support me as I navigated these major changes. With the support of my sister and my ability to function on little to no sleep, I was able to return to work after only a few months off.

I don't think I slept for about a year after that. Learning how to juggle my work commitments with the new responsibilities that had been thrust upon me was harder than I could have ever imagined. By then, I was so well-known that my often abrupt and unexpected disappearances from Hollywood began to make me an enigma—a puzzle that everyone competed to be the first to solve. The harder people tried to uncover my secret, the more determined I became to conceal it. I found it ironic that each time I shunned the limelight, interest in me spiked, propelling me back into the spotlight I was trying to avoid. Gradually, my need to party into the early hours, consume excessive alcohol, partake in dick swinging contests, and engage in short-term romances dwindled away, becoming a thing of the past. None of it held any interest for me anymore. I still went out on occasion. Although when I did, I drunk in moderation and tended to pick my battles, avoiding confrontation rather than instigating it, hence my walking away from Mitchel's little display of aggression earlier. I still wasn't a monk, far from it, but I was much less impulsive and more discerning over who I invited to share my bed these days. I'd learnt the hard way that impetuous actions could have unforeseen consequences.

After tossing the bag of now defrosted peas in the sink, I jump in a cold shower to help wake myself up for the drive ahead. I throw on some old clothes, jeans and a T-shirt, and don't bother to shave the five o'clock shadow that is already starting to dust my features. It's a struggle to squeeze my frame into the T-shirt I grab. It feels at least one size too small as it clings to me like a second skin. There's no point in changing, all my clothes are getting snug thanks to the hours of rigorous training I've been putting in at the gym instead of going out. If truth be told, I need a whole new wardrobe. It's not that money is an issue, my burgeoning bank balance is nine figure healthy, it's just that shopping isn't really my thing. If I can put it off I will, all the time I can squeeze into what I already own, it will just have to do.

I grab my grey hold-all from the top of the wardrobe and throw in a few more clothes, then don an old baseball cap and head out of my apartment to the lift that takes me straight to the underground garage. I pause in front of the bright green Lamborghini that has been a gift to myself thanks to my expanding bank balance. Bypassing the supercar, I head for the vehicle parked next to it. It's covered, not because it needs protecting, more to prevent nosey neighbours from recognising it and associating it with me. It makes it easier to run around unnoticed if no one knows I own the beat-up, black pick-up nestled underneath. It's registered in my sister's married name. Even so, with a tiny bit of detective work, anyone could forge it's connection to me. I'm surprised I've managed to keep it under wraps, no pun intended, this long. I grab the end of the cover, yanking it off with one determined pull, rolling it haphazardly before throwing it in the back of the vehicle. It's nearing half past two in the morning. If traffic is on my side, I should be able to reach my destination sometime before six, even allowing for the stop I'll have to make along the way to pick up the double espresso that will help keep me alert enough to drive.

I jump into the cab of the truck, putting my bag on the seat beside me, and opening the driver's side window before placing the key in the ignition impatient to be on my way. The ageing engine splutters a couple of times before roaring into life on my third attempt to get it started.

"I'm on my way baby," I whisper into the darkness, as I put my foot down and creep out into the night.

I make good time and pull into the driveway of the ranch-style home I bought for my sister, half an hour earlier than anticipated. I fumble in the glove box of my ride until I find the remote that opens the garage door, then drive inside. Once parked, I climb out, forgetting to take my bag, knowing that if I hurry, I will be able to grab a couple of hours of shut-eye before all hell breaks loose. There is a jar of nails on a shelf by the door that leads to the inside of the house. I upend the jar over a workbench, the nails spill out, and with them, the key my sister hid there so I can let myself in without waking anyone.

I don't have the strength to drag myself to one of the guest rooms. Instead, I flop on the first couch I meet in the living room, kicking off my trainers before stretching out along the cushions, and pulling my cap down over my face to block out the sunlight filtering through the shutters. I fall asleep almost instantly. I need to conserve as much energy as possible for the day ahead, things are about to get brutal.

Chapter Two

※

"**J**ared, are you awake?"

"No!" I open one eye and squint at my sister, who is perched on the coffee table beside me. She is still in her nightclothes and holding two mugs of something that smells deliciously caffeinated.

"Well, you soon will be. Here, fortify yourself," she giggles, offering me one of the mugs. I swing my legs to the floor and sit myself upright before I accept it. "What time did you get here?"

"About quarter to six." I take a deep draw from my drink as I try to drag myself to full consciousness.

"Seriously? Why didn't you hide out in one of the guest rooms? I could have made up an excuse and bought you a few more hours of sleep. Bro, for someone that was once voted second sexiest male on earth, you look like shit."

"I'm wearing a disguise to boost your self-esteem. I know how depressed you get over how I got the looks as well as the brains in the family." I grin as my sister grabs a cushion and whacks me with it. It's about the same time as a tiny human rounds the corner rubbing the sleep from her eyes. She looks too damn cute in her crumpled pink pyjamas. Her head sports a tangled mass of dark brown hair, and she has the teddy bear I brought her on my last visit tucked under her right arm. She looks up, and as her eyes focus on me, they go as wide as saucers before she launches herself at me squealing excitedly.

"Daddeeee."

I'm on my feet in an instant and swinging her round in the air before flopping back down on the sofa with her sat in my lap, "Morning peanut, how's my best girl?"

"You came for my party." She clings to my neck, squeezing so tightly I have to prise her little arms open before she strangles me.

"Wouldn't miss it for the world," I tell her jovially. It's a half truth, spending time with my daughter is precious, spending the afternoon trapped in a garden full of four-year-old's surfing the wave of a sugar rush, not so much.

"I missed you daddy."

"I missed you too, peanut." My heart clenches when she pulls back to give me 'the look', a precursor to what I know is coming next. Big brown eyes gaze at me full of hope before looking down at the hands which are playing idly with the neck of my T-shirt. "If I come live with you, you wouldn't miss me anymore."

"Don't you like staying with Aunt Ava and your cousins?"

"I do, but…"

"But what peanut?"

"I wanna live with you! Please daddy, I'll be a good girl. You said I could when I was bigger and I'll be four tomorrow." She puffs out her chest proudly, before flinging her little arms around my neck again and burying her head into my shoulder. I hold her close, hugging her tight, inhaling the familiar scent that wafts under my nose. Her hair smells of coconut, it's soft and sweet just like her. "Connor says you don't want me to live with you coz nobody likes me and I have a funny name."

What the fuck!

A red mist descends and I frown at my sister, waiting for an explanation. I'm seconds away from finding Connor and ripping his tongue from his mouth so I can smack him around the head with it. Ava glances at me smirking, she can read my mind, she shifts position so she is sat beside us on the sofa and can look my little girl in the eyes.

"I told you sweetheart, boys can be weird sometimes, just look at your cousins. When they are mean to you, it's usually because they really like you. If Connor didn't like you, why is he coming to your party later?"

"You invited him?" I ask my sister incredulously as I feel my eyebrows shoot up beyond my hairline. My daughter interrupts before Ava gets the chance to respond.

"I asked him why, like you said."

"What did he say?" I growl, my eyes still trained on my sister.

"The free food."

My sister chuckles and I throw silent daggers in her direction. I'm glad Connor is coming; I *really* want to meet this kid.

"Jared, he's four." My sister warns me smiling.

"He won't make five." I mutter.

"Connor's dad says you have your pie... pie-rit-tees all wrong."

"Pri-or-ities," Ava steps in, I'm not sure if it's to help my child with her pronunciation, or to help me understand what she is saying. I understand all right, it seems Connor learnt being an ass from his father. I can't wait to meet this pair. I open my mouth to speak but I'm interrupted by my daughter again.

"Connor says when his mom left him at least his dad loved him enough to stick around. Don't you love me? Why don't I have a mommy? Did she leave because she didn't love me?"

Fuck! That's new, she has never asked me about her mother before. I knew this day would come, but I was hoping it would be a few years from now and when I'd worked out the best way to handle the situation. I didn't expect to be blindsided thanks to Connor and his big mouth. I look across at Ava and can tell from her shocked expression that this is the first time the subject has been raised. At least she didn't have to deal with this shit fest without me. I feel like the worst parent in the world right now, and when I see the tears starting to well in my daughter's eyes it slays me.

"Tia..." Ava starts to speak but I raise my hand to

stop her. She does more than enough for me already. I turn Tia in my lap so she is facing me head on, she averts her eyes and looks down to her knees.

"Peanut." She doesn't look up, so I gently tickle her ribs until she starts giggling. "Look at me."

Tia finally makes eye contact. When she does, I turn serious, speaking slow and deliberately. I have to be sure she understands the importance of what I'm about to say.

"Connor is an idiot."

"Jared!" Ava snaps. I give her the stink-eye while Tia giggles.

"And his father is clueless. Feel free to tell them both that." I ignore my sister who glares at me and flaps her arms in disbelief. I turn my attention back to Tia. "You do not have a funny name. You have a beautiful name. Do you want to know why I chose it?"

Tia nods her head enthusiastically.

"Because in another language it stands for happiness, joy and princess. It was a wonderful surprise when you came into my life. I couldn't have been happier." *Well, once the shock wore off.* "You are as pretty as a princess and every day you bring me oodles and oodles of joy. I love you more than anything or anyone in the whole wide world."

"I'm a princess?" Tia's eyes go wide.

"You are to me." I grin at her. "Do you know what I think Connor's dad's name stands for?"

Tia shakes her little head.

"Jared!" Ava half shouts.

"Never mind." I scoff, pulling my daughter in for another hug.

It's about this time we hear a stampede approaching, before my sisters eight-year-old identical twins come crashing into the room saving me from a more complicated conversation.

"Uncle Jared!" They both yell in unison.

"Morning boys. Can you not do that thing where you speak at the same time and finish each other's sentences, it freaks me out."

"What's it..." Starts one twin.

"Worth?" The other one finishes. They both stand in front of me with their arms crossed. A huge mischievous grin across each of their faces.

"Morning T." They both coo fondly to my daughter. One of them ruffles her hair affectionately. Tia turns in my lap so she is facing them.

"Morning." She grins back at them.

My heart swells at the sight of their obvious love for her, and her for them.

"Can you refrain from addressing my daughter like she is a hot beverage?" I joke to the boys, before leaning forward so I can pretend to whisper in Tia's ear. "Which ones which?"

"Daddy," Tia giggles, and it's the best sound in the world. She raises her arm and points to the twin on the left. "That's Jacob," she points to the other twin, "That's Taylor." How she can tell them apart I'll never know. Even Ava looks a little relieved to have been enlightened.

We all hear the front door open and we are joined shortly after by Grant, my brother-in-law.

"Hi honey," Ava walks over and greets her husband, wrapping her arms around his neck and pulling him in for a kiss. "I wasn't expecting you until later."

"My next flight got cancelled." After high school, Grant successfully followed his dream of becoming a pilot. He takes mostly short commercial flights now, as he doesn't want to stray too far away from his home and family. Before she got pregnant, Ava was a flight attendant for a while and the pair of them got to travel the globe together. Spending time in some of the most romantic cities in the world gave them the opportunity for some pretty spectacular dates. I was worried that when Ava got grounded to have the twins their marriage would suffer. I couldn't have been more wrong, and it makes me happy to know Tia has such a pair of healthy role models in her life.

"Why?" Ava pulls back to look at Grant for an explanation.

"Who cares?" He tugs her back in for another kiss.

"Eww," I mouth to the twins as we all share a look of disgust at their sudden public display of affection. I may only be joking, but I can tell by the boys' faces they are clearly traumatised at the sight of their parents' canoodling.

"Right!" I clap my hands decisively. Everyone jumps and turns to look in my direction. "Sorry peanut," I whisper in my startled daughter's ear before addressing the rest of the room. "Everyone under the age of ten, get washed and dressed because I'm taking you out for breakfast."

"Yeah!" Jacob fist pumps the air, before he and Taylor each take one of Tia's hands to help her climb down off of my knee. The three of them rush off to get ready.

"Why only those under the age of ten?" Ava rounds on me with her hands on her hips and frowning. I stand and walk over to her, kissing her on her temple while I share a look with Grant. "Because I think your husband is tired and he's hoping he'll get breakfast in bed."

"Not that tired." Grant comes up behind Ava, whispering in her ear as he wraps his arms around her waist and pulls her flush against him.

"Oooh," Ava's eyes go wide.

"Just wait until me and the kids are out of the house." I sigh, I don't want to think about what they are going to get up to while we are gone. "Married or not, that's still my sister dude."

Grant chuckles and starts to nibble my sister's neck. I can't get out of there quick enough. "Sis, I need to borrow your car." It's already set up for transporting minors of multiple ages around.

"Mm hmm." She murmurs, clearly distracted.

I roll my eyes and make a hasty exit calling, "I'll wait in the kitchen," to anyone willing to listen.

Chapter Three

Half an hour later, I pull up into the parking lot of Daisy's, a sixties themed diner five minutes' drive from my sister's place and one of our favourite haunts. The whole family love it here. Grant, my sister and I love the atmosphere. There's always music pumping from an old-style jukebox, more sedately in the mornings than the evenings when it's cranked up to generate more of a party atmosphere. It's one of the only places I can come where I feel I can fully relax. We've been here so often the waitresses are used to seeing me around, which means I'm a familiar face rather than a famous one, no-one questions my identity. Even so, I turn in my seat to address the three youngsters in the back. Tia is sat between the twins, who helpfully decided to wear identical outfits. Blue jeans with white T-shirts, and the designer trainers I bought them for their birthdays last month. Note to self: Next time, buy them different variations of the same stuff so you have a slight hope in being able to tell them apart. Better still, buy them shirts with their names on.

"Right, so while we're here…" I start with my practiced speech and am cut off by Taylor… or is it Jacob?

"Call you Uncle James." James is my second name. Although most of the staff pretty much leave me alone, I have occasionally been confronted by a customer who recognises me when they just happened to be passing through. Since no one expects to see my Hollywood persona, unshaven, dressed in casual sweats, and wrangling three kids in a town two hundred and twenty-nine miles away from where I'm expected to be, by the time you throw in a change of name, even if I am recognised, it's relatively easy to convince strangers they've stumbled on a pretty good replica rather than the real deal.

"Cept me, I still get to call you daddy." Tia's little brow furrows, "Right daddy?"

"Right peanut." I smile, no matter how many times I tell her, she always feels the need to check. It has to be confusing, but the least I can do is try to give her a childhood out of the public eye. It can be hard enough being a kid without every move she makes being scrutinized and torn to shreds by either the media, or rich, pretentious jerks like those who terrorized my sister and me when we were younger. However, as much as I want to protect her privacy, there's no way I'll ever get her to pretend I'm not her dad. It was bad enough that her mother bailed on her; I'll never make her feel like I'm ashamed of her, or like I never want her around. She's my world.

We all pile out of my sister's minivan and Tia immediately takes my hand, it feels so small and delicate in my large paw, I look down to see her gazing up at me in awe and adoration. I'll always cherish that look she gives me, the radiant smile that lets me know she believes I can conquer the world for her. It's hard trying to live up to her expectations, but no matter how I fare, she always makes me feel like I just swooped in and hung the moon for her. My chest clenches, despite her being my biggest cheerleader, I never feel like I'm enough for her, she deserves so much more than just the moon; she deserves the sun, moon and every star in the whole fucking universe. Every day I kill myself trying to be a better man because of her.

The twins dash off and push through the large glass doors of the restaurant. They love it here because it caters to their love of every food their mother tries to steer them away from on a regular basis. Unlike Tia, who loves it because, apart from the black and white checkerboard flooring and the chrome fixings, the whole place is decked out in different hues of what I assume to be Daisy's favourite colour, which also happens to be my daughter's favourite: pink! It's like a flamingo flew in and threw up all over the joint.

Tia and I follow the twins inside. The diner hasn't gotten that busy yet, and it's easy to find an empty booth by one of the large windows. Tia slides in across from the twins, who are already scouring the menu and eagerly debating how to best spend my money. I slide in beside her, smiling, and take a cursory glance around. There are a few diners sitting on the chrome stools that align the curved counter, which runs along the back wall and in front of the food pass from the kitchen. A couple is seated in a secluded booth in the far corner of the room, and a lone female is hunched over the table, staring into her mug morosely a few booths away. She is wearing a sweatshirt that looks at least three sizes too large. If I had to guess, I'd say she got dressed in a hurry after fleeing or getting kicked out of the lover's bed she'd been warming the night before. I'd lost a lot of sweatshirts that way, although before now, I'd never had to bear witness to the events that may have followed any of my companions' hasty departures. Even though I wasn't the source of this woman's distress, having my daughter beside me makes me feel quite contrite at this moment.

My thoughts are interrupted when the kitchen doors swing open to reveal the one waitress I was hoping to avoid. Her eyes lock onto mine instantly, and I force a smile as her predatory gaze rakes over my body before she almost sprints to my table.

"Hi handsome," she purrs, retrieving her small note pad from the pocket of her white apron. She tears her pen from where it is clipped to the seam of her uniform, and in a practiced move, she manages to pull her top button loose at the same time. The pen falls from her fingers with too much force to be accidental, and it obediently rolls across the tabletop in front of me. Before I get the chance to retrieve it, an ample bosom is thrust in my face as she leans across me at a rather unnecessary angle to grab it.

"Hi Gina," I sigh, trying my best not to get suffocated by her tits. I ignore the giggles of the twins as they hide behind their menus. Thankfully, Tia is watching out of the window, blissfully unaware of what's happening right beside her. Gina pulls back so she can look me in the eyes, stopping to hover menacingly in front of my face. When she smiles, it's like looking at a viper ready to strike.

"Would you like to hear the specials?" She murmurs seductively. "There are a few things you might fancy that aren't on the menu."

One of the twins bobs his head up to roll his eyes at me dramatically before he ducks down again. The other's menu is shaking so spectacularly, he is either sitting in the epicentre of an earthquake, or laughing so hard it wouldn't surprise me if he'd peed himself. I look under the table and give the floor a cursory glance. Clean and dry. Shame, I'd love for him to pay penance for wallowing in my misfortune. At this point, I'm saved by the bell —or more specifically, my mobile as it starts to chime. I don't even bother checking to see who's calling. Hopefully, it's the IRS, or someone offering me an appointment for a rectal exam. Anything will be better than continuing to endure my current torture.

"Sorry Gina, I need to take this." I wait for her to step aside and let me pass. When she doesn't, I have no option other than to squeeze past her with our bodies colliding awkwardly. "I'll just be outside," I gesture to the window before pointing two fingers at my eyes and one back at the twins to let them know I'll be watching. Rapidly turning on my heel, I call over my shoulder as I make my escape, "Let them order whatever they want, Gina. I'll have the pancakes."

It's only when I'm safely out of Gina's clutches that I look at my phone and see it's Jerry calling. As I answer, I make my way outside to the window in front of the booth I've just vacated, in order to keep an eye on what's happening inside. Gina has slipped into my seat and is writing down whatever the kids are ordering. Mollified, I take the call.

"Hi Jerry, what's up?"

"Jared, I just wanted to check you are free next Saturday. Henrietta Greenslade wants to schedule your date in as soon as possible."

I groan. Henrietta was the winning bidder in last night's bachelor auction. She had dropped a cool half a million without even blinking for the opportunity to spend a few hours with me. It had all been done under the guise of her making a sizable charitable donation, but the moment we'd stepped off stage together, her roving hands and salacious comments told an altogether different story.

"No, tell her I'm out of town and won't be free until the week after." It's definitely not a date I'm looking forward to, but I know I can't put it off indefinitely. It's probably better to get it booked in and out of the way with.

"Out of town? Where the hell are you? I need you here."

"Why?" Sometimes less is more. I know Jerry gets frustrated when I disappear without telling him, especially since even he doesn't know the cause of my mysterious absences.

"You might get a call about the part in 'Wildly Adrift'. What if the producers want to meet with you again? What do I tell them?"

"Tell them I don't want the part, let Dalton have it. Find me something that doesn't involve me leaving the country for the next six months."

"But…"

"Jerry, I know it was a coup getting me a meeting and I can't lie, the thought of stealing the part Mitchel wants so badly is rather appealing, but it doesn't negate the fact that I don't want to be out of the country filming for that long at the moment. Not to mention the fact that I'd be working with that damn wolf." The role was set to be filmed in the wilds of Canada and the wolf in question was to be the co-star. I'd been invited to meet him and one of the producers, Caitlin Archer, to see how we all gelled. Let's just say we didn't. I'd expected a highly trained and amenable animal. Instead, I met a surly, belligerent beast that seemed intent on savaging me —and the canine hadn't been much better. Since there was slightly more meat on Mitchel's torso, I thought it best if he was the one thrown to the wolves (pun intended). It might work out to be the perfect way to eliminate my fiercest competition entirely.

"Rumour has it, until you threw a hissy fit when he nipped you, there was a good chance you were going to be offered the lead. Now, the powers that be are rethinking, and Dale has managed to arrange a meet and greet for Mitchel to see how he gets along with the animal. I'm doing my best to keep you in the running, but since I'm pretty sure Mitchel and Caitlin have been bumping uglies, she'll probably try to persuade the rest of the crew that Mitchel is the better fit to give herself unlimited access to his cock. By the way, I sent Dale some flowers on your behalf."

"That explains why Caitlin was being such a bitch when we met. It doesn't matter about the movie, there'll be other jobs. I told you, even if it's offered, I'll have to decline. Find me something better and filming locally. I don't want to be away for more than a couple of weeks at a time right now. Oh, and I know about the flowers. I can't say I'm not surprised though, why did you send them?"

"To piss Mitchel off. How did you find out?"

"Because I swung by the hospital in person to check Dale was Ok and spotted them."

"Why?" Jerry asks incredulously. Dale is Mitchel's personal assistant and probably the last person in the world Jerry would think I'd want to visit.

"Because before I knew what the role would entail, you told me Mitchel was in Vegas and it was the ideal time to make a play for it. Since I knew Mitchel wasn't around, I thought I'd check in on Dale to make sure he was being looked after. After my minor altercation with the wolf, Caitlin took me out for a drink, I think she was worried I might sue. Anyway, I think it was when Dale spotted me talking to her in the club, he lost his footing and fell. I guess I felt guilty. I wish you'd told me about the flowers, I'd arranged for a separate bouquet, he was probably confused when a second one arrived a few days after the first." I don't think it prudent to mention that during my visit, I made Dale a lucrative offer to leave his current post and become my personal PA. The man had connections within the industry that Jerry was never likely to forge. Not only was he well-revered, but as I found to my detriment, he was also unequivocally loyal, politely declining my proposal to remain with his current employer.

"Guilty?" Jerry blows out a long breath. "For a hard ass you can be a cupcake at times."

"That's what having a four-year-old..." I stop myself abruptly. *Fuck*! That's what having a four-year-old daughter does to you, is what I was about to say. Scrambling to finish the sentence, I add, "... conscience does to you." It was the best I could come up with.

"Four-year-old conscience?" Jerry repeats clearly confused. I turn and bang my head on the window beside me in frustration. On the other side, Tia jumps at the sudden noise.

"Sorry, peanut," I mouth to her as my eyes go wide. I watch as a vast array of plates is delivered to the table. There are so many dishes they won't all fit on. The twins wave at me mischievously as

Tia struggles to pour syrup over a ginormous pile of pancakes. Eventually, her tiny arm proves to be no match for gravity and the weight of the jug, which upends, spilling its contents all over the pancakes as well as the tiny person in front of them.

"Fuck!" I exclaim again, out loud this time. "Jerry, I have to go, I'll call you in a few days when I get back in town."

I don't wait for a response before hanging up and running back inside, grabbing a handful of napkins on route back to booth that appears to have ordered enough food to sustain a small country for at least a week.

"Tia," I sigh, wiping the worst of the sticky substance off of her arms and clothes. The boys are too busy devouring everything in sight to take much notice of what is going on around them.

"I'm sorry daddy," she looks up at me and all I see is her big brown eyes glistening with tears as her bottom lip quivers. Any negative emotion I was experiencing immediately evaporates. The girl has me wrapped around her tiny finger; she's going to be a heartbreaker when she hits thirty, maybe forty, and I finally grant her permission to date.

"That's ok peanut," I tell her, "I blame your cousins for not helping you."

"Sorry Tia," one boy murmurs, while the other swops out her plate of sodden pancakes for a fresh batch.

"C'mon, we need to get you cleaned up." Tia and I wander hand in hand to the toilets, and I push her behind me while I peer inside the gents to check it's empty. It's not, and there's no way I'm taking my young daughter inside when some hairy-assed dude has his trousers around his ankles with his meat and two veg on full display. I knock on the door of the ladies and am pleasantly surprised, as well as thankful, to find it empty. I lift Tia and sit her beside the sink before starting to get her cleaned up the best I can. We aren't there long before the door opens and the lone female diner I'd spotted when we first arrived strolls in. Her eyes widen in shock, and I'm not sure if it's because she recognises me, or because she has just found a man standing in the middle of the female facilities. Neither of us speak as we eye each other warily. I can't help but think she looks vaguely familiar. She's tall, at least five-nine, and her baggy sweatshirt dwarfs her slim frame. Even with her long blond hair scraped back into a messy knot, and the red rimming her piercing blue eyes, she's devastatingly pretty. My eyes automatically drift to her left hand, and I smile to myself when I see there's no ring. Another look at her face reminds me to keep my distance; if I were a gambling man, I would've set odds on the fact that she'd been crying. Now definitely isn't the time to try and arrange a date to ease the ache that's been brewing in my balls for the last few weeks.

"I'm sorry," I tentatively break the silence, "My daughter had an accident and the mens' was otherwise engaged." I raise my eyebrows, hoping the gesture conveys the underlying meaning behind my words. The stranger smirks, a gesture I take to mean: Message received.

"No problem," she whispers in a tone as smooth as silk. "Do you mind?" She nods to a cubicle. "Or would you rather I wait?"

"Go ahead." I watch as the stranger disappears behind the door, completely mesmerised until Tia starts tugging on my shirt, reminding me why I am there.

"Daddy, my jumper is all sticky."

"I know peanut, but I don't have a change of clothes for you. We'll have to wait until we get home before you can change it."

"But I need to take it off," she whines, scrunching up her little nose. "Please, Daddy, I don't like it."

I drag my hand down my face. "Alright, arms up." Tia dutifully obliges and raises her arms so I can pull the sweater up and over her head. Thankfully, she is wearing a T-shirt underneath and it has been spared from harm. Even so, I'm worried she isn't going to be warm enough. It's a bridge I'll have to cross when I reach it.

"Daddy."

"Yes peanut." I cheer and raise my arms in triumph as the spoiled jumper flies through the air and hits the trash can a few feet away with surprising accuracy. It narrowly misses the stranger's nose as she chooses the exact moment it passes to emerge from her cubicle.

"I'm cold."

I appear to have reached the bridge sooner than

anticipated.

"Um. Sorry," I mutter to the blond beauty who is now at the sink washing her hands. She looks up into the mirror above the sink and her reflection smiles back at me. I turn back to Tia. "Did you bring a coat? Is it in the car?"

She shakes her little head dejectedly.

Cosmic!

I scan the room and pick up the only viable option, waving it in front of Tia's face. "Do you remember last Halloween when daddy and aunt Ava wrapped you in bandages?"

Tia nods.

"How about we do that again but this time I use this?"

I hear an amused snort from beside me and turn to see we are being watched by the stranger who seems to be in no hurry to leave. In fact, she appears to have settled in to watch the show, leaning her hip against the counter without a care in the world as she stares at us, unable to tear her eyes away from the car crash about to happen in front of her.

"You can't be serious." Blondie looks like she is biting the side of her cheeks as she tries not to laugh.

"You got a better idea?" I snap. "It's not like I have a pair of knitting needles and a ball of yarn in my back pocket."

"No, but I thought you might have at least bought a spare sweater." Blondie smirks, "It looks like you've had what, three, maybe four years to prepare yourself for these sorts of emergencies."

Smartass!   I narrow my eyes at the stranger and side eye my daughter before reluctantly swallowing an undignified retort.

Blondie rifles in her bag and hands me a ball of material. "Here, try this."

I take the scrap of material being proffered, shaking it out to see it's a square silk scarf and quite a bit larger than I was expecting. It looks expensive, unlike the rest of the clothes she is wearing. Other than the fact I don't feel right accepting it, I don't know what the fuck she expects me to do with it. I can feel her eyes on me, watching, if I didn't know better, I'd say she was setting me up for an even bigger failure. Well, fuck you sweetheart.

"Thank you but we can't take this," I try to pass the scarf back but she waves my hand away.

"You would rather your daughter suffer the indignity of being mummified in toilet roll? That only works one day of the year and that day is not now. On behalf of under-fives everywhere, I have to make a stand."

"Um… thanks." I look at the material, staring at it quizzically. I drape it over Tia's head before standing her on the ground and wrapping it round and round her tiny body. I secure it in place with a knot behind her back. She squeals with laughter as she is cocooned until you can just about see her eyes peeking out from between the swathes of material.

"Daddy," she chuckles manically, "How am I gonna eat my pancakes?"

Good point. Her arms are bound to her sides

underneath the scarf. "We can get them to go. Won't that be nice?" Since her legs are also bound, I swing her up into my arms as she starts to protest.

"Noooo," Tia wails. If I could've seen her lips, I'm pretty certain they would've been pouting. I rub my temple.

"Can I help?" I turn to the sniggering woman beside me and frown.

"You think you can do better?" I place my daughter back on the ground, stepping back and gesturing to the wriggling pupa. "Be my guest."

What happens next is nothing short of a miracle. I watch in fascination, as after carefully freeing Tia, the material is folded a few times, knotted, flipped and fitted around Tia's frame until she is wearing something that resembles a trendy wraparound top. With sleeves! It's still a little loose, so to help hold it in place, blondie removes the clip from her hair and uses it to pin the folds of material in place.

"Yeah," I murmur, totally awestruck, "That's what I was going to do next."

"It's not perfect, but it should hold you until you get home." The woman kneeling in front of my daughter looks up at me and smiles. With her hair now loose and falling in soft curls down her back and shoulders, she looks even more beautiful. Right now, I could kiss her... purely in gratitude for helping me out of this sticky situation of course.

"Thank you..." I pause and tilt my head as I wait for her to give me her name. She seems to think about it before finally offering it to me.

"Mackenzie. But my close friends call me Mac."

"You're hoping we'll become *close* Mackenzie?" I drawl seductively, "I don't usually let strange women pick me up in bathrooms, but I'll make an exception just this once. What's your number?" I get my phone out, opening the contacts before looking back at her. She looks shocked and if I'm honest, a little uncomfortable. It's a reaction I'm not used to, usually women are either throwing their numbers at me or begging me for mine.

"Um…"

"So I can return the scarf." I add hastily when her reaction isn't the one I was expecting. Her shoulders sag in relief and my ego weeps.

"It's fine. Keep it…" She pauses and cocks her head waiting for me to give her my name, mirroring my action from earlier.

"This is Tia," I offer immediately, presenting my daughter with a hand flourish, avoiding the question but answering it at the same time.

"Pleased to meet you Tia," Mackenzie turns her attention back to the pint-sized human trying to hide herself behind my leg. Mackenzie is still kneeling on the floor so is at Tia's level as she greets her, a shrewd move, it makes her seem less intimidating. Tia peeks out from behind my knee before emerging and taking the hand being extended to her. As soon as she has it, Mackenzie shakes Tia's little hand formally. Tia giggles and beams at her, her shyness preventing her from speaking. Mackenzie stands to look me square in the face, "And you would be?"

I'm not sure if she recognises me, but the way she phrases the question makes it sound more like a dare. I don't want to lie but I'm not ready to reveal the truth either.

"That's daddy," Tia offers timidly, saving me from both.

"That's right, I'm daddy," I respond seriously.

"You want me to call you daddy?" Mackenzie asks incredulously as she stares me down.

I smirk as my mind instantly drops to the gutter, then lean in to whisper my response so young ears can't hear. "I don't know what sort of kinks you think I'm into beautiful," I try to sound shocked, "but let's get one thing clear right now," I lower my tone to what I think is a dangerously sexy level and move even closer, close enough for my lips to brush Mackenzie's ear as I speak, "I'm a show not tell kind of guy, so unless you're willing to play, don't tease me." I pull back and wink before grabbing Tia's hand and adopting my fun dad voice, "C'mon peanut, let's go get some pancakes before the boys eat them all." We walk away together, leaving a very flustered Mackenzie standing open-mouthed and at a loss for words in the middle of the room.

Chapter Four

J eez! What is wrong with me? I've never done anything like that in front of my daughter before. Now I have yet another example to add to my long list of failings as a father. Good job Tia didn't hear. Granted, it's been a while since I've been with a woman in the biblical sense, I've been too busy and too tired of late to even entertain the thought. Maybe that's the problem, my balls are so full their contents have started leaking into my bloodstream creating some sort of hormonal imbalance. My brain misfired and stopped communicating with my mouth. What kind of example am I setting for Tia by flirting with a woman I've known for barely five minutes, while trying not to get hard, in the female toilets of a family-themed restaurant mid-morning? I'll take care of the situation when I get back to Hollywood and am out of dad mode. Hook up with someone willing to help me release the tension that's been building within me for far too long. The models Jerry arranged to attend the gala with me the other night were clearly up for a good time, but with a three-and-a-half-hour drive ahead, I didn't have the chance to take advantage of their hospitality.

Tia and I make our way back to our seats. Gina's hovering, I glance at her and my dick shrivels in fear. There's no doubt she's a beautiful, curvaceous woman that would provide a quick and easy solution to my current problem, but I've a feeling she'd want a lot more than I'd be prepared to give and then things would get awkward. I can't risk not being able to come back to my favourite diner. I slide along the bench first this time, wedging myself between the window and my daughter, shielding myself from the huntress who has me in her sights. The twins are still eating. I'm not sure they even noticed we were gone. A few minutes later Mackenzie emerges and resumes her position a few tables down. Gina brings her a fresh drink and she either stares into her cup or out of the window as she tries to avoid making eye contact with me. I can't help but watch her, wondering what her story is. I've definitely not seen her here before which means she is either new to the area or just passing through. When our eyes connect briefly, she blushes furiously before snapping her gaze away. Her mobile starts to ring and when she answers it, I turn my attention back to the kids at the table, not wanting to eavesdrop on her conversation.

"I hope you two aren't about to throw up." I tell the twins who finally seem to have reached their limits. The boy sat opposite me is slouched back in his seat looking rather green. The other looks fine and smacks his lips the way you do after you've been blessed with a fine meal.

"I'm fine." Says the one sat opposite Tia. "I bet that lightweight he couldn't eat more pancakes than me. Loser had to drink what was left of the syrup straight from the jug. Guess who won." He thumps his chest proudly.

I blow out a long breath. "Go and ask Gina for some more will you, Tia and I will need some syrup for our pancakes, and ask for another coffee while you're at it, this one's got cold."

"You sure you don't want to ask her?" He grins, and when I scowl back at him, he scurries off giggling.

The other twin groans as he holds his stomach.

"Tyler, are you ok?" Tia asks, her voice full of concern. Ahh, so that one's Tyler.

He grunts offering her a weak grin. Tia smiles back, before continuing to concentrate on piling her plate with food.

Jacob returns, and shortly after Gina follows with my coffee, a fresh batch of pancakes and some more syrup. Tyler takes one look at the pancakes and pushes past his brother to make a dash for the bathroom. Jacob sighs and shakes his head solemnly. "Sometimes I can't believe we're related," he groans. "I think he was adopted."

I huff out a laugh. "How do you explain the fact that you look so alike?" I go to take a sip of my coffee only to see a love heart has been etched into the top of the steamed milk. I look at Gina and she smiles around the top of her pen as she pushes it in and out of her mouth salaciously. As I try to ignore her, my attention is drawn to Tia when she walks across my line of sight carrying a plate stacked full of pancakes. I hadn't even realised she'd slipped out of her seat.

"Tia," I call, as I start to shuffle out of my seat to go after her. "Where are you going? Jacob, can you go and check to make sure your brother hasn't slipped into a diabetic coma?"

Jacob races off and I follow Tia as she carefully carries her loaded plate over to Mackenzie, gently setting it down on the table and pushing it in front of her. It's obvious she's been crying again. It must be something to do with the phone call she's just taken.

"Is this for me?" Mackenzie asks surprised as she grabs a napkin from the dispenser on the table and starts blotting her eyes in embarrassment.

Tia nods bashfully.

"Why honey?"

"Coz when I'm sad, daddy buys me pancakes and says they make everything better." Tia pushes her hair back from her face. I couldn't be prouder of her in this moment. My mind flicks back to Ava when we were at school, remembering all the times someone could have shown her even the smallest amount of kindness and respect—just like my four-year-old has just shown to an almost complete stranger. I can't help but think my sister is doing an incredible job of raising her, much better than I could ever do.

"But if I eat your pancakes, won't you be sad?"

44

Mackenzie asks.

Tia shakes her head, "My daddy's here," she says matter of factly, "I'm not sad when he's home."

Which means she *is* sad when I'm not? My heart bursts and shatters all at once.

I crouch down beside her trying to talk around the lump in my throat. "Peanut, you might not be sad right now, but you must be hungry?"

Tia shrugs.

"How about I share my pancakes with you," I tap the end of her nose and she beams brighter than the sun. "And you know what else makes people happy when they're sad?"

She shakes her head, her mouth hanging open in anticipation of the wisdom I'm about to impart. "Company." I stand and hold one hand out to Tia and the other out to Mackenzie, "Would you like to join us?"

"Pleeease." Tia begs Mackenze as she takes my hand.

"C'mon." When Mackenzie doesn't move, I grab her hand anyway and pull her out of her seat. "I don't bite." When she is standing beside me, I can't help myself and lean in to whisper playfully, "Unless you want me to."

"No… It's fine…" As she starts to protest, I ignore her and stride off with her hand in a vice like grip. She has no option other than to follow, scrambling to grab her plate with her free hand as I pull her back to my table with me.

"You girls get yourself settled and tuck in, I'm

just going to check on the boys." It doesn't take me long. Tyler's stomach ache has subsided and while he is still feeling queasy, he hasn't actually been ill. Jacob has been keeping him company, ready to bait his brother should any display of pyrotechnics occur. When I head back to the table, they both follow. I sit beside Tia who has trapped Mackenzie against the window. The boys sit opposite us again, this time making sure Tyler is on the end in case he needs to make a sudden break for freedom. After introductions have been made, everyone settles down to enjoy the rest of the food set out. Everyone except Tyler, who watches on while gingerly sipping at a glass of iced water. There's no awkwardness; conversation flows effortlessly as we all engage in idle chatter, sharing amusing anecdotes and delighting in playful banter.

It's not long before I feel a shadow looming over me. I take a quick glimpse expecting it to be Gina, and am surprised when I see a guy I don't know stood beside me but staring intently at Mackenzie. He doesn't look happy, but I'm still surprised by his venomous tone when he speaks.

"Kenzie." He snaps tersely. When he says her name the penny drops. I knew I recognised her, she's a model, or used to be. Kenzie Kingsley is her professional name. I don't know if she is still in the business, I do know that she has her own makeup brand since my sister usually leaves copious amounts of the stuff scattered around her home.

"How did you find me?" Mackenzie jumps before

visibly slumping in her seat.

"I'll always find you," he sneers. "Let's go."

"I don't want to go with you." Her words are barely more than a whisper.

"You don't have a choice," he snarls. "What else are you going to do? You've no money, no friends, no other place to go."

"I do," she counters sadly.

"Who the hell would have you? Especially now," he spits. "You should be grateful I've been dragging all around this god forsaken place searching for your sorry ass. Quit bitching and move."

I stretch my neck from side to side until it cracks. I don't want to get involved in whatever this is, but this guy is really pissing me off with his attitude. I don't want Tia or the twins growing up thinking that this is acceptable behaviour. I look at him, sizing him up. He's slightly shorter than me, at a guess I'd say about six feet tall, sandy blond hair that's slicked back with gel. He is wearing a T-shirt and his muscles lack definition, his hands look unbelievably soft. He obviously doesn't work out often or do any kind of manual labour. His clothes are all designer. Yep, rich prick. Thinks he can stride in here, ignoring me and my family, rudely interrupting our breakfast, while he attempts to throw his weight around by shouting at our guest who clearly wants him gone. I start breathing slow and deep in an effort to control my temper as it starts to rise.

"My brother," Mackenzie replies. As she says the

words, I see the prick's face blanche. Interesting, he is obviously wary of her brother.

"Nice try sweetheart. Your brother is on his honeymoon and do you think he would want to see you after you couldn't even be bothered to show up for his wedding? Now pull yourself together we're fucking leaving."

"That wasn't my fault and you know it." Mackenzie snaps half-heartedly. When I see the tears glistening in her eyes, threatening to fall, I can't hold my tongue any longer.

"Watch your language in front of my daughter." I growl as calmly as I can muster.

"Who the fuck are you?"

I close my eyes and let out a breath before I start to push myself out of my seat.

"I don't want any trouble," Daisy shouts from behind the counter. "Take it outside." Her partner, George, emerges from the kitchen with a meat cleaver in his hand. He is a big guy, in his fifties, tall and stocky with a slight paunch. He's a lot bigger than me if I'm honest, but anyone who is familiar with him will know he is a gentle giant that hates confrontation. I raise my hand to signal to them that I'm not looking for any trouble so there's no need for them to get involved.

As soon as I step out of my seat, the angry stranger shoves me out of his way, lunging across the area I've just vacated in an effort make a grab for Mackenzie. I seize his forearm before it can get anywhere near my daughter, let alone reach the woman cowering in her seat the far side of her. "I suggest you leave," I warn him. "She clearly doesn't want to go with you."

"Fuck off!" He snaps, shaking my hand from his arm without even bothering to look at me. He is still facing Mackenzie, staring at her with a renewed fire in his eyes that makes her try to slink further back in her seat.

"I told you to watch your mouth in front of my daughter." My voice automatically morphs into being low and threatening. Finally, he deigns to turn his head to look at me.

"Are we going to have a problem?" He barks.

"Only if you create one." I growl as I feel myself starting to unravel.

"This doesn't concern you." He snarls back.

"I think it does," I rumble. "Do you want to discuss this outside?"

He wrinkles his nose derisively as he sizes me up. It's a look I used to see all through high-school. "I do," he growls. He obviously needs to vent, and I'd rather it be with me than risk him lashing out and hurting anyone else in the room.

"Leave my daddy alone." Tia suddenly shouts angrily. It's only then I notice she has pulled herself up onto her seat so she is now kneeling sideways and right in front of the idiot causing the scene. As he looks down at her she draws her right arm back and hits him with all her might. Unfortunately for him, due to the way they are positioned, she is at the perfect angle for her tiny fist to give him an uppercut between his legs and at the apex of his thighs. She hits the bullseye and I can tell by the way he folds she must pack one hell of a punch. I make a mental note to ask my sister what she has been feeding her. Her victim doubles up in agony, squealing like a pig and clutching his junk as he staggers backwards.

"I taught her that." Jacob tells me proudly, and as I look at him, I struggle to curtail my grin. Maybe Tia can start dating before forty after all.

When I look back, I realise my daughter isn't done. She has grabbed the ketchup bottle off the table, pointed it at her target and squeezed. Red sauce shoots out of the bottle. Considering he is stumbling about I'm surprised she hits him, but hit him she does, right in the face. Instinctively, he uses his arm to try and swipe the condiment away, but all he ends up doing is smearing the ketchup over himself and inadvertently getting some in his eye. I wince as he screams out in pain.

"I taught her that." Tyler deadpans before the colour drains from his face. "I think I'm gonna..." He doesn't get to finish as he projectile vomits all over the prick dancing about beside him.

"It's just not your day, is it?" I chuckle as I throw a wadge of notes on the table and jerk my head, motioning for the kids to head out to the car. The twins grab Tia and run out laughing. I grab Mackenzie and drag her out with me. There's no way I'm leaving her behind with that jerk, especially now. I wave to Daisy as I leave, mouthing, "I'm sorry." She smiles back to let me know she doesn't blame me and that I'll still be welcome back in the future.

We all pile into the minivan and I take off. Mackenzie is sat up front with me. The twins are in the back excitedly commending Tia on her performance. I smile and glance over at Mackenzie, she looks so sad and despondent. My face falls and I put my hand on her knee to try and console her.

"It's ok," I reassure her. "It's over."

"For now," she whispers. "I'm so sorry."

"There's nothing to be sorry for," I say. "What do you mean 'for now'? Who is he?"

"His name is Dan," she murmurs. "And he'll never give up. He'll just find me again, and next time I won't have you around to step in and protect me. He's right, I don't have anyone left anymore. He has destroyed every relationship I've ever had, taken everything. He'll find me again and be even angrier next time. He'll convince me to go with him because I don't have any other option. It's how this will all play out in the long run. I should have just gone with him now."

I glance across at her perplexed.

"The fuck you should have." I half-shout.

"Daddy, you said a bad word." Tia calls from the back seat. The twins chuckle.

"Sorry peanut." I glance at her in the rear-view mirror and she smiles back at me, satisfied with a job well done.

"Who is this Dan anyway?" I ask, prompting Mackenzie for more information.

"My husband."

What the hell!

Chapter Five

✧

"**Y**ou married that prick?" I ask incredulously.

"Daddy," Tia calls. "Bad word."

"Sorry peanut." I look in the rear view again, making sure I get my smile before addressing Mackenzie once more. "I think we had better talk about this later. Every time I swear in front of the kids my sister makes me put ten bucks into each of their college funds, and there's no getting away from it because my own daughter sells me out every time." Like Ava thinks I'd never pay for them to go anyway... yeesh! "And let's just say your husband is making me want to swear a lot right now. We'll park this conversation for now while we deal with the more pressing matter."

"Which is what?" Mackenzie cocks her eyebrow at me.

"In a little under five hours you've just been volunteered into helping my sister and me corral twenty or so four-year-olds, as they wreak havoc in my sister's back yard while attempting to O.D on sugar."

"Come again?"

"It's Tia's birthday tomorrow but she is having her party today since it's the weekend, that's why I had to haul ass..."

"Daddy."

"Sorry peanut." I sigh, tilting my head up to glance in the rear-view mirror. I'm going to get repetitive strain injury at this rate. "It's why I had to high tail it back here from the gala last night."

"Gala? What Gala? Where?" Mackenzie asks with interest.

Shit!

"Oh, it was just a work thing, nothing important, although it was out of town so I had to rush back."

"So, Tia stayed with your sister?" Mackenzie asks slowly as she looks at me thoughtfully.

"Um... yeah. That a problem." I answer a little too defensively, not liking the direction this conversation is heading.

"No... No, not at all." Mackenzie stutters, suddenly looking sheepish. "I'm sorry, I didn't mean to pry."

I glance across and frown, she looks nervous and is fidgeting in her seat uncomfortably.

"What's wrong?"

"I didn't mean to upset you." She whispers.

I drag my hand down my face. What the fuck! She thinks I'm about to kick off like that idiot back at the diner. When we pull into the garage at my sister's house, Mackenzie and I stay put while the kids pile out and rush inside. As soon as we are alone, I turn in my seat to look at the woman beside me. I rest one arm on the top of the steering wheel while the other gently reaches across so I can take one of her hands in mine. She can't, or won't, look at me. Her gaze stays fixed on the windshield in front of her. "Can I ask you a personal question?"

She shrugs softly.

"How long have you and despicable Dan been married?"

"Fourteen years."

"I'm not him Mac," I whisper, "You don't need to be afraid of me. I won't lie, I'm no saint that's for sure, and I'm sure my sister will confirm that when you get to meet her in a few minutes, but I'll never hurt you."

We sit in silence for a few minutes before I have to ask, "Has he... has he ever hurt you? Physically I mean?"

Her tears give me the answer I need. She doesn't move or make a sound as they roll down her cheeks. I wonder if she has conditioned herself that way, so she is able to hide the pain and sorrow he causes her. I should have kicked his ass when I had the chance. I drop her hand so I can wrap mine around her neck, pulling her head into my chest while she cries her silent tears. I have so many more questions but I know now's not the time. It's uncomfortable, the way we are contorted in the front of the car. When she finally stops shaking against me, I pull back. "So, are you ready to brave my sister and help us prepare for Tia's party?"

"Why would I need to brave your sister?" Mackenzie gives me a weak smile.

"She's a bit of a fan, I'm afraid."

"Of me?" She gasps, genuinely surprised.

"Yeah, of you." I smile, "C'mon let's go inside." I turn to get out of the car but Mackenzie grabs my arm.

"Wait, I don't have a present."

"What?"

"I can't go to Tia's party empty handed. Is there a mall or something nearby?"

"It's fine," I smile, "She'll probably have so many gifts she'll never know."

"But I'll know, and after she was so sweet to me at breakfast it just wouldn't feel right."

"This really means a lot to you, doesn't it?"

Mackenzie nods, "And don't take this the wrong way, but we could get you some new clothes while we're there."

"What's wrong with my clothes?" I ask indignantly.

Mackenzie blushes and smiles shyly, "Your T-shirt's a little... snug, don't you think? You look like you're about to burst out of it like the hulk."

"You been checking me out Mac?" I smirk.

"Well, it was hard not to...I mean... um..." She shakes her head clearly flustered, "...never mind."

"Buckle up." I chuckle. I call my sister on the hands-free to let her know I just need to run a quick errand as I back the car out of the garage again.

It doesn't take us long to find what we need. I

stop at a thrift store and purchase a couple of T-shirts with Mackenzie's guidance. I never knew I should be taking so much into consideration when buying such a simple item. Colour, style, fit, fabric —the woman really knows her stuff. While I couldn't give a shit about any of it, her energy and enthusiasm are a joy to watch. She is positively glowing, and it completely changes the way she carries herself. She radiates beauty and strength as she passionately strives to make the entire clothes shopping experience enjoyable for me. I try to hurry her along as she becomes completely consumed in rifling through the stock, and I am more than a little surprised when she chooses a few pieces to buy for herself. After I finally manage to get her to leave, we head to Tia's favourite toy store, where I help Mackenzie choose a gift for her before we head back home.

By the time we arrive it's like I'm with a different woman. All trace of nervousness has disappeared. Mackenzie is oozing confidence and charm. We park up and I lead her into the house and through to the kitchen, where we find Ava on her hands and knees with her back to us as she searches for something in the back of a cupboard.

"Hi sis," I call.

"Hey bro," she calls back. "Take care of what you needed to?"

"Yeah," I laugh as Ava starts throwing the contents of the cupboard out behind her, "What are you looking for in there?"

"Fairy dust." Comes the muffled reply as she delves deeper into the back of the cupboard.

Mackenzie looks at me horrified. I snigger, "She doesn't mean the drug; she means glitter, which Tia likes to think is a magical, shimmering powder she can scatter to make everyone's wishes come true." Mackenzie nods her head clearly relieved, so I can't help myself and lean in to whisper, "We keep the drugs in one of the top cupboards, out of the reach of the kids." Her eyes go like saucers and I mirror her look to let her know that I'm only joking.

She's smiling when she punches me on the arm softly and rolls her eyes at me. "Very responsible of you," she mutters.

"I like to think so." I grin back her.

"What was that?" Ava shouts, obviously thinking I was talking to her. When I don't answer straight away, she carries on, "Jacob told me what happened at the diner. Trust you to swoop in and rescue a damsel in distress."

"Actually, she rescued me." I call, as I wink at Mackenzie.

"Yeah, right," Ava replies in disbelief. Then I hear her say, "Thank fuck," as she emerges from the cupboard with a box containing all sorts of fairy-like paraphernalia. She places the box on the floor beside her and starts throwing the rest of the scattered contents she'd previously ejected back into the cupboard without turning.

"That's ten dollars for each kid." I bark out a laugh.

"Nope, kids are up the garden with Grant, though according to Tia you owe the kitty ninety bucks."

I look at Mackenzie, raising my eyes and nodding sadly at my daughter's disloyalty. "Told you she'd sell me out." I grumble, and Mackenzie rolls her lips trying not to laugh.

"Who was the woman anyway? Tia said she was *really* pretty; I suppose that had nothing to do with the fact you asked her to join you for breakfast." Ava rattles on as she finally closes the cupboard door and stands. "Did she know who you were?"

"Ava." I snap, trying to shut her up. I can feel Mackenzie's eyes suddenly boring into me.

"What?" She finally turns and registers I'm not alone. Her hand flies to her mouth and she gasps, "Holy shit!" Before she screams so loud, I check behind me to see if we are under siege.

"Jeez, Ava!" I exclaim, "You really need to come with a warning label." She is bouncing up and down on the spot in excitement as Grant and the children come barrelling into the room.

Grant runs straight to his wife, knocking me out of the way in his haste to get to her. I huff out a laugh as he grabs her shoulders, stooping to look her in the eyes. "Babe, what's up?" He cries in a panicked voice.

Tia runs over to Mackenzie and throws her arms around her legs. "You came for my party," she gushes, and starts bouncing up and down on the balls of her feet like Ava."

Jacob punches his right fist into the palm of his left hand, "We got a problem in here?" He shouts, while Tyler just looks at him shaking his head with his arms crossed.

"Who do you think you are? The Rock?" Tyler asks him bemused.

"Some day!" Jacob tells him seriously.

"What're you gonna call yourself? Pebble?" Tyler deadpans, clearly unimpressed by his brother's bravado.

"Whatever!" Jacob counters, "Better than pancake!" He sniggers, referencing the bet his brother lost earlier.

Once they realize their mother is fine, the boys take off bickering, leaving the rest of us in the kitchen. I try to pry Tia off Mackenzie's leg while Grant, still perplexed, inspects his wife for any signs of injury. "Babe?" he asks, his voice filled with concern.

"It's Kenzie Kingsley," Ava finally squeals. "In my house!"

Grant looks at me in confusion noticing Mackenzie for the first time. "Oh, hi," he says totally unaffected by the towering beauty, exhibiting the one quality I most admire about him for the second time within the space of two minutes. No-one will ever stand in his way or turn his head when it comes to his love for Ava, no matter who they are. If only I could find someone to love me half as much as he loves her. He walks over and shakes Mackenzie's hand. "Welcome to the mad house. I'm Grant."

"Mackenzie, but please call me Mac."

"Not Kenzie?" Ava asks breathlessly.

"Kenzie Kingsley is my professional name. Family and friends call me Mac." She extends her hand to Ava, who takes it like she is accepting something so fragile and precious it will break if she grips it too hard.

"Ava."

I grab a grape from a ginormous bowl of fruit salad my sister has made in readiness for Tia's party, throwing it in the air and catching it in my mouth. It's tasty so I go in for a second. "Well, now the introductions are out of the way with..."

"Not all the introductions." Makenzie interrupts, tilting her head to look at me speculatively. "Although, I've worked it out."

I raise my eyebrows at her, encouraging her to finish.

"You're that actor, aren't you? What's his name?" She snaps her fingers as she thinks.

I'm not sure if I'm pissed she doesn't immediately know who I am, or relieved there's still a chance my anonymity could remain intact. I throw another grape in the air ready to catch it.

"Mitchel Dalton," Mackenzie declares triumphantly.

Her shock announcement causes me to lose focus and the grape catches in my throat. Ava and Grant contort in hysterics as I manage to stop myself from choking. "You've got to be fucking kidding me!" I splutter.

"Daddy." *Shit!* I forgot she was still here.

"Sorry peanut." I look down at my daughter and

she smiles back at me as my sister wipes the tears from her eyes and holds out her hand for the cash I owe. "I'll make a transfer at the end of the day." I tell Ava. "I've got to get through the party yet."

"Speaking of which," Grant interjects, slapping me on the shoulder. "I could do with a hand outside man."

"Sure," I follow him out of the room, glancing back to frown over my shoulder at a grinning Mackenzie as leave. I know she'll be fine with my sister when Ava stops fangirling.

"So?" Grant asks, when we are out of earshot. "It's not like you to pick up a woman and bring her back here, or to introduce her to Tia so early in the game. In fact, this is the first time you've done either. Man, I know she's hot but…"

"It's not like that," I interrupt. "She's married for a start. As are you." I remind him.

"Relax. You know your sister is the love of my life. Even so, I'm married not dead, I've got eyes just like you have. If you want to try and convince me your reasons for bringing her here are totally innocent, you'd better start explaining." The fucker smirks, so I fill him in on my morning before we engage in general chatter while we finish decorating the garden.

A couple of hours later, Mackenzie emerges with a couple of beers which she hands to me and Grant. "Wow. You guys have done a great job," she praises the pair of us. "Grant, Ava has asked for your help when you are finished out here." He takes off leaving us alone. "Why didn't you just pay someone to come in and do all this for you?"

I side eye her, not wanting to speak until she at least acknowledges I'm not the ass Mitchel Dalton.

She smiles. "Chill, I know who you are, Jared James Jones."

"Glad to hear it," I reply gruffly. "To answer your question, Ava and I enjoy doing it. Our parents didn't have a lot of money when we were growing up but it never mattered. They always put in the effort to make sure our birthdays and the holidays were really special. Those are the sorts of memories I want to create for Tia. I don't want her growing up thinking everything can be bought, or that her dad doesn't care enough to get involved."

"You're a good father." Mackenzie touches my forearm lightly so I look at her.

"I'm glad you think so," I tell her honestly, "Although most of the time, with Tia, I feel completely out of my depth. Speaking of," I drag my fingers through my hair as I prepare myself to ask for the impossible, "All her life I've tried to protect her by keeping her out of the public eye, by trying to keep her existence a secret. I'll admit it's getting harder and harder to achieve every day, but I want her to have a normal childhood for as long as she can. I'd appreciate it…"

"If I didn't let the cat out of the bag. I get it," Mackenzie's smile drops, "My parents, they were the opposite of yours. Always too busy for me and my brother. It was just the two of us for as long as

I can remember. Neither of us could wait to leave home, so when I hit eighteen and got offered a modelling contract, I jumped at it. My only regret is I had to leave my brother behind because he was younger than me and still at high school. I called him every day until he met his best friend and they became inseparable. I didn't have to worry about him so much after that. He spent more time at his friend's house than he did our own, and there was a wonderful woman called Elena there, she kept an eye on him and helped mould him into the man he is today. It's not that our parents were bad people, it's just they were so career orientated."

"Don't make excuses for them Mac." I snap, "They chose to be parents."

"Did you?" She throws back immediately sensing she's hit a nerve.

"Honestly, no. Although I wouldn't it change it for the world. That little girl is the best thing that's ever happened to me."

"I always wanted children." She sighs wistfully. "Dan kept putting it off."

"Maybe that's a blessing." I blurt out before I can stop myself. When I see her getting tearful, I instantly regret my outburst. "There's still time." I add softly.

"Maybe," she gives me a weak smile and I drape my arm across her shoulders, pulling her into my side for a hug. "I won't say anything, I promise. What about the parents coming to the party though, how do you know they will be so discreet?"

"Those that have got any sense will drop their kids off and bolt for a couple of hours down time. Those that don't have any sense," I shrug, "They're easier to fool, and I've gotten pretty good at becoming invisible."

"How?"

"You'll see," I laugh. "Especially since I don't want you drawing attention by anyone recognizing you, we'll have to make you invisible too."

We fall into a companiable silence until our peaceful interlude is shattered by a tiny tornado barrelling outside and flinging herself at me. I pick her up and swing her up into my arms. "Hey peanut, 'sup?"

"Aunt Ava said to tell you it's time to get ready."

"She did?" I act surprised.

Tia nods her little head enthusiastically.

"Well, I guess we better get changed then."

"I'm going dress like a fairy." Tia tells Mackenzie, before the rest of her words come out in an excited rush. "Daddy brought me a pink dress with silver wings that sparkle, and I have a wand and aunt Ava wrote to clitoris to ask for her to send me some fairy dust so I can make wishes for everyone at my party."

"I think you mean Chloris." I correct her whilst trying not to laugh. "When Aunt Ava was little, she used to know a fairy called Chloris, peanut."

"Swat I said, daddy." Tia looks at me indignantly before turning to our guest.

"What are you going to be?"

Mackenzie looks over at me in amusement.

"Invisible apparently."

Chapter Six

꙰

W hen Ava suggested making the party fancy dress, it seemed like such a great idea. "It'll be so much fun. The kids can choose what they want to wear and then we can have a theme for the adults. It'll be the perfect way to disguise you so you don't get recognised," she said. "The children will love it if all the adults wear costumes as well," she said. "Remember your seventh birthday party when everyone dressed as superheroes and how cool that was?" It was cool, and to this day it remained one of my favourite memories growing up, that's why I agreed. "You've been so busy lately; I'll go and hire our costumes. You can trust me," she said.

I scowl at Ava, who is dressed perfectly respectably, since she had to bequeath her own outfit to Mackenzie so that she, too, could attend the party incognito.

The theme she chose for the adults. Not superheroes, or pirates, or anything remotely cool. Fruit and fucking vegetables. "It'll be educational," she giggled, when I went in to get changed and lost my shit when I saw the outfits for the first time. "It'll help promote healthy eating." I'd trusted her! I'd trusted her so much it never occurred to me doubt her. I'll never make that mistake again. I flat out refused to put the damn thing on until she played her ace, said the words guaranteed to make me fold every time. "Do it for Tia."

"How you holding up?" Grant waddles over, sweating and looking about as happy as me. He is dressed as an aubergine. His face, which pokes out of the hole cut into the costume so he can see, has been painted purple to blend in with the colour of his foam suit. His arms and legs also match the colour of the outfit, thanks to the purple jumpsuit he is wearing underneath. If I wasn't in exactly the same predicament, I'd be taking great delight in telling him how he'd handed my sister his balls, for years to come.

"Just so you know, one way or another I will make Ava pay for this." I growl.

"Duly noted." He tells me. "Just so you know, next time we have the house to ourselves; I'll be making her pay enough for the both of us."

"Eww. How many times do I have to tell you? That's my sister dude! And don't even get me started on the fact she dressed you like a giant walking dick emoji. I mean, it's not as if any these kids even know what an aubergine is, why the hell did she pick that?"

"She worships my cock. What can I say?" He jerks, which I think is due to the fact he shrugs, it's hard to tell. "Did you remember to put some sunscreen on your nose?"

"What?" I snap.

"Wouldn't want you to peel." He bursts out laughing.

"Fuck off!"

"Daddy, you said a bad word."

Fucks sake! Where did she spring from? I swear she should be dressed like a ninja!

"Sorry peanut." The cutest little fairy beams up at me. She is wearing the outfit I bought her. Much to her delight, Mackenzie curled her hair and tastefully painted her face with pink and silver glitter to match her dress. "What can I do for you?"

"Aunt Ava said to tell you she has never seen a banana do the splits before."

"She did, did she? Go tell her she won't be seeing it today either." I look over at my sister, who is dishing out drinks and avoiding my gaze as she rolls her lips trying not to laugh.

Tia skips off merrily as I scan my surroundings, I've been to some wild parties in my time, but nothing compares to what I'm experiencing now. Music blares from the speakers Grant and I set up earlier. I feel like I'm tripping as I watch a bunch of grapes and giant strawberry dancing with a group of children in the middle of the lawn. There's a giant sprig of broccoli trying to maintain some semblance of control over at the bouncy castle, and a giant orange is using a variety of props to take comedic photos at our specially constructed booth. There is a lot going on, but it's the carrot that has set up a face painting table and is currently working on turning a small child into a tiger, that holds my attention.

"I'm just going to check on Mac." I tell Grant, before one of the twins pushes between us as he tries to stomp past.

Grant and I grab an arm each to stop him.

"Looks like we have an escape-pea." I tell my brother-in-law who chuckles.

"Where do you think you are going?" Grant asks his son.

"I can't suffer the indignity of being dressed like this any longer." A painted green face whines.

"You and your brother can't be peas in a pod if there is only one pea." Grant reminds him.

"I don't care."

"Where is your brother anyway?" I ask, as the second twin comes flying out of nowhere, yelling "Geronimo!" before flinging himself at his brother and attaching himself courtesy of the Velcro on the sides of their costumes. Individually, they are dressed as one pea poking out of half of a pod; together, they look like two peas in a single pod. Even I have to admit their costume is a stroke of genius.

"C'mon Jacob, stop being such a buzzkill," Tyler laughs at the grouchy expression on his brother's face. It's then it hits me: Jacob is a lot like Grant and me, whereas Tyler is a lot more relaxed like Ava. Maybe that's the key to finally being able to tell them apart. "TIA," Tyler suddenly yells so loudly that she looks up and comes running over. Tia takes one look at them and doubles over laughing, wrapping her arms around her little body as she chuckles uncontrollably. Every time she looks at them since they dressed up, she reacts the same way. It's the best feeling to see her unrestrained laughter.

"You look so funny." She chortles.

"This isn't about you," Tyler whispers to Jacob, "Look how happy she is."

"Fine," Jacob grumbles.

I couldn't love either of them more for their desire to please my daughter, and make a mental note to reward their selflessness by getting them the new bikes I know they've been wishing for. Ava will fight me on it if I tell her what I'm about to do, but maybe if they just magically appear, she'll believe me if I tell her Tia's fairy dust actually worked.

"C'mon Tia," Tyler says, "Let's go and get our picture taken, then you can sprinkle Jacob with some of your magic powder and make him less grum'pea' and more hap'pea'."

Everyone groans, except Tia who jumps up and down in excitement. The three of them disappear and Grant waddles off to check on Ava. I make my way over to Mackenzie who has just finished her latest masterpiece.

"And what noise do Tiger's make?" I hear her say.

"RARRRR." The little boy in front of her shouts.

Mackenzie raises her hand for a high five, and the lad slaps it before running off. She has been hard at it all afternoon, firstly by helping Ava, Grant and I with the party preparations, and now by working her way through a queue of raucous children begging her to make them up to look like their favourite animal, superhero, or similar.

When she is finally finished, I creep up behind her and whisper in her ear, "I bet this is the first time in your career you've been asked to model as a giant carrot."

She turns to me and grins. "It is actually. Is this the first time you've agreed to dress as a giant banana?"

"First, *and* last." I sigh, "I was hoping I'd never have to sink this low but my sister feels the need to keep me grounded. I'm sorry, I bet this wasn't the sort of day you had planned when you got up this morning."

"To be honest, I didn't have much of a plan at all when I got up this morning. Today has been... unexpected, in a good way, and so much more fun than I thought it would be. I can't thank you enough."

"You're actually being serious, aren't you?" I have to admit I wasn't expecting that. I thought that once the shock of what happened with her husband at the restaurant had worn off, she was more than likely going to run for the Hollywood hills.

"I am," she tells me sincerely. "Everyone has been so kind. Despite my ruining your morning, and the fact I'm a virtual stranger, everyone has welcomed me with open arms and let me experience what it feels like to be part of a loving family for a little while. It's a memory I will always treasure for the rest of my life."

"Mac, you do realise we aren't just going to disappear at the stroke of midnight? We still need to pick up our chat from earlier, but I don't feel like I can have a serious conversation with you while I'm trying to salvage some pride from being encased in a bright yellow, elongated piece of foam and a body suit so tight I think I'm going to have to wait for my balls to drop again."

"I think you look very a-peel-ing," she chuckles.

"Don't you start," I roll my eyes. "How's my face?"

"Holding up. You could lose the frown though; this is supposed to be a party," Mackenzie sniggers. Like Grant, my face has been painted to match the colour of the suit I'm wearing. I'm sweltering and worried my sweat has started to make the colour run. I don't want to ruin my disguise. "How's mine?"

"Still a bright and vibrant shade of orange," I confirm. "Since we are obviously looking our very best, shall we immortalise this momentous occasion?" I jerk my head to the photo booth.

"Can we?" I've never seen a carrot get so animated. The green plume on the top of her head is shaking madly as she bobs up and down in excitement, clapping her hands. "You wouldn't mind?"

"As long as you promise not to run off with the pictures and sell them to the highest bidder."

"I promise." She raises her right hand as if taking an oath when she speaks.

"C'mon then."

What is supposed to be a single photograph turns into what feels like a hundred. After the first couple of shots, Tia comes running over demanding to be included, then the twins, then Grant and Ava. We lark around with the props until a little girl comes running to tell us a boy called Michael has a grape stuck up his nose. How it got there, I have no idea. I give Ava the look that tells her she owes me, and she immediately scoots off to deal with the problem, hopefully getting covered in snot at the same time. After that catastrophe is resolved, the rest of the afternoon goes like clockwork. Ava lights the candles on the fairy castle cake, and we all sing happy birthday. Then we play games until the parents that didn't fancy staying to be stripped of their dignity arrive to pick up their offspring, so the big clean up can commence.

It's seven o'clock before I finally head inside to shower and change. Removing the face paint is harder than I thought it would be. I climb out of the shower and pause to look in the mirror, checking to see if I look human again or if I still resemble someone with a bad case of jaundice. Just then, the bathroom door flies open and Mackenzie strides in, catching me in all my glory. I know I should be a gentleman and cover the essentials, but the shocked expression on her face as her eyes skate over my naked body provokes the devil within me.

"Like what you see?" I try to hide my smirk, but don't think I do a very good job of it.

"I'm s... sorry," she stutters, "A... Ava said I could come in here to get cleaned up. I guess she didn't realise you were already here."

Sure she didn't!

"It's fine." I slowly wrap a towel around my waist and when Mackenzie's eyes finally drift up to my face, I tell her, "I was just about done. Are you?"

Even though she is blushing furiously, she composes herself pretty quickly, stepping forward to trace her index finger across the ink covering my left pec as she admires the design. Her touch is electric when it hits my skin, surprising me and throwing me a little off kilter. "I didn't know you had a tattoo."

"It's pretty new." I admit.

"It's beautiful." Mackenzie seems entranced as she continues checking out the detail in the artwork. "It's a phoenix, right? Wrapped around Tia's name. But it doesn't look quite finished, why is there a void here?" Her fingertip dusts over the patch of skin she is referring to as her questioning eyes hold my own. The sensation causes most of the blood in my system to drop south.

"Because someday I want more kids," I tell her simply. I'm struggling to keep my voice level and the words come out huskier than I would have liked. "I got them to work it so I could add in more names if it happens."

"Kids?" She asks breathily, looking back down to fixate on my chest. "How many more would you like?"

"I haven't thought that far ahead," I answer honestly as I try to focus on keeping my dick in check. "I just know that someday I'd like more, and I can't rule out the possibility that if it happens, I might be blessed with more than one. As you've already seen, having twins runs in the family. The gene is on our side; my grandmother was a twin.

"Why a phoenix?" Her voice is barely more than a whisper while my cock throbs harder with every passing second.

"So many reasons," I murmur, the tension between us is thick and heavy, suddenly crackling with unfulfilled desire.

"Tell me, I want to know."

"It can represent, protection and strength which is why it wraps around my daughter's name. I'll always do whatever I can to keep her safe, and it also serves as a reminder that no matter what happens in my life, I have to stay strong for her sake."

"Mhmm." Mac's hand seems to have drifted down to my abs, tracing the ridges between the muscles.

"It's also the symbol for rebirth and renewal. I had to figuratively rise from the ashes a better man when Tia came into my life."

"Anything else?" She breaths, as her finger makes its way to the top of my happy trail.

"Healing, resilience, courage and hope." I grind out as I'm about to lose all control. Mac looks up and her eyes go wide. She steps back horrified, as if only just realising how intimate her touch had become.

"I'm sorry." She says, her panicked eyes darting

around the room.

I step forward and gently place my hand under her chin, raising it so she has to look me in the eyes.

"If I minded you touching me, I would have stopped you before now."

She swallows, her pupils have dilated so much, the colour of her iris is barely visible.

"I'm married," she says sadly. "Even if he was never faithful to me, I've never cheated, not once."

"Why am I not surprised to hear he's cheated?" I growl menacingly.

She steps back and I step forward closing the gap between us again.

"They mean something to me, the vows I took."

"But nothing to him evidently." I challenge.

"He wasn't always... I mean in the beginning..." Her voice trails off as I lean in to her.

"Save it," I bark irritably. "I'm not the bad guy here..." I really don't want to be talking about her jerk of a husband right now. I can't explain why I'm drawn to her the way I am. My mouth descends like a magnet, my lips hovering so close to hers we are almost touching. I wait impatiently for her to grant me the permission I need to put us both out of our misery. "...unless you want me to be."

"I can't." She steps back again, and this time, although I'm disappointed, I don't follow. "I should go."

"Stay. You get cleaned up while I put Tia to bed, and then we can talk." I don't want her to leave, but I know I can't stop her if that's what she really wants to do.

The bathroom door closes behind me and I lean against it, taking a few deep breaths to try and tame the beast that's risen beneath my towel. I could really do with jerking off, but now that the bathroom is occupied, the only option left is to fight to regain my control, throw on some clothes, and go in search of my daughter."

I find her curled up on the couch, cuddling her teddy and fighting to keep her eyes open.

"I was just going to put her to bed," my sister whispers. "She's exhausted."

"I got it," I tell her, gently picking Tia up. She cuddles into me sleepily and I melt. "Where are Grant and the boys?"

"They've gone to grab us some burgers," Ava replies.

"They didn't eat enough earlier," I ask bemused.

"It seems the twins are always hungry these days," she chuckles. "I can't keep up. Plus, we adults have been so busy that I'm pretty sure none of us have eaten. I'm too tired to cook and I'm craving a quarter pounder with fries."

"Thanks sis." I lean forward and kiss her on the cheek.

"For what?" She looks at me confused.

"For being you," I tell her. "I couldn't have pulled all this off without you."

"Sure you could." She laughs as her eyes dance with mischief, "I take it you've forgiven me for your choice of wardrobe."

"Not even a little." I give her my fiercest look. Far from frightened she just laughs harder. "I'm putting my daughter to bed," I say indignantly before telling her seriously, "Don't let Mac leave until I've had a chance to see her." I walk away before she has a chance to respond.

Twenty minutes later I'm back in the kitchen. Grant and the boys are unpacking a pile of food and setting it out on the table, Ava is grabbing some napkins out of a drawer, and Mackenzie is watching the whole scene, transfixed.

"I should go," Mackenzie says as I enter the room, "I was just waiting to say goodbye."

"You can't go," Ava cries, "Not yet, you haven't eaten since breakfast, we weren't sure what you liked so we got you a chicken, beef and vegetarian option."

"You did?" Mackenzie looks surprised.

"Of course," Ava matches her surprised look before her face clouds with a sudden realisation, "unless you have other plans. I'm sorry, we should have checked instead of holding you hostage all day."

Mackenzie smiles, "No, I don't have to be anywhere else. But you have to let me pay for my food."

"I don't think so," Ava tells her resolutely. "You've worked your butt off today helping us out, this is our treat."

Will all sit around the table, stuffing our faces and reminiscing about the day.

"Did Connor come? I was on the lookout for him,

but it seems our paths never crossed," I ask Ava seriously. "I was looking forward to meeting him... and his dad," I add as an afterthought.

"Yes, Connor was there." Ava smirks, "He was the one dressed as a fireman. His dad didn't hang around though."

I jerk my head in acknowledgement, a gesture she knows means they're not off the hook as far as I'm concerned. "He should have got his priorities right and been there for his kid. Bet he sloped off to play with himself," I mutter. Ava laughs while everyone else just looks confused.

I muse to myself petulantly, "I would have liked to have been a fireman today." I glance at Mackenzie to see her grinning at me. I frown back puzzled.

"Maybe next year," Ava giggles, making me realize I had unwittingly verbalized my thoughts. Suddenly, she blurts out the one question I desperately wanted to know the answer to, but was too afraid to ask, "So, Mac, where are you staying tonight?"

"I... I hadn't really thought about it," Mackenzie answers, dropping the last of her burger like she has suddenly lost her appetite.

"Will you be coming back tomorrow?" Ava presses on, God bless my sister.

"Tomorrow?" Mac asks, confused.

"For Tia's birthday silly," Ava says. "She'll be upset if you disappear without seeing her. I was thinking, after what happened this morning, you probably won't be heading home. If you haven't already arranged somewhere else to stay, you could stay here tonight and surprise Tia in the morning."

It seems like time stops as everyone stares at Mackenzie while she squirms in her seat uncomfortably. "I couldn't."

"Why?" Ava goes on. "Jared said you picked up some clothes when you were out with him today. The kids are always having friends over who forget to bring something or other, so I have a whole cupboard full of new toothbrushes and toiletries. Plus, you can borrow anything of mine if you can't find what you need."

"No one would mind?" At such a simple gesture of kindness, Mackenzie looks like she is about to burst into tears.

"Why would we mind?" Grant chips in. "I think we would all feel happier knowing you are safe and not on your own tonight."

"He's right." Mackenzie's hand rests on the table beside me, and I cover it with my own, feeling it shake beneath my touch. "Please stay, Tia would love it if you were here when she wakes."

"O...ok." Mackenzie smiles at us all. "I'd like that too. Thankyou." She picks up a couple of fries and pops them in her mouth.

I take a huge bite of my burger and start chewing to hide my glee.

"Fabulous," Ava declares. "Just so we're clear, you can stay with us as long as you need to. Although, when Jared goes back to Hollywood, it would probably be best if you go with him and stay at his apartment there."

Grant chuckles as Mackenzie and I start to choke on our food. Unperturbed, Ava continues, watching me with a mischievous look on her face. "I'm sure it'll be closer to work for you, and he could do with some company. That place is far too big for just one person. I worry about him rattling around in it all on his own. It's also got top notch security so he'll be able to keep you safe and make sure your husband doesn't bother you while you take some time to consider your future."

I narrow my eyes at my sister.

Too far Ava.

"Uncle Jared and Mackenzie sitting in a tree, K-I-S-S-I-N-G," one of the twins sings.

"Shut up Ty," Jacob snaps before anyone else can intercede.

"Why? You were thinking the same thing." Tyler tells him.

"No I wasn't," he replies staunchly, "I was thinking: Man, Gina's gonna be pissed."

"JACOB!" Ava and Grant both shout to reprimand their son for swearing.

"That's thirty bucks." I grin and hold out my hand to Ava, who just stares at me open mouthed as her husband bursts out laughing.

Chapter Seven

✧

When Ava invited Mackenzie to stay, I hadn't realised it would mean I would get relegated to the box room. I suddenly regretted getting Tia so many presents when I opened the door to see they had all been hidden behind a huge façade of boxes, crammed beside the small single bed. Squeezing into the bed was a mission, but once there, exhaustion took hold, and I slept like a baby for the rest of the night.

It was the screams at about six the following morning that ripped me from my sleep, and had me tearing across the hall in no more than my boxers like my life depended on it.

"What's wrong?" I burst into the guest room to see Tia bouncing up and down on the bed in excitement. Mackenzie is rubbing the sleep from her eyes and looking adorably ruffled as Ava and Grant also appear. Ava is wearing a pair of pyjamas, and in his haste, Grant has obviously grabbed her matching pink dressing gown and thrown it on. I shoot him a dubious look, and he returns it with one of his own—an undisputable *'fuck off'*, which makes me chuckle.

"I'm sorry," Mackenzie says as she sits up in bed, "Tia must have thought I was you and jumped on me. I forgot where I was for a sec and she surprised me."

"M'kenzie's here." Tia screams as she continues jumping on the bed, "Best. Birthday. Ever!"

"Is that my shirt?" I ask Mackenzie as I raise an eyebrow, my daughter's enthusiasm is shaking the mattress so violently I can't help but notice Mackenzies breasts bouncing with the movement. I snag my daughter around the waist and swing her into my arms as a distraction. "Morning peanut, happy birthday."

"Um... yeah, sorry I needed something to sleep in," Mackenzie murmurs. "I hope that was OK?"

"Well, it certainly fits you better than it ever did me," I tell her. She blushes as she looks down at herself, before grabbing the bed cover and pulling it up under her chin.

"Happy birthday Tia," Ava and Grant both coo as they surround me to each kiss one of Tia's cheeks.

"I'm older now daddy," she giggles happily, throwing her arms around my neck and hugging me tightly.

"You are peanut." Her excitement is infectious and I can't help but smile.

"How about we give Mackenzie the chance to wake up? While she does, you can put some of that energy to good use by helping me get the boys out of bed so they can have breakfast with you before they have to leave for school," Ava giggles.

Tia nods and Ava takes her from me, "Which one shall we attack first?" Ava asks as they disappear from the room.

"Jacob!" Tia yells.

"Good choice." I hear Ava say as they burst through a door further down the hall.

"Dude?" I look at Grant and gesture to his outfit.

"What? You'd rather I'd come running to save your girls in the raw?" Grant grumbles. "It's all I could lay my hands on." He flaps his arms and disappears with my laughter ringing in his ears.

My girls? Plural! Must have been a slip of the tongue.

I cross my arms and lean on the door jamb. "I'm sorry, Mac. I should have warned you. Tia's always been an early riser. With the excitement of her birthday, I should have known she'd be up with the sun and on a mission to find me."

When she doesn't answer, I smirk, realising it's because she's distracted as she checks me out. "Hey," I half shout, startling her so her eyes snap up to my face.

"S...sorry," she gasps. I'm not sure if the apology is for not listening or for the way her eyes were unabashedly roaming my body.

I laugh and push myself off the door frame, "We're having a birthday breakfast for Tia, if you want to join us, I'll see you downstairs in fifteen." I leave closing the door behind me.

Mackenzie does join us, when I make my way to the kitchen after having showered and changed into a plain white T-shirt with blue jeans, she is already there, leaning over the stove in the black jeans she picked up at the thrift store and another one of my shirts. Her hair is pulled back into a high pony tail, secured by one of Tia's hair ties—a pink band with a unicorn attached. As she cooks, she chats amiably to Ava, who is busy making the boys' packed lunches.

I sneak up behind Mackenzie and without thinking, snake an arm around her waist as I pear over her shoulder to see what she is frying in a pan. Her neck smells of soap and her hair is still slightly damp from a recent shower. She gasps and jumps slightly at my touch, but doesn't pull away as I reach over with my free hand to steal a small piece of bacon right from under her nose.

"Hey!" She scolds as I smile and pop the contraband into my mouth. I huff as the hot meat sears my tongue, "Serves you right," she laughs as she swats me away playfully with her spatula, "Go and sit down, it's almost ready."

Grant comes striding into the room with Tia hot on his heels, "Your mobile was going off so I brought it down for you in case it was important," he says as he tosses it onto the kitchen counter.

"Cheers." I pick up the phone to see who was calling me, but soon realise the phone must belong to Mackenzie.

"Mac," I call.

"Hmm."

"This must be your phone and you've eighteen missed calls," I tell her.

"I don't care," she says gruffly without looking. "I know who it'll be. I'm not ready to see him, not yet."

"I get that," I tell her gently, "But you have voicemails and texts too. What if they're not all from him? What if there's an emergency and someone is trying to get hold of you?" Since Tia came into my life, I've never missed a call, ever!

"Who else could it be?" She whispers sadly.

"Someone from work?" I suggest.

"I doubt it, I've been let go." She still won't turn around.

What?

"When?" I frown in confusion.

"I got the call just after I met you in the diner. I haven't been getting many modelling gigs for a while now. Truthfully, I've been lucky to have lasted this long. I started to diversify in my late twenties when I could see the writing was on the wall, but I got the call yesterday to tell me I'd lost my endorsement contracts. Without them, I can't afford to continue producing and advertising my makeup brand, so now I'm pretty much screwed financially."

"M'kenzie." Tia calls.

I know what's coming.

"Yes baby," Mackenzie calls back.

"You said a bad word and I'm not a baby anymore. I'm older now."

Far from being upset, Mackenzie bursts out laughing, she finally looks up and over to where Tia is sat at the table. "You're right, thank you for reminding me on both counts. I'll square up with your dad or aunt in a little while for the bad word."

Tia beams at her as she kicks her legs back and forth beneath the table.

"HAPPY BIRTHDAY!" The twins holler in unison as they charge into the room with an armful of presents. They rush over to their cousin and start smothering in her in kisses. She giggles as she tries to bat them away with her hands.

"Couldn't you get a louder pair?" I gripe to Ava who just smiles.

Everyone carries the food that has been prepared over to the table, and we sit and eat while Tia excitedly rips into her cards and gifts.

Her favourite present of the morning appears to be a back pack with a toy Koala strapped to it. "I really wanted one of these," she gushes.

"We know, you only told us a million times and pointed them out every time we went passed them in the store." The withering tone lets me know this must be Jacob.

Tyler just gazes at her, happy that she is happy, mirroring the same look his mother is sporting.

"What are you guys going to do today?" Jacob asks as he inhales a piece of toast.

"I don't know, what would you like to do Tia?" I ask my daughter.

"THE ZOO!" She yells animatedly.

"Couldn't you get a louder one?" Ava mocks me, as I poke my tongue out at her.

"Sure, we can do that." I tell the birthday girl.

"You guys want to come?" I ask Grant and my sister.

"Why would I want to go to a zoo when I live in one?" Grant replies.

"I can't," Ava chips in, "I have to drop the boys' at school then I have some errands to run. How about you and Mac go with Tia, and then we all meet back here later for a special dinner?"

"Sure, would you like to join Tia and I, Mac?" I ask hopefully, thinking this could be the ideal time to find out more about her.

"Pleeeease?" Tia pleads.

"I'd love to." Mackenzie grins.

We finish our breakfast and it's a race to get ready. Tia decides she wants to see penguins, and the closest place is an aquarium in Monterey Bay, a good two hours' drive away. To save time, I take the minivan and drop the boys off at school on the way, leaving Grant and Ava the truck so they can get around during the day. Ava arranges for the twins to be dropped back by another parent she knows from their school, so I don't have to worry about making sure I'm back in time to collect them.

The day passes by in a blur. Tia is too amped up to fall asleep on our journey in the car, which means I can't ask Mackenzie all the questions that are rattling around in my brain. At the aquarium, we spend three and a half hours just mooching around and spending quality time together. Tia insists on taking her new backpack, which Ava fills with healthy drinks and snacks for the day. As she runs ahead of Mackenzie and me, I can't help but laugh at the cuteness of the koala as it stares back at me, looking as if it is holding on for dear life. We spend an inordinate amount of time at the penguins. Tia becomes mesmerized by their antics as they swim and waddle about.

"Penguins. They mate for life you know," Mackenzie whispers sadly at one point.

"Not all species," I correct her, before grabbing her hand and squeezing it gently. "Besides, who would want to be hitched to something that's slippery all the time and obviously fishy. Now wolves are a totally different story. When they decide on their mate, they're monogamous and usually stay together for life. The males are playful and protective dads that usually have four to seven cubs in their litter."

"Four to Seven?" Mackenzie looks at me wide-eyed.

"Just saying," I tease, before I'm dragged away by Tia.

It's the journey home where I seize my opportunity. As soon as Tia drifts off in the back of the car, I tentatively start a conversation that I hope will give me some of the answers I desperately need.

"So, did you get around to checking your phone messages?" I start hesitantly.

"Nope." Mackenzie tells me resolutely as she turns to stare out the window beside her, clearly signalling she wants to avoid this conversation.

"Mac..."

"I know what you are going to say ok? But trust me, there is only one person that would be phoning me that many times and we both know who that one person is going to be."

"Your brother?" I quip, raising a reluctant smile.

"He is on his honeymoon right now, so I very much doubt I'll be at the forethought of his mind."

"Yeah, that jockstrap mentioned it. He also mentioned you didn't go to his wedding." When she doesn't say anything, I press further, "Want to tell me why?"

She sighs heavily. "Dan and my brother don't get along. They used to, when Dan and I first got together. That all changed when he found out Dan was being unfaithful. I can't go into details because it's not my story to share, but Jack, he has a real problem with cheaters."

"I like him already." I glance across at the woman beside me and smile, "Go on."

"Although I left home at eighteen, nothing prepared me for the reality I was about to face. Sure, I got to travel a lot and made a ton of money, but the industry can be tough. I wanted to be the best of the best and couldn't afford to fail. My parents and I fought before I left, so going home with my tail between my legs wasn't an option. While most of the other girls partied hard and took recreational drugs, I preferred early nights, sensible diets, and exercise. When I started getting all the top assignments because they were always late or off their heads, they got jealous and started to turn on me. I'd never felt more isolated and alone. I used to look forward to my daily chats with my brother, but then he met his best friend and was always off and up to some mischief with him. Our calls became less frequent, and I missed him so much. That's when Dan came into my life."

She falls silent for a few moments and I wait patiently for her to continue.

"Dan worked for a catering company in New York when I met him. He was good looking..."

I snort.

"...and popular, all the girls flirted with him, but he only had eyes for me. I was lonely and if I'm honest, loved the attention. We started dating, and things got serious pretty quickly. When the time came for me to move on, he asked me to marry him. I was only twenty-two, and even though we'd only known each other a few weeks, I didn't want to be alone again. I was torn between him and my career, but he convinced me I could have both. If I married him, he would leave New York to be with me. It would mean I would have to support him while we travelled, but I made enough money for that not to be an issue. So that's exactly what happened.

For a few years, life couldn't have been better. Then one day, I got called into work because one of the other models, a girl named Cassandra, had phoned in sick. The shoot didn't go well, and it finished early. I got home to find Dan and Cassie wrapped around each other in our bed."

"Shit, what happened?" The pain in her voice

makes me grip the steering wheel so hard my knuckles turn white. I want to pull the car over so I can take her in my arms and give her a hug, but we are on the freeway so that isn't an option.

"There was a lot of shouting and throwing things. Then I left and holed up in a hotel for a couple of days. Dan tracked me down and begged for my forgiveness. He said Cassie had come onto him, and I'd been so busy working he was feeling neglected."

"Are you fucking kidding me?" I snap, then automatically say, "Sorry peanut," before checking my rearview to see she is still fast asleep in the back.

"We reunited and although I didn't catch him cheating again for another couple of years, with hindsight there were plenty of signs I chose to ignore."

"What sort of signs?

"He would often disappear for long periods of time, and when I'd ask where he'd been, he'd be evasive and say I was being clingy. Sometimes, I would smell perfume on his clothes, and he would brush it off, saying it must have rubbed off on him while he was hanging around on a shoot. Then, one day, I followed him and saw him heading into a hotel with another woman. When I asked him where he had been all day, he lied and said he had been drinking with his buddy, Marcus, who had been in town for the day.

Things started going from bad to worse after that. As agencies began searching for younger, new talent, work started to dry up. Dan liked the flashy lifestyle and hanging around beautiful women, so while I was at home, he continued to go out more and more. He'd excuse his behaviour by saying he was keeping his ear to the ground, so I'd be one of the first to hear about any potential new gigs.

All of a sudden, the loneliness I feared so much was back, and this time, there was nothing I could do about it. Even though he wanted to be free to do as he liked, in Dan's mind, I was still his wife and had to remain committed to him. There was no way he would ever let me go; he couldn't face the stigma of anyone thinking I'd left him. On some level, I did still love him, and my wedding vows meant something to me. I wanted to make it work, but I was starting to realise I was barely more than a meal ticket for him.

I decided to transfer the money out of our joint accounts. If he was going to screw around, I couldn't stop him, but there was no way I was going to pay for him to have the privilege. I was just a tad too late. He'd already taken everything there was. I didn't even own my house or car; all the assets I thought we co-owned had been put into Dan's name when they were bought.

One day, when I was feeling particularly low, my brother phoned. Since we were in the same town, he took me out for dinner. I tried to put up a front, but he knows me too well. He knew something was wrong and kept picking at me until I admitted I'd caught Dan cheating on me. Jack went ballistic. He attempted to get me to leave with him then and there. He wanted me to contact our parents, who are both attorneys, and file for a divorce. I was embarrassed, ashamed, and too scared to let him find out the full extent of Dan's betrayal, so I refused, and we got into a huge fight.

We're both stubborn people and didn't speak for a while. Then Jack suffered his own tragedy, which made mine seem tame in comparison. It took him a long time to heal, and he shut himself away from the world for years. If it hadn't been for his best friend, who stuck by him through thick and thin, I don't even want to think about what might have happened.

A few weeks ago, I got offered a job that required me to fly to London and then onto Rome. Imagine my surprise when Jack phoned me to say he would be in London for the few days I was there, and he asked if we could meet for coffee. I was so happy he was finally getting out and about, of course I agreed. We met in a tiny café, and it was a bit strained at first. Just as I was starting to relax, he presented me with a dossier of all Dan's indiscretions.

I think he thought that I'd only ever known about Dan's first affair, and that by proving there had been others, he could persuade me to leave him. Of course, things were so much worse, but I couldn't confess. I was just so pleased Jack was finally getting on with his life, that I didn't want him to start worrying about me. I ended up provoking another fight and storming off.

Jack co-owns a small flat in London that hardly anyone knows about. I hid out there until it was time for me to fly to Rome. I just needed some time and space to think things through. Dan followed me to Italy, and when he caught up, he had a shiner that he said Jack had given him. I was surprised Dan had the nerve to take him on; my brother can be a force to be reckoned with at the best of times.

Anyhow, it seems Dan had almost burnt through our savings. Now that I was having my earnings diverted into an account solely in my name, he was very remorseful about the way things were between us. He tried to charm me into giving him more money, and when I refused, he got angry. He busted my mobile, so when Jack left me a message to say he was getting married, I didn't get it. I only found out about the wedding during an argument when Dan let slip that Jack had phoned him because he couldn't reach me. Dan was obviously still pissed at Jack, or me, or both of us, and decided not to pass the message on. I doubt that even my own brother, the one person I had left who cared about me, would want anything to do with me now. I guess that's what Dan was hoping for.

So you see, Dan's all I have left. I've no job, hardly any money, no home to call my own. If I leave Dan, I'll have failed at my marriage too."

When I don't speak, I can feel Mackenzie's eyes drawn to me. "Jared, are you Ok?"

"No." I grind out trying to not to wake Tia, "I'm fucking furious!"

"W... Why?" She stutters nervously.

"That idiot has manipulated you from day one. He

took advantage of a lonely, vulnerable, and beautiful young woman, convincing her to marry him so he could give up his menial job and travel the world. He's fulfilled his narcissistic fantasies by financing the high life on your dime. And before you try to tell me he gave up his job so you could be together, how many other jobs has he had or even applied for since you married him? Even part-time or short-term gigs. None, I'll bet. And whose idea was it to put all your assets in his name? I'll bet it wasn't yours.

He swans around, shagging anything with a pulse, while he has the girl millions would kill to have waiting at home for them, pining for him. He thinks he is some kind of supreme being. Not only that, he makes you think you are to blame for his shortcomings by slowly chipping away at your self-esteem, destroying it to the point where you are virtually condoning his behaviour. Now you're trying to tell me that you think you are the one who has failed in your marriage and pretty much everything else in life.

The reality, sweetheart, is that not only are you incredibly beautiful, you are also kind, smart, funny, hardworking, and so much more than he ever deserved. I've managed to work that out in the short time that I've known you. That's the reason he has you isolated. He is scared—scared that if you ever left him, he wouldn't be able to hide behind you anymore, and people would see him for what he really is: a selfish, arrogant motherfucking freeloader with what I highly suspect is an infinitely small prick."

Rant over, I glance at across at Mackenzie who is staring at me with her dropped jaw swinging in the breeze from the cars HVAC system.

"I've one more question?" I snarl. My blood is boiling so hot I feel like my head is about to explode.

"W... what?" She stammers after a second.

"Just how many times has the fucker hit you to try and keep you in line?"

"Daddy, you said a bad word." A little voice pipes up from behind.

Chapter Eight

⋆

Mackenzie and Tia chatter the rest of the way home while I sit and fume in silence. I daren't open my mouth for fear that I'll be bankrupt by the time we get home now the vocabulary police are awake.

When we park up, I help Tia out of the car and she goes running inside to tell Ava about her day. I go to follow and Mackenzie grabs my arm to stop me.

"Only once," she whispers. "It was my fault. He'd been drinking and I provoked him..."

"Don't!" I growl, immediately cutting her off, "Don't you fucking dare try to justify what he did."

She goes quiet and looks at her feet, which are shuffling back and forth uncomfortably. I'm just about to leave when she starts speaking again. Her voice sounds strained and is barely audible. "The night before the morning I met you, Dan came home drunk. He was furious because his card had been declined while he was out... entertaining. He blamed me for not having the money I'd been earning paid into the joint account. When I asked him where all our savings had gone, he totally lost it. He was shouting and screaming at me for embarrassing him because he had to ask whoever he had been with to settle his tab. The argument got really heated. The more I challenged him, the worse he got. Everything escalated so quickly." She pauses for a moment to collect herself before continuing. "He caught me off guard when he slapped me. I saw him raise his arm, but I never imagined he would actually follow through. I stumbled back from the force of the blow and fell, crashing into a unit and shattering the glass. I cut my shoulder, and suddenly there was blood everywhere. I think Dan was more shocked than I was. He immediately tried to apologize and help me up, but for the first time in my life, I was actually afraid of him. I ran out the door, not knowing where to go or what to do. I jumped in the car and drove around for hours until I ended up in that diner, where I patched myself up in the bathroom just before you arrived. I was lucky there was a first aid kit in the boot of the car, together with some clean clothes that I must have taken to a job and forgotten about."

I gently put my hand on her shoulder and she looks up at me. "We can go and get your car tomorrow."

She shrugs, "It's not my car, not on paper anyway. I don't want it. I wouldn't be surprised if Dan either took it or had it towed away after we left, just to leave me stranded." I watch as her eyes fill with tears and can't help myself as I pull her in for a hug. We stand in silence as she clings to me until one of the twins comes charging out to see where we are.

"Jeez, not you as well," he grumbles.

"What do you mean?" I ask, mystified. I feel Mackenzie raise her head off my shoulder to look at the boy, and I assume it's because she's also baffled.

"When Jacob and I got home from school, Mom and Dad were making out in the kitchen," he says, contorting his face in disgust. "Jacob was so traumatized he had to go and lie down. He even made me put a cold compress on his head. He's so dramatic!"

"We aren't making out," I assert, as Mackenzie tries not to laugh.

"Not what it looks like to me." Tyler says, as he folds his arms across his chest defiantly. "I'd definitely say you're at first base."

"How the hell do you even know what first base is?" I ask incredulously.

"Duh, this is the twenty-first century, you know," Tyler counters. I try to fathom how this actually answers my question as he carries on, "Can you hurry it up? We're hungry, and Tia still has a mountain of presents to open before bed."

"Yeah, yeah," I say, taking Mackenzie's hand as we follow Tyler into the kitchen. Ava is already there, dishing up Tia's favourite: spaghetti bolognaise, to be followed by ice cream sundaes. After we eat, we grab drinks and head to the living room, where Grant has accumulated and arranged all of Tia's presents. It takes her a couple of hours to unwrap them all. She absolutely loves Mackenzie's gift—

a pink case containing a children's hairstyling kit, complete with a tiny battery-operated hairdryer. After throwing herself at Mackenzie for a hug, Tia turns into a very bossy hairdresser who insists on grooming everyone in turn. I'm granted a reprieve for my efforts in hastily constructing a salon in the corner of the room. At seven o'clock, I'm just about to take Tia to bed when Ava stops me.

"Wait! We have one more present, but it's for everyone," she announces out of the blue.

I take a seat beside Mackenzie with Tia on my lap. Tyler and Jacob look at each other, confused, as they sit on the floor in front of their parents. Grant moves over to perch on the arm of his wife's chair. He drapes his arm across her shoulders, and they share a look before Ava speaks again.

"I'm pregnant," she suddenly blurts out.

The whole room falls silent.

"What's pregnant?" Tia asks Mackenzie.

"It mean's Aunt Ava is going to have a baby sweetie, you are going to have another cousin. Isn't that wonderful?"

Suddenly Tia squeals so loud I'm surprised everyone's ear drums remain intact. "It worked." She climbs off of my lap and launches herself at my sister.

"What worked?" I ask, bemused, as I watch Tyler attempting to administer first aid to his brother, who appears to have keeled over and is now pretending to be unconscious as he lies spreadeagled on the floor. Every now and then he twitches for effect.

"My fairy dust!" Tia claps her hands excitedly. "I sprinkled it on aunt Ava and made a wish. It come true."

"What did you wish for peanut?" Everyone, except Jacob, who is still obviously reeling from his mother's recent revelation, stares at my munchkin in wonderment as I wait for her to answer my question.

"I wished that aunt Ava would have a baby and it would be a girl that she could call clitoris…"

"Chloris." Tia frowns at me for correcting her, and huffs at me for interrupting her ramble. I try to keep a straight face as my daughter stares at me, annoyed. Around us, I hear a ripple of giggles.

"…now she and uncle Grant and Tyler and Jacob, won't be sad when I come and live with you now I'm older daddy."

Ava, Grant and I look at each other. I drag my hand down my face and stand. "C'mon peanut, time for bed.

"Can M'kenzie read me a story?" Tia asks as she takes my hand.

I look to Mackenzie for confirmation, she nods.

"Sure, just one though, you've both had a busy day and like you, Mackenzie's tired."

"I'm not tired." Tia tells me seriously.

"I am though," Mackenzie backs me up by faking a yawn as she stands and takes Tia's other hand.

The three of us leave so Grant and Ava can help Tyler try to resuscitate the newest aspiring actor in the family. I've got to hand it to Jacob; Tyler's right, and he really does have a flair for the dramatic.

About twenty minutes later, I leave Tia snuggled up in her bed with Mackenzie lying beside her. Mackenzie is reading her a story I've already had to read numerous times in the past, and I'm grateful to be able to hand the responsibility over to someone else for the night. I wander into the kitchen and catch Ava there alone.

"Hey," I call as I enter. She is sitting at the table eating ice cream straight from the tub. I grab a spoon and go join her.

"I'm sorry Jared." She whispers.

"What for?" I shrug.

"I never knew what Tia was doing when she kept dancing around me, throwing glitter at my feet. I thought she was just playing. Now she really believes all this has magically happened so you'll be able to take her back to Hollywood with you. Talk about the worst timing ever. Grant and I thought it would be nice to tell everyone tonight, you know, as we were all together. We thought if you were there and we announced it on her birthday, it would make it more special for Tia. She has been missing you more and more recently. I was worried she would get upset or feel like she was being sidelined. Especially now she has started asking questions about her mom."

"Ah, don't worry about it." I tell my sister affectionately. "Look at it this way. It appears I have a daughter with the ability to wave a magic wand

and make a woman pregnant. With a bona fide hundred percent success rate, I can make a killing when word gets out."

Ava snorts. "She's going to be crushed when you have to leave and you don't take her with you. What are we going to do? She'll be starting kindergarten soon, and Connor won't be the only kid asking questions about her parents."

"I don't know," I answer honestly. "But we'll figure it out. We always do. I'm more worried about you?"

"What do you mean?" She asks as we both take a spoonful of ice cream.

"If you have a girl, she'll expect you to call her clitoris," I tell her seriously.

Ava almost chokes on her ice cream as she bursts out laughing.

"How do you feel about it? The baby that is, not the fact that if it's a girl you'll have to call her clitoris."

"Can you stop saying 'clitoris'," Ava wipes the tears of laughter from her eyes and smiles at me, it's then I notice for the first time that she is actually glowing, "Excited. Grant and I weren't expecting this to happen but we couldn't be happier. I was worried about telling the boys, you saw how Jacob reacted."

I kiss her on the temple as I steal the tub of ice cream from her. "I wouldn't worry about him, although he certainly loves his theatrics. I'm not sure where he gets it from."

"If I had to guess, I'd say it was his uncle." Ava

steals the ice cream back.

"Well, I have always thought he was exceptionally talented. Seriously though, they'll be fine. Look at how they both dote on Tia. Even though they make out she doesn't, she has them wrapped around her little finger. It'll be the same with the newbie, I can pretty much guarantee it. How far along are you?"

"Almost thirteen weeks. That's why we couldn't come to the aquarium with you, while you were there, we went and had our first scan. Everything is fine, and before you ask, there is only one bun in the oven this time."

"I'm really pleased for you sis. Aside from the fact it's gonna cost me an extra ten bucks every time I swear in front of the kids."

"I can help you with that."

"Yeah?"

"Yeah! Don't fucking swear!"

I laugh as we clink spoons.

"What's going on in here?" Grant asks as he breezes into the room. "Did I miss the invite?"

"Where are the boys?" Ava enquires.

"In Jacob's room," Grant tells her. "Tyler is excited and hoping for a brother he'll like for a change. Jacob says he isn't sharing his room, changing poopy diapers, or babysitting when we want to go out. He also said if we have a girl, to never buy her one of those kits like Mac gave Tia today because he can't be expected to wear pink bows in his hair on a regular basis—it'll ruin his street cred. He also wants his room soundproofed so his sleep doesn't get disrupted. When I left them, they'd decided it was all Jared's fault for spawning a daughter with magical powers, and they were trying to decide on what they were going to demand he buy them in compensation."

Grant and I smirk at each other.

"They're on board with the idea then," I say.

"It seems they've come around." Grant confirms.

"Seriously, I'm really happy for you guys." I stand, leaning down to give Ava a hug before going and clapping Grant on the back. "I'm off to check Mac has managed to escape Tia's clutches then I'm going to bed, it's been a long day and I've plenty of sleep to catch up on."

I gently push open the door to Tia's room. From under the soft glow of her nightlight, I can tell she is sound asleep and that Mackenzie must have tucked her in before she left. She is swaddled under her comforter with her teddy tucked under her arm. Her hair is splayed across the pillow and I creep in and kiss the top of her head. "Sweet dreams peanut," I whisper. She doesn't stir but once she's out for the count, she rarely does. I leave quietly, closing the door behind me.

I check on the twins next. They are both in Jacob's room, so engrossed in their video game that they don't even realize I'm there. Probably because they are wearing headphones, a prerequisite for playing the raucous racing game they favour after Tia has gone to bed. I close the door and wander down to the guest room, knocking gently.

"Mac," I call. When there's no answer, I call again and press my ear to the door. I don't want to wake her if she is sleeping but after her emotional confession earlier, I feel obligated to check on her before I turn in myself. I call her name again as I open the door. The room is empty, but I see the door to the en-suite is slightly ajar, steam billows out of the small gap and I can hear the shower running. I figure I'll just wait for her to finish. Once I know she is okay, I can head to my room and rest easily.

I sit on the bed with my back against the headboard, resting my head on the wall behind me. I stretch out and relax while I wait for her to appear. There is a television above the dresser at the end of the bed, it's on and playing a nature documentary. I'm just watching a pride of lions on the Serengeti when Mackenzie strolls out of the bathroom completely naked and looking like a goddess. Her hair is pinned up in a messy pile on top of her head, with soft tendrils hanging loose and framing her pretty face. Her breasts are jiggling provocatively as she walks, exquisite tiny orbs in proportion with her slim frame, and down below I can't help but notice she is clean shaven, I guess it's a habit formed from constantly being asked to showcase skimpy bikinis in the past. The sight of the tiny droplets of water running down her perfectly toned, porcelain skin, makes me almost blow like a horny teenager.

When she spots me and our eyes connect, she freezes in shock for a few seconds before we both move simultaneously. Mackenzie makes a grab for the towel she had obviously forgotten to take in with her, snatching it off of a chair and wrapping it round herself. I grab the pillow beside me and rest it in my lap to hide the growing evidence of my attraction. I know I should apologise, look away or even leave, but instead I lace my fingers together and place my hands behind my head as I smirk. What is it they say about never looking a gift horse in the mouth? I'll be able to dine off these new images, safely stored in my spank bank, for months, possibly even years to come.

"I... I'm sorry." She stammers, "I wasn't expecting anyone to be in here."

"One. Why are *you* apologising when I'm the one who snuck in here uninvited? Two. When you live in a house like this you learn to lock the door if you don't want to be interrupted. Trust me, you're lucky it was only me out here."

"Lucky?" She smiles, even if she is blushing furiously. There seems to be as much blood rushing to her cheeks as there is rushing to a different part of my anatomy. "Why are you here?"

"I just wanted to check on you before I head to bed. To be honest, I was still expecting to find you being held hostage by my daughter."

She smiles nostalgically. "She was asleep before I got to the end of the book. Isn't it a little early to be going to bed?"

"That means I'll have to read the same book to her again tomorrow night, just once I'd like her to pick a story about something other than fairies," I groan.

I've not had much time to sleep recently, I figured I'd stock up while I have the chance. Tia's an early riser, and I want to help Ava out as much as I can while I'm here."

"So, what you're actually saying is, you don't have much stamina?" She teases as she looks at me with one eyebrow cocked. Our eyes lock, and we embark on a staring contest as sparks start flying between us. I desperately want to launch myself at her and prove just how much stamina I have got, but I also want to challenge her. I want her to find the courage to fight for what she wants, give her back some of the self-respect her husband stole. A battle of wills ensues, and it's no surprise to me when she suddenly deflates and looks away. "Can I borrow another shirt to sleep in?" She murmurs. "I think Ava must have put the other one in the wash."

This time I do go to her. I let the pillow fall from my lap as I stand so she can clearly see the effect she has on me. She swallows audibly as I invade her space, closing the gap between us so I can whisper in her ear. My lips are so close they almost skate across the shell, my warm breath on her cool skin causes her to shiver when I speak. It takes every ounce of willpower I have not to touch her.

"You can," I whisper, "feel free to use anything of mine while you're here."

"A...Anything?" She stutters, as I flex my hips so my hardness gently nudges her thigh."

"Uh huh," I confirm, "See how easy that was, Mac? Don't be afraid to ask for what you want, not with me." I hold my position, hovering in front of her until she starts to tremble with the anticipation of what could happen if she's brave enough to take a chance. Then I pull away before she can make any kind of move.

The duffel I brought with me is still on the floor where I left it before I switched rooms. I walk over and grab a shirt, holding it up and open for her like a coat. Much to my disappointment, she doesn't remove the towel when she slips her first arm into one of the sleeves. I figure she is going to wriggle out of it once she is covered. However, when she spins to put her second arm into the empty sleeve I'm still holding, I notice her shoulder for the first time and stop her.

"Jesus Mac." I exclaim, pulling the shirt back off her. "You need to go to hospital."

Her face blanches as she suddenly remembers the deep gash on her back. It's surrounded by a cluster of smaller abrasions and deep purple bruises. The main wound is so long it starts in the middle of her right shoulder blade and disappears beneath the towel hugging her frame. It looks red and angry but isn't bleeding. "No, it's fine." She turns and starts to back away from me. "I'll patch it up, it's already starting to heal."

"Throw some clothes on, we're going to the ER," I yell, and immediately regret it when she flinches.

"N... no. Please Jared." She looks as if she is about to burst into tears.

I cross my arms, taking a few deep breathes to

calm myself down and even my tone. "Mac, that looks like it needs stitches. What if there is still glass in there? It could get infected, you could scar."

"It'll be fine. It's really not that bad. Please, I don't want to go to the hospital."

I'm torn. I really think she should seek professional medical attention, but if I force her to go, she'll think I'm no better than the dick she married. It has to be her decision, whether I agree with it or not.

"Please," she pleads.

I shake my head, hating what I'm about to say. "Fine." I think for a second before adding, "But I have conditions."

"Name them."

"You let me clean the wound thoroughly, dress it, and check it daily until it's healed. I'm also going to photograph it every day with my phone, because I'm not a fucking doctor and I need to compare the pictures to ensure it's not getting any worse. If it hasn't improved after a couple of days or you start to feel unwell in any way, you agree to come with me to get it checked out without argument. I can use the pictures as a timeline to make sure you get the best possible treatment."

"I don't know." She frowns while she contemplates which is going to be the lesser of two evils, my demands, or agreeing to go to the ER immediately. "Do you promise not to show the photos to anyone without my permission?"

"I do. Unless it's necessary."

"Ok, then," she agrees unenthusiastically.

"Right," I sigh. "Wait there, I need to go and find the first aid kit. Ava probably has more supplies than the hospital anyway."

"Wait!" She calls panicked as I attempt to leave. "What are you going to tell her?"

I wink as I turn to go out the door. "Not to disturb us as you've seduced me into playing doctors and nurses."

"You can't say that," she gasps horrified. "I'm married, what will she think?"

"That you've upgraded." I growl, before I disappear.

Chapter Nine

✴

It doesn't take me long to return with what I need. I know exactly where it's kept, so Mackenzie doesn't have to worry, there's no need for me to bother my sister. Ava's first aid supplies are so comprehensive that they have to be stored in a large backpack, which is stowed under the bed in the room I'm staying in. When I get back, Mackenzie is sitting on the bed waiting for me. She has changed into a loose-fitting tank and a pair of tight-fitting shorts. I dump the bag beside her and watch as her eyes go wide.

"You weren't kidding," she says, "When you said Ava had a lot of supplies."

I snort. "She likes to be prepared, she's the organised one of the family."

"What qualities do you bring?" She asks mischievously.

"The looks, talent and…"

"Ego?" She finishes for me.

"Ha ha. I don't think you want to upset your physician before he is about to administer treatment, do you?" I mock. She laughs at me before turning so I can look at her back more closely.

"You're going to have to take your top off Mac. I need to get a proper look."

She gives me a coy, disbelieving glance. I hold my hands up in defence.

"Seriously, I can only see the top of your injury."

She peels off her top and holds it tightly to her bare chest as I sit behind her inspecting the cut.

"Shit, I think there is still a piece of glass in here. Please Mac, let me take you to see someone who actually knows what they are doing?"

"No," she tells me resolutely. "I trust you to get it out."

"But I don't have any anaesthetic, it's going to hurt if I start poking around in there, or worse, I could do even more damage."

"It's Ok." She tries to soothe my fraying nerves, "I trust you."

"Let me at least get Grant to take a look, he is a qualified first aider."

"No." She tells me again, firmer this time. "It's you or nothing."

"Fine," I sigh. I take my mobile out of my pocket.

"What are you doing?" Mac snaps, and her body goes taut.

"Easy tiger," I grin, grateful she is asserting herself, even if it is taking the abomination on her back to make it happen. "You agreed I could take some photos remember. Then I want to google what I need to do. I thought you said you trusted me."

She relaxes. "I'm sorry, I do, take care of whatever

it is you need to."

I take several photographs from different angles and do a quick internet search, before riffling through my kit to find a pair of latex gloves. I position myself on the bed behind Mac, sliding my legs either side of her body to make us both comfortable, and to put myself at the best angle to take care of her. With the gloves on, I check to make sure there is only one piece of stray glass before using a pair of tweezers to carefully remove it. Mac doesn't make a sound, even though she must be in pain with me fumbling around inside her. Unfortunately, my actions cause the wound to start bleeding again, so I gently hold some gauze over the top, applying direct pressure until it stops.

"I know you've just showered, but under the circumstances I'd feel more comfortable if you would let me clean this again. You obviously couldn't see to do it properly or you would have known the glass was still in there."

I'm grateful she doesn't fight me. She simply stands and walks back into the bathroom. I follow, noticing how her face is pale and drawn.

"Are you ok?"

She nods weakly and I know I have to try and lighten her mood, distract her somehow, give her something else to think about while I finish taking care of her. I remove the gloves I'm still wearing, throwing them in the trash before starting to strip.

"What are you doing?" She giggles.

"The best way to flush that cut is to use the

shower. If I'm getting in there with you, I don't want my clothes getting soaked," I tell her. "I'll keep my boxers on."

"Do you have to?" She jokes.

"It would be unethical if I didn't." I respond with feigned shock. If she wants to play, I'm game. "I wouldn't want to get my medical licence revoked ma'am. Although, if some patients get a bit handsy, who am I to complain?"

She laughs, confirming my diversion is working.

I step into the cubicle and take the shower head off the wall, turning on the water until the spray reaches a comfortable temperature. I hold out my hand for Mac to join me. She is still clutching the tanktop she previously removed.

"Do you really want to get that wet?" I cock an eyebrow as I gesture to the scrap of material she is holding to her chest. She hesitates for a second as if unsure of herself. "It's not like I haven't already seen you naked." I remind her casually, "and you still have your shorts on."

She drops the tank outside the shower as she steps in with me. I immediately spin her so I can avoid being taunted by the rosy pink nipples begging for my lips. My cock is painfully hard as I try to concentrate on thoroughly flushing the tear in her back. She whimpers, placing her hands on the wall in front of her and bowing her head as she tries to deal with the pain. She doesn't complain or beg me to stop, even so, I don't want to be remembered this way, as the beast that did little more than torture her.

"I'm done here," I murmur, when I'm confident her wound is clean.

She exhales in relief before slowly righting herself. I put my free hand on her hip to help steady her. She doesn't turn around but stays standing with her back to me.

I move the shower head across her neck to the top of her good shoulder. "Are you sure you managed to wash the rest of yourself properly, or did you get distracted when you were in here before." I slowly move the shower down until I can use the spray to circle her left breast.

"Ohhh." She hisses. "I may have been a little remiss, missed some areas."

"Want me to help you?" I breathe in her ear.

She pauses, then nods slowly. I don't move.

"Tell me what you want baby," I whisper.

"I... I..." She can't seem to find the right words.

I wait, moving the shower head over to the other side of her chest, teasing her with the spray. I take my hand from her hip and fill it with soap from the dispenser on the wall. As I glide the water back across her body, I palm her left breast under the guise of washing it. She shudders as I tweak her nipple before moving my hand down to soap up her belly.

"I want you to..."

"You want me to what?" I prompt, washing away the suds by slowly trailing the spray of water down her sternum and over her shorts, before deliberately letting it rest just below the apex of her thighs. Her legs part, and I change my aim to deny her the pleasure she seeks. She writhes in front of me, pushing her ass back and gasping when she feels my erection behind her.

"I want you to help me forget," she groans, rubbing her ass cheeks up and down my length. I'm starting to flounder, clinging to the thinnest veil of restraint.

"How?" I manage to grind out.

"It's been so long since..." She whimpers, "Make me come."

I'm gobsmacked. How a man can have this woman and not want to pleasure her, is beyond me. I don't require further invitation. The hand I have on her belly seems to move of its own accord, dragging her shorts to her knees before my fingers slide up the inside of her legs, slowly making their way to the soft folds of flesh nestling at the top. She's slick with arousal when I use my thumb and fourth finger to part her lips so I can push my middle two fingers inside her. She whimpers and puts her hands back on the wall in front of her to brace herself, pushing back against me harder, grinding her ass against me. I let her set the rhythm as I pump my fingers in and out of her warm silken core.

"Shhh baby," I whisper as her moans get louder. "You have to keep it down."

I'm not sure if she hears me, her eyelids flutter as she loses herself amidst the sensations overpowering her body.

"Look at me," I growl, trying to break through her haze.

As she tilts her head back and forces her eyes open, I move the shower head I'm still holding in my other hand, positioning it so the force of the spray caresses her clit. She falls apart almost instantly. I dive to cover her mouth with my own, swallowing her screams of ecstasy until she is completely spent and collapses back against me. I hold her trembling frame, being careful to avoid touching her injured shoulder, until she has regained enough strength to stand on her own.

I reach around her to turn off the shower, and silence reigns. She doesn't speak, or move, and not knowing what she is thinking is killing me.

"Everything Ok?" I nip the side of her neck playfully.

"No."

Fuck!

"What's wrong?" I ask, petrified I've done something wrong. My heart is thumping so hard in my chest I think it's about to break through the skin.

She turns slowly and looks me dead in the eye, "I think I may want to do that again."

She smiles, I take in her flushed face and the plump red lips swollen from my assault. She couldn't look any more beautiful, and I grin back like an imbecile.

"We need to finish patching you up." I help her discard the shorts still tangled around her knees before pulling her out of the shower with me and gently wrapping her in a towel.

"But…" She gestures to my straining boxers and pouts. As much as I want her to take care of my situation, it's more important that we get her fixed up while she is still riding the high from her orgasm.

"No buts." I quickly towel myself dry and lead her back into the bedroom, resuming the same position from earlier by sitting her on the edge of the bed and between my thighs. I find some steri-strips and use them to close Mackenzie's wound as best I can, before smothering the whole area in antiseptic cream and covering it with gauze.

"Done." I exclaim proudly as I survey my handiwork.

"Thank goodness," Mackenzie gripes, "I was starting to wonder what you were doing back there you've been taking so long."

I tickle her ribs lightly and she squirms, giggling, before pulling out of my grasp and standing. "Careful." She puts her hand out to stop me when I try to follow her, "You don't want me to undo all your hard work." She uses her thumb to point back over her shoulder.

"You're right, I should go." I pull myself up and she closes the gap between us.

"Do you have to? Can't you stay a while?"

I drag my hand through my hair. "I'm not sure it's a good idea, Mac."

"O…Ok." Her insecurities overwhelm her and she shrinks away from me, scared and confused. I should have seen it coming and curse myself for being so insensitive.

"Hey," I step forward, gently cupping her face and raising it so I can gaze into the piercing blue eyes that are searching my own. "Don't think for one second I'm walking away because I want to."

"Then why?" She asks sadly.

I grab her hand and slide it over my straining boxers. "Because we both know what will happen if I stay, and it's too soon."

"But in the shower..."

"You asked me to help you forget. The pain. The hurt. The past. I could help you do that, even if it was only for a short while. You never said you wanted *me* and I get that, we've only known each other a couple of days. You're dealing with a lot right now and tomorrow you might even regret what we did..."

"I won't." She continues searching my face.

I smile softly, "I hope not, because it was one of the hottest experiences I've ever had, with one of the sexiest women I've ever had the pleasure to meet. A few years ago, things would have been very different, but I've got responsibilities now, I have to think about Tia. If I stay, I know I won't be leaving any time soon, then when Tia comes looking for me in the morning and finds me here with you..." I pause, choosing my words carefully, "She's never seen me with a woman before and I don't want to confuse her Mac, her life's complicated enough as it is. I can't risk her heart by becoming your rebound guy. At the moment you're just a friend having a sleepover, she knows you'll be leaving soon. If she gets too invested..." I kiss her long and slow and deep. Pouring all my emotions into that one kiss in case it's the only one I'll ever get from her. When I finally pull back, I know she understands. "I'm not going anywhere Mac," I tell her, gently swiping her bottom lip with my thumb. "When you've taken some time to process everything that's happened and you're ready, if you decide i'm what you really want, I'll be waiting."

Then I do the second hardest thing I've ever done in my life. I walk away.

Chapter Ten

⚡

It feels like it's the longest night of my life as I lie in the dark with my hands behind my head staring at the tented sheet covering me. All I can think about is the angel sleeping peacefully a couple of doors down. The memory of her naked body squirming, before falling apart at my touch, haunts me. There's no way I'm getting any sleep until I go and take care of business.

I glance at the clock on the nightstand beside me just as the digits change to 4.37am. The whole house will be up soon. If I don't go now, I will have lost my chance. I toss the sheet back angrily and climb out of bed. After cracking open my bedroom door to check the coast is clear, I don't bother with any clothes before I creep across the hall and into the family bathroom. I lock the door and immediately take myself in my hand, letting the images I was previously trying to suppress flood my brain. Relief comes a lot faster than I was expecting, a testament to the irresistible power of the carnal desires ignited by my earlier tryst.

After, I lean on the sink and gaze into the

mirror above it. My eyes are drawn to the phoenix etched into my skin. Considering the subject, it's not a colourful piece. It's a majestic and poignant depiction, weaved betwixt an intricate web of grey strokes, highlighted and shaded to create a striking work of art. As I continue to stare, I remember what it symbolises, and wonder if maybe it's time for me to find the courage to rise from the ashes once more.

I wrap a towel around my waist and go back to my room. I'm too wired to sleep, so throw on some underwear and head to the kitchen. I don't expect to find anyone there, and jump when a familiar voice startles me.

"Finished in the bathroom?" Grant smirks over the top of the mug he is holding.

Fucker! With two sons fast approaching their teenage years, he'd better get used to the bathroom being occupied.

He is sat at the table drinking coffee, and like me, he is just in his boxers. He jerks his head to the percolator on the counter behind him. "There's more in the pot if you want one."

"What are you doing up?" I ask, as I pour myself a cup of joe and take a seat beside him.

"Couldn't sleep and didn't want to wake Ava, she needs all the rest she can get right now."

"Can I ask you a question?"

Grant looks at me quizzically before waving his mug at me, "Shoot."

"Do you think taking Tia back to Hollywood with me would be a huge mistake?"

He regards me thoughtfully before speaking. "If you are asking me as Grant, your brother-in-law, I do. Tia has lived here full time since the day she was born and not having her around..." He shakes his head sadly. "Ava and the twins will be devastated, but..."

"But..."

"If you are asking me as Grant, a father, no I don't. I think it would be the smartest move you've ever made. Provided you agree to bring her back on a regular basis."

"Like I can keep away," I laugh.

"Seriously Jared, I honestly don't know how you've survived without her this long. I can't bear being away from Ava, the boys and Tia, for more than a few hours at a time. When she first arrived, granted it was a huge shock. Your career was just taking off, and you needed our help while you created a solid foundation for yourself and ultimately for her. Now though, you can pick and choose your roles, where you go, and how long you are away. You have enough money stashed to never have to work again if you don't want to, yet you still kill yourself trying to live this double life that doesn't suit you anymore."

"I'm not sure I get what you mean?"

"You live in that fancy party pad, but when was the last time you held a party? You live modestly these days; most of what you spend is on Ava and the kids. I mean, when was the last time you took a good look in your wardrobe? These days you walk around looking like all your clothes have shrunk in the wash."

"Jealous?" I tease, as I flex my arm to show off my bicep. Grant rolls his eyes and carries on regardless.

"That's another thing, you hardly go out unless it's for work. When you aren't here, you spend all your time in the gym. Before Mac, I hadn't seen you with a woman for months, not including the ones hired to make you look good at one of Jerry's events. You ditched the playboy lifestyle a long time ago. Every chance you get, you spend hours on the road, scurrying back here to be with Tia. You even skip sleep, like the other night, to do it. It's not healthy. When you can't be here, you video chat with her every day, but you still end up missing out. Her first word, her first steps, the first time she thought the Easter Bunny had hopped by and she woke us all at five o'clock in the damn morning, bursting with excitement to tell us she'd been left a special treat— you missed them all. I'm not saying all this to make you feel bad; I just don't want you to miss out on any more, not when you don't have to. Maybe this is the right time for you to have this epiphany. I'm not saying the new baby will replace Tia—I love that kid like she's my own—but it will certainly help fill the huge void she'll leave by not being here."

We sit quietly drinking our coffee as I consider his words. Finally, I break the silence. "How do you feel about the new addition?"

"Honestly? I couldn't be more thrilled. It was Ava that kept holding back, I always wanted a big brood. Lots of little Grant and Ava's running around. I was the one worried about how your sister would deal with the news. I mean, the pregnancy wasn't planned, Tia had the sniffles a while ago and Ava caught it. She had to have antibiotics and I guess they messed with her contraception."

"How does she feel now? Has she come to terms with it?"

"Yeah, before we went for the scan, she was more worried we'd have another set of twins and she wouldn't be able to fit five kids in the car," he laughs, "I told her you'd have just bought her a bus."

"Was it because of me?" I ask horrified.

"Was what because of you?" Grant looks at me confused.

"Did Ava put your plans for a larger family on hold because you were helping me by taking care of Tia."

"No, she didn't feel ready to put her body through another pregnancy until now. She had a rough time of it with the twins, the morning sickness was relentless, then she worked hard to get her body back in shape after the birth. Now the boys are older and not so dependent on her she feels more equipped to deal with it all again."

"You know, when Tia came into my life, everything was so messed up for a while. I don't know what I would have done if you and Ava hadn't automatically stepped up to help me out. I'll always be eternally grateful, we both will, but I'm ashamed to say I don't ever recall asking you how you felt about taking Tia in."

"You never needed to."

"I should have."

"I love you like a brother, but the decision was never about you, or Tia for that matter."

"What do you mean?"

"I'm going to tell you something now and I don't want you to go off the deep end."

"Okaaaay?"

"I mean it. Ava knows everything."

As I wait for him to elaborate, I start deep breathing to control the temper that's rising even before I know what he is about to say. Grant smirks me.

"Just remember we've been married for over ten years now."

I grunt.

"Back in the day, when I transferred to your high school, even though I put up a good front, I was struggling to fit in. When I joined the football team, Parker Johnson befriended me."

I snort. Parker and I had never gotten along. He was rich, and people said he was good looking, even if I could never see it, but he was also arrogant and cruel. The pair of us had been in more than one fight, and his sister, Mira, had been one of the ringleaders in harassing Ava.

"I thought he was popular and hanging with him and his mates would help me fit in. I didn't know it at the time but you'd just screwed his sister and by all accounts left her heartbroken. Anyhow, he bet me five hundred bucks I couldn't pop Ava's cherry. I guess he wanted an eye for an eye but knew she'd never give him the time of day."

I can feel my nostrils flaring and stretch my neck from side to side until it cracks. "Go on," I snarl.

"Well, I took that bet so he'd like me and started to pursue your sister. Which, I hasten to add, you didn't make easy for me. Thing is, the more time I spent with her the more I started to like her. The night she snuck out of your house to meet me was the night everything changed for me. We talked for hours, one thing led to another and we..."

"Can we go with held hands?" I growl, not wishing to know the finer details of their encounter.

Grant chuckles, "Sure, we held hands. After I," Grant uses his fingers to invisibly air quote his next three words, "held her hand," he laughs as I wince, "I knew she had me. I knew then she was the only girl I'd ever want or need. I knew I would do whatever it took to convince her to marry me someday. She had my balls in a vice back then just as she does to this day. So, you see my friend, if Ava told me she wanted me to help look after a hundred Tia's, there's no way I'd ever refuse."

"You're a good man, Grant." I clap him on his shoulder.

"So are you," he tells me. "Have you forgotten how you were there for us when the twins came along. We thought we were so prepared but it was so much harder than Ava and I ever thought it would be. They never seemed to sleep, and it was a constant round of feeds and diaper changing. We were exhausted.

As soon as you could afford to you bought us this house, we had a constant stream of food deliveries because we couldn't get out to shop, and you were convinced we weren't eating properly. You came over as much as you could and did your best to give us a break from it all. You helped me hold the fort so Ava could get her hair done or grab a few hours' sleep to feel human again. You stayed to help Ava get into a routine so I didn't have to worry when I had to go back to work. That's what families do—when the going gets tough, we band together and kick ass.

We fall into another companionable silence.

"What happened about the bet?" I say after a while.

"I told Ava about it; she was pissed at first and I thought I'd lost her. Even when she told me you knew and were going to kick my ass into the next century thinking it would make me disappear and leave her alone, I never gave up. I think that's when she finally realised I was serious about her. Eventually, she admitted she'd lied about telling you, and then she told me to take Parker's money. I didn't want to, I wanted to tell him where to shove it, but she was insistent, so I did, but I told her I didn't want it and gave her every penny. She used it to buy all those mysterious presents you found under the Christmas tree that year."

"What? So there really is no Santa Claus?" I ask, pretending to be shocked, "Don't tell Tia, she'll be devastated."

We both chuckle.

"You're a good dad Jared. I know whatever decision you come to will be the right one, and I'll back you one hundred percent. We all will."

"Thanks man." His words mean more than he'll ever be able to comprehend. We finish our drinks, and I ask, "What's the time?"

Grant looks at his watch, "Quarter past five."

"I feel like I need to clear my head. Fancy going for a run? We could be back before the others are up."

"Sure. Get dressed and I'll meet you back here in five."

We both throw on our running gear and head out. It's something Grant and I like to do whenever we get the chance. Grant's no slouch, and we cover approximately 5K in a little under an hour. We are laughing and bantering as we get back and stroll into the house. As we enter, I hear loud wails coming from the kitchen. My stomach drops instantly. I rush in to see Tia, red-faced and sobbing, clinging to Ava. Ava is holding her, with both Mackenzie and the twins hovering around, trying to help pacify her. I quickly move to take Tia from my sister.

"Hey, hey. Peanut, what's wrong?"

As soon as she sees me, Tia let's go of Ava and reaches for me. "I... I..." She's crying so hard she can barely speak. Her cheeks are streaked with tears and tiny droplets hang from her long dark lashes. "I... c... came... t... to... find... you... and... you'd gone." She forces out between sobs.

I hug her tightly, "Uncle Grant and I went for a

run. That's all peanut. When have I ever left you without saying goodbye?" She buries her head in my shoulder, and I feel her whole body shudder as she starts to calm down. I look at Grant and he knows my mind's made up. He nods in understanding. Now all we have to do is tell the others.

Chapter Eleven

E veryone bustles about as I sit at the kitchen table with Tia on my lap, trying to soothe her. She only releases her grip when the twins bring her breakfast and play-fight over who gets to sit next to her. A clever ploy to get her to sit between them so I can get up and go shower. When I return, Grant hands me a coffee. I lean on the countertop beside him, and we watch everyone else interacting as they sit at the table, still in their nightclothes, eating.

"How do you want to play this?" He murmurs while we are out of earshot.

"I have to be back by Saturday," I whisper, grimacing, "I have to take the woman who won me at the auction out on her date."

"Who's going to take care of Tia while you're off socialising?"

"I've been thinking about that." Grant follows my line of sight to Mackenzie.

"Do you think that's a good idea? Maybe come and get Tia after the weekend."

"You saw her this morning. What are the chances Tia is going to let me get out of here without her? At least she knows Mac, and I trust her. There's no way I'm leaving Tia with a stranger."

Grant chuckles, "Tia will play her like a fiddle." Then he turns more serious. "What if Mac's husband shows while you're not around?"

"I've thought about that too. Security at my place is pretty tight, so I know the girls should be safe when they are home, but I can't keep the pair of them cooped up forever. I'm going to hire some extra security for when they are out and about. I know someone who can put me in touch with a reputable firm. I'll try to shield Tia for as long as I can, but there is bound to be some kind of backlash when people start to find out she exists. I'll make sure whoever gets hired is filled in on Mac's situation too. That's if she even agrees to come back with me."

Grant snorts in amusement.

"What?" I look at him curiously.

"The way she looks at you, let's just say, I'd be very surprised if she didn't."

"How does she look at me?" I glance over at Mackenzie who seems to sense we are talking about her. She looks up and smiles coyly at me."

"Like that."

"Hmm." I murmur, distracted by the beautiful woman holding my attention.

Grant bursts out laughing, drawing my awareness back to him. "And you, you're not much better. You look at her like a horny teenager about to have his first wet dream. Put your tongue back in your mouth."

"I do not," I grumble belligerently.

"If you say so," Grant smirks back at me. "Look, I'll talk to Ava. I'll go with her when she drops the boys off at school, and then take her out for a bit afterward to break the news to her gently. Give her the chance to wrap her head around it."

"Are you sure? I feel like I should tell her."

"I'm sure. You focus on your girls; I'll focus on mine."

"Are you and Ava having a girl?" I ask in amazement.

"It's too early to tell, and I'll be happy as long as whatever we have is healthy, but I've just got this weird feeling. I can't explain it."

"I want to speak to Mac and Tia separately. I don't want Tia to get upset if Mac does say no, or for Mac to feel like I'm using Tia to coerce her into agreeing to something she doesn't want to do. Although, I doubt that I'll get the opportunity to get Mac alone before Tia's in bed tonight. Can you ask Ava not to say anything until then?"

"Sure. I'll take Ava and the boys out for dinner later, maybe catch a movie after, give you guys some space to talk it out."

I jerk my head in grateful acknowledgment. I have a recurring thought that terrifies me, and even though I dread the answer, I ask Grant anyway. "What if I'm not enough? What if Tia hates it in Hollywood and wants to come back?"

"Then you bring her back, or call me, and I'll come get her. But I can tell you right now that's not going to happen. That girl adores you. She'd live on the streets in a tent, as long as it was pink and she was with you." Grant sounds so certain, I believe him and relax.

"Thanks man."

"You may have one teeny tiny problem though." Grant holds his thumb and forefinger up, millimetres apart, to emphasise his point.

I groan and feel myself tensing again. "Already? What is it?"

"She wants a puppy."

"Fuck no!" I exclaim.

"Daddy, you said a bad word." A little voice come sailing across the room as Grant bursts out laughing again.

"Make that two problems," he sniggers, before we join the others for breakfast, "She also has ears like a bat."

When everyone has finished eating, the twins start their usual process of stalling to get ready for school. Grant claps his hands loudly to garner the entire tables attention.

"Ty, Jacob, get a wriggle on will you, or you'll be late." He frowns at Tia playfully, "Stop holding them up missy."

Tia giggles shamelessly.

"Do we have to?" One twin whines. If I had to guess that would be Jacob.

"The sooner you get there, the sooner you'll be home." Ava tells him.

"The later we are, the less time we're there." He

throws back without missing a beat.

Tyler giggles and offers his brother a high five. Ava sits glaring at them, open mouthed, as she struggles to conjure up a suitable retort. The look on her face is so comical the rest of us hide our smiles as we try not to laugh.

Grant steps in to save her. "I'm coming with you today as I'm taking your mom out after we've got shot of you two."

"You are?" Ava interrupts.

"I am." Grant rests his hand over hers, "We are going to go and look at some stuff for the new baby."

"We are?" Ava's eyes go wide with excitement.

Grant ignores her as he continues addressing his sons. "And if you don't get a move on, we are going to wait until all your friends arrive, then make out in front of them at the school gate."

"You wouldn't?" Jacob looks like he is about to faint.

Grant leans across and kisses a grinning Ava chastely on the mouth.

"Gross." Both twins shout, before shooting off as fast as their legs will carry them.

"What would you like to do today peanut?" I ask Tia.

Her lips purse, and her brow furrows as she ponders the question seriously. She looks adorable. "Can we go to the park?"

"We surely can," I confirm, and she grins at me.

"Can M'kenzie come?" She asks.

"If she wants to. She might be busy. Why don't

you ask her?"

We both look at Mackenzie who is smiling in anticipation of her invite.

"M'kenzie, would you like to come to the park and feed the ducks with me and daddy?"

"I'd love to." She looks almost as excited as Tia. I briefly wonder if I can send them alone, while I put my feet up in front of the tele and catch up on the shut eye that eluded me last night.

"Daddy pushes there and gets you really high." Tia tells Mackenzie earnestly.

"W... what?" Mackenzie stammers, looking at the cupboard where I'd previously joked we kept a stash of class A pharmaceuticals.

"The swings," I chuckle, deciding it would probably be wiser to go. There could be a good chance of Mackenzie reporting me to child services if I'm not around to translate Tia's ramblings.

"Oh," Mackenzie chuckles, "Of course."

"Wait." Ava says suddenly. "Will Tia's car seat fit in the truck? If Grant and I are going out straight after dropping the boys, we'll need the car."

"It doesn't matter." I tell her, "It's not far and it's a nice day, we can walk."

I look at Grant and he reads my mind. I need to trade the truck in for a more suitable vehicle and quickly.

"Tomorrow." He mouths to me. I nod back subtly.

"Come on wifey." Grant drags Ava up and out of her chair. "If you hurry and are ready before the boys, I'll let you make out with me before we have to leave." He slaps her butt and she squeals before he chases her out of the room.

"What's make out?" Tia asks innocently.

"Nothing you need to worry about until you're at least thirty," I tell her gravely.

Mackenzie scoffs and starts collecting up the dirty dishes.

"I'll do that." I tell her taking them out of her hand. "Unless you want a slap on the ass too, I suggest you go and get yourself ready."

Our eyes lock and I can't help but notice a lustful heat in hers. My cock twitches as she opens her mouth to speak, before looking at Tia and closing it again. She smiles, holding her hands up in surrender as she backs away, before disappearing.

It's always a mission to get out of the house and today is no exception. Tia is wearing a cute dress and is all ready to go, until she sees Mackenzie dressed in a pair of joggers and one of my sweatshirts, then she insists on changing so she matches. I huff in annoyance as I riffle through the closet trying to find something suitable. Mackenzie leans on the doorjamb watching in amusement as Tia vehemently disagrees with every new outfit I present to her. Finally, Mackenzie steps in to help, her first suggestion appears to be the right one, never mind it was the same choice I showed Tia at the beginning. After that, Tia has to decide on which essential items she needs in her backpack before we can leave. Call me crazy, but I'm not sure we really need to take a magic wand, some fairy dust, half a dozen marbles, a pair of socks and a photo of the twins, then again, what do I know?

We end up being out for most of the day. When we get to the park, I realise I had forgotten to take any food for the ducks. Tia is convinced they will starve if we don't find some immediately, so we take a detour to find a store that sells some. Mission accomplished; we head to the playground where I learn that Mackenzie isn't a fan of heights. Tia kneels on the grass with her hands on her knees, rocking back and forth in laughter, squealing "higher," as I push Mackenzie out of her comfort zone on the swings. She lets me torture her for my daughter's amusement, and as a reward, I treat us all to ice creams afterward.

It's at that point Mackenzie learns that neither Tia nor I are fans of cotton candy flavour ice cream. After a lengthy decision-making process and despite my reservations, Tia chooses that particular flavour because she likes the colour. Two minutes after leaving the store with our cones, and one lick later, I'm persuaded to swap for my butterscotch. One lick of that, accompanied by a disgruntled sigh from Tia, and Mackenzie willingly trades her strawberries and cream. I lose the pink monstrosity I'm left with at the first trash can I meet, but I don't care since the other two are so happy.

When Tia gets distracted by a puppy walking past, she twirls so fast she ends up wearing what's left of her cone. It's then I realize that Mackenzie is far more organized than I'll ever be, having thoughtfully grabbed a spare jumper for Tia and concealing it in her oversized bag before we left home. She hands me the sweater with a knowing smirk as we endeavour to clean up my child with a handful of napkins she also produces, after having previously stashed them in Tia's backpack when neither of us were looking.

We spend the rest of our time meandering in and out of a few stores before stopping for burgers and fries for tea. After that, we head home. Tia walks between Mackenzie and me, already holding my hand as she always does when we are out, but I'm startled when she reaches across and shyly takes hold of Mackenzie's too. I wonder if this is normal for her, if it's how she behaves when she is out with Grant and Ava. How will she feel back in Hollywood with only my hand to hold? Mackenzie glances across, as shocked as I am. Her expression belies her need for some kind of approval, and I smile back. I can't explain why, but my own personal feelings for Mackenzie aside, this feels right.

When we get home, Grant and Ava have evidently been back and left again. There are mountains of bags strewn in the living room. It's hard to tell if this is a good sign. Are they the product of Grant trying to pacify Ava after he dropped the bomb about Tia leaving? Or simply the result of an excited, expectant couple shopping for the baby they recently discovered was on the way? My questions are answered when I wander into the kitchen and see a note left for me on the worktop in Ava's handwriting. It's the last four words that ease my mind. It's a term we used all through high school to reassure each other when times were tough, and one, or both of us, were feeling uncertain about the future we faced.

We've gone out to the movies and
for something to eat.
Be back by nine as the boys have school tomorrow.
I've got your back. XOXO.

The three of us hang out until Tia's bedtime. Mackenzie is so patient, playing every weird and wonderful game Tia's vivid imagination concocts. When Tia is finally tucked up in bed, she can't decide if she wants Mackenzie or me to read her a story. I suggest Mackenzie and I take on the task jointly, and we both lie on Tia's bed side by side, facing each other with Tia sandwiched between us. It's a tight squeeze, but no one seems to mind as Tia listens intently while Mackenzie and I act out the story, adopting different characters and assigning them mad and over-exaggerated voices. I'm glad we managed to find a new book in one of the stores we visited earlier in the day. It gives me a welcome reprieve from the usual suspects Tia insists upon. When Tia finally drifts off to sleep, Mackenzie and I creep out of her room.

"Thanks for today," I whisper gratefully, turning to face her as I pull the door closed behind us.

"I should be thanking you," she replies. "This has far and above been one of the best days I have had in a very long time."

"You should set yourself higher standards," I joke. "Although I shouldn't complain, when the fact you don't could be about to work in my favour."

She completely catches me off guard when she unabashedly grabs my junk and cops a feel. "I don't know," she teases, giggling at my wide-eyed look of disbelief. "From what I can tell you don't appear to be lacking in that department."

She starts to slowly and rhythmically stroke me over my clothes. I know I should remove her hand, but I find crossing my arms is a more appropriate move.

"Mac," I growl, as I unsuccessfully try to stop myself rising to the occasion. "I thought we decided this wasn't a good idea."

"You decided," she purrs. "I didn't get the chance to say anything before you left the other night."

Something in me snaps.

I grab the hand she was using to pleasure me and drag her away from Tia's room, not stopping until we reach the guest room in which Mackenzie is staying. I pull her inside and close the door behind us.

Somewhere along the way, sanity prevails, and I manage to temper the flames of desire that are starting to ravage my body.

"Look Mac," I tell her decisively, making sure I stand a few feet away lest I do something I'll later regret. "There's something I really need to discuss with you before the others get back."

"I'm listening," she pulls off her sweatshirt,

throwing it on the bed as she closes the gap between us. She is wearing a thin T shirt with a scooped neck, it's obvious she isn't wearing a bra, and I immediately lose my train of thought.

My eyes roam appreciatively over her body, "How's your shoulder?" I ask. At least, I think it's me speaking; I don't recognise the low, husky voice coming from where I'm standing.

"I'm not sure," she tells me seductively. "I guess you'd better take a look." She pulls off her T-shirt and I feel myself starting to unravel.

"Mac," I plead.

"What?" She asks innocently, her hand is back at my groin and her hard nipples are crushed against my chest. When her lips brush mine, I lose my resolve, forcibly claiming the mouth that's been goading me.

Once the fuse has been lit there is not stopping it.

There's a frantic removal of clothes between hot feverish kisses. As much as I want to pick her up and take her like an animal against the wall, I know I can't, I don't want to hurt her, or make her injured shoulder any worse. It's been so long since I've been with a woman all restraint goes out the window. I need this, probably more than she does. I walk her backwards towards the bed before spinning at the last second so I fall down with her on top of me. She moves fast, desperate to take what she wants, pulling out of my kiss so she can sit up and straddle my hips. Our eyes connect before she slowly starts to push down on me. As I feel myself sliding into her warm, slick embrace, I swear I almost black out. She moans in pleasure as she swallows me whole, her ass cheeks coming to rest on my balls. Neither of us move while she adjusts to my size, and the feeling of having me inside her. Then, if I was anticipating a slow and easy ride, I was going to be disappointed. As every nerve ending in my body lights up like a Christmas tree, and I become concerned about how long I'll be able to last, I'm relieved to find she seems as eager to chase her release as I am. She raises herself once, sinking back down again, before her body starts working like a piston, frantically picking up the pace. I use my hands either side of her ass to help support her movements, gently pulling her cheeks apart to heighten the sensations her whimpers confirm she is already experiencing. Both our bodies are swathed in sweat by the time I feel the muscles in her core fluttering around me. I'm physically shaking and making noises I never knew I could as I throw my head back into the mattress, trying to delay the inevitable until she's ready. Every fibre of my being is strung taut, my balls are burning like white-hot coals ready to make the rest of my body combust. It takes considerable effort for me to focus long enough to move one of my hands between Mackenzie's legs. With skill and dexterity my fingers close in or her clit, I've barely touched her before she shatters with my name on her lips. Her body clenches, gripping me so hard I follow her lead instantly. The intensity of my orgasm consumes me, making me question every other romantic interlude I've experienced up until this point. Even the one that resulted in my daughter. A string of obscenities falls from my mouth as my hips rise automatically, driving me in deep so I can plant my seed. This is more than just sex, I feel an unfamiliar and primal, uncontrolled urge to mark her as mine. My body spasms out of control, repeatedly jerking as my seemingly inexhaustible release continues pumping relentlessly into her. She takes everything I've got before she collapses like a rag doll on top of me. I know how she feels, and I swear I'm seeing stars as my limp arms automatically splay out on the bed either side of me while I fight to catch my breath. I'm still panting heavily and trying to organise my scrambled thoughts when Mackenzie starts to move. Raising herself slightly, she rests her chin on her crossed arms atop my chest so she can look down at me with hazy, smouldering eyes.

"Now," she sighs dreamily. I'm still buried inside her, and she's still battling to stabilise her own breathing when she puffs, "What was it you wanted to discuss?"

Chapter Twelve

Ava leans into my new ride and hands Tia her teddy. "Be good for daddy, you hear?"

"Uh huh." Tia beams back at her from where she is strapped into her new car seat. I decided to leave the old one with Ava. A symbolic gesture on my part to remind my sister not to be sad, because Tia will be back visiting on a regular basis. My daughter is too excited about coming to live with me to notice the red rimming Ava's eyes or to catch the way her voice wavers when she speaks.

"I'll call you later." Ava tells her, and Tia nods her head enthusiastically.

Mackenzie is next. Ava pulls her into a hug and judging by the expression on Mackenzie's face, Ava must have jarred her sore shoulder in the process. "Thankyou for agreeing to go with Jared and help him out for a while."

"It's not like I had anywhere else to be." Mackenzie jokes in a light-hearted manner. "Thankyou for letting me stay this last week."

"Anytime." Ava gives her a weak smile. "I mean that. If staying with Jared's Hollywood alter ego gets a bit much, come back. If only to remind yourself the big banana that you met here is the real deal, all the rest is smoke and mirrors. Deep down all he's ever wanted is to settle down and have a family like Grant and me."

"Ava." I roll my eyes and stare at her wide-eyed in the hope she'll stop speaking.

She doesn't. "What? It's true. Sure, you switched careers because you found something you were more passionate about doing, but your long-term goal never changed. You've always wanted to get married and raise a few kids, live nearby so we could spend all the holidays together as one big happy family. You never cared for the fame, you just wanted to be successful enough to be able to provide for your family and make sure your children never had to fight to survive like we did. When you got the unexpected news that Tia was on her way, it came way before you were ready, even so, I watched you bust a gut trying to make that..." She spells out the next word so little ears don't pick up on what she is saying, "B-I-T-C-H happy..."

"Ava!" I bark. Ava snaps her mouth closed but she glowers at me. I glare right back.

"Can I ask you to remember me the same way? When you think of me, remember the woman you've gotten to know now," Mackenzie asks Ava, deflecting the conversation before it escalates enough for us to part on bad terms. "I don't know how Dan will react to me not going back to him. He has made a lot of influential friends over the years, and as I've recently discovered, has a nasty streak. I know he is low on funds, and I wouldn't put it past him to try and make a fast buck by selling a story about me. If he decides to do that, heaven knows what tales he could try and spin."

"Of course." Ava smiles sadly, before hugging Mackenzie once more. "Look after them both Mac."

"I will. I promise." Mackenzie lets go of Ava before giving Grant, who has been standing quietly on the sidelines all along, a quick hug goodbye and going to sit in the passenger seat of the car.

Grant steps forward and gives me a bro hug, thumping me on the back. "Good luck, you know where we are. Although why Ava is making all this fuss when you'll be back in a couple of weeks, and she'll be phoning you every day in between, beats me."

I smile and jerk my head in response as he steps back to leave Ava and me face to face.

"Don't forget, Tia's favourite dinner is..."

"Spaghetti Bolognaise." I finish.

"I've put my recipe in your bag, she doesn't like the readymade ones which is just as well because they are full of preservatives."

"I thought you would have made me a couple I could've put in the freezer," I joke.

"I have, they are in the cool bag in the boot."

"Of course you did." I laugh, shaking my head.

"And I've framed one of the pictures of us all together at her party for her bedside, so she doesn't forget..."

"Ava." I pull her into a hug as her tears start to flow. "She isn't going to forget you. We aren't leaving the country. We are literally only going to be a couple of hours drive away in the same place I've been living for the last five years. Plus, you're kind of annoying, not to mention emotional. You leave an impression."

Ava huffs out a laugh between sobs.

"Why's Aunt Ava crying?" Tia calls from the back of the car.

"She's troubled by your dad's lack of dress sense." Grant quips before calling, "Seriously Mac, take him to get some new clothes would you?"

"Got it." Mackenzie laughs, while I flip Grant off behind my sister's back.

Ava pulls back and looks up a me, "It must be my hormones."

"Glad I'm leaving then." I tell her with a smile as I wipe the tears from her cheeks with my thumbs. "Keep crying on me like this and my shirts might shrink."

"Even more?" Grant scoffs incredulously, "You know Jacob checked your bag this morning before he left for school. He's convinced you're having a mid-life crisis and have started borrowing his stuff to try and look cool."

"It's true," Ava confirms as she breaks out into a grin.

"And you think I've got problems?" I chuckle. "Honestly sis, let's not pretend this is the end of the world. We'll still see each other. A lot."

"Promise?"

"Promise. You and the twins are just as important to me as Tia."

"What about me?" Grant asks indignantly.

"You, not so much." I tease with a smile that prompts him to flip me off in return. He steps forward, tucking Ava under his arm, and kissing the top of her head as she burrows into his side. I get into the car and buckle up.

"Everyone ready."

"Yeah!" Mackenzie and Tia shout excitedly.

I open the garage door, put my shiny, new, black SUV into gear, and pull out into the driveway. Grant and Ava wave us off as I turn into the street, relieved to finally be on our way.

"Daddy," Tia calls from behind me.

"Yes, peanut." I call back.

"I need a wee."

I sigh, stopping the car and reversing back the few feet I'd managed to cover. Mackenzie won't meet my eye as she pretends to look out the window beside her. Even though she has strategically covered her mouth with her hand, I can hear her sniggering.

And so it begins.

I've made this trip so many times I've lost count. On the worst day, it's never taken me more than three hours. Today, I pass security to pull into the underground garage of my apartment block four hours after setting off, courtesy of two unplanned bathroom stops and forgetting to pick up the snack pack Ava had prepared for Tia's journey.

Mackenzie and I grab as much stuff as we can carry out of the car. Tia puts on her back pack and seizes her teddy, before I take her hand and we all bundle into the elevator. Tia is uncharacteristically quiet as she takes in her surroundings.

"You Ok peanut?" I shake her little hand gently as I smile down at her. She looks up at me and smiles nervously as she nods.

The elevator stops and we all climb out, there are only two residences on this floor, so we step out into a short passage. A few feet away, two heavy doors sit across from one another.

"Which one?" Mackenzie whispers.

"The right," I tell her as I drop Tia's hand to fish my keys out of my pocket. "Why are you whispering?"

Her cheeks flush in embarrassment and she shrugs. I chuckle as I reach my door and open it to let us in, immediately dumping the bags I'm carrying and tossing my keys in a dish on the consol by the entrance. "I'll show you guys around and then I'll get the rest of our gear out of the car."

Tia is hanging back and white knuckling my jeans, so I scoop her up and feel her instantly relax into my arms.

The apartment opens into a hallway with two doors opposite each other. "That's a closet and this one is a shower room." I point at each in turn before striding forward. The passage opens out into a huge, empty space with a sleek, modern kitchen at one end. A large, elongated island defines the space, separating the kitchen from the rest of the room. Panoramic windows wrap around the south side, with a pair of large sliding doors in the centre opening out onto a wide terrace. Fear grips me at the thought of Tia wandering out there alone, so I stroll over to make sure the doors are locked before removing the key.

"Where's the garden?" Tia looks at me confused.

"We don't have a garden baby. We are eight floors up so we have this balcony and those wonderful views." Tia doesn't look impressed.

"Where am I going to play?"

"I think that's the least of our worries," Mackenzie pipes up from behind us, clearly astounded.

I turn to face her, frowning.

"What's that supposed to mean?" I ask defensively.

"Where's all your furniture?"

Ok, so other than the couch and a kick ass TV, the room is bare.

"When we first came in, I thought you were being surprisingly calm for someone whose place looks like it might have been burgled," she murmurs, raising her eyebrows.

"I just wanted to leave plenty of space for Tia to be able to play inside." I reply indignantly.

Tia grins at me; she appears to be appeased even if Mackenzie doesn't since she knows I'm fibbing.

"Sure you did," she mutters.

I cough and lead the girls to far end of the room where there is another passage with five doors leading off of it. I open the first door on the right. It's the smallest room and the one I use as an office. There is only a small desk in the middle of the room and nothing on the walls.

"Mmm, minimalist." Mackenzie rolls her lips trying not to laugh as I glare at her.

I walk past the other rooms, straight to the door facing us at the end of the hall. "This is my bedroom." I open the door, and two pairs of inquisitive eyes peer inside at the huge bed and its single side table, which has one lone picture perched on it.

"What's in there?" Tia points to a door.

"That's my bathroom. Want to see?" She nods her head and we all trail over so the girls can look inside.

Mackenzie appraises the space with a smile, "The grey tile must provide a welcome relief from all the other white walls in the place."

I ignore her and pull the door closed.

"What's in there? Tia points to my closet.

"That's where I keep my clothes peanut."

"This I've got to see." Mackenzie takes off before I can stop her. She slides the door open and gasps. It's a huge walk-in wardrobe with a few clothes stored in one corner. "I see you were leaving room for Tia to play in here too."

"Fuck off!" I mouth over Tia's head, much to Mackenzie's amusement.

"Where's my room?" Tia asks.

"You can choose any of the others."

She squeals in excitement and scrambles to be put down. As soon as her feet hit the floor she takes off, flinging open doors to inspect any room we haven't yet visited. The remaining three rooms are all approximately the same size, although two have en-suites. They feature the same white walls as the rest of the apartment, and the same lush cream carpet as my own bedroom, but they are completely empty and devoid of furniture. I'm waiting for her to ask me where her bed is, and am shocked when she doesn't. Instead, she runs off back through the apartment towards the front door.

"Hey, peanut," I yell. "Where are you going?"

"Probably back to your sister's." Mackenzie quips.

I throw her a look of exasperation but don't have a chance to formulate a reply before Tia is back, brandishing her magic wand. She chooses her room —the one with the en-suite and a bath; the other just has a shower—and stands in the middle of the floor, twirling around. "Fairy clitoris..."

"Chloris," I call. Tia stops and stares at me with her hands on her hips, infuriated.

"Shhh daddy. I'm wishing," She chastises me. I bite my lip, as Mackenzie who is watching from behind me buries her head in my shoulder to prevent Tia from seeing her giggle.

Tia starts spinning again, wielding her wand like a sabre. "I wish for a pink bedroom with a pink bed," she calls. It's too cute until she starts tossing handfuls of glitter in the air and I have to make a dive for her.

"Shit!" I exclaim before I can stop myself, carefully prising the pot Tia is holding out of her tiny fingers. "That's enough Tia, I think she got the message."

"Daddy, you said a bad word," Tia informs me.

Like I didn't know!

"I'm sorry peanut." I think for a minute as I try to brush copious amounts of glitter off myself and my child. "Since you live with me now, there's no need to tell aunt Ava I slipped."

"That's right." Mackenzie calls from the safety of the glitter free zone. "Before we left, Aunt Ava said you have to tell me now so I can be sure your dad pays up."

I stand and stomp over to where Mackenzie is sniggering in the doorway. "That mouth needs to learn it's place." I growl low enough that my daughter doesn't hear.

"Promises, promises," she smirks as she wanders off, "I'll go find the vacuum."

I could tell her I haven't got one. I don't. Instead, I listen to cupboard doors opening and slamming shut until Tia and I wander back into the living room a few minutes later. Mackenzie has obviously realised her search will be fruitless, and is now sat on the sofa scrolling through her phone.

"What's this address?" She asks.

"Why?"

"I'm ordering you a vacuum."

"Don't bother," I smirk. "I'll go and fetch our things from the car, then if you don't mind watching Tia, I need to pop out to get a few bits, I'll pick one up then?"

"Shall we all go?" Mackenzie asks.

"I'm coming." Tia pleads.

"I'd rather you stayed, if that's ok." I speak to Mackenzie but roll my eyes in Tia's direction. "It might be nice not to draw unnecessary attention to yourself while you get used to the place."

"You might be right," Mackenzie picks up on what I'm really asking. "I'll start unpacking. It's a big job though, I wish I had someone to help me."

"I can use my fairy dust," Tia blurts out excitedly.

"Or," I look at my daughter as I crouch down to whisper conspiratorially in her ear, "you could wait here with Mackenzie and help her while I'm gone. You've already made one big wish today; one so big the fairies might even have to ask me to help them out."

"But then you'll be on your own," Tia whispers back.

"I've got some of your fairy dust on me, look." I point to myself. That damn glitter gets everywhere, it's stuck all over me. "Fairy Chloris will protect me."

Tia nods in understanding. "Kay," she whispers, before announcing loudly, "I can stay and help you M'kenzie."

"Would you?" Mackenzie smiles and feigns surprise, before going on excitedly, "We can bring all the bags in here and put the television on while we sort everything out. If we can find a music channel, we can sing and dance while we work. I think the fairies will like that; if they can sing and dance too, it might make your wish come true quicker."

"Yeah." Tia fist pumps the air as I mouth, "Thank you."

∞∞∞

I'm gone a few hours, dashing from shop to shop, hunched over with my collar pulled up and my cap pulled down so nobody recognises me. When I get home, Mackenzie is curled up on the couch watching TV, Tia has crashed out beside her. Tia's head is resting on Mackenzie's lap and she has one of my jackets thrown over her for a blanket.

"Everything OK?" I ask, taking a seat beside them.

"Did you think it wouldn't be? We've unpacked, danced, sung, and put as much of the spilt fairy dust as we could back in the tub to use again another time. Then Tia was hungry, so I reheated one of those meals Ava prepared for her. We made a video call to your sister and after, Tia got tired, I didn't know whether to put her in your bed or what the plan was."

"I've got some paint and the brushes I'll need to decorate her room tomorrow. I'll put them in there tonight for her to find in the morning. I've ordered her a bed which will hopefully arrive in a couple of days. I thought you might like to choose your bed yourself so we need to take care of that later. Until they arrive, you and Tia can bunk in my room. I'll take the sofa."

"You don't have to," Mackenzie sighs.

"Yes, I do." Since the night Mackenzie and I were intimate, I've made sure to keep my distance. I can't help but feel like I took advantage of a vulnerable woman, even if she was the one to make the first move. It didn't stop me from asking her to accompany me to Hollywood though, for Tia's sake. My little girl is comfortable around her after seeing how well she fit in with the rest of the family, but I've had to set boundaries for this arrangement to work.

I don't think Mackenzie shares my opinion that she isn't ready to embark on any kind of new relationship. She tries to tempt me every opportunity she gets, testing my resolve as I'm forced to remember the night we were together, and how perfect it felt to be buried deep inside her. She thinks that I don't notice the sly, flirtatious glances she casts my way, the skimpy outfits she wears when we are alone, or the subtle touches that drive me insane with desire. My feigned detachment is an award-winning performance. A beautiful, sexy woman keeps trying to seduce me and I go to great lengths to make sure I appear impervious to her charm. I must need my head examined even if I know deep down it's for the best. I can't stand the thought of her resenting me at a later date, walking away like we weren't ever friends.

"Did you pick up some groceries while you were out?" Mackenzie swiftly changes the subject.

"Shit. I forgot."

"That's ok, I'm not a great cook." She smiles at me and I return it with one of my own.

"Me either."

"I got that impression when I couldn't find any saucepans."

"Chinese?" We both say simultaneously.

Could this woman be any more perfect?

Chapter Thirteen

✦

I carry Tia to my room and put her to bed while Mackenzie orders us both take out. After we've eaten, we slump on the sofa together, watching television in companionable silence until it's time for bed. We aren't late, it's been a long day and I've a feeling it's going to be an even longer one tomorrow. I need to check in with Jerry, find out if I can postpone Saturday's 'date' with Henrietta Greenslade, break the news of said impending 'date' to Mackenzie, set about hiring some extra security for the girls, and pretend to my daughter I was visited overnight by a mystical being, who craftily persuaded me to start painting Tia's new room so she could fly off in search of the perfect pink bed.

I lie on the couch thinking about it all. The surface is hard and unforgiving, I've never spent enough time at home to realise how uncomfortable my sofa really is. The room, bathed in moonlight due to the lack of blinds, makes it impossible to fall asleep despite the darkness outside. About three in the morning, I give in, getting up and silently trudging down the hall to what will be Tia's room.

Imagining the delight on her tiny face if she thought her wish had actually been granted, I set to work.

It's an easy enough job, I cover the carpet with a plastic sheet before painting three walls pale pink, working as quickly and quietly as I can. The fourth wall I make a feature of, by using a darker hue. I try to imagine where Tia's new bed will go before stencilling just above where her head will be, using the last of the pale pink to create a design on the darker surface. The cabin bed I've ordered has a fairies play tent, tunnel and tower. The bed is raised with a pink curtain hanging from its base to create a covered den beneath it. It has a wide sturdy ladder one end, and a slide emerging from a pink tower the other so Tia can get in and out easily. I smile to myself as I think of how happy she will be when it finally gets delivered. When I'm finished, I throw all the used equipment into a black garbage bag, and stow it together with the unused paint in the shower room by the front door, cleaning myself up while I'm in there. It will be easy enough for me to sneak the evidence out later when Mackenzie has Tia distracted. As I final touch, I grab a pen and paper from the kitchen, trying to disguise my handwriting as I write quick note which I leave folded on the floor underneath the picture I've painted on Tia's wall. I leave the door to the room open enough for Tia to see inside when she gets up and comes to find me.

Exhausted I look at my watch, it's nearing 6am. I go and lie back down on the couch; this time I fall asleep almost instantly.

I'm woken by a high-pitched screaming and the patter of tiny footsteps.

"DADDEE!" I prise my eyes open just in time to catch Tia as she launches herself at me. She can't contain her excitement as she shouts in my ear. "DADDY! SHE CAME!"

I try to look confused. "Who came?"

She doesn't answer, she's already racing off down the hall.

"M'KENZIE! M'KENZIE! SHE CAME!" A distant voice yells.

I look at my watch and groan. 6.18am. When Tia comes running back, her face radiating pure joy, it reminds me why it was worth staying up all night. She tugs at my hand. "DADDY COME ON."

"Why?" I pretend to be baffled as I let her lead me to her bedroom. We get there at the same time as a yawning Mackenzie. She is wearing one of my T-shirts and looking as adorably ruffled as Tia.

"LOOK!" Tia squeals, as she jumps up and down, she's so excited she is almost in tears. "LOOK DADDY. LOOK M'KENZIE."

"I see, honey." Mackenzie looks around the room in wonderment before kneeling down so Tia can fling her arms around her neck and hug her tightly. "She left you a note, look."

While Tia grabs the paper Mackenzie gives me a look so warm it almost brings me to my knees.

"Can you read it M'kenzie," Tia hands her the paper.

"Well, it has your name on it," Mackenzie tells her

seriously, "How about you sit by me and we read it together?"

I watch as Tia settles beside her and while Mackenzie helps her read the note, explaining the letters and sounding out the words until Tia knows what it says.

Dear Tia,

I caught your wish and have started on your room.
I had to leave so I could check in on your aunt Ava
before going in search of the perfect bed for you.
It will be here soon. I promise.
I left a magical picture of my fairy friend Angelina.
She will watch over you and keep
you safe while you sleep.
Love Chloris. xxx

"Angelina." Tia whispers, gazing up at the picture of the fairy on the wall above where her bed will go. The fairy's wings appear to be flapping in the air, helping her to hover with a magic wand in her hand. Tiny little sparkling stars shoot from the tip of the wand, thanks to me finding Tia's pot of glitter and being inspired to mix it into the paint at the last second.

"Daddy, I *have* to show Aunt Ava." Tia implores.

"I think she would like that. Go grab my phone and we'll call her."

No sooner has she left than Mackenzie is by my side. "Did you sleep at all last night?" She asks me sternly.

"I don't know what you mean," I reply. "I'm as shocked as you are."

"Shame," Mackenzie sighs.

"Why?" I look at her curiously.

"Because I'm kinda turned on right now, and if it had been you going out of your way to make that little girl so happy, you could have been getting so lucky later."

I swallow as she sashays out of the room, just as Tia arrives back with my cell to stop me following.

∞ ∞ ∞

"Where the hell have you been?" Jerry yells, as I walk into his office.

"Out of town." It's my go-to response for situations like this. I know I need to tell him about Tia now she is living with me, but I'm not ready yet. Not until I have some additional security measures in place.

"Well, while you've been off fuck knows where, I've been working my butt off trying to cover your ass."

"Isn't that what I pay you to do?"

"Not enough." He glowers at me from across his desk.

"What have you got planned for your outing with Cath tomorrow?"

"About that…"

"Don't you try and cancel Jared," he shouts. "She paid the charity a cool half mill to spend a few hours with your sorry ass. You've already postponed once. How's it gonna look if you try and do it again without good reason?"

"Fine," I sigh. "Any suggestions about where I should take her?"

"I'll sort it. I'll get a car to pick you up outside your building tomorrow. 1pm sharp. Be ready."

"Why so early?" I groan.

"Because for the price she paid she expects more than a pit stop at a fast-food joint and..." He looks me up and down scathingly, "...she'll expect you to be wearing something that fits. Look at you."

"Jeez Jerry, what's got stuck in your craw this morning?"

"You! Disappearing all the time without a damn word." He stares at me, waiting for me to fill him in on where I've been.

I stand and get ready to leave.

"Wait," he shouts a little more calmly. "I've got six new job offers for you to review."

I sit back down.

"I'm still waiting to hear about the part of Connor in 'Wildly Adrift,' but I've also been contacted to ask you about these." He takes a pile of folders, removing one from the top and setting it to the side, before pushing the rest across the desk in my direction."

"I told you; I'm not interested in the role of Connor." I point to the pile of folders. "Which of these are being filmed locally?"

Jerry rubs the back of his neck." Two of them are being filmed at Universal but require you to be out of the state for at least three months."

"No can do. Not at the minute."

"Jared…"

"It's non-negotiable Jerry," I tell him forcibly. "What about that one?"

I jerk my head to the file Jerry removed from the pile.

"It's no good, not your sort of thing. Some kids film and they're offering peanuts. If you ask me, they had a hell of nerve sending it over in the first place."

"Let me see." Jerry thrusts the file into my hand, and I leaf through it. It's a movie about an enchanted forest where a host of good fairies are held under siege by goblins intent on stealing their magic to create chaos in the human world. The script appears well-written and contains subtle adult humour. I chuckle, "What part did they want me to play?"

Jerry mistakes my laughter for derision. He smiles, "The goblin king. Can you believe it?"

"Looks like it's primarily being filmed here, just a couple of random weeks out on location in the national forest, and a week in the everglades subject to the relevant permits getting approved."

"Jared…" I can tell by his tone Jerry doesn't like the way this conversation is headed, so I cut him off.

"I trusted you at the beginning of my career and it paid off. Neither of us were expecting it, but we made a shit ton of money based on little more than your gut instinct and a little luck. Now I've got a similar feeling about this one, and I'm asking you to trust me this time."

"Seriously?"

"Seriously. I do have a couple of stipulations though before I give them my final decision."

"And they would be?"

"If they can't get the necessary permission to do the remote filming, they have to run any potential location changes past me. The longest I can be away from home is one week at a time for the foreseeable. Anything longer has to be mutually agreed in advance. And, I will only consider playing the part of the king to the good fairies."

"The fairies are led by a queen, there is no king."

"You did read the script then?" I quirk my eyebrow at Jerry.

"Glanced at it." He starts shuffling papers on his desk in order to avoid my gaze. "Enough to know there is no king."

"Get them to switch the roles around, the king of the fairies versus the malevolent goblin queen, instead of a goblin king. It shouldn't be hard to do, and I know a few females that would be good for the role if they struggle to fill it."

Jerry snorts. "You and me both. Okay, if you're sure about this, I'll see what they say."

"Great." I stand again. "One more thing. Tell them if they agree to the changes, I'll do it for half of what they are offering and a percentage of the profit."

"You've got to be joking." Jerry leans so far back in

his chair it almost topples over.

"Isn't that what I said to you the day you negotiated the deal that got us here." I sweep my hand around Jerry's palatial office.

"Point taken."

I turn to leave pausing at the door to glance back, "I tell you Jerry, I've got a really good feeling about this one."

Jerry jerks his head in response as I disappear out the door.

As soon as I'm in my car I call Mackenzie.

"Hi," Such a small word, but it's said with such warmth I can't curtail my grin.

"Who is it M'kenzie?" A little voice sings.

"Daddy. Do you want to say hi?" I hear Mackenzie ask, before a familiar little voice greets me.

"Hi daddy. I'm showing M'kenzie where all the groceries go."

"Maybe you can show me when I get home." The joke's lost on my daughter.

"Kay." She says, before she's gone again.

"Me again," Mackenzie purrs, the sound travels straight to my dick.

"The groceries got delivered Ok then?"

"Yep, just in time too, a tiny tearaway was getting hangry and the breakfast leftovers just weren't cutting it."

I laugh. "I was calling to see what colour you wanted your room. I'll pick up some more paint while I'm out."

"Whatever you want, it's your place remember."

"But I want you to feel at home Mac, think about it, and I'll call you when I get to the store."

I disconnect before she has the chance to argue with me.

∞ ∞ ∞

I knock tentatively on the door of a private hospital room before opening it and peering inside.

"Jared Jones as I barely live and breathe. Back again?"

"Hi Dale, is the coast clear?" He is lying in bed wearing a pair of luminous green silk pyjamas. One arm is in plaster where he has broken his wrist, and one leg is raised at a forty-five-degree angle where it is in traction. He has a straw about a mile long tucked in the corner of his mouth as he sips from a vat of water on a side table. He spits out the straw when he sees me.

"As clear as my conscience," Dale retorts. "If you've stopped by to try and persuade me to jump ship and come work for you again, you are going to be disappointed."

"I wouldn't dare, not after the lecture you gave me last time, but I would appreciate your help with one thing. Mind if I come in?"

"If you are going to beg me for a date, I'll have to decline that too. The boss wouldn't like me fraternising with the enemy."

"Your virtue is safe, I promise." I chuckle, as I take

a seat beside Dale's bed. "How are you doing?"

"I should be happy. Since I've been in here, I've had more pricks in me than a hooker handing out free samples." He shows me his arm, bruised from where the medics keep drawing blood.

"Ouch." I wince. "Is there anything you need?"

"And here I was thinking you needed something from me?"

"I do," I admit. "I need to hire some security for... personal reasons. I need someone reliable, trustworthy and stealthy enough to blend in to the background. I was hoping with your contacts, you might be able to recommend someone."

"You do know I'm not your PA, right? Mitch would have a hissy fit if he knew I was helping you out."

"What's the guy's problem? Seriously, I'd like to know."

Dale shrugs, "Asked him once but he wouldn't say, shut me down. Must be pretty bad though, the boss doesn't usually hold a grudge without good reason."

"I honestly don't know what his beef is and I don't mean to put you in an awkward position, but I need a man with integrity to point me in the right direction. The situation I'm in is kind of sensitive, and I need to hire someone I can count on to be discreet. Someone with a proven track record."

Dale thinks for a minute. "Ok, I'll help just this once. In return for the flowers, and the job offer, even if I didn't take it, and the date, even if I declined it."

I breathe a sigh of relief, "Thanks Dale, although I never wanted to date you."

"You would have. I'm irresistible the more you get to know me."

"Maybe, but not to me I'm afraid," I laugh.

"Crap. You prefer muff over buff, don't you?" He sighs as the penny drops.

I nod solemnly.

Dale rolls his eyes like he disapproves of my life choices. "There's a guy called Josh Stone, ex SEAL. He sounds like what you need, although it will cost you. He is in high demand and extremely selective over which jobs he takes. I don't even know if he is available right now, but there was a rumour floating around that he was looking to set up his own security firm with some pals he used to serve with. If he can't help you, he can probably put you in touch with someone who can. It might work in your favour if you agree to let him mention your name when advertising his services after the job's done."

"Thank you, I appreciate this more than you know. How do I reach him?"

"Good question. I'll ask around, see if I can get a number I can forward to your cell. He can't be that hard to track down if he is starting up a business."

"Dale you're a star."

"Tell me something I don't know."

I get up and leave with one parting shot, "If you need anything while you're in here, call me. I mean it."

Dale waves his hand in acknowledgement; he is

already busy scrolling through the contacts on his mobile.

∞ ∞ ∞

I'm laden with bags again when I climb out of the elevator back home. I hear Mackenzie's giggle before I see her. The sound makes my heart pound and cock twitch. I start concentrating on banal tasks to try and stem the urges that are becoming harder and harder to resist. I wonder why she is stood in the hallway, then I see the door to the apartment opposite is open and realise she is chatting to my neighbour. Tia is clinging shyly to her leg, and Mackenzie is stroking the back of my little girl's head to reassure her.

I smile until I see who she is chatting to.

"Who the hell are you?" I snap. I'm in front of the girls in an instant, a protective shield between them and the six-foot-four, tattooed mass of muscle, who has his arms folded across his chest as he leans on the doorjamb, flirting with my girls while wearing little more than a pair of shorts.

"Assuming you live across the hall and aren't just visiting this gorgeous woman and child, I'm your new neighbour." He extends his hand for shaking. I ignore it. There aren't many men I look up to in this world, but I definitely have to tilt my head upwards to make eye contact with this guy. I feel Mackenzie's hand on my arm.

"Where's Mrs Elliott?" I bark.

"Gone to live with her son in Iowa, I think. I'm not really sure, like you, we weren't that close."

"What makes you think we weren't close?" I growl.

"Oh, maybe the fact you weren't even aware she was moving."

Ok so he had me there. *Smartass.*

"Anyway, I just knocked to introduce myself." He rattles on, as he looks over my shoulder to smile at Mackenzie. "I wouldn't want your wife and kid to get worried if they came home to find me lumbering around outside your place. I work odd hours, so I never know when I'm going to get home. If someone bumps into me late at night, I've been told I can look a little intimidating."

Wife?

The fact he thinks Mackenzie and I are married relaxes me, her not correcting him elates me, until I glance behind me and notice she is blushing furiously as she stands there unashamedly ogling his naked torso.

"Well, if you'll excuse us, I need to talk to my *wife* urgently." I bundle the girls back into our place and close the door before he has the chance to say anything else. "That's if she can put her tongue back in her mouth," I tell Mackenzie abruptly as soon as we are alone. "We'll discuss this later," I huff, as I storm off with Tia hot on my heels and Mackenzie's laughter ringing in my ears.

Chapter Fourteen

✦

I t's official! Neither Mackenzie or I can cook.

After her little display in front of our 'hot' new neighbour earlier—her description, not mine— I thought I'd better up my game. My plans of a romantic dinner for two and a half are dashed when I swiftly realise that creating the perfect Michelin star meal doesn't just involve throwing a load of random ingredients into a pot and then wandering off, expecting it to create magic. When the smoke detector goes off, the three of us rush to find the charred remnants of what was supposed to be chicken casserole stuck to the bottom of one of my new dishes. It's then Mackenzie decides she needs to take charge.

An hour after that, Tia and I are sat at the kitchen island while she plops spoonfuls of a congealed brown substance on the plates in front of us. She tells us it's beef stroganoff, although it looks and smells suspiciously like the prime fillet steak I'd ordered with our groceries has been substituted for an old tire rolled in some brown, foul-smelling gloop without my knowledge.

Thankfully, Mackenzie looks neither hurt nor surprised when Tia wrinkles up her nose and asks if she can have nuggets instead. I order us another take out before either the apartment burns down or one of us succumbs to food poisoning.

After eating, I leave the girls sitting at the island drawing, while I go to make a start on Mackenzie's room. She's chosen a pale green paint and asked for a grey feature wall. I'm three-quarters of the way around the room when my mobile warbles, signalling I have an incoming text. It's from Dale and contains the number he said he would try to get for me. His accompanying message is straight to the point:

Good luck!

I go straight to my office to make the call. Since it's already early evening, the best I think I can hope for is to leave a message for someone to get back to me. I'm taken by surprise when my call is answered. There is no company name offered, no aimable greeting, just a gruff voice barking, "Yeah."

"Is that Josh Stone?" I ask after a couple of seconds' uncomfortable silence.

"Nope."

"Do you know how I could get hold of him?" I ask, wondering if some time in the near future I might be graced with an answer of more than just one syllable.

"Who wants to know?"

Success. "My name is Jared Jones and I would like to meet with Mr Stone with regard to hiring his services."

Whoever is on the end of the line bursts out laughing. Not a chuckle or any form of constrained hilarity—a full-on, 'that's the best joke I've ever heard' belly laugh.

I wait patiently, and if I'm honest, more than a little pissed off, until the laughter stops. Before I can say anything further, the man at the other end titters, "The boss doesn't babysit actors. He says they're too high maintenance and have more money than sense." There's more laughter and then the line goes dead.

I look at my phone mystified, then call back immediately.

"Yeah." A voice sniggers.

"I'm afraid we got cut off," I say politely, even though I'm feeling anything but.

"No," he laughs, "We didn't. Nothing left to say so I terminated the call." He hangs up on me a second time.

I call back again.

"Yeah. What now?" He asks.

"Fuck you!" I yell, before disconnecting.

"Daddy..." A little voice calls. I turn to see Tia standing in the doorway all ready for bed. Mackenzie is standing behind her smirking.

"I know peanut," I sigh, "I know!" Since my mobile is in my hand, I use it to transfer fifty bucks into all the kids' college funds, and then turn the screen to Mackenzie as proof. "I'm forty bucks in credit." I warn her.

"Thirty." She corrects me.

"Huh."

"You dropped one after the fairy dust explosion." She reminds me smiling.

"Can you and M'kenzie read me a story?" Tia interrupts, saving me from eating further into my reserves.

"Sure peanut."

Mackenzie and I lie on my bed with Tia between us, reading her a tale about a fairy called Blossom. The story tells of how all the flowers in the forest where she lives start to suffer when she accidentally sits on her magic wand, breaking it. It's a new book I picked up on today's travels, and when Tia falls asleep midway through, Mackenzie and I pretend not to notice so we can finish the tale and find out what happens in the end.

When I close the book, Mackenzie looks over my shoulder to the picture beside my bed. "I take it that's Tia?" She whispers so as to not wake up the sleeping beauty.

I reach behind me and grab the frame, bringing it forward so we can both look at the picture as we continue our conversation in the same hushed tone. "Sure is. Can't you see the resemblance?"

Mackenzie chuckles, "Not really, no."

The picture is actually one of the first sonograms taken back when Tia was developing inside her biological mother. I point to a tiny curved shape amongst the blurred black and white backdrop. "What does that look like to you?"

She stares for a few seconds before her face lights up, "a peanut."

"Exactly." I smile back.

"What happened? To Tia's mom."

I feel my face cloud over as Kendra's face appears in my mind. "Nothing." The word comes out a lot harsher than I intend it to as I gently climb off the bed and make a hasty exit.

I stomp back into Mackenzie's room and flip open a paint can to start decorating again. I fill the roller and use brisk, aggressive strokes that leave more paint on the floor than they do on the walls. It's a good job I took the time to cover the carpet carefully. I tense when I feel Mackenzie's arms circling me from behind.

"Tell me," she murmurs. "You know everything there is to know about me, and I can't imagine for one second any woman in her right mind would just walk out on that precious little girl in there."

"She didn't. She walked out on me," I snap, slopping paint everywhere, including all down myself.

"Baby, stop." Mackenzie manoeuvres herself to capture my arms in her embrace. Gently pinning them to my sides as she presses her front to my back, resting her head on my shoulder, "What happened?"

I sigh and hang my head. I've never talked about Kendra to anyone. Of course, my parents, Ava, Grant and the twins were around when it happened, but the moment Kendra walked out of our lives for good, was the moment I refused to ever have her name mentioned in my presence again. "I met her at a party just before I hit the big time. She was dressed to kill and obviously out to have a good time. My popularity was rising and she made a play for me, ignoring every other guy in the room. There were plenty of others soliciting her attention but she wouldn't give them the time of day. I was flattered and cocky with it, one thing led to another and we ended up in bed."

"You didn't use protection? When we…"

"I did," I say quickly, "With Kendra I mean, I always have in the past and would've with you if you'd given me half a chance." I feel her chest vibrating against me as she chuckles. "In all seriousness, if you're worried, I'm clean. I had a medical a couple of weeks before we met."

"I wasn't worried, you're too good a man to put me at risk. Just so you know, even though Dan and I hadn't been sleeping together for quite some time, I kept up with my birth control. Before the night I ran out on him, I guess, deep down, I always hoped he would find his way back to me. Given his history, I made sure to get myself checked and I'm healthy. That said, if you were careful with Kendra, how was Tia ever possible?"

"I asked myself the same question for months after she dropped the bomb. The morning after Kendra and I hooked up I told her I wasn't interested in anything long term. I wasn't the same guy back then Mac, and it's not as if she was the love of my life or anything. She said she was fine about it but we didn't exactly part on the best of terms. I never saw or heard from her again until she knocked on my door a few months later and handed me that sonogram. She told me outright she didn't want to be a single mom and either I stepped up to the plate or she would get a termination. Since I knew we'd used condoms..."

"Condoms.' As in plural?" Mackenzie teases, to try and lift the dark cloud that's descended.

"Let's just say you caught me off guard and didn't get my best performance."

"If you say so," she giggles, giving me a squeeze. "Although, you didn't do too bad."

I snort. "Anyway, since I knew Kendra and I had used protection, I never thought the baby could be mine. The money had just started rolling in and I thought she wanted a piece of the action, so I made her take a paternity test before the baby was born. We got the results the same day she was booked in to..." My voice catches, I can't even bring myself to say the words out loud, the thought of my peanut never being born eviscerates me. "Anyway, I begged her not to do it. Apologised for my behaviour and said I'd stand by her, which I did. She told me that she forgave me and that she wanted to make a go of things for the baby's sake.

We stayed in Hollywood, but to help her avoid the stress of becoming headline news, we kept the pregnancy on the down-low. Everything continued much the same as normal until she started to show. By then, I was busier than ever and while we never made our relationship public, she insisted on accompanying me everywhere. I thought it was because we were having this child together and she genuinely wanted to spend time getting to know me. So, I let her tag along. It soon became obvious she wasn't taking proper care of herself; she still wanted to be out partying every night and was clearly overdoing it. I was worried she was going to end up harming herself or the baby. I thought if we moved out of the city, she would slow down a bit and we could really get to know each other, settle down, and build our little family together without any interference.

I bought a place near Ava and secretly moved Kendra in with me. She fought me on it at first, then one day she looked at herself in the mirror, saw her burgeoning belly and it's like something in her mind clicked. She was suddenly eager to get out of town and I believed it was because we were finally on the same wavelength. I cared for her throughout the whole pregnancy. There's nothing I wouldn't do for her, anything she asked for, I gave her. Looking back, I suppose that's when I first started living this crazy double life. When I went off to work, Kendra insisted on staying behind and out of the public eye. I got Ava to check in on her regularly because she went from one extreme to the other. She was like a recluse, barely setting foot outside the door. Although I must admit, Ava never really trusted her, so they never hit it off.

I stayed home as much as possible, but work was

suddenly piling in thanks to my agent, Jerry. He had been instrumental to my success so I felt obligated to try and keep him happy as well. I was on my way back from a promotional photoshoot when I got the call to say Kendra had gone into labour. I got home just in time to witness Tia coming into the world. She was overdue, but when she decided she wanted out, she came fast. Kendra never made it to the hospital, and the midwife delivered her on the floor of our living room. She was perfect. The midwife placed her in my arms and I'd never felt a love like it. When it was all over, Kendra wanted to lay on the couch rather than go upstairs to bed. I took Tia upstairs to watch over her while Kendra got some rest. I called Ava who was so excited she asked if she could come straight over to meet the new addition. Of course, I said yes. She arrived just as Tia started fussing. We walked into the living room to find her mom, but Kendra had gone."

"Gone?"

"Up and left. The worst of it is she'd obviously been planning it. She'd folded up the blanket I'd used to cover her and left a note on top. When I ran upstairs and looked in the closet most of her clothes were already gone. She must have packed them up while I was out and left them somewhere so she could leave in a hurry. I don't know if she called a cab or if someone picked her up. She was just gone."

"The note, what did it say?"

"Something along the lines of, 'I'm sorry, you're not the man I thought you were and this isn't the life I want for myself'. Turns out she wanted the wild Jared with all the celebrity trappings, not the one that wanted to settle down and become a family man. In trying to protect her, I ended up shielding her from the life she craved and she resented me for it."

"Even if you turned out not to be the man she wanted, how could she just walk away from her daughter like that?"

"That's the best bit."

"What do you mean?"

"I couldn't understand it either. I was worried she was suffering from postpartum depression or something similar. When she didn't come back, while Grant and Ava stepped in to help Tia and me, I hired a private investigator to track Kendra down so I could make sure she was ok. Let's just say she wasn't hard to find. She'd basically thrown herself straight back into the party scene, picking up her old lifestyle from where she left off. I honestly thought she would be back. If not for me, for Tia, but it was like we never existed.

After a month I went to see her. She was vicious. Told me I meant nothing to her; she'd moved on and so should I. She made it clear that she had set her sights higher and that she didn't want my kid dragging her down. We had one hell of a fight, during which she let slip that she'd 'arranged' for at least one of the condoms we'd used to break. I never noticed it at the time; she'd gotten rid of the evidence but had basically set me up. She thought

I wouldn't want a child any more than she did, and that after she got me to marry her, she could hire a nanny and jet off with me to start sharing the lavish, exhilarating lifestyle she presumed I wanted to lead and had always planned for herself. When she started to get to know me well enough to realise that wasn't going to happen, she said she agreed to move away with me because she didn't want anyone getting wind of the fact she'd been expecting, and she was too far gone to take care of the problem herself. After the birth she couldn't get away quick enough. I told her I wanted sole custody and for her to waive all her parental rights. There's no way I could let anyone that toxic be around my peanut. She agreed, on the condition I didn't go around advertising the fact she was Tia's biological mother. I walked out the door and received the legal paperwork renouncing her rights three days later. We haven't seen or spoken to each other since."

"I'm sorry Jared." Mackenzie hugs me a little tighter.

"It's never been a problem up until now." I grind out.

"What do you mean?"

"Bringing Tia back here with me, people are going to ask questions. The truth is bound to come out eventually, and when it does, I'm not sure how Kendra will react. Then there's Tia herself, the morning I met you she asked about her mom for the first time. She got distracted before I had to answer but the topic will come up again, and when it does, I don't know what I'm supposed to tell her."

"You said Kendra agreed to sign over her rights as long as you kept schtum about her. Was that written in the contract anywhere?"

"Originally, and if I broke my promise, I'd have to pay Kendra some pretty hefty compensation. I was so desperate to get her out of my life I almost signed it."

"What stopped you?"

"Not what. Who."

"Ava?"

"Grant. I think he could see what I couldn't. That the future would pan out the way it has. Grant made me get my own set of papers drawn up, making sure they were watertight with no obligation to anything on my part. Kendra can't have checked through them very well either, because I had a special little clause of my own added and I'm sure if she'd spotted it, she never would have signed. Grant sent everything to Kendra with a note stating the basic changes and saying that if she didn't sign, he would not only make it known far and wide that she was Tia's mom, but he would also paint her in the worst possible light when doing it. He also hinted that he would persuade me to go after her for child support. I doubt very much I would have got it given my situation, but I guess fighting it out in court could have cost her a bomb in legal fees. Grant got the signed papers back by return with a note of her own."

"What did it say?"

"Fuck you!" I let out a long sigh. "There's something else I need to tell you."

"Go on."

"I need you to watch Tia for me tomorrow."

"Of course."

"You might not want to when I tell you why."

"Why?"

"I have a date." I wait for an explosion, or any sort of reaction that will indicate she doesn't want me to go. I think the arms that are holding me tense, but the reflex is so slight, I wonder if it's wishful thinking.

"Tell me about it?" She whispers.

"I participated in a bachelor auction for charity and the woman who won, Henrietta Greenslade, wants to go out tomorrow. I've already postponed once and she's paid a lot for the privilege, so Jerry says I have to go this time."

"Henrietta Greenslade," she mutters almost to herself, before addressing me again. "You do, you can't let the charity down."

"There's bound to be photos Mac, Jerry made all the arrangements so he'll be after publicity, and Henrietta, well, the last time we met she was kind of handsy. I don't want you getting the wrong idea. Oh, and there's something else."

"Go on."

"You and Tia have been pretty good about being holed up in the apartment all this time…"

"Babe, it's only been a couple of days."

Babe. I like the way the word rolls off her tongue

when she says it.

"Even so, I don't want either of you to feel like prisoners here. I want you to be able to come and go as you please, but I'd feel happier knowing I had some support in making sure you guys aren't going to get bothered when you do. That's why I'm in the process of hiring some extra security, just for a while. When she becomes public knowledge Tia will be a novelty for a bit, I don't want her to get frightened or overwhelmed if she starts generating extra attention. I chose this life, she didn't."

"All this has been weighing pretty heavy on you, huh? As well as the fact you've had to take care of me as well."

I shrug as Mackenzie slides around my body so she is in front of me. She doesn't seem bothered that she gets covered in paint in the process.

"Maybe it's time for me to help you forget. The pain. The hurt. The past. I can help you do that, even if it's only for a short while." She uses my own words against me while her nimble fingers unzip my jeans. She releases the button and pushes them down with my boxers. Then she sinks to her knees, and suddenly, I'm able to block out everything bar her exceptionally talented mouth.

Chapter Fifteen

⭒

I couldn't face another night on the sofa I bought for style rather than comfort. So, while on my shopping spree earlier in the day, I had the foresight to pick up a double air bed as a temporary fix. The store had a choice of two colours; I grabbed the blue. At the checkout, I was just about to hand over my card, when I had a sudden change of heart and dashed off to switch it out for the pink version, much to the amusement and fascination of the assistant checking me out in more ways than one. I knew a pint-sized person who would continue to get enjoyment from the purchase long after I was finished with it, and the blue one just wouldn't cut it.

After Mackenzie had blown more than just my mind, I thought it only fair I provided her with a similar level of satisfaction. Much to my dismay and confusion she declined my advances.

"No," she'd muttered, "Tonight was about you, not me."

"If it's about me, then get on the floor and spread, I need to be inside you." I'd growled back.

She hesitated, eye's full of longing, before murmuring, "Not tonight." Shaking her head softly as she walked away from me, pausing at the door to look back and say with a smirk, "You're not ready."

I'm not ready!

What the fuck was that supposed to mean?

I finished decorating before getting cleaned up and inflating my new make shift bed in Tia's room. I lay staring at the ceiling, with Mackenzie's words and my rock-hard dick keeping me awake for most of the night.

Now, I was painfully aware of tiny fingers trying to prise my eyelids apart in a vain attempt at waking me.

"Daddy. Wake up."

"What time is it peanut?" I grumble.

"Wake up. Do you like the picture I drawed?"

"Drew. Picture I drew." I correct her sleepily, as I try to rouse myself into action.

"No, I drawed it, not you?" She tells me confused.

I chuckle and force my eyes open, not alert enough to argue. Tia is holding up a picture right in front of my face. Three colourful stick people of varying sizes are sporting grins so big that they literally can't fit on their faces. Their clothes are way too large for their painfully thin bodies, and the material appears to be so thin, it wouldn't come as a surprise if they got arrested for indecent exposure in the very near future. They are all stood in a row like soldiers, with their elongated fingers touching, I assume they are supposed to be holding hands.

There is a giant brown blob behind the largest of the three people so it looks like he's shit himself. I say he, but my daughter is obviously being careful not to offend any demographic with her artwork, since all three people appear gender neutral, and are wearing a vibrant array of different colours. I'm not sure why the brown blob has huge wide eyes. Maybe because it thinks the giant stick figure standing alone and behind it, is about to step on it. The giant person, he isn't smiling. His mouth is set in an unimpressed straight line. I guess the shit he is standing behind smells toxic. If it doesn't, it certainly looks like it should, the way it appears to ooze down the page in four long thin streaks. Hovering above the whole scene is a stick person with large a pink triangle for a body and one extra-long arm. She has blond hair and two humps on her back. Random.

"It's beautiful." I tell my daughter. "Who are all these people?"

"That's you," she points to the stick figure with the bowel problem. Cosmic. "That's me and that's M'kenzie. That's fairy Angelina."

"Why has she got one really long arm?"

Tia giggles like I'm playing, but I really want to know.

"That's her wand."

Course it is.

"What's that?" I point to the brown blob.

"Bob."

Okayyy. Perhaps she means blob, since despite my best efforts, she refrains from dropping the S-bomb.

"And that's M'kenzie's new friend," she finishes.

"Who?"

"The man." Tia tells me innocently.

If I wasn't awake before, I am now.

"What man?" I sit bolt upright knocking Tia over in the process. She is on the air bed beside me, and bounces back on the mattress, unhurt and giggling as if it's a game and I meant to do it. It makes her lose focus, so to jog her memory, I repeat as calmly as my sky rocketing blood pressure will allow, "What man?"

"The man with pictures painted on him like you." She points to my tattoo. "We are taking it to him but I wanted to show you first."

She scrambles up, the picture forgotten as she puts her hands on my face by my mouth, squeezing so my lips bunch up and it's hard for me to speak. "When?" I mumble.

"Now silly." She races off forgetting to take the picture with her.

I'm up, pulling on a pair of sweats and after her in seconds, taking the picture with me.

I find her in the kitchen with Mackenzie.

"Well, I was wondering if you were going to join us today." Mackenzie chuckles, as she takes in my dishevelled appearance.

It's then I notice that everyone else is already washed and dressed. "What time is it?" In the absence of my watch I scan the room searching for a clock. I guess that's something else I need to buy.

"Half-nine." Mackenzie smiles at my shocked expression, I can't remember the last time I stayed in bed this late. "We've been up since six, haven't we?"

Tia nods while focusing on her next masterpiece. It's the first time we have been together without her coming to find me the minute she wakes up. I'm a little gobsmacked, and I think Mackenzie can tell. It's also feels like the first time in the last four years I've had nearly six consecutive hours of uninterrupted sleep.

"Tia thought you would like to lie in today," Mackenzie tells me as if reading my mind. Code for, I persuaded her to leave you be a while, "You looked a little weary yesterday." In other words, I looked like crap. She turns her attention back to Tia but carries on speaking to me, her previously jovial tone is replaced by a much chillier timbre, "I told her you had a big day ahead of you, Chloris stopped by overnight to say she had found the perfect bed for her room, but it was in an evil queen's lair who demanded you go wrestle her for it this afternoon."

The corner of my mouth twitches happily. So, she is jealous over my date.

"We thought we would draw a picture for our new neighbour while you were sleeping. We are just going to walk it over."

Mackenzie's new friend. If she is trying to make me jealous, it's working. I walk up to where the girls are sitting, standing between them so I can drape an arm across each of their shoulders. They both look up at me, Mackenzie looks more worried than Tia.

"You know you have absolutely nothing to worry about, right? There won't be any wrestling with the evil queen, just cool, calm negotiation."

Tia nods and goes back to her colouring. "It's Ok daddy, I can use my magic wand to 'tect you."

"I'm more worried about your dad having to whip out his own magic wand." Mackenzie mutters dryly, unfortunately Tia's acute hearing picks up on it.

"You have a magic wand too?" She asks excitedly, "Let me see."

Fuck!

I give Mackenzie a sideways glance, she returns my unimpressed look with an apologetic one.

I bend to whisper conspiratorially in Tia's ear while holding Mackenzie's embarrassed gaze, "I can't peanut. It's a gift I have to keep hidden."

"Why?"

"So other men don't get jealous," Mackenzie huffs out a laugh as I scramble to come up with a story that will appease my daughter's inquisitive mind. My thoughts stray to the folder I thumbed through in Jerry's office. "I wouldn't want any goblins to find out about it and for them to try and steal it away. Mackenzie is just worried I might get it out unnecessarily and that it gets stolen before she has the chance to see it again."

"Did you show it to M'kenzie?" Tia whispers, checking around to make sure there are no goblins listening in.

"Not exactly," I narrow my eyes at Mackenzie who rolls her lips in amusement. "She knew I was hiding something big and made me show it to her."

Tia nods in apparent understanding before going back to her sketching. I kiss her on the cheek and turn my attention back to Mackenzie.

"Sorry." She mouths to me.

I hold her eyes, "You don't need to worry, I promise I'll keep my wand out of the evil queen's clutches." When she smiles, I lean forward and peck her quickly on the lips. The heat between us is palpable, and I only drawback slightly before I can't resist diving back in. The second kiss is still chaste, but it lingers. Her lips part by a small degree, and my tongue is about to accept her invitation when we are halted by an unrestrained bout of giggling beside us. We both pull apart and look at the source.

"Uncle Grant kisses Aunt Ava like that," Tia chuckles.

"Like what peanut?" I cock my head, smiling.

"On the mouth. Can we take my picture to your friend now M'kenzie?"

"No." The word shoots out a little harsher than I was expecting. Tia frowns.

"I think what your dad is trying to say, is that he wants to be the one to go with you." Mackenzie smiles at me, "I'm ok with that."

"Kay." I help Tia shuffle off of her chair and she grabs my hand. "C'mon."

"Can I grab a shower first peanut?"

"We could make our cakes while daddy's getting ready." Mackenzie waves a box at Tia who grins and nods enthusiastically.

"You sure you want to risk it?" I murmur in Mackenzie's ear. The close contact makes her shiver.

"It's pre-mixed," she giggles, "How hard can it be?"

Exceedingly apparently. I emerge from the bedroom three quarters of an hour later to the obnoxious smell of burning, and my pristine kitchen surfaces covered with all sorts of baking paraphernalia that must have ordered without my prior knowledge.

Mackenzie is watching, as Tia is attempts to cover the charred remains of whatever they have been baking, in white icing. Mackenzie has rolled the sleeves of Tia's top up to her elbows, good call, since Tia has more icing on her arms than the burnt crisps she is trying to cover.

"Went well then?" I ask Mackenzie, who pokes her tongue out at me in jest.

Tia is concentrating too hard to respond. She is carefully shaking silver edible glitter on to the top of one of her creations. When she has finished, she pushes it in my direction.

"Daddy, this one's special, I made it for you."

"Thank you peanut," I tell her graciously. "I'll eat it later."

Tia pouts and I know she expects me to have it straight away. Reluctantly, I pick it up, looking at it suspiciously. "If I chip a tooth I'm sending you the bill." I tell Mackenzie before taking a tentative nibble.

"Lovely." I tell Tia, putting it back on the counter top.

"You have to eat it all," she replies assertively. I see Mackenzie enjoying the show and decide she shouldn't be missing out.

"What about a special one for Mackenzie?"

Tia claps her hands in glee and sets to work. As soon as she is distracted, I catch the look of terror on her next victim's face.

I sidle up beside Mackenzie, and as I lean in to snake my arm around her to unobtrusively drop my spoils in the trash, I let my mouth graze her ear, "If you promise to wait up for me tonight, I'll create a diversion." I can almost feel the heat from her blush. She nods, and I smirk.

"Tia, grab your picture, let's take it across the hall." I call.

"Can I take a cake too?"

"Sure." I grab a piece of kitchen towel to rest it on.

"You can't." Mackenzie grabs my arm horrified.

"Oh yes I can." I laugh, as Tia and I wander towards the door.

Tia's little knuckles don't make much of an impact on the sturdy door of our new neighbour's apartment. After two tries, she concedes and lets me knock for her.

A few seconds later, the door swings open and the giant from yesterday appears before us. He and I lock eyes as we size each other up, neither of us wanting to be the first to speak. He suddenly looks down and I follow his gaze to see Tia pulling on his trouser leg. He immediately crouches down to her level.

"Well, what can I do for you little lady?"

Tia wraps one arm around my leg for security, as she shyly hands over the piece of paper she is carrying. "I drawed this for you," she tells him quietly.

"I drew this for you," I correct her.

"No daddy, I drawed it." She looks up as she reminds me.

The stranger chuckles even though he looks a little taken aback. "You did?" He takes the picture and surveys it with a practiced eye. "This is an exceptionally fine masterpiece."

Tia looks a little confused but it doesn't stop her, "That's you." She points at the giant in the picture.

"I know, I can see the resemblance." The way this guy interacts with my little girl makes me warm to him. "Who are the others?"

"That's daddy, M'kenzie, me, Bob…"

The stranger frowns, "Who's Bob?"

"That's my puppy but I haven't gotten him yet."

Puppy? I drag my hand down my face.

"Ahh, I see, and who's this?"

"That's fairy Clitoris, she 'tects us."

The giant bursts out laughing.

"CHLORIS," I half shout, "Fairy Chloris peanut, and she is so busy, you have fairy Angelina now, remember?"

"If I hang this on my wall, will she protect me too?" The big guy asks Tia.

She thinks for a minute. "I don't think so," she tells him seriously before following my lead, "Fairies are really busy you know."

My neighbour chuckles, "Shame, I could do with a magical clitoris in my life."

"Chloris." I correct the man still crouched on the floor with an exasperated sigh.

"Do you need 'tecting?" Tia asks.

"Every day." The man replies earnestly.

"I can help." Tia dashes back inside our apartment and the man stands.

Feeling magnanimous in light of his kindness towards my daughter I try to introduce myself, "Hi, I'm..."

"If I'm not very much mistaken, you're Jared Jones." He cuts me off but doesn't offer his name.

"I'm afraid you have me at a disadvantage." I prompt.

"I do, don't I?" He smirks arrogantly as Tia returns with her magic wand. She tugs on his trouser leg to make him lower himself back down to her level again. When he does, she taps him on his shoulder with her wand.

"I 'tect you Mister," she tells him solemnly.

"Why thank you."

A second later, she pulls her hand from the pocket of her skirt and showers him with glitter.

Fuck's sake!

I feel myself tense as I wonder if I'm about to be hospitalised. The big man coughs and sparkles like an ethereal being at my feet.

"Make a wish," Tia tells him.

"I wish I wasn't covered in glitter," he murmurs.

"It's fairy dust," I correct him.

He looks up at me with his eyebrows raised and sighs, "Well that's ok then."

"What's your name?" God bless that child.

"Mr Stone, but you can call me Josh." Josh says, as he turns his attention back to Tia.

I feel my hackles rise instantly as I remember the phone conversation I had yesterday. This was the man I was trying to reach before I realised he was a judgemental ass, no better than the jerks I used to go to school with, blatantly refusing to 'babysit' actors because he assumed they were all arrogant, alcohol-fuelled party animals. Maybe I was five years ago, but I never would have wanted someone like him hanging around back then, telling me what to do and cramping my style. I lock my annoyed eyes with Josh's amused ones, as I crouch down to join him and my daughter. "What about your cake peanut?" I extend the gift my daughter wishes to bestow, all traces of guilt at its less-than-appealing nature vanishing.

"I made this for you." Tia smiles shyly, taking the cake from me and offering it to Josh.

"Well, today really is my lucky day," he grins, accepting the gift.

I wouldn't bet on it.

I try not to act smug as he pops it straight in his mouth whole, much to Tia's delight. The myriad of emotions that flutter across his face are priceless. Delight rapidly descends into confusion, disgust, and then feigned happiness for my daughter's sake.

I watch as he struggles to crack the tiny slab of concrete with his teeth. After a few seriously intense moments of crunching and chewing, he finally manages to swallow. I try to conceal my glee as he runs his tongue over his teeth, presumably checking to make sure they are all still there and intact.

"Fuck!" He finally splutters before looking at me.

"Mister," Tia sings, holding her hand out, "You said a bad word."

"No peanut," I tell her gently, "Mr Stone doesn't have to pay, he's not family, he doesn't know the rules."

"What are the rules?" Josh speaks to Tia, ignoring me completely. I can't say I blame him, he is probably going to need to see a proctologist to remove the results of what I've just fed him.

"When Daddy says a bad word Aunt Ava makes him pay for my school when I'm older."

"How much?"

"Ten bucks."

Josh pulls some notes out of the back pocket of his jeans handing Tia a ten dollar note.

"You really don't…" He raises his index finger to silence me as he concentrates on my daughter, who is still standing in front of him, waiting.

"Tyler and Jacob too," she tells him.

Josh's eyes shoot up into his hairline and he casts me a glance.

"Her cousins," I tell him.

"Aunt Ava's kids?" He asks for confirmation.

I nod.

"Shrewd woman, Aunt Ava," he mutters as he hands Tia another couple of notes. "We done here?" He asks a smiling Tia. She nods. "You better run and give that cash to your mom then."

Fuck!

Tia freezes and looks at me with her little brows furrowed. "Go give it to Mackenzie honey." I tell her before she grins and runs off.

Josh and I both stand. He folds his arms across his chest and just stares at me without speaking. With Tia gone, the atmosphere becomes heavier, thick with tension.

I feel I need to speak first, "Thank you for being nice to my daughter." Josh doesn't react; he just watches me with an unnerving, assessing stare. Feeling uncomfortable, I turn to leave. When I do, he breaks his silence.

"I hear you've been trying to find me," he growls.

I turn back and match his tone, "I'm surprised. Your receptionist didn't seem to be all that efficient. In fact, he was quite dismissive and rude."

"My receptionist?" Josh's face crinkles in amusement as he guffaws, "Wait till I tell Kurt that. You'll have to excuse him; he has a flea up his ass that I'm making him man the phones until I can hire someone to do it. Kurt by name, curt by nature. Sounds like I'd better act fast, or my business will crash and burn before it even takes off."

"I shouldn't worry too much," I tell him calmly. "Hiring someone should be easy since he isn't exactly setting the bar high. In fact, Tia's available for the right price. She might need a little training before you let her loose answering calls, but as you've just witnessed, her accountancy skills are top notch."

Josh drags his hand down his face, "I might take you up on that." He finally extends his hand for shaking. I hesitate before taking it, deciding if we are going to be neighbours, it makes sense to be cordial.

"So, why did you want to see me?" Josh asks.

"It doesn't matter," I sigh, before blatantly calling him out. "I hear you don't work for actors. I'm told you think they're too high maintenance and have more money than sense."

He sucks in breath. "I'm afraid that wasn't a lie. The ones I've met in the past didn't really give me cause to think otherwise. They said they wanted protection from someone or something, then did everything in their power to put a target on their own back, and by default, mine in the process. I don't need the aggravation when there are people out there in genuine need of my help and grateful for it."

Unimpressed, I turn to leave.

"But..." He calls, I stop and turn, intrigued as to what's coming next, "Depending on the circumstances, I might be persuaded to help out a cute little girl who can't cook for shit, and who's just hustled me out of thirty bucks."

We exchange a chin tip as a little voice pipes up,

"Mister Josh, you said a bad word."

"Make that sixty," I say with a smile.

Chapter Sixteen

Tia comes running out of the apartment opposite with her hand outstretched once more. Josh chuckles as he shakes his head and hands over another thirty dollars. "When you're ready to start work, I'll have a job waiting for you at my firm. I could retire on the money you extort from the guys' swearing alone."

"Kay." Tia takes her spoils and runs away again.

"Shall we take this inside?" Josh jerks his head towards the door of his place, "Either your daughter has an acute sense of hearing or she has this hall bugged. Either way, I'd prefer not to lose any more cash today."

I chuckle. "Sure, I just need to let my girls' know where to find me, then I'll come over." That statement was half true. Of course, it was the polite thing to do, to let them know where I'd be, but I'd carefully worded my statement to let Josh know Mackenzie was mine and he could forget about making any romantic overtures to her now or in the future. That woman was spoken for.

Five minutes later, I'm ensconced in Josh's living

room, surrounded by moving boxes and drinking coffee.

"So," Josh starts, "Since I don't have a lot of time for bull, it's probably best if I tell you what I already know, then you can fill in the gaps."

I nod, since we only formally met about ten minutes ago, I figure he won't know much.

"Full name Jared James Jones, thirty-two years of age with one sister, Ava, who lives in Morro Bay with her husband Grant, and two sons, Tyler and Jacob. No other siblings."

I frown, my full name and age is common knowledge, but I'm pretty sure neither Tia or I have mentioned Grant, or where he and Ava live, within the past few minutes.

"We'll skip over your parents, since they are currently in Bali as part of the world cruise you bought them for their wedding anniversary last year. You bought the apartment opposite, around about the same time as your career began to skyrocket. Probably chose to buy it for the same reasons as I did. As well as having relatively good security, it's close enough for work to be convenient, but far enough away not to have to bring it home with you. We'll also skip over everything up to approximately four and half years ago, as I'm pretty sure that's when your problems all started."

"Wait!" Gobsmacked, I hold my hand up to silence him. "Where are you getting all this? I never mentioned Grant, my parents or when I bought my home."

"When I first showed interest in this place, I made some initial enquiries as to who else lived on this floor. After learning your name, I did some basic internet research. When Kurt mentioned you called yesterday looking to hire me, I dug a bit deeper to understand what trouble you might be in, and gauge the likelihood of it coming to knock on my door."

"Wow, I don't feel violated at all. Is that legal?" I try not to bark.

"Do you want my help or not?" He definitely barks back.

"Point taken. Please…" I wave the hand holding my coffee cup signalling for him to continue.

"As I was saying, just over four and a half years ago, something changed. Your life was pretty much an open book up until that point—exactly what I expected: a career orientated party animal leaving a string of heartbreak in your wake. Then, it was like you woke up one morning, and everything changed. I was trying to figure out why until I met you yesterday. I must admit, I initially thought your frequent and sudden disappearances from Hollywood were due to you needing to slip away for some kind of rehab. I guessed one of your entourage was helping you avoid negative publicity by covering your tracks, so as not to tarnish the reputation you had been fighting so hard to build. The last thing you would need is to create any sort of bad press that would stop the big bucks from rolling in. Now though, since I've recently received confirmation that you are her father, I'm pretty sure it has something to do with the miniature moneymaker living with you that no one seems to know about. You're needing my assistance seems to coincide with her sudden appearance, however, there's the other factor to take into consideration."

"What other factor?"

"The fact that Mackenzie Kingsley is also staying with you—happily married to Dan Kingsley for the last fourteen years—yet suddenly turns up at your place not wearing her wedding ring and comfortable being called your wife. Neither of you corrected me yesterday, and interestingly, you referred to her as one of 'your girls' today. Thus implying you two have something going on, and that you wanted me to know before I discovered she'd ditched her husband and decided to make a play for her myself.

So, which is it you need protection from? The jilted ex-husband after your balls for seducing his wife, or the pissed off ex-partner hunting you down for parental kidnapping?"

I chuckle dryly, "Neither. I can take care of myself."

Josh seems to like that answer. "What do you want with me then?"

"Work and other commitments prevent me being around the girls 24/7. I need someone to look out for them when I can't be there. Just until things are more settled and people get used to Tia being around. I'll be honest, she hasn't been living with me because I wanted to give her the chance of a normal life, but circumstances changed and the decision to bring her here was a spontaneous one. It was the right one, but until I know how it's going to play out, I want to make sure any further disruption to her life is minimal. At the moment, not even my agent knows I have a daughter, when people find out about her..."

Josh holds his hand up to stop me, "I hear you. Things could get a little crazy. What about Mackenzie where does she fit into all this? If you want my help, you have to tell me everything."

So, I do.

Even after spilling my guts, Josh won't commit to giving me the help I need. He said he had other job offers to consider, as well as a new business to get up and running. He promised to get back to me, even though I made him a very generous offer for his services. Something about the way he couldn't be bought makes me want him all the more. It gives him an air of integrity that reassures me I can trust him and that my girls will be in safe hands. I'm back home, mulling over the situation, when my thoughts are interrupted.

"Penny for them."

I turn to see Mackenzie leaning on the doorframe to my bedroom, when I'm facing her, she gives me a low wolf whistle.

"Do I look ok?" I've showered and changed into one of the few outfits I own that fit properly: a black designer shirt and dark grey suit, ready for my afternoon with Henrietta.

"I'd go out with you." Mackenzie's downcast eyes don't share the same enthusiasm as her voice.

I crook my finger, beckoning her over to me before wrapping my arms around her. "I'm glad, because I thought next weekend we could all go back and visit Ava. While she is spoiling Tia, I thought you and I could have our first official date."

"You did?" Her eyes immediately light up.

"Uh huh. If you feel you're ready and you want to that is."

"I am and I do." She gazes at me bashfully and I steal a quick kiss. I pull away before things get too heated. The last thing I need is Handsy Hetty thinking I brought a boner along specifically for her to play with.

"Wait up for me?" I ask softly.

Mackenzie nods as my cell starts to chime. I answer, thinking it's my driver letting me know he has arrived and is waiting for me outside. It's not.

"Jared, I have news." It's Jerry.

"Good or bad?" Mackenzie tries to pull away to give me some privacy, but I tuck her under my arm so she can't escape. Unlike her douchebag husband, I've got nothing to hide.

"Depends on whether you're you or me."

"Go on," I laugh.

"The producers of that fantasy film you're

interested in, they've agreed to everything in principle. I didn't even have to cut your fee. In fact, I had the devil of a time trying to convince them I was on the level. I think they believed I was just toying with them. They want me to arrange a meet with you for next week. I'm pretty sure it's just to prove our offer is genuine. They want the chance to look you in the eyes to make sure I'm not just raising their hopes."

"That's great news."

"Is it? I still don't think this is your best move."

"I told you Jerry, I've got a really good feeling about this. Set it up, but only when they have a copy of the modified script that I can bring back with me. I want to run it by a target audience. If they approve. I'm in."

"Target audience? Who?"

"I'll tell you soon, I promise."

"Jared, tell me now!" I can feel Jerry silently fuming at the other end of the line.

"I can't, I have to go and schmooze Henrietta for you. Where are we going?"

"After you pick her up, you are taking her for a behind the scenes tour of Universal, dinner and cocktails, followed by a concert with fireworks at the Hollywood bowl. Your driver has the itinerary and anything you may need."

"In other words, you're getting me to parade around town on a publicity stunt."

"Listen, you need all the help you can get if you are seriously considering becoming the king of fairyland."

I laugh as my mobile lets me know I have another incoming call. "Jerry, I have to go, I think the car is here."

"Make me proud." Are the words I hear just before I hang up.

"Where's peanut?" I ask Mackenzie, after speaking to the driver of my ride.

"Curled up on the sofa watching television."

I push a lock of hair back from Mackenzie's face, tucking it behind her ear. I can tell she's worried, and if I could cancel going out to stay home, I would. "I'll be back as soon as I can." I try to reassure her.

"I'm fine." She shrugs unconvincingly.

"Liar," I growl in her ear, pausing to nibble her neck. She shivers and my cell warbles again. I pull back to answer it and listen for a few moments. "Send them up." I say before disconnecting. "Guess what?"

"What?" Mackenzie asks curiously.

"Tia's new bed has arrived. Delivery and install has all been paid for, so is it Ok to leave you in charge?"

"Yes." She claps her hands excitedly. I think we are both relieved it will give her something to concentrate on while I am out. Suddenly, I have another idea to keep her occupied and hand her one of the cards out of my wallet. She takes it with her brow furrowed.

"Perhaps when they are done you can go online and order some furniture for the rest of the place."

"But don't you want to…"

"I cut her off with another kiss. "I trust you. If it were left to me the place would still be empty."

She giggles, and there is the same fire in her eyes that I saw when I took her foraging for clothes in the thrift store that first time, shortly after I'd met her.

"What sort of style are you going for? What do you like?" Mackenzie asks eagerly.

"Minimalist," I deadpan, before yelling, "Peanut! Chloris just called to say she found you the perfect bed."

I hear a squeal and shortly after Tia comes hurtling into the room. "When's it be here?"

"She said soon, and you know with her magic, soon could be anytime now." I tell her just as there is a knock on the door.

"It's here, M'kenzie it's here!" Tia jumps up and down in excitement, it's hard not to get swept up in her enthusiasm.

"Quick, let's go see." Mackenzie holds out her hand and Tia takes it. They rush off together and I follow. I'm just about to slip out the door when Tia stops me.

"Daddy wait!"

I pause while she dashes off, returning with her magic wand. "I 'tect you," she shouts, as she bashes me on the back of the leg.

I crouch down and give her a hug. "Take care of Mackenzie while I'm gone peanut."

She nods just as the door behind me opens and Josh appears. "What's all the noise out here little lady?"

"My new bed is here!" Tia screams excitedly.

I stand, "I have to go out," I tell him.

He nods in understanding. "I'll be here tonight."

I jerk my head in gratitude. It's good to know, even if I'm sure the girls will be safe enough indoors on their own.

"I've been meaning to ask," Josh scratches his chin thoughtfully. "How would you feel about me fitting a security device in the hall."

"What sort of device?" I ask, my interest piqued.

"Nothing too extreme, just something that would give me the heads up if anyone were to be loitering about on our floor uninvited."

"I think I would feel…" I search for the right word, "reassured."

He nods and I turn to leave again.

"Daddy."

"Yes peanut." I crouch back down.

Before I realise what's happening, a shower of glistening dust reigns down, covering me, as well as my black shirt and dark suit.

"I wish you safe from the evil queen."

"Thank you peanut," I grind out, as Josh bursts out laughing behind me.

With no time to change, I head off sparkling like a disco ball.

Chapter Seventeen

✧

T he outing with Henrietta goes a lot smoother than I'm expecting. When I pull up outside her house to collect her, she climbs in the car, giving me an odd look. I'd dusted myself off as much as I could, but I thought her initial reluctance to get too close might have had something to do with not wanting to get glitter on her haute couture. However, as the evening wears on, I start to think her overzealous affection the night we met had either been driven by alcohol fuelled bravado or Tia really did have magical powers, and her fairy dust is indeed protecting me from a hands-on harlot. Whichever it is, I don't care. Much to my relief, the hours we spend together are perfectly amiable. Even when we are frequently asked to huddle together for photos, Henrietta keeps her distance and we barely make contact. She eyes me almost warily before we even touch.

By the time I get home it's edging past midnight. I step out of the elevator and am making my way to the front door when Josh appears from his apartment as if expecting to see me.

"Are you stalking me?" I quip, when I see him, "Do I need to hire someone to protect me from you?"

He chuckles, "No, if I were going to stalk anyone it would be the babe you're living with. She's not wearing a ring, so I guess that would be Ok."

I feel myself tense and he obviously picks up on it.

"Relax, would you feel happier if I told you I have a girlfriend?" He laughs.

"Yes," I confirm, "It would. Have you?"

"Nope," he grins.

Jerk!

"I just wanted to show you what I've installed." Curiosity makes me follow him into his place where, just inside the door, he points to a small screen displaying the lift doors and the entire hallway we share. After a few seconds, the screen flicks off automatically. "Watch."

Josh walks out into the hall. The minute he does, an audible alert sounds and the monitor comes alive again. Josh looks at a hidden camera somewhere and waves before coming back inside.

"Neat," I tell him.

"I have an app on my phone that lets me review any footage remotely, if you want me to, I can install it on yours too so we can both use it."

"That would be great." I'm just going to hand over my cell when I whip it back out of reach, "Wait, you're not going to put any dodgy tracking devices or bugs on there while you're at it are you?"

"Paranoid much?" He chortles. I narrow my eyes and make a point of watching over his shoulder while he downloads and configures what he needs to. "I've turned the alerts off as they can get a bit annoying, but you can just tap the app to see what's going on or change the settings here, if you want to switch the notifications on."

I nod, "How did you obtain permission to get the camera installed?" I stick my head out of his door to glance up and down the passage, wherever he hid the device, he did a good job, I can't see any evidence of it.

"Let's just say, what property management don't know, won't hurt them."

"Is that legal?" I ask before I can stop myself.

Josh just smirks.

"Never mind," I sigh. "Head's up, we are all going away for a few days next weekend?"

"Anywhere nice?"

"Visit my sister."

"For her birthday? Need any of my crew to keep you company?"

"You agreeing to my job offer?"

"Maybe, it did get me thinking. I can't be around much personally, but I've a crew of about eight lined up and chomping at the bit to start working for me. They're all sitting around twiddling their thumbs while I'm trying to get organised. Not having anything to do isn't good for them, idle hands being the devil's workshop and all that. It's not good for me either, having to keep listening to them bitch about being bored before I have to eventually bail them out of trouble. So, how about I loan them to you for the next three weeks?"

"What do you mean loan them?" I ask intrigued.

"You decide how you want to go about introducing your family to the public, I keep my guys' occupied by getting them to skulk around in the background making sure it all goes smoothly. I reckon interest will die down in you after a couple of weeks, and I should be more or less ready to assign the team to their new positions by then. We can review any further requirements you may have and take it from there after I launch my business."

"That will be great." I try not to sound as relieved as I feel.

"How much pocket money does your kid get?"

I laugh, "I've haven't had to start paying that yet, except when I swear. Why?"

"I told you. I don't work for actors and I have a reputation to uphold. I'll be employed by Tia and no-one else, so I guess it means I'll be doing this job pro bono."

"I can't ask you to do that."

"You didn't."

"What about your crew, won't they mind?"

"Like I said, you'll be doing us all a favour. I just need to find someone with a modicum of sense to handle our calls first. I know we joked about it, but it's harder than you think trying to find someone polite, who's intelligent enough to recognise a timewaster, as well as being able to take an accurate message while maintaining discretion."

"And you thought Kurt was the answer?" I scoff.

"No," Josh laughs, "Everyone is having to muck in, but I do need to focus on keeping him busier than the others, and I keep him around because he has a lot of other useful skills."

"Getting coffee, that sort of thing?" I ask seriously. "What about Mac? Would you consider her? I'm not talking long term, just to help you for a few weeks while you get yourself sorted."

"Hasn't she got enough on her plate?" He pauses for a moment, "She doesn't have any experience in our line of work, but I could teach her the basics to hold us over until I find a permanent replacement."

"As far as I know she hasn't been offered any work since her agency dropped her, with her shoulder still healing it's limiting her opportunities. I can't promise she'll want to do it, but I'll ask if it will help."

"Sure, yeah, see what she says. If she's interested, get her swing by tomorrow for a chat. I reckon Kurt would pay her out of his own pocket, just to get himself off the hook."

"What about me? When do I get to meet your crew?"

"You don't. Not unless I think it's necessary, or they have to step out of the shadows and blow their cover. It's safer if you don't know who they are, then you can't draw attention to them. It makes their job easier if no-one knows they are watching, it makes any potential threats easier for them to spot, plus they can concentrate on keeping Tia safe without any other distractions. Besides, I'm still hiring so the team will be expanding.

I'm thinking I can use this job as a practical assessment, you know, send any new recruits out with the squad so I can assess their strengths and weaknesses to place them in the right roles going forward.

Give me twenty-four hours to brief the team, then just go ahead with your usual routine knowing we've got your back for the next few weeks. The guys that are with me already, they're all ex-SEAL's, and I can personally vouch for every one of them," he chuckles, "even Kurt. You may not be able to see them all the time, but they're be around, your family will be safe. I promise."

I do a head tip and walk towards the door. "Oh, it's not Ava's birthday, you got that little fact wrong," I tell him smugly, just as I'm about to leave, "makes me wonder if you're the right guy for the job after all."

"Oh, I know it's not Ava's, her birthday is in July," he throws back arrogantly. "I was referring to Mackenzie. It's her birthday next Saturday, that's why I thought you were taking her away. Don't tell me you forgot?"

"No." I snap unconvincingly. How could I forget something I never even knew? At least now I had a week to plan a surprise for her.

I creep into my apartment hoping to find Mackenzie waiting for me. The living room is empty so I presume she got tired of waiting and took herself off to bed. I wander down to my bedroom and find it empty. I check the bathroom before turning and heading back to Tia's room. Pushing the door open, I have to chuckle. From the soft glow of a nightlight, I can see Tia's new bed has been erected and made, but it lies empty. The air bed I have been using, has been pushed as far as possible into the den underneath. Two pairs of legs protrude from the bottom of the curtain that conceals the recess beneath the bed.

I gently peel back the curtain to find Mackenzie and Tia snuggled together, with a book lying open across Mackenzie's chest. Tia is in her pyjama's, but Mackenzie is still is her day clothes. It's obvious they both fell asleep while Mackenzie was reading. I grab the comforter from the top of the bed and throw it over the pair of them, before sneaking away to grab a drink and head back to my room. At least I can sleep in the bed there and be comfortable tonight. I don't bother with a light, I'm just starting to strip, when my sixth sense tells me I'm being watched. In the dim light, I see a shadow standing in the doorway as I toss my shirt to the side of the room.

"I'm sorry," I say in a low voice, "Did I wake you?"

"No. How was your date?"

"It wasn't a date, not in the way you're implying, and it was fine actually. I must have got her all wrong, Henrietta was very well behaved."

"I thought she might be," Mackenzie murmurs, walking over and letting her hand ghost over my tattoo. Her touch is electric, blood starts surging through my veins.

I tip her chin up with my fingers so I can look her in the eye, "What's that supposed to mean?"

"I may have…" She tries to avoid my gaze but I don't let her, "I may have given her a call."

I bend and kiss the corner of her mouth, smiling against her lips as I ask, "I didn't know you knew her. What did you say on this call?" She starts to squirm uncomfortably, so I grab her behind with my free hand, pulling her against my body and holding her tightly in place. She whimpers as she becomes aware she isn't the only one suffering from the effects of our close proximity. I grind against her gently as I encourage her on, "What did you say?"

She looks ashamed as she admits the truth, "I told her that if she didn't want her husband to find out about the affair she had with Dan last year, it would be in her best interests to keep her paws to herself tonight. I was worried she wouldn't listen, but I guess the thought of being cut off from her expense account made her think twice about trying to feel you up."

I laugh out loud. "Why Miss Mackenzie," I growl, "I do believe you are trying to stake a claim."

"What would you say if I were?" She asks nervously.

I squeeze her ass, "I'd say you'd have to mark your territory."

She looks at me confused. "How?"

"Coming on my face would be a good way to start."

She gasps and shudders at the same time, "You've

got a filthy mouth."

"And it's about to get filthier." I drop her chin and use both hands under her butt to hoick her up and into my arms. She instinctively wraps her legs around me as I carry her to the bed, claiming her mouth in a searing kiss as I do. When we reach the side of the bed I stand her on it. She starts to lower herself down, but I grasp her hips to hold her firm. "Don't move," I smirk.

She looks down at me inquisitively, and I slowly slide my hands under the skirt she is wearing, pushing it up her legs to her hips, so I can hook my fingers into the sides of her panties. I take my time dragging them down, teasing her soft skin with kisses as I lower them. When her underwear hits the top of the bed, she obediently steps out of it and when I straighten, it's then she realises my face is almost perfectly aligned with the apex of her thighs.

"Jared..." She murmurs apprehensively, the soft mattress on which she is standing doesn't provide a very solid foundation. When I lift one leg to hook it over my shoulder, her balance falters, and she tries to find purchase by reaching above herself to plant her hands on the ceiling. When that fails, she grasps handfuls of my hair to steady herself. The sting as she tugs isn't as painful as the erection straining to break free of my pants.

"Jared..." She mutters again, "I'm not sure this is a good idea."

I look up and see her dark, lustful eyes gazing down at me, "Which? This?" She cocks her head not understanding, so I give her a hint, sliding one finger inside her hot, soaked core. She quivers slightly and bites her bottom lip as she tries to remain silent. I pump her a couple of times before removing my wet finger and using it to circle her perfect hole, "Or this?" I look up at her grinning wickedly, and she makes a strangled sound I've never heard before. "Or, maybe this?" I don't give her a second before I bury my head between her legs and set to work. She whimpers and tenses, gripping me harder as she tries to remain upright on the undulating surface she's stood on. Her balance regained, I feel her relax and start to enjoy the ride. Her moans are muffled as she fights to contain them. It doesn't take long before I feel her muscles fluttering around my tongue letting me know she is close. I work harder, eager for her to finish so I can chase my own release by lying her down and sinking deep inside her.

As she starts to shudder a little voice carries down the hall, "M'kenzie. Where are you?"

Fuck! Out of time, I give it all I've got, plunging two fingers inside her so as to free up my mouth for her bud. I start sucking and teasing like man possessed.

"I'm coming baby!" Mackenzie screams in a trembling voice.

I'm not sure which of us she is talking to.

"Wait there so I can find you." She grinds out a second before she climaxes. Her body tenses and shudders violently before collapsing like a Jelly on top of me.

"Kay," a little voice calls.

I pull back, setting Mackenzie's leg back on the bed before smoothing down the skirt that I didn't bother to remove. Her legs are still trembling as I help her climb down off the bed. Her flushed face and dazed expression make me smile. "Want me to go and see to her?"

She shakes her head numbly, "I got it," she mumbles with glazed eyes.

"Hurry back, I've not finished with you yet," I warn.

She nods her head in the same anesthetized manner she just shook it.

"You sure you're Ok?" I laugh, as she staggers away.

While Mackenzie is off seeing to Tia, I disappear into the bathroom to clean myself up. I strip off the rest of my clothes and am ready for action when I hear voices coming from the adjoining room. Wrapping a towel around my waist and frowning, I go to find out what's happening. I'm just in time to catch Tia climbing into the bed.

"Hey, what's going on in here?" I try to keep the frustration out of my voice.

"M'kenzie was scared so I said I would sleep with her tonight." Tia tells me seriously.

"I can understand why." I lock eyes with Mackenzie before flicking mine down to my towel, or more specifically what's hiding beneath it. When I look back at her, she giggles, we both know Tia was really the one scared. "I'm going to take a shower," I announce dramatically. "A cold one."

I saunter off to Mackenzie's en-suite so no one can overhear while I make myself infinitely more comfortable under the spray of the shower there. After, with all hopes of spending the night inside Mackenzie dashed, I go and settle back on the airbed, where instead of counting sheep, I try to come up with 101 ways of encouraging Tia to sleep in her own bed.

Chapter Eighteen

✧

The next week goes by in a flash.

Sunday the three of us have a lazy day. Tia kept Mackenzie so busy while I was out the night before, she didn't get the chance to look for any new furniture like I suggested. After creating an in-door cinema experience for Tia, she settles under a blanket on one end of the sofa watching her favourite movies, while I settle on the other with Mackenzie snuggled into my side as we look for suitable pieces on my tablet. We don't end up ordering anything. I know I have to bite the bullet and let the girls leave the apartment eventually, with Josh's offer of help on the table, I figure it's better to grab the bull by the horns while I know I have some highly trained professionals watching our backs. In light of that, I tell Mackenzie we should go to a store to pick out some items personally. I've never seen a person look so excited to be going shopping. She wants to leave straightaway, but to ensure Josh gets the twenty-four hours he asked for, I tell her how he needs someone to help him handle some calls for a while and send her next door for a chat. While she is gone, I take the opportunity of calling Ava to ask for a small favour.

Monday through Thursday is hectic.

Shopping has to be put on hold when Mackenzie agrees to help Josh out with his telephony issues. I start to regret mentioning her name when I lose her to him all day Monday for 'training purposes'. I mean, how long does it take to teach someone how to answer a phone? While she is gone, Tia and I go to visit Jerry. I don't want him finding out about her second-hand, not after all the mysterious disappearances and vague excuses he has had to put up with over the years. To say he's surprised is an understatement. When I first walk in, he surmises I must be child sitting for a friend. As I start to explain and the pieces of the puzzle fall into place, his eyes grow so wide they almost eclipse his face. I swear he is frozen in shock for a solid two minutes. Tia gets bored waiting for him to respond, and whacks him on the head with her wand, then she sprinkles him with fairy dust wishing he could speak, after that we can't shut him up. He paces his office, excitedly rambling about how he can turn the situation to our advantage. Suddenly, my considering the role of the fairy king in the movie he had originally dismissed was a shrewd move. He goes on at length, animatedly describing the various publicity shoots and marketing campaigns he could put together in order to capture a previously untapped audience. Tia sits on my lap watching him bemused, while I mostly ignore him until he pauses to take a breath. Only then, can I interrupt him long enough to quash his dreams and make it abundantly clear that my daughter is off-limits as far as all his imaginative ideas are concerned.

Over the course of the rest of the week, Mackenzie gets me to hit the shops with her not once, but three times. The first time, we go in search of a couch that doesn't cripple you after more than five minutes use. I end up buying three. One for our apartment, and two more to appease the store manager after they get suspiciously covered in glitter. Despite our best efforts it proves impossible to completely remove. Tia swears she isn't to blame. When I challenge her, Mackenzie leaps to her defence, assuring me that fairy Chloris must have flown in when I wasn't looking, tested the cushions on my behalf, and dropped some fairy dust in her wake. Even though I'm not convinced, I arrange for the one with the least amount of sparkles to be delivered to Josh, since on my various visits to his place, I've had to perch on boxes where he doesn't appear to have gotten around to purchasing anything more substantial yet. The other I tell the manager to take straight to the closest thrift store.

On our second trip, we look for additional pieces of furniture and various accessories. Eating at the kitchen island isn't always comfortable or practical, so we buy a round table for the dining area. Then, since Mackenzie has agreed to work for Josh short-term, I give her free-reign to kit out the office any way she sees fit. While she and Tia are debating desks and lamps, I disappear and treat myself to a state-of-the-art multi gym for the room opposite. For some unknown reason, and despite my best efforts at bribery and corruption, Tia refuses to settle in her own bedroom, making alone time with Mackenzie impossible. I need something other than my right hand to help me work off the frustration that's consistently building night after night.

The third spree is all my worst fears realised, as Mackenzie takes Tia and me out to buy a wardrobe full of new clothes. I'm a mobile mannequin that's dragged from store to store as Mackenzie fulfils Grants previous request to her.

One morning, Mackenzie asks to borrow the car so she can go and visit her parents. I think that seeing how close Tia and I are to my family makes her want to reconnect with her own. I know it must be hard for her, after being estranged for such a long time, so suggest I go with her. She declines my offer with a grateful kiss, saying she feels it's something she needs to do alone. I act unconcerned, but then worry until she is safely back home with me. When she returns, I try to gauge her mood. She seems happy, if a little quieter than usual. With little ears constantly around us making it difficult to have an adult conversation, I decide to give her some time, but only after making it known that I am willing to listen whenever she is ready to talk.

Ever since I moved Tia in with me, Ava has been on my case about registering her for pre-school. She already has a place set in Morro Bay, but since that's no longer viable, Mackenzie and I do some research before the three of us go on an outing to scope out her options. The one's near us are all good schools, but something just doesn't feel right. I'm not sure what it is, but I just can't bring myself to pick one.

Finally, I get the call from Jerry to say the producers of the fantasy film I'm interested in are ready to meet with me. At the same time, Josh asks if he can borrow Mackenzie to scope out some commercial premises with him. Tia asks to go with Mackenzie, I figure Josh will keep them both safe, and Tia will keep Josh from getting up to any mischief with my woman, so I agree. They take my SUV since Tia's car seat is already installed, presenting me with the opportunity of being able to peel out of the parking lot in my luxury sports car. When I cruise up in time for my appointment, the reactions are priceless. It's clear everyone thought they were being punked by Jerry, never really expecting to see me stride through the door. After I leave with the revised script tucked safely under my arm, I make a pit stop on the way home to pick up the gift I'd ordered as one of the surprises for Mackenzie's birthday. I knew I was taking a huge gamble, and it made me nervous to think about what might happen if it didn't pay off.

Ever since we first set foot out the front door together, I'd been expecting Tia to be a bigger sensation than she actually was. I guess that saying is right, fear of the unknown is greater than the fear itself. Our excursions were blissfully uneventful, with only a few curious looks and the odd awkward question I was able to artfully deflect. If either Mackenzie or I were recognised and approached for either autographs or selfies, Tia always found a way of stealing our thunder. She won the hearts of everyone she met with her sweet nature and quirky behaviour. Even so, she was headline news for little more than a couple of days. I did wonder if the sudden decline in attention had something to do with Mackenzie, since it coincided with the visit she made to her attorney parents, or with Josh and his sometimes unorthodox ways of getting any job done. It didn't matter; what did was that we were mostly just a regular family, out doing regular chores and I couldn't have been happier. Mackenzie and I would walk side by side while Tia danced around us pointing out things she found interesting. I'd watch Mackenzie looking at her with such fondness, encouraging her inquisitive nature and never once getting tired of her relentless questioning. If Mackenzie's hand accidently brushed against mine, I took it every time. More than once, I wished we'd met earlier, that Tia had been blessed from birth with the kind of mother she deserved and found in Mackenzie, and that her father had been a better man in not fucking up the first four years of her life.

By the time Friday rolls around, in my mind, we have solidified into one perfect, happy little family.

Throughout the week, I never saw any sign of Josh or his band of merry men when we were out and about. Yet, every so often, my skin would prickle and the hairs on the back of my neck would stand on end, leaving me with the eerie feeling that my family and I were being watched. It made my protective instincts kick in and I'd huddle my girls around me a little closer. Then as suddenly as the fear arose, it would disperse and I'd relax, reasoning that I was sensing Josh or one of his comrades, and blaming my own neurosis for the uneasy feelings that had descended.

It makes a change for me to be able to get a good night's sleep before we all make the drive back to Ava's Friday morning. Even though we don't need to leave under the cover of darkness and I tell Ava not to expect us before noon, we depart early to miss the heavier traffic. We reach our destination at about nine in the morning, parking in the garage and letting ourselves in with the hidden key. Ava's car is in the garage, so I know she is back from dropping the twins at school. We were hoping to catch them before they left for the day, but my plans to set off from home even earlier after simply bundling Tia into the car in her pyjamas, were disrupted when she woke up and insisted on getting dressed and having breakfast before she left.

We all pile into the kitchen expecting to find Ava there. When she is missing, Tia runs off in search of her while Mackenzie starts a fresh pot of coffee. As soon as we are alone, I take the opportunity to test her resilience by sidling up behind her, cupping her breasts with my hands and nibbling her neck to see how she performs under pressure. She does her best to remain focused on the task in hand, as she remembers where we are and the likelihood of us being discovered at any given moment. It's Ava's piercing scream that interrupts us and sends us both charging through the house in search of her. Mackenzie and I burst into her bedroom to find an excitable Tia jumping on the bed, while Ava peers out from beneath the sheets looking mortified. Grant is sat up beside her, the covers draped across his mid-section as he contorts in laughter. Without looking too closely in case my retinas burn, they both appear to be naked. My mind combusts as I try not to imagine what Tia interrupted.

"Uncle Grant was hiding under the covers but I found him, even though he said he took all his clothes off to make himself invisible," Tia announces proudly. "Aunt Ava said two bad words..." She holds up two little fingers for emphasis, "but she says you have to pay for coming early and making her say them."

"At least you got to come at all," Grant sniggers, and Ava whacks him as she stares at us all speechless.

"Dude, what were you doing to my sister?" The question tumbles out in shock, even though the answer is obvious.

"Giving her a gynaecological exam, I needed to check on baby clitoris." I shrivel on the spot and my look of horror causes Grant to burst out laughing again. "Your face, seriously? You do remember we're married, right? How do you think the twins got here?"

"The stork," Tia chimes in helpfully, "Daddy said she delivered them to the hospital by UPS."

Grant roars with laughter before he finally manages to wheeze, "Fancy a run? I suddenly have some excess energy I need to burn off."

I hear Mackenzie snigger beside me and frown at her unimpressed. She rolls her lips and looks away as she tries to control herself. "Um..." I don't really know how to respond without choking on the words, "Don't you want to... um... finish up here? We can pop out for breakfast and come back later."

"We've had breakfast silly." Tia reminds me as she continues jumping up and down on the bed, "I want to play with Aunt Ava."

"So does Uncle Grant," Mackenzie mutters before she can't contain her laughter any longer. Ava throws me silent daggers as Grant and Mackenzie try unsuccessfully to curb their hilarity.

"That ship's sailed for now," Grant tips his head toward Ava who is still too traumatised to speak.

To be honest, I'm not fairing much better than my sister. "Right... um... see you in ten," I mumble, as I grab a giggling Tia around the waist, lifting her and carrying her under my arm with her body parallel to the floor, as I make a hasty departure with Mackenzie hot on my heels.

Chapter Nineteen

"So, how do you stop yourself from being constantly cock blocked by a four-year-old?" I ask Grant while we are out pounding the neighbourhood pavements.

"You get her to move out and find a new hiding place for your spare key." Grant side eyes me mischievously.

"Yeah, about that…"

"Don't worry about it." Grant chuckles as he cuts me off. "What's the problem? Ava told me you bought her a fancy bed with all the bells and whistles, once Tia's asleep not much wakes her."

"I did, I just can't get her out of my bed and in it. When we first all moved in together, Tia had to share my room with Mac while I got hers decorated to her liking. She loved her new bed when it was delivered, but the first night she spent in it, she woke up scared and ended up climbing back in with Mac. I expected her to be a bit unsettled for a few days while she got used to all the changes she's been going through, but now it's become the norm. And it's like she has this sixth sense, she'll be out like a light, then as soon as Mac and I sneak off for a bit of alone time, she's awake and seeking one of us out. I painted a fairy on the wall above her bed to help her feel safe, and I've tried everything I can think of over the last week to get her to move into her own room, but nothings worked."

"Who does she try to find first?"

"What?"

"You said she comes looking for one of you. Who does she try to find first?"

"Does it matter? I think you are missing the point here?" I huff.

"Humour me," Grant chuckles.

I think for a minute. "Mackenzie. But then she would, wouldn't she? She is used to waking up with Mac beside her."

"Did you ask her what she was actually scared of?"

"Monsters and shit I suppose."

"But you never actually asked?"

"Well, no."

"Where are you sleeping?"

"I tried the couch but that didn't work, so I bought an air bed and put it on the floor in Tia's room."

"Why not the bedroom across the hall from her?"

"I've been decorating that for Mac."

"So, this thing between you and Mac, it's just a fling?"

"What?" I bluster more than a little aggrieved. "No! It's much more than that."

Grant rolls his eyes at me.

"What?" I snap.

"Did you ever stop to wonder why, when Tia says she is scared, she climbs into bed with Mac for security—a woman she has known for a little over two weeks—rather than coming to look for you, her dad, the man she adores and who has always been there for her, protecting her since the day she was born?"

I cast him a look of bewilderment.

"Stop thinking like a horny teenager trying to get laid, and start thinking like a father." Is the only wisdom he imparts before he shakes his head and jogs off, leaving me more baffled than ever.

When we get home, and Ava and I have gotten over the awkwardness of me having walked in on my sister attempting to have sex with her husband, the rest of the day runs smoothly. Ava gives Mackenzie a cooking lesson, where she educates her on how to make Tia's favourite spaghetti bolognaise. After chatting with Ava, Mackenzie feels that it makes sense for us to be able to prepare at least one dish for Tia that we don't have to order in. I have to agree since Ava and I planned the whole scene in advance. While Ava keeps Mackenzie busy, Grant, Tia and I excuse ourselves to go to the park. Since my daughter leaks like a sieve as far as secrets are concerned, Grant takes her to feed the ducks while I go off to pick up a cake and some other bits to surprise Mackenzie with. She hasn't mentioned it's going to be her birthday once. So, I'm pretty sure we are going to be able to make it a pretty memorable occasion for her. The three of us stop to pick the twins up on our way home after making a quick pit stop at Daisy's. When we walk through the door, we enjoy a healthy home cooked meal curtesy of Ava, before we all spend the rest of the evening catching up over a variety of family games at the kitchen table. It's endearing how the twins want to spend time fussing over Tia, I guess I hadn't really given much thought as to how much they would miss her not being around.

When I catch Tia yawning and look at the clock to see it's almost half past seven, I push my chair back and stand, holding out my hand, "Time for bed peanut."

Tia climbs out of her chair taking my hand before holding her other one out for Mackenzie. Just as she is about to take it, Grant speaks. "Actually Mac, can you stay, I'd like to talk to you about something."

"Noooo." Tia's face scrunches up in fear and she starts panicking, bobbing up and down on the spot. "You have to come."

Mac stands, "I'll just go up with Tia and get her settled, then I'll come back," she tells Grant.

Grant shakes his head. "No," he tells her firmly. Everyone stops to stare at him, except Jacob, who seems completely clued in to the situation, and Tia, who goes into complete nuclear meltdown. I glare at Grant and he widens his eyes at me. I know he expects me to do something, I'm just not sure what it is. If he wasn't family and I didn't trust him as much as I do, I probably would have punched him for making my little girl so upset. Instead, I stay frozen to the spot staring at him blankly. After watching me flounder for a few seconds, he puts me out of my misery by calling Tia over to him, and sitting her on his lap. "Hey, hey," he soothes, as Tia sobs into his chest, "Why all the tears?"

"I should have thought that was obvious," Jacob chips in. All eyes turn to him, but he just rolls his eyes and slouches back in his chair.

"M'kenzie h... has to s... sleep with m... me?" Tia bawls.

"Why baby?" Grant asks softly.

"C... coz if she wakes up and I'm not t... there, she gets scared." Tia wails.

"I can understand that." Grant tells her patiently.

"You c... can?" Tia sniffs, and looks up at him.

"I can," he confirms. "I think you get a little scared too, don't you? If you wake up and Mackenzie isn't there."

Tia won't look him in the eye, but she nods.

"What are you scared of baby girl?" Grant asks.

Everyone except Jacob watches Tia intently, waiting for her answer.

"That she doesn't love me anymore."

Fuck me! I collapse back down in my chair with my head swimming. My first instinct is to find that kid Connor and shut him up. Permanently! Then I realise the blame for this situation lies much closer to home and become furious with myself, knowing I should have had the conversation with Tia about her mom as soon as the subject was raised. I look across at Ava and can tell she gets it too.

"What makes you think that?" Grant presses on softly, even though I know what's coming.

"Because Connor said my first mommy left because she didn't love me."

I look at Mackenzie who is rolling her lips, trying to keep quiet as her eyes start to leak. I glance at Ava who also looks on the verge of tears.

"Have you asked Mackenzie if she loves you?" Grant whispers in Tia's ear.

Tia shakes her head.

"Why don't you ask her now?" Grant persists.

Tia shakes her head again.

"Why not?"

"She might say no." Tia mumbles, "and then she'll leave."

"Baby, people leave sometimes, but it doesn't always mean it's our fault when they do. If Mackenzie wasn't here, you'd still have your dad, and me, and aunt Ava, and Tyler, and your new cousin when they arrive, and..." Grant pauses for effect before teasing, "*Even* Jacob," making Tia giggle. What if she says yes?"

Tia shrugs.

"Are you worried she might change her mind and leave without telling you?"

Tia nods.

"Do you remember when you lived here with me and Aunt Ava, your daddy had to leave sometimes, but he always came back didn't he? You didn't get scared then, did you? Why is that?"

"Because he always said he would be back silly."

Tia chuckles.

"So, if Mackenzie were to promise to never leave without telling you first..." Grant leans in and whispers conspiratorially in Tia's ear, "and you sprinkled some magic fairy dust on her while she wasn't looking to make sure she kept that promise, do you think you wouldn't be scared anymore?"

Tia hesitates before nodding.

"You do know that even if Mackenzie does love you, she can't be your new mommy right now, don't you?" Grant goes on. Mackenzie, Ava and I all go to speak at the same time. He raises his hand to silence all of us.

Tia's little brow furrows and she looks like she is about to burst out crying again, "Why?" She whines.

"Because mommy's and daddy's usually sleep in the same bed, like aunt Ava and me. But you take up so much room, daddy has to sleep on the floor even though Chloris found you a beautiful bed of your own."

Tia thinks about this for a minute, then her eyes go wide before she speaks, "If I sleep in my bed, daddy could sleep in the big bed with Mackenzie and she could be my mommy."

"Maybe," Grant smirks as he casts me a sly look.

I shake my head slowly in disbelief as a broad grin spreads across my face. However, my joy is short-lived when Tia continues, "I think I would like to sleep in my bed if I had a puppy.

"Let's take this one step at a time, shall we?" Grant chuckles, before lowering his voice so Tia thinks she is the only one that can hear, "Go and ask Aunt Ava if she has some fairy dust hidden that you can borrow, then we can speak to Mackenzie together, yeah?"

Tia slides of off Grant's knee and runs round to Ava. While Ava is rummaging around in a cupboard, Grant ousts Jacob from his chair and turns it so it is facing him. Once Tia has what she needs, she runs to climb back up on Grants knee. "Ready?" He murmurs.

Tia nods.

Even though we've all only been a few feet away watching the whole scene play out, Grant calls Mackenzie as if he didn't know she were there, and she has no clue what to expect. "Mac, could you come here for a sec please?"

Mackenzie assumes her role, and walks round the table to Jacob's recently vacated seat; Grant extends his hand in invitation, and she sits in front of him.

"Tia has something she would like to say to you?" He says.

Tia squirms in his lap.

"What is it honey?" Mackenzie asks kindly.

"Um," Tia looks at me anxiously, and even though I know Grant has everything under control, it makes me want to go to her. Ava reads my mind and comes up beside me, gently holding my arm to stop me barrelling in and derailing Grant's well-executed plan. Instead, I just give her an encouraging nod. Tia looks up at Grant. He nods his head too.

"M'kenzie," Tia starts, as she plays with her hands and avoids eye contact, "Promise to never leave me without saying goodbye first?"

My eye's start to feel a little scratchy. I think I'm more nervous than Tia now.

Mackenzie takes Tia's little hands in her own, and leans forward to be at eye level with her. "Tia, will you look at me for a second, it's really important."

Tia nods and looks up shyly, as soon as she makes eye contact, Mackenzie continues, "I promise that I will never leave you without saying goodbye first. Sometimes I might have to go to work like daddy does, or I might have to go to visit my family like I did the other day, or I might have to leave for some other reason, but if you are asleep, or at school, or somewhere else and I don't get the chance to speak to you before I go, I promise with all my heart, I will always come back. Daddy, Aunt Ava and Uncle Grant all have my telephone number, and if I'm not with you, and you get scared, you can ask any of them to call me at any time, so I can speak to you so you won't be scared anymore."

What does she mean 'leave for some other reason'?

"Promise?" Tia asks hopefully.

"Promise." Mackenzie tells her resolutely.

"Close your eyes," Tia tells her. As soon as she does, Tia pulls one hand from Mackenzies grasp, showering her in glitter that she grabs from her pocket. "I wish M'kenzie has to keep her promise," she mutters.

"Can I open my eyes now? I have something I would like to tell you."

Tia nods.

"You have to speak to her sweetie. She has her eyes closed remember," Ava whispers.

"M'kenzie, you can open your eyes now," Tia says seriously. "What did you want to tell me?"

"Well," Mackenzie looks at me, her face is filled with emotion and I'm petrified that it's all been too much. I fear she thinks she has to leave before Tia gets even more attached to her, and that she is about to make good on the promise she has just made, by saying goodbye before explaining she can't stay. My heart sinks knowing my daughter will be crushed and it's all my fault. Deep down I knew things were moving too fast. Grant was right. I was thinking like a horny teen, and instead of having my daughter's best interests at heart, I let myself get blinded by my own feelings, which were amplified by the last two weeks of family bliss. I start to feel bile rising to the back of my throat, my heart starts to pound, and I'm pretty sure I forget to breathe as I wait for the axe to fall. "I haven't known you very long..." Here it comes, I brace myself, waiting for the confirmation that I've failed as a father yet again. I can barely watch as I'm sure my daughter is about to be shattered thanks to my own selfishness. I look to floor ashamed. "...but I think I've got to know you pretty well, and, well, I just wanted to say that I love you very much and I hope that one day you might love me too."

What?

"You do?" Tia squeals.

"I do, and I was wondering, would you promise to

never leave me without saying goodbye first?"

"Promise!" Tia yells, flinging herself at Mackenzie and hugging her tightly.

I sit there more than a little stunned. Ava bursts into tears and has to be consoled by Tyler, Grant folds his arms across his chest looking smug, and a distinctly unimpressed Jacob rolls his eyes before exclaiming, "Girls!"

"Love you too!" Tia shouts in Mackenzie's ear.

"Right, how about we get you to bed now that's sorted?" I tell Tia in a hoarse voice. It's a valid excuse to be able to disappear for a few minutes to pull myself together. She runs over happily and grabs my hand. "Where shall I put her?" I ask Grant.

"In her room doofus," he mocks me. "What did you think? We would turn her room into a nursery the minute she walked out the door?"

"No that's your room." Jacob points at me laughing.

"What? Wait! Where am I supposed to sleep?" I ask indignantly.

"Well, there's always the couch if you can't find anyone willing to let you bunk in with them," Grant tells me nonchalantly, pausing before adding, "You're welcome," with a cheeky smile.

Chapter Twenty

I do sleep on the sofa that night, not because Mackenzie wants me to, but because the evening has been a bit intense. I want her to have time to digest everything that's happened. I don't want Tia finding us in the morning, seeing us sharing a bed, and instantly upgrading Mackenzie into fully-fledged mommy status before she is good and ready. She has to be feeling overwhelmed; I know I am.

It doesn't mean to say that when I check her shoulder before she turns in, there isn't a great deal of kissing and heavy petting before I finally manage to wrangle her into bed and walk away.

Awake and restless, I get up at five. I retrieve the decorations I picked up while out with Grant and kept stashed in the boot of the car, then festoon the whole house.

It's customary to do presents as a family, either in the living room or at the table in the kitchen. Since the plan is to provide Mackenzie with breakfast in bed, I pile her gifts in the living room—all except one, which I hide in my jacket pocket. I knew it was always going to be a risk, and now, yesterday's shenanigans with Tia before bed have made me even more cautious. I had a plan, and a whole speech prepared. Tia unwittingly derailed both, and I decide it's not one I'm willing to take anymore.

I put the coffee on and Ava appears to help me with breakfast just after six. Since we have had such a busy week, I capture Tia when she wakes to let Mackenzie sleep in. Although I do let her peek in Mackenzie's room to confirm she hasn't vanished overnight. I think we both needed that reassurance. At eight, after I check she is decent, everyone bundles into her room to stand at the bottom of her bed. I'm carrying a tray laden with coffee, juice and all sorts of edible breakfast goodies, Tia is holding three pink, heart shaped helium balloons, and the twins are either end of a large banner which reads 'Happy Birthday'. Tyler is smiling cheerfully, while Jacob looks as if he's asleep standing up, I've seen more enthusiasm in a zombie. Grant is carrying a handful of birthday cards, and Ava is holding a party cannon she is planning to shoot streamers and confetti out of, when she is sure Mackenzie is awake enough that surprise won't give her a heart attack. Everyone is still in their nightclothes except Grant and me who have thrown on some sweatpants, although we have all complemented our look with silly party hats. I'm sure it's Tia's loud giggling that finally causes Mackenzie to stir.

"HAPPY BIRTHDAY!" Everyone choruses at the same time.

Mackenzie's eyes shoot open, and she sits up in bed panicked until she sees us all and realises what's happening. Ava shoots her cannon in the air above Mackenzie's head, so colourful ropes of sparkly, shredded paper come raining down on her. Tia squeals in excitement before climbing on the bed and jumping about enthusiastically, scooping up the fallen debris and throwing it back over Mackenzie. At the sudden noise, Jacob startles like he has just been shot.

"How did you know?" As the shock wears off, Mackenzie's face drops and I see the tears before they start to fall.

"M'kenzie what's wrong?" Tia's little face falls and she drops to her knees on the bed. She puts her hands on either side of Mackenzies face, squeezing so her lips purse and she looks like a fish.

Mackenzie murmurs something inaudible, while I hand the tray I'm holding to Grant and rush over to the pair of them. I peel Tia off of Mackenzie so she can speak freely. "Babe, what's up?"

"Nothing, these are happy tears," Mackenzie says in a wobbly voice. "I didn't expect... I haven't celebrated my birthday for the last few years."

"Why?" Ava frowns.

Mackenzie shrugs, "No-one to celebrate with I guess, Dan never remembered and usually had plans that didn't include me. Over the years, I lost touch with most of my friends."

"What about your family?" Ava looks at me concerned.

"I've only just reconnected with my parents. We were estranged for quite some time. My brother always calls, or he used to, this year I'm not sure that he will," Mackenzie answers sadly.

"Well," Ava tells her matter of factly, "You have us now, and we have a house rule that everyone gets spoiled on their birthday, so, Jared…" She clicks her fingers at me and gestures to the tray of food Grant is holding. I take it back and place it on Mackenzies lap while Grant swings a giggling Tia into his arms before one of her flailing limbs causes a spillage. I move the balloons that Tia has abandoned and place them beside the bed, then everyone perches around its edge while Mackenzie opens her cards. Ava helped Tia make hers. The words 'happy birthday' have been neatly written in pencil before being unevenly traced over in crayon. Below, there is half a stick person being dwarfed by a huge cake with so many candles that a few of them appear to have toppled off, setting fire to the stick person's hair. Far from upset, the stick person looks remarkably calm about it. Mackenzie gushes over how the card is her favourite, leading me to believe she has hidden sadistic tendencies.

When Mackenzie is done, Ava claps her hands loudly. "Right, we've got a busy birthday planned so everyone washed and dressed please. Let Mackenzie enjoy her breakfast in peace and then we'll do presents."

"Presents?" Mackenzie murmurs, confused.

"Everyone has presents on their birthday silly,"

Tia tells her.

Grant tickles Tia's ribs and she screams with laughter as she squirms in his arms. "That's right. Everyone has presents on their birthday silly," he repeats for Mackenzie's sake before turning his attention back to Tia, "C'mon little girl, let's find the perfect outfit for you to wear."

"I want to wear my special party dress," Tia tells him excitedly.

"You can later," he tells her, as he carries her out of the room whispering something in her ear.

One by one, everyone follows them out until just Mackenzie and I remain.

"What does she mean there is a busy birthday planned?" Mackenzie looks at me in wonderment.

I lie on my side next to her, resting my elbow on the bed and my head on my hand. "If you eat your breakfast like a good girl, then get you sweet ass up and dressed, you'll find out." I steal a bit of bacon from her tray and pop it in my mouth as I smile up at her mischievously.

"Shouldn't you be getting ready?" She teases. I can see her trying to fight the fact her eyes are roaming unashamedly over my body. I love that she can't help herself; it feels good knowing I have that effect on her. Her heated gaze warms my blood and I fight to stop a certain part of my anatomy from showing its appreciation.

"I can't leave you. We are on a tight schedule, and Ava has tasked me to make sure you keep to it. I need to have you ready and downstairs by half nine so we can do presents before we leave."

"Leave for where? And it's almost nine now, we'll never both be ready on time unless you jump in the shower while I try and get through this feast."

"Or, I help you finish here," I grab some more bacon and hold eye contact as I say nonchalantly, "then we save time by jumping in the shower together."

I see the lust and longing cloud Mackenzie's face before she quirks her eyebrow at me, "Stop stealing my bacon, and if we do that, do you really think it will save us time or make us even later?"

"Good point." I push myself up and lean across to gently claim her lips, as I pull away, I smile against them, "You'll just have to wait until tonight to take advantage of me."

"I didn't think you wanted to be taken advantage of since you didn't stay last night." She calls me out in a hushed tone, "Was it too much? Did I overstep with Tia?"

"That depends." At this point I have to be honest and hope she will be too. "Did you mean what you said? I know you were suffocated in your marriage, and now you're free, eventually you'll find your wings and want to fly again. My life's complicated, and my responsibilities make it way less exciting than it's made out to be in the tabloids. Even so, I'm happy and wouldn't want to change a thing. I'm not ashamed to admit I'm happier here around my family than I ever am back in Hollywood without them. I love what I do and I'm lucky to have made such a good living out of it, but if I had to give it all up tomorrow for any one of them, I would. I wouldn't blame you for wanting more than I can offer, you deserve so much more..." Than me, is what I was going to say, and even though I know it's true, I can't bring myself to admit the fact out loud. I know she'll end up walking away, because I'm certain I'll never be enough to make her want to stay, "...what I'm trying to say is, whatever happens between us, do you promise not to break her heart?"

She stares at me for a few seconds before she answers my question with one of her own. "Do you promise not to break mine?" She murmurs softly.

That's not what I was expecting to hear. She takes the tray off her lap, and carefully places it on the floor before lying down beside me, on her side, so we are facing one another.

"When I went to see my parents the other day, I probably wouldn't have gone unless I needed to," she admits.

I frown, "I don't understand."

Mackenzie cups my cheek in her hand, "I went to tell them I was getting a divorce. My mom is one of the best attorneys in the state and I wanted to ask her if she would represent me. I want this all settled quickly and since Dan wiped me out financially, I can't afford anyone else of the same calibre. I want *you*, baby. You. I know everything's happened really fast, but before I met you, I'd not been happy for a long time. I've spent years wishing my life would change and imagining what it would look like if I had the ability to choose the perfect outcome. Then fate directed me to that diner where you found me when I needed you the most. The more I got to know you, the more I got to see you are everything I ever wanted, and so much more than I ever dreamed of. Tia is just the icing on the cake. I could never hurt her, because in doing so, I know I would be hurting you. Don't get me wrong, I didn't lie, I do love her. But I'm also falling for you pretty hard, and I was hoping that if I were free, you'd stop trying to push me away by telling me I'm not ready for another relationship. I really think it's you who isn't ready and I'm scared you might never allow yourself to love me back. I get why you've built this impenetrable shield around yourself, but I'm so afraid that I'll never be enough to make you want to let it down and let me through."

I search her eyes for any signs of deception but all I see is sincerity and hope. I smile and she mirrors my reaction. Suddenly, the atmosphere between us changes, and it's as if something magical is happening. I almost want to look above me to see if Chloris really does exist, and she is there waving her wand, making the impossible, possible. "C'mon, birthday girl." I climb off the bed and pull her up with me, if I kiss her now, I might never stop. "We better get a move on."

I leave Mackenzie to get ready, while I disappear down the hall to get changed myself. Everyone is ready and waiting in the living room when we finally appear. Mackenzie marvels at all the decorations before spying the pile of gifts waiting for her.

"Are they all mine?" She gasps.

"This one's from me." Tia barely waits until Mackenzie has sat down before she thrusts a foot long box in her lap. It's sporting a pink bow and copious amounts of glitter. I bite the inside of my cheeks to hold back my smile as Mackenzie pulls the lid off the box. Inside is child's toy, a pink glittery stick with a gold star attached to one end. "It's a magic wand. I chosen it." Tia jumps about in excitement.

"I chose it." I correct her.

"No daddy, I did." She frowns up at me.

Mackenzie laughs. "Thank you, sweetheart, I'll treasure it always."

"Is it like daddy's?" Tia asks.

"Say again?" Of course, Grant picks up on what she says.

Tia turns to him with her hands on her hips, "Mackenzie says daddy has a magic wand but he has to keep it hidden."

"Really?" Grant smirks, "So Mac, how did you happen to stumble upon it?"

Mackenzie blushes furiously and Ava tries not to laugh as she hands her another gift to open. The rest of the presents are much more practical and carefully thought out. Mackenzie receives everything from a home cookery course, to a new scarf to replace the one she gave Tia the first time they met. It takes us over an hour to get through them all. It's amazing how much you can learn about a person in such a short period of time.

At eleven, we all pile into two cars and head out for a boat trip around the bay. I had managed to hire a private charter in advance, which allows us to set our own agenda for the journey. We hop off to search for seashells along the way and stop to enjoy a picnic lunch on a secluded beach. There, we also play a game of softball before taking the trip back to shore. The whole thing was Ava's idea; she thought it would be fun to take a nature cruise so Mackenzie could take in the local sights and hopefully fall in love with Morro Bay, just as she had before she moved here. In addition to spotting a variety of birds, Tia is so excited when we see some seals swimming not far from the boat and several otters playing along the coastline. We are home by three, so everyone has time to get changed for dinner.

"Where are we going? What should I wear?" Mackenzie asks as soon as we get home. She's positively glowing.

"Daddy got you a special party dress," Tia tells her eagerly, "He got me one too, aunt Ava is going to do my hair, if you ask her, she will do yours too."

"You bought me a dress?" Mackenzie looks at me in wide-eyed disbelief. "You actually went shopping without me?"

I'm not sure if she is disappointed she didn't get to go with me, or amazed that I even went at all.

I peck her on the nose. "It's different to your usual style but I'm hoping you'll humour me."

She frowns. "What's that supposed to mean?"

"You'll see," I laugh, "It's in your room, I'd appreciate it if you could get yourself ready then wait until I come to get you."

She runs off and the rest of us disperse to get ourselves ready.

Dinner isn't going to be anything ostentatious; it's hard to find a restaurant that caters to the twins and Tia's particular palette, so we are all going to Daisy's diner. What Mac doesn't know is Daisy is throwing a surprise fifties themed birthday party for her. Ava has invited a few of the more discreet parents she knows from school, and Daisy has let her regulars know that they are welcome to join in the fun.

An hour later, everyone except Mackenzie starts to accumulate in the living room. I'm dressed in a tailored, dark grey flannel, single breasted suit, with a crisp white shirt and slim tie. I'm wearing suspenders and a pair of polished brogues. I got Ava to style my hair even though I have a matching trilby to complete my look. Grant almost looks the same, except he is wearing a brown suit and brogues, deciding against the hat. The twins are in a pair of cuffed jeans with button down plaid shirts, trainers and slicked back hair. After learning from my previous mistakes, I ordered the boys different coloured shirts, one is predominately blue, the other red. It's too early for me to tell who's in what. We are all complementing each other on how we look when Ava strolls in holding Tia's hand. Ava is wearing a yellow dress with a fitted bodice, and a full skirt that falls from her middle in soft pleats, she has a thick white belt loosely fastened around her growing belly and is wearing a delicate pair of white gloves. She has a small white handbag slung over her arm and a pair of white shoes with a small heel on her feet. Her hair is in a high ponytail and she has done her makeup to reflect the era. When Grant sees her, he lets out a low whistle of appreciation, but it's Tia that makes my heart swell. She looks adorable in a dress the same style as Ava's, its pink with large black polka dots, and a black ribbon around the waist fastened into a sweet bow at the front. She is wearing a cute pair of white pumps and Ava has curled her hair before fastening it half up. She comes running over and I pick her up.

"Thankyou for my pretty dress daddy, I love it!" She throws her arms around my neck and gives me a smacker on my cheek.

"I have another surprise for you." I tell her and her eyes go wide.

"What?" She whispers.

"Wait here and I'll go get it." I hand her off to Grant and leave to fetch Mackenzie.

I knock on the bedroom door and when she opens it, she finds me leaning on the frame with my head bowed and my trilby balanced on the fingers of my right hand. I look up, and when our eyes connect, Mackenzie's breath catches while mine is completely stolen away by the vision in front of me. She looks stunning. Her hair and makeup are flawless, the dress I bought her fits perfectly. We stand in silence for a few seconds, just staring at each other, both at a loss for words. Without speaking, I extend my arm and she takes it for me to be able to lead her to where the others are waiting. When we round the corner so Tia sees Mackenzie, she squeals and wriggles in Grant's arms until he sets her down on the floor. She comes running over.

"M'kenzie, we have the same dress," Tia screams so loud I think the guys on the international space station hear her.

"I see, I see," Mackenzie kneels down to give her mini-me a hug, looking up at me with watery eyes when she does. The pair of them look like they should be starring in some kind of commercial.

"Photo's," Ava calls, getting out her phone.

Mackenzie stands and I put my arm around her waist, Tia positions herself in front of us and we each place a hand on her shoulder. Ava takes a few pictures before everyone wants to get in on the act, and we spend another half hour snapping fun shots of each other in various situations around the house until it's time to leave.

Everyone is in the garage, piling into the cars when I make a split-second decision to run back and grab the gift I had previously hidden in the pocket of the jacket I was using earlier. If the right moment presented itself, maybe I would give it to Mackenzie after all. I transfer it to the pocket of my suit just in case.

Daisy's is already buzzing when we arrive. To be able to keep the venue a surprise, Mackenzie is blindfolded in the seat beside me. Grant pulls into the parking lot behind me as I'm helping her out of the car. I wait while Ava corrals the rest of the family so we can make our way inside together. Daisy spots us through the large glass windows and hushes everyone before turning out the lights. Only the soft glow from the kitchen pass illuminates the room. As we push through the doors, I whip off Mackenzie's blindfold, the lights snap back on and everyone yells happy birthday. Music starts to blare from the jukebox and Mackenzie's hand flies up to cover her mouth as she gasps in shock. Everyone has joined in the spirit of the occasion and dressed according to the theme. People come flying over and Mackenzie looks a little over whelmed as Ava introduces her to everyone she knows. Even the relative strangers Daisy invited, wander over to bestow their best wishes. I keep my arm clamped firmly around her waist for support as we navigate through the crowd to the table that has been reserved for us at the end of the room. Daisy has gone all out with the decorations, and she totters over to take our order personally after helpfully giving Gina the night off. She too, has joined in on the festivities, by wearing a baby pink dress with short capped sleeves beneath a white apron, and sporting a small hat atop her head.

The whole evening turns out to be a complete success, the longer Mackenzie stays the more she relaxes. People scatter about eating, laughing, and generally having a good time. After our main course, Daisy brings out the cake I dropped off in secret. Everyone gathers around to sing before Mackenzie enlists Tia's help in blowing out her candles. Tables get pushed to the side of the room to allow people to mingle and converse more easily, while the cake is cut and handed out for guests to enjoy. After the cake, Daisy ranchettes the music up a notch and the dancing begins. Tyler paves the way for our group when a cute little brunette in a blue dress comes over and asks him to join her. We all hide our smiles as he gracefully accepts and saunters off after throwing Jacob a smug look.

"Who's that? And what was that look about?" Grant asks Jacob, jerking his head in Tyler's direction.

"Melissa, some chick from school, she's got the hots for me," he grumbles. "She's in my class, always wants to sit next to me and borrow my stuff. Ty reckons she's cute and I should get in there."

"Chick?" Grant mouths to me.

"Get in there?" I mouth back, as we try not to laugh.

"If she likes you, why is she dancing with Ty?" Ava frowns at him, "And what do you mean by 'get in there'?"

"He owes me." Is all he replies.

"Jacob, what's going on?" His mother asks him sternly.

Jacob sighs heavily, "You won't like it."

"That may be so, but tell me anyway," Ava replies in her, 'what have you done you little fucker', voice.

"She thinks she's dancing with me right now. I

let her know in advance what colour shirt I would be wearing so I could avoid her by passing her off to Ty. He thinks I'm crazy as her dad owns that fancy car dealership in town and he reckons if we play our cards right, one of us can get a good deal on a Porsche when we get older."

"I told you before, you and Tyler have got to stop pulling that shi…" Ava corrects herself at the last second when she sees Tia flexing her fingers ready to pounce, "shenanigans, you can't keep strutting around swopping identities. Other than the whole car thing, why did he agree? Why do you think he owes you?"

"Because at school the other day, Toby was giving Ty a hard time at break and I got in his face telling him to back off, and he did."

"Why was Toby giving Ty a hard time?"

"Because Toby's pants are so tight they must have cut off the circulation to his brain." Jacob tells her seriously.

Everyone bursts out laughing at the incredulous expression on Ava's face. I give Jacob a fist bump for standing up for his brother.

"Jacob, will you dance with me?" Tia asks him demurely.

"I don't dance T," he tells her sulkily.

"Pleeeease," she begs, batting her eyelashes at him.

"Fine!" The corners of his mouth twitch as he pretends to take her hand under duress. Tia skips beside him merrily as they wander off hand in hand.

"Wifey," Grant holds out his hand.

"You need to have a conversation with your sons?" Ava tells him gravely.

"That may be so," he laughs, "but not right now. Now I want to dance and, 'get in there', with my girl."

Ava fights back her own laughter as she takes his hand. They disappear just as, 'Oh Boy' by the crickets, starts booming out of the jukebox.

"Birthday girl, would you like to dance?" I offer Mackenzie my hand and she slips hers into it.

"Depends," she giggles, "Are you trying to 'get in there' too?"

"You're damn right I am," I growl.

"Then lead on Romeo. Let's see what you've got," she taunts me, grinning.

Chapter Twenty-One

E veryone is having such a great time we end up staying much later than we anticipated. Tia crashes at about half eight. We settle her along one of the benches, using my jacket as a pillow and Grant's as a blanket to keep her warm, and although we never ask them to, the twins take turns sitting beside her, protecting her from harm. At one stage, Tyler has Melissa sat opposite him—the girl who asked him to dance and who used to think he was his brother until Ava made him come clean. They look to be in deep conversation, while Jacob sits at an adjoining table with a group of young females vying for his attention. I catch Ava watching him with her hands on her hips and Grant wiping the tears of mirth from his eyes. Mackenzie and I dance over and pause to find out what's going on.

"What's so funny?" I ask Grant. It's Ava that answers.

"Nothing!" She snaps. "Look over there, it seems Jacob inherited more genes from his father and you than he ever did from me. Look at him. I'm telling you now Grant, I'm buying a bunch of bananas and a packet of condoms on my next visit to the store. "You two," she waves her finger between us, "better make sure he can wrap it before he gets the notion he might want to do anything else with it."

"Ava, he's eight." Grant pinches the bridge of his nose as he tries to control himself. Mackenzie and I burst out laughing.

"And you two," she barks, as she waves her hand between Mackenzie and I, "be grateful you have a girl."

Mackenzie stops laughing immediately and tenses in my arms. I can sense her trying to gauge how I'm about to react. I give her a reassuring squeeze, "We are," I tell my sister, "I won't have to worry about Tia dating for at least another twenty-six years."

Ava rolls her eyes at me as Grant folds his arms around her and whispers something in her ear that makes her blush. I turn my attention back to the woman I'm holding. As soon as I do, her lips crash against mine. I don't need any further prompting to take what I've been hankering for all night. I swipe my tongue along her lower lip, and her mouth opens inviting me in. Time stops as I surge forward, kissing her with a passion I didn't know I had in me.

"Hey, get a room you two." Grant calls from somewhere nearby. "Oh, that's right, you did!"

Mackenzie pulls back. "What does he mean? You did?"

I lean in to whisper, so no one else can hear, "I've booked us in a hotel overnight. Grant and Ava are taking Tia back with them."

"Why?" She wants to hear me say it.

"Because beautiful," I murmur, pausing to nibble the shell of her ear, "My cock's been weeping ever since you opened that door and I saw you standing there, looking oh so fucking sexy in that dress. Nothing is going to stop me burying myself as deep as I can get inside you later, and when I do, you'll be screaming my name so loud it's probably best if the rest of the family aren't around to hear."

She shudders as I pull back, her face is flushed and her eyes are dark pools of desire. "Best birthday ever," she mutters, before I claim her mouth again.

Suddenly my skin starts to prickle and the hairs on the back of my neck stand on end. I feel his presence even before he speaks.

"Well, isn't this cosy?" An irate voice snaps. I spin, instinctively tucking Mackenzie behind me. My eyes flit to Grant and then Tia. Thankfully he sees my grave expression and instantly knows something is up. Without drawing attention, he carefully manoeuvres himself and Ava, between me and the rest of the family. Mackenzie's husband stands before us holding a huge bouquet of flowers and a gift bag. He is well-groomed and immaculately dressed in all the latest designer gear, courtesy of all Mackenzie's hard-earned cash, no doubt. I think of her shoulder and the days I've spent trying to repair the damage he caused. Everything turns red as molten fire starts coursing through my veins

"I guess I spoke too soon," Mackenzie sighs.

"What are you doing here? You need to leave, you're not welcome here," I growl, I don't see any reason to beat around the bush, he needs to fuck off. I guess that must come across in my tone because he looks me over in disgust.

"I came to speak to my *wife*." He definitely gloats over the last word. "So, if *you* wouldn't mind fucking off and leaving us alone for a moment, I'd appreciate it."

"No!" I think that one word covers about everything.

"Kenzie," he snivels, "Baby, can we talk for a second..." He throws me a dirty look. "In private."

I'm about to tell him where to go when Mackenzie steps up beside me.

"Anything you've got to say, you can say here and now, before you leave. This is the best birthday I've had in a long while and I'm not about to let you spoil it."

Dan rears back in shock, and I'm proud of Mackenzie for standing up to him. Would she be as brave if she were alone? I don't know, and quite frankly I don't care, it's not something she'll ever have to worry about.

"Happy birthday," he gushes, "I got you these."

He tries to hand the flowers and gift bag to Mackenzie but she refuses to take them. "After fourteen years I would have thought you'd remember I'm allergic to lilies."

His face drops, and he tosses the flowers onto a

nearby table. He pushes the gift bag into her hand.

"Please," he simpers.

She pulls a framed photo from the bag, looking at it wistfully. It's the pair of them together on their wedding day. They are standing on some stone steps outside a building of some description. With most of the backdrop cropped out, it makes it difficult to tell where the marriage took place. Mackenzie looks beautiful in a simple white gown, gazing up at him adoringly, while he looks happy and is smiling for the camera. My heart clenches at the sight.

"I miss you baby," he whispers. She looks up at him with tears in her eyes and I panic.

"Which part do you miss the most?" I hiss and narrow my eyes threateningly, "The money or the punch bag."

He gives me a death stare but doesn't deign to answer, redirecting his attention back to the woman beside me.

"You need to come home baby," he whimpers.

"She is home," I bark, and I feel Mackenzie's hand on my arm.

"He's right," she says, "I am home." She hands him back the photo. Her voice speaks with renewed determination, "Have you heard from my mother?"

"Jeanette? No why would I..." His voice trails off as he must realise what she's insinuating. "NO FUCKING WAY!" He shouts, and everyone in the place freezes, then turns in our direction to see what the commotion is all about. "You can't have a fucking divorce. Not to shack up with this prick."

"ENOUGH!" I shout, this has been a long time coming, "Outside now!"

"My fucking pleasure!" He growls, glaring at Mackenzie before storming towards the door.

"Don't, please," Mackenzie begs, gripping my arm as Grant appears beside her.

"Want me to come?" Grant asks.

I shake my head. "No, I don't know if he came alone. I need you to stay here and look out for everyone else."

"If you think he could've come mob handed, that's even more reason for me to go with you." Grant growls.

"I need to know you've got me covered in here." He looks back at the rest of the family and nods.

"You coming." The weasel yells from the door impatiently.

I start to leave and Mackenzie tries to follow.

"No, baby." As I push her into Grant's arms, I can see the panic in her eyes. "Stay here, I won't be long."

"But..."

"This needs to be settled Mac," Grant mutters, "Or he'll just be back. Better that it's taken care of now than left to fester."

"Keep them all in here," I tell Grant. I know he'll do as I ask, and it makes it easier knowing I don't have to worry about anyone else.

Once I know my family is safe, I follow the jerk outside and round to the side of the building. Everyone gawps at us through the large windows as we march past. I look across and see Mackenzie and

Ava being both comforted and restrained by Grant. Then Jacob catches my eye, he punches his fist in his hand and I jerk my head back in response. I sigh as I wonder what sort of example I'm setting here?

We step off of the paved surface of the parking lot and the ground suddenly feels soft underfoot. The area isn't well lit and the trees lining the back of the property stand tall and imposing, blocking out what little moonlight there is. The foul stench of rotting food swamps me before I notice the dark commercial bin standing on the sidelines, waiting to be emptied. I stretch my neck from side to side until it cracks, and as soon as I stop walking Dan rounds on me, incandescent with rage.

"I'm only going to tell you once. Stay the hell away from my wife." He flies at me, jabbing me hard in the chest.

"She won't be your wife much longer," I snarl. "But since she is right now, and I'm fucking her, you get one shot." I'm bigger, fitter, and stronger. He knows it, but his eyes flash with fury and he comes at me anyway. He rears back before taking a swing and landing a right hook on my jaw. The force of the blow is greater than I was expecting and it forces me to stumble back a few paces. "That's the only one you get jerkoff, unlike your *ex*-wife, I'm not about to run."

"Bring it on prick," he spits.

After that it's game on. He lunges at me, snagging me around the waist and using the entire weight of his body to push me back onto the bin behind me.

It slides at the force of the impact, crashing against the wall behind it. A bag rolls from the top, splitting at it hits the floor. The contents spill out at our feet making the surface slippery as we start to struggle. I shove him off me and land a hit of my own. He staggers back, momentarily stunned, before flying at me again and punching me hard in the abdomen. I feel a searing pain as one of my ribs cracks, but I don't miss a beat before tackling him. We both go down, wrestling in the mud and debris on the floor between violent punches. He is like a man possessed, screaming obscenities as I get the upper hand and straddle his waist, pinning him down in order to get a couple of good punches in and end this.

"That's for hitting Mac," I growl, as I land the first punch and definitely the hardest. "That's for bleeding her dry financially," I say as I land the second blow. "And when I said you'd get a freebie, I lied. This one's for me." After the third punch he groans and goes limp. His face is a mess, covered in blood from his split lip and broken nose. I roll off him and sit on the floor while I catch my breath. I drag my hand down my face and look at my knuckles which are torn and bleeding. I'm just thinking it's been a while since they have been this messed up, when I see Dan in my peripheral vision, pulling himself up ready to make a dive at me again. I dodge his fist and lunge at him again, failing to see the rock he is holding in his other hand. He whacks me hard on the temple and everything goes black for a second. I wake up to see him hovering over me, the bloody rock raised in his hand once more. I'm dazed and my reactions are slow. My brain knows what I need to do, but my body is too sluggish to respond. Dan's eyes flame with hatred as he smiles down at me manically. He raises his arm even more and I brace myself for the inevitable. Just as I see the rock heading towards my face someone catches his wrist.

"Na ah. I know we're not exactly playing by the marquess of Queensbury rules here, but that's definitely cheating." A familiar voice tuts.

The next thing I know Dan is pulled off me and thrown to one side like he is weightless. I'm hoisted to my feet and an unfamiliar face appears in front of mine. Whoever it is checks me over, then takes a step back, leaning against the wall with his legs crossed at the ankles as he lights a cigarette and takes a drag. "Carry on," he tells us calmly, while Dan and I both stare at him in confusion. He has to be at least six foot three with a sleeve of tattoos running up both of his highly muscled arms. He is dressed entirely in black, black combat trousers, boots, T-shirt and cap. I'm pretty sure I've never seen him before even though his voice definitely sounds familiar. He looks at Dan and I in turn. "We done here girls?" He smirks, "Or are you going to finish this? I've got a job to get back to."

It's Dan who moves first, pushing himself up off the floor and surging forward. I don't underestimate him again and he runs straight onto my waiting fist. He ricochets back and stumbles before dropping to his knees. He stands on wobbly legs and even though I know he's done; the fucker just won't quit.

"Fuck you!" Dan mutters from where he's swaying back and forth unsteadily. I'm not sure which of us he is talking to until he continues, "You'll never have her. She'll always be mine; I'll make sure of it."

His threat tips me over the edge again and I charge at him like a bull, thrusting my shoulder into his stomach, winding him as I pick him up to launch him into the bin with the rest of the garbage. He lands heavily and groans as his eyes finally flutter closed.

I turn to our audience. "We're done," I confirm, "and thanks."

The stranger jerks his head in acknowledgement. "Bet that hurt to say," he laughs, and I frown. Who is this guy? "I wasn't going to get involved, but I hate dirty tactics and I'm not sure my client would like it if anything happened to you."

"Who are you?" I ask, "Have we met before?"

He avoids the first question. "I shouldn't have thought so," he chuckles while walking away. His outfit blends seamlessly into the darkness, rendering him almost invisible as he vanishes. "I'm like the boss, I don't usually babysit actors."

Suddenly the penny drops.

I think I just met Kurt!

I know how I must look—covered in dirt from rolling around on the floor and with my white shirt, stained crimson with blood—but I can't get cleaned up just yet. There's something I have to do first. I just hope my peanut is still asleep and doesn't get to see me this way, I need my phone and I left it inside. I walk round to the front of the building and glance in the window, Mackenzie is pacing back and forth, I smile when I realise she is trying to find a way around Grant, who is blocking her access to the door. They both spot me at the same time, and as I walk back inside, Grant finally sets her free to run over to me. I hear some startled gasps as I appear, I ignore them and focus on the one person who matters. Tears start streaming down her cheeks. I hope they're for me but I have to be sure.

"He'll live." I tell her.

"I'm not worried about him," she murmurs, cupping my cheek as she surveys the damage to my face and hands.

"Then don't cry beautiful," I swipe her tears away with my thumbs, "I'm fine."

"You don't look fine," she challenges softly, "You look like you could use a doctor."

"Do I?" I grin, "Good."

She cocks her head inquisitively.

"Grab my phone and meet me in the bathroom."

She hesitates, then scurries off.

I lock eyes with Ava, who heaves a sigh of relief and visibly relaxes. Back in the day she used to see me in far worse states of disarray, she knows once the fight is over, I bounce back quickly. I glance across to check that Tia is still sleeping, Tyler is still beside her looking distraught. I nod at Grant who follows my line of sight to his son, nodding back before strolling over to check he is alright. Jacob is the total opposite, punching the air in glee at my apparent victory. Mackenzie comes back and I grab her hand taking her into the vacant gents' toilets with me.

"I need you to take some photos of my injuries, and for you to make them look as bad as you can."

"That shouldn't be difficult," she sighs.

"Babe, I'm fine." I try to reassure her as she starts taking pictures.

"Why are we doing this?" She winces, as I lift up my shirt for her to take a record of my battered torso.

"Because I've a feeling when your ex wakes up, he'll try to discredit me and raise a few bucks in the process by selling his story with some pics of his own. I'm going to send these to Jerry so he can get ahead of the game."

"If it even gets that far," she barks, she doesn't seem to be overly concerned about the fact her husband is lying unconscious somewhere. "Do you mind if I share these with my parents?"

I shrug. "If they get in the paper, they'll see them anyway."

"I'm going to ask them if there is anything they can do, slap him with an injunction or something, at the very least my mom can use them to get me a quicker divorce."

"You don't have to do that." I know her relationship with her parents is rocky, I don't want to create any more angst. She doesn't say anything, just hands me back my phone when she is done. I stare at her transfixed. "You really are beautiful."

"You look kind of a mess." She smiles at me, her face alight with love and warmth. In still high on adrenaline, and it amplifies my arousal as I feel it start to thrum through my veins, invigorating every part of me that matters.

"Are you ready to get out of here?" She can see the heat in my eyes and her pupils dilate as her own lust starts to take hold.

"I am." She gives me a coy look, then her eyes go wide with concern, putting me on instant alert. I glance behind me half expecting to see someone there.

"What's wrong?"

"We can't go," she tells me firmly.

"Why?" I cross my arms and glare at her.

"Because Tia is asleep."

I relax even though I'm still confused, "I don't follow, she is staying with Grant and Ava tonight, they've helped me take care of her for the last four years, I think they can manage one more night."

"But I promised I would never leave without saying goodbye first. What if she wakes up and I'm not there?"

I shake my head in awe at the way she is putting my daughter's needs above her own, "You're incredible you know that?" I step forward and brush her hair back over her shoulder with my hand to give me easy access to her neck, bending to nibble and kiss the sweet spot just above her collar bone.

"Jared," she squirms at my touch, "I mean it."

"Do you know what I do?" I whisper, before I nip her then sooth the sting by swirling my tongue over her sensitive skin.

"What?" She croaks huskily as her body arches towards mine.

"Anytime I have to go anywhere before she wakes, I leave her a note saying when I expect to be back and asking her to call me as soon as she can. One of us sticks it on her bedroom door for her to find when she gets up. Ava or Grant usually text me a heads up before I get the call. I'm sure she would be super excited if there were two notes for her to find tomorrow morning," I murmur, as I fondle her ass while dragging her close enough for her to feel the growing bulge in my pants.

"O...Ok," she stutters. "Do you want to get cleaned up before we go?

"I was kinda hoping my nurse would give me a sponge bath back at the hotel."

"That I can do." She answers with a smirk.

And it turns out to be far and away the best one I've ever had.

Chapter Twenty-Two

☆

It's quarter to seven in the morning and my mobile starts ringing. I reach across blindly to grab it from the top of the bedside cabinet. I don't need to look to know who's calling. Mackenzie is passed out half across me with her leg tangled around mine, she is resting on my bruised ribs but the pain is nothing compared to the feeling of having her naked and on top of me. After joining me in the bath and spending an inordinate amount of time ensuring I was thoroughly cleaned—everywhere, I reciprocated her attentive behaviour by fulfilling my promise to make her scream my name in pleasure multiple times throughout the night. She's exhausted, we both are, but I know Tia won't settle unless she gets to speak to us. I answer the phone at the same time as I tickle Mackenzie's ribs to try and wake her. She doesn't flinch.

"Morning peanut." I try to sound chirpy and not like I've been up all night screwing.

"Mornin' daddy, when you and Mackenzie be home?"

"Today, we'll be back in time for dinner."

"Kay."

"Did you have fun at Mackenzie's birthday party?" Silence.

"Are you nodding, peanut? Remember daddy can't see you, we aren't on video call."

"Yes."

"Do you want to speak to Mackenzie?"

"I call her. Love you."

The line goes dead before I can tell her I love her back and I grin, huffing out a laugh.

"Mac," I call, gently shaking her.

She sighs and wraps her body around me tighter. It's the best feeling, one I'll never get tired of.

"Mac," I raise my voice and shake her a bit harder until she stirs.

"Again?" She mumbles, "I guess I can take one for the team."

She starts lazily kissing down my chest as she wraps her hand around my morning wood. Just as things start to get interesting, her mobile starts to ring.

"You need to get that," I groan. I really don't want her to stop what she's doing, but I know she needs to answer that call.

"You get it, I'm busy." She murmurs as her lips arrive level with my dick.

"It's for you," I grunt.

"Thankyou, I like it," She smirks, taking me in her mouth. She does something amazing with her tongue, swirling it around the tip of my cock. My head arches back into the pillow as my hips flex involuntarily, forcing her to take me deeper. She hums in satisfaction and the feeling reverberates up my spine almost short circuiting my brain.

"I meant the call. It's Tia."

"Fuck." She's wide awake instantly, hurriedly climbing off of me and dragging a sheet around herself. She scrambles for her phone while using the fingers on her free hand as a comb to try and make herself look presentable. "How do I look?"

"Well fucked!" I laugh at her horrified expression, as I place both hands behind my head so I can watch her more easily. She is kneeling on the bed facing me when she swipes her phone screen to take the call. "Relax, it's not a video chat."

"Morning honey," Mackenzie calls jovially.

"M'kenzie, I can see your ear," Tia giggles.

"Oh, it's a video call," Mackenzie widens her eyes at me before moving the phone round so Tia can see her on the screen, "silly me."

"I miss you." Tia's little voice sings out. Mackenzie's hand flies to her chest and her eyes start to water.

She coughs as if trying to clear her throat, "I miss you too."

"Didn't tell me she missed me." I grumble good naturedly.

Mackenzie smiles.

"When you and daddy be home?"

"Dinner." I mouth to Mackenzie.

"We'll be back in time for dinner honey."

"Kay. Love you."

Mackenzie's eyes hold mine. "Love you."

"Can I speak to her?" I hold my hand out for the phone. I want to see her little face, when we are apart, I look forward to receiving her calls as much as she likes making them—as short as they sometimes are.

"She's gone." Mackenzie shows me the phone screen for confirmation.

Wait! Had Tia gone before Mackenzie murmured those last two words? I look at her face searching it for any sign of regret. I see a hint of nervousness and a lot of warmth, but no sorrow. She's definitely waiting for me to say something as I climb out of bed.

"Where are you going?" She asks, her tone laced with disappointment.

"I need to get something." I can feel her eyes on me as I grab my jacket from where I had thrown it over a chair, riffling through the pocket until I find what I'm looking for. I pull out the small velvet pouch and go back to sit on the bed. "It's a belated birthday present," I tell her as I hand it over.

She tips the contents into her open hand, and the light catches the diamonds, projecting tiny rainbows around the room as the ring falls into her palm. Her eyes go like saucers, "Is this..."

"It's a promise ring," I correct her as she stares at the platinum band with three diamonds set across the top.

"Promise ring?" She echoes in shock.

I take the hand not holding the ring and tip her

chin up so she is facing me. "I can't propose properly, not yet, not while you're still married, but I love you, Mac," she gasps, and this time the tears do start flowing. "I'm yours, I think I have been ever since the first day I met you back at Daisy's diner, I was hoping that you would wear this now to show the world that someday, you promise to be mine."

My heart stutters nervously as she stares at me with her mouth opening and closing like a goldfish.

"Yes!" She suddenly squeals, launching herself at me. I grab her by her shoulders before she can make contact, gently pushing her away from me. She looks at me, startled by my reaction.

"Wait, there's more."

"More?" She inclines her head quizzically.

"Tia and I are a package deal…"

She cuts me off. "I know that, I adore…" I press my finger over her lips to stop her speaking.

"I know you do, but what I'm trying to say is I don't want us sleeping apart any more, ever! And I don't want to be sneaking out of our room every morning before Tia wakes. If she sees us in bed together, she is going to think she has a new mommy." I need to get to the point before I drown in the tears Mackenzie is shedding. "It's a big ask and I get it if you need more time, it's a lifetime commitment… I guess what I'm trying to say is, are you ready to be a mommy to my little girl Mac?"

She nods enthusiastically and murmurs, "Yes," against the finger that is still pressed against her lips.

"One more thing," I grin as I remove my finger, and Mackenzie stays quiet while she waits to hear what it is, "We might have to get a puppy."

"I love dogs," she tells me with a broad smile.

I take the ring and she holds out her left hand so I can place it on her third finger. Once that's done, I gently push her back down on the bed, removing the sheet between us so we can have the skin to skin contact I'm craving. I rest my forehead against hers as I hover over her and cup her sex, "How sore are you?" We were pretty frantic last night.

"A little," she admits, "but not enough to stop me wanting you right now."

"I'll go slow," I whisper against her lips before I kiss her.

And I do, more than once, which is why I get charged a late check out fee by the hotel.

Chapter Twenty-Three

A fter dinner the pair of us spend the evening playing games with Tia and the twins while Grant takes Ava out for some alone time. At nine, with the kids finally in bed, Mackenzie and I are alone, snuggled on the sofa, when her mobile starts to ring. She grabs it off a side table and glances at the screen. Her face lights up immediately.

"It's Jack," She tells me excitedly, "He's calling."

I grin at her, "I'll go and make us a drink while you take it, give you some privacy."

She smiles at me gratefully and answers the call. She sounds really happy to hear from him and I'm glad he called, even if he is a day late. While I'm in the kitchen my own phone starts buzzing. It's Josh, I answer immediately, concerned he is about to deliver some bad news.

"What's up?" I ask anxiously.

He chuckles, "Why does anything have to be up?"

"No reason."

"I was just calling to let you know something really strange happened to me today and I was wondering if you knew anything about it."

"Go on." I have absolutely no idea where he is going with this.

"I got a call from the concierge of our building about three this afternoon, notifying me he had a large delivery downstairs with my name on it. I tried to tell him it couldn't be for me as I hadn't ordered anything and that the company had made a mistake, but he said the men were insistent and wouldn't leave before I'd signed for it. Because of the business I'm in, it piqued my interest and I thought I'd better go and check it out. You know, just in case someone had decided to send me some illegal firearms, or a severed ear, that kind of thing..."

I feel my eyebrows shoot up beyond my hairline, "Please tell me you're joking?"

"Of course I'm joking," he laughs. "Anyhow, I went downstairs to help him sort things out. Imagine my surprise when I found a brand-new couch waiting for me in the lobby."

I smile, I'd forgotten about that. "Why would I know anything about it?" I say, trying to act confused.

"Well, funny thing is, it seemed to be adorned with patches of this sparkly, iridescent powder that looked suspiciously familiar. Kind of like the stuff your kid loves throwing around all over the place. The delivery guys said they got off as much as they could, but what was left had weaved its way into the fabric and it would hopefully work its way out naturally over time. When I asked them what it was, they gave me a really weird look, burst out laughing, and said it must be fairy dust."

"I still don't see what that has to do with me. Did you ask to see the delivery slip?" I'm fighting to keep my voice level as I know what's coming.

"I did, and they couldn't stop laughing as they handed it over. It appears someone called fairy clitoris ordered it on my behalf."

"Wow," I try to act surprised. "I guess she must have wanted to thank you for helping her look out for Tia free of charge."

"Mmm." He doesn't sound convinced. "When you speak to Tia, can you ask that next time she speaks to her fairy friend, she lets her know that while the gift is appreciated, it was unnecessary. Especially since every time I use it at the moment, I end up all glittery. I'm getting some really funny looks from the guys."

"Oh, I don't know, she probably thought she was doing you a favour, adding a bit of sparkle to your usual mean and moody look to make you seem a bit more approachable. Plus, you have less furniture than I did before Mac moved in, and believe me that's saying something."

Another laugh, "I'm not usually home long enough to warrant anything other than a bed."

"What about when you have guests over?"

"I don't."

"I've been over, so has Tia, and Mac.

"I wasn't planning on inviting you back." He deadpans, I can't tell if he's joking.

"Well, you're just have to come to us then."

"Only if you promise to let me cook."

It's my turn to laugh, "You got it."

"I hear you met Kurt the other night?" I know he's smirking; it comes across in his tone.

"I did."

"How'd that go?"

"Like you don't already know." I scoff.

"Just wanted your take on it," he chuckles. "I checked up on the trash to see if he was planning on making a song and dance over what happened. The good news is he went straight back home with his tail between his legs, the bad news is he packed a bag, took off, and now we can't find him."

"Mac dropped the bomb she was divorcing him; he's probably sloped off to be consoled by one of his many mistresses. Or, he could've gone into hiding so Mac's mother can't serve him with the papers, he did say he wasn't about to just let her walk away. I suspect it was just an idle threat made in the heat of the moment, so I'm not too worried. I bet he just wants to lie low and lick his wounds for a bit."

"Maybe, I'm not so sure. We can usually find someone pretty fast when we need to, but this guy seems to have vanished off the face of the earth. In my experience it's never a good sign when that happens. If he's planning on making another move, he probably won't wait too long. We'll have eyes on the girls for a while longer in case he does, but not you when you're not with them. I guess what I'm saying is, watch your back."

"Ahh, you worried about me?" I tease. "The high

maintenance actor with more money than sense?"

Another deep laugh. "Not me, but Kurt was definitely concerned."

"I bet he was."

"See you around hot shot." Is the last thing I hear before Josh disconnects.

I carry the drinks I've made back to the living room, and arrive just as Mackenzie's disconnects from the call with her brother. She is glowing and it's a joy to see.

"How'd it go?" I ask, as I resume my position beside her on the sofa.

"Wonderfully," she gushes. "He apologised for not phoning yesterday but he was upset that I didn't show for his wedding. I told you he can be really stubborn, but his new wife, Jaime, could see that the fact he hadn't called was eating away at him, and she persuaded him to pick up the phone. She must have some sort of magical powers to get him to do something he didn't want to do; I can't wait to meet her."

"Wait, you've never met?"

"No, it was kind of a whirlwind romance."

"Must run in the family," I kiss her on the nose and she grins.

"And I just learned I'm going to be an aunt." Her smile fleetingly falters. I don't think she realises as she carries on, "Anyway, I got to explain why I wasn't there and that Dan had hidden the fact he was getting married from me. I told him I was finally getting a divorce and he was over the moon. He has been trying to talk sense into me for years, ever since he learnt of Dan's inability to stay faithful. He has invited me to visit, and I told him I would in a few weeks when he and Jaime have settled into married life. They've just got back from their honeymoon and last thing I need to see is my brother chasing his new wife around the house."

"I hear ya." We clink mugs. "Did you tell him about us?"

"Not yet," she starts to look a bit uncomfortable, and I'm concerned about her reaction, "Why?"

"Jack abhors cheaters and I'm still married, so effectively that's what I am. He was badly burned in the past, and it almost destroyed him. That's when his best friend stepped up and without him, I don't know what would have happened."

"Sounds like a good guy."

"He is. A really good guy when you get to know him," she smiles wistfully. When I go and see Jack, I want to be able to take you and Tia with me, but I suppose I'm nervous as to how he'll react about us being together right now. It's really important to me that you guys get along. So, when you meet for the first time, I need it to all go smoothly. I want us all to be on good terms from the start."

"Do you think your brother will have a problem with me even though he knows what your ex was like?"

"I don't know but I don't want to risk it. My brother can be pretty scary. He was never a fan of Dan, and because their relationship never got off to strong start, it deteriorated rapidly when Dan constantly tried to keep us apart to avoid being around him. Dan would never let it show, but he is terrified of Jack. Other than you and your family, Jack is probably the only other person I can go to who will make me feel safe. I *really* want you guys to get along from the get go, I'm so happy right now, I don't want anything to spoil it."

"Won't he have seen the recent pictures of us together in the gossip column or on the news?"

"I doubt it. Like I say, he has been away on his honeymoon and he avoids the press like the plague. He certainly isn't shy. I would've thought if he had seen anything that made him suspicious, he would've come right out and asked me about it."

"Babe, I promise, whatever happens, everything will be Okay." I tell her seriously before trying to lighten the mood. "Are you forgetting Tia gave you your very own magic wand for your birthday, give it a wave and see what happens."

"As much as I love it," she chuckles, "I much prefer the magic wand you gave me."

I smile and lean in for a kiss.

"Ava, the child minder is making out with his girlfriend on our couch." Grant calls from the doorway. Mackenzie and I spring apart not having heard them return. Ava appears beside him ginning like a cheshire cat a few seconds later. She looks at us and her eyes immediately zoom in on Mackenzie's hand, as soon as she sees the ring she lets out a blood curdling scream and throws herself at us.

"You've got engaged!" She cries, she so excited the rest of her words come out in a rush. "When? What happened? Jared, you didn't say? When's the wedding? Will it be here or in Hollywood? Large or small? Where will you live?"

Mackenzie and I burst out laughing, and I hold up my hand to stop the barrage of questions.

"We're not engaged," I say, and Ava's excitement immediately morphs into disappointment.

"But, the ring?"

"It's a promise ring." I enlighten her.

"A what?" Grant looks at Ava confused, just as two young boys come hurtling round the corner, yelling fiercely while dressed in pyjamas, and with their hair sticking out in all directions. Both are ready for battle, one is leading the charge carrying a raised hockey stick, the other is following holding a deodorant spray at the end of an outstretched arm.

"Stay away from our mom." The one with the hockey stick yells. Grant swipes it out of his hand mid run before he can do any accidental damage. As he unexpectedly loses his weapon, he stops in his tracks startled, causing his brother to crash into the back of him.

"It's Okay Jacob, your mom just lost control of herself for a moment," Grant chuckles.

Jacob fails to see the funny side as he rounds on Ava with his hands on his hips. "What the hell do you think you're playing at?" He yells, "Do you know what time it is?"

Ava checks her watch puzzled. "Quarter to ten."

"Exactly, and I've got school in the morning," he tells her frowning. He looks around the room. "What exactly is the problem here?"

"Your uncle just... didn't get engaged." She tells him mournfully.

"This is exactly why I need my room sound-proofed." Jacob grumbles to Grant. "And why you need to give me a new brother," he jabs his finger in the direction of Ava's stomach before jerking his head in Tyler's direction, "I yell at him to arm himself and what does he grab? A can of deodorant. I think my mom's being attacked and want to take the guys knees out, he wants to make him smell nice."

"Hey!" Tyler says indignantly, "I was going to aim for his face."

"In case he had bad breath... Whatever!" Jacob snaps, "Go and check on Tia."

Tyler rolls his eyes and wanders off, while the rest of us try not to infuriate Jacob further by laughing.

"And if you've woken her," he growls at Ava, "you can read her that damn book she loves so much. I'm going back to bed."

He stomps off and everyone laughs out loud, except Ava who turns to Grant, "you really need to talk to your sons."

"I'm not going to tell them off for wanting to protect their mom, she's precious." He replies and pecks her on the lips.

"Grant, someone could've got hurt the way Jacob came tearing in here, or he could've put himself in danger. Violence isn't the answer, teach him to use his words…"

"Or how to bribe any potential threats with toiletries," I chip in, casting Grant a teasing look.

Ava glares at me, "You're not helping." She looks back to Grant, "Teach him how to use the phone…"

"Yeah, that can do way more damage than a hockey stick," I tell him with a smirk.

Grant is struggling to keep a straight face as Ava continues seriously, "I meant to call the police."

He pulls her into his side, and as he hugs her, she finally lets herself chuckle.

"So, what exactly is going on here?" Grant asks me. "What's a promise ring?"

"Exactly that," I tell him. "She promises to never leave me without saying goodbye first," I joke.

"So, you're together but not planning on getting married?" He asks with his brows furrowed.

"No, we will when Mac's divorce comes through."

"So, you're engaged." Grant informs me.

"Not exactly." I don't know how to explain what we are.

"Mac, where's your purse," Grant asks her.

"In the kitchen I think, why?"

"I'm just going to go and see if that's where my brother-in-law hid his balls."

"Fine," I sigh. "We're engaged."

Ava beams. Mackenzie giggles beside me, and Grant smirks.

"And we might get a puppy," Mackenzie suddenly pipes up, everyone turns to look at her. She glances at me coyly, "Although, I was thinking, it wouldn't be fair for him to be cooped up in the apartment back in Hollywood the whole time."

"What are you saying?" I ask.

"I was thinking, that maybe we should think about moving somewhere out of the city, somewhere a bit more dog friendly. I was also thinking that since we couldn't settle on a good pre-school for Tia, and she was already registered here, that maybe you might want to relocate to your house in Morro Bay?"

I hear Ava squeak but my eyes are firmly fixed on the woman in front of me. "Are you sure?" I ask hopefully, "I presumed you'd prefer to be based in the city."

"I'll be happy as long as I'm wherever you are," she offers me a contented smile. "I travelled the world when I was modelling and I've never felt more at home than I do when I'm here. It might mean you have to travel for work a bit more, but you could still keep the place in the city and we could split our time around Tia's schedule. I really think she would like to be nearby when Ava has the baby, and we need to be close enough to be able to offer our support when Jacob gets arrested for aggravated assault."

This woman! I hear Ava and Grant chuckling behind me.

"Mac's parents are attorney's," I tell them with a smile.

"You chose well," Grant laughs, and Ava swats him playfully.

"There's one major problem." I hold Mackenzie's eyes and she tips her head inquisitively.

"Nooo!" I hear Ava gasp.

"I sold that house years ago," I say with a smile, "But I guess we could look for a new place together."

Mackenzie's lips twitch and I can't help myself as I lean in and kiss her again, pouring every ounce of emotion she's incited into the action.

"Ava," I hear Grant say in amusement. "The child minder is making out with his fiancée on our couch again."

I pause to long enough to growl, "Get used to it," then resume exactly where I left off.

Chapter Twenty-Four

⋆

"**D**ADDEE!" I hear Tia calling me as she goes barrelling round the house looking for me. A few minutes later she comes crashing through the door. "M'KENZIE, I CAN'T FIND..." She stops mid tracks when she sees me. I put my finger to my lips to silence her and point to the sleeping body beside me. In anticipation of our discovery this morning we are both wearing more clothes than we would do on a normal day. Although I did manage to persuade Mackenzie to do a lot of naked snuggling before she finally insisted we get dressed in the early hours.

"Morning peanut," I whisper.

She clasps both hands over her mouth and her eyes go wide. "Daddy," she whispers louder than she normally speaks, "Did you and M'kenzie sleep in the same bed?"

I nod and smile.

"Does that mean I'm not different any more and have a mommy now like my friends?" Her voice cracks and her little face scrunches up.

I wasn't expecting tears and I'm out of bed and

cuddling my daughter in an instant.

"Hey peanut," I soothe, "What's wrong? I thought you would be happy?"

She buries her head in my shoulder and I sit on the edge of the bed cradling her.

"What if she doesn't want to be my mommy?" Tia murmurs so low I almost don't hear what she says.

I thought we covered this the other night. Where's Grant when I need him? "Shall we ask her?" I murmur back.

"But she's sleeping." Tia pulls back and looks at me as if disturbing Mackenzie would result in an apocalypse.

"With a question as important as this one, I bet she wouldn't mind if we wake her. Go on give her a nudge."

Tia shakes her head nervously so I do it for her. When Mackenzie starts to stir, Tia's grip on me tightens.

"Mac," I call.

"Hmm?" She mumbles sleepily.

"Tia has something she would like to ask you."

Mackenzie is awake in an instant, sitting up and clutching the sheet around herself until she remembers that we got dressed in the middle of the night. "Morning darling, how are you?" She asks Tia.

"M'kenzie, wooble youble me mymommee?" The words are lost as Tia buries her head into my chest.

Mackenzie looks at me and frowns with an uncomprehending expression. I try to peel Tia off of me and when that doesn't work, Mackenzie reaches down the side of the bed and produces the magic wand Tia give her for her birthday. She thinks for a second, then swirls it above Tia's head before bopping her gently and announcing in an authoritative tone, "I wish Tia would ask me to be her mommy."

Tia's grip loosens immediately and she turns to look at Mackenzie, "You do?"

"I do," Mackenzie tells her kindly, "But only if you want to, and only if you promise it's for ever."

"M'kenzie, will you be my mommy for ever I promise?" Tia gets her words muddled in her excitement.

"I would love to be your mommy," Mackenzie tells her. I recognise the voice even if her image has gone a little blurry, I must have suddenly contracted allergies.

Tia squeals and throws herself at Mackenzie, while they are cuddling, I wander off to rinse my face in cold water from the sink in the adjoining bathroom. I stare at myself in the mirror above and wonder how my life changed so dramatically in such a short period of time.

"I'm going to tell Aunt Ava, and Uncle Grant, and Tyler, and Jacob." I hear a little voice yell before what sounds like a herd of baby elephants stampede out of the room next door. Moments later a pair of arms wrap around my waist.

"You Ok baby?" Mackenzie asks tenderly.

I turn and take her in my arms so her head rests

against me, "I'm more than ok, it's you that I'm worried about?"

"Me? I'm so happy right now I just can't describe it. I have you, your family—who have gone out of their way to make me feel welcome from the first second I met them—and now you've just made me a mommy for the first time to a beautiful little girl. We are starting a fabulous new life together, one that you've always dreamed of, here, surrounded by the people we love."

"Is it enough for you?"

"What do you mean?"

"You're right, it is the life I've always dreamed of. What about your dreams? I don't want you feeling you've sacrificed them for mine."

"I don't." She cups my face in her hand and I lean in to her touch. "I promise you, everything you are giving me now is all I've ever wanted for as long as I can remember."

"Except one thing maybe?"

She pulls back to look me in the eye, "I don't follow."

"I've seen the way you look at Ava, and I caught the way you spoke yesterday about becoming an aunt. You've always said you wanted kids, as in plural. Do you want to try and make a baby with me Mac?"

She gasps and I can see the waterworks brewing before they arrive. All I seem to do is make this woman cry.

"D... Do you want more children?" She stutters

nervously.

"You know I do. I even left a space for them." I grab her hand and place it over my tattoo. "But this isn't about me right now, this is about you, your needs, and what you want. You've given me so much already."

"I would love to try and make a baby with you," she nods tearfully. "But what about Tia? This is all so new, everything is changing so fast for her. She might not be ready."

"We'll have to go about it sensibly, keep her involved as much as we can and hang fire from mentioning anything until we're confident we can deliver. The fact that you're even considering her needs right now, proves you are going to be a great mom to her and any other little person that might happen to come along. Being a mom to a four-year-old, a puppy and potentially a newborn won't be easy. There will probably be a lot of sleepless night and don't even get me started on the amount of poop we'll have to deal with. When you sit down and consider the reality of it all, you might not feel ready. You might never feel ready. But if you are, and it's what you want, I'm not about to make you wait longer than you have to. I'm pretty certain Tia will love being a big sister and I know she'll make a good one, but whatever happens, I'm sure Grant will be able to deal with it." I joke, and Mackenzie bursts out laughing.

"Are you sure?"

I shrug and wink mischievously, "Well, we're

about to get a puppy, what's one more mouth to feed? I have a new project lined up that I was planning to run past everyone later. I've made sure I'll be filming locally most of the time, but I could be away for a week or two on occasion. I could always cancel or try to convince them to postpone. I haven't signed any contracts yet, although I did give my word I wouldn't back out at the last minute. If we move here, I know the gang will help out where they can. In fact, you might even try to follow me back to Hollywood just to get away from Ava."

Mackenzie chuckles. "I don't want you to pull out of the movie. I know it won't be easy, and while I'll appreciate any help I can get, I bet I could handle everything on my own if I had to, as well as keep Jacob out of jail and make sure my man is always satisfied," she tells me with lascivious smile, cupping my balls though my shorts and rolling them gently.

I kick the door closed with my foot and flick the lock.

"Interesting, I'm particularly curious as to how you intend on doing that last part," I muse with a smirk, "Perhaps you would like to join me in the shower and provide me with a practical demonstration."

Chapter Twenty-Five

✧

T he next few months unfold seamlessly.

Over the course of one evening, I tell the whole clan the story of a fairy king who defeats an evil goblin queen in an enchanted forest. It has plenty of intrigue and battles to keep the twins from wandering off, enough romance to keep the girls enthralled, and plenty of humour to keep Grant amused. At the end I ask my panel if I should formally accept the role of the fairy king in the movie I'd been considering. Everyone loves the story so I get five enthusiastic thumbs up and one bewildered look. I crouch to ask my youngest, yet harshest critic, if she thinks I would be a good fairy king. She taps her chin thoughtfully before saying, "You do have a magic wand daddy, if I come live in the forest can I have a puppy?" While everyone else laughs, I take that as an affirmative and tell Jerry it's all systems go the following day. Contracts get signed, permits get approved, and soon the only thing we are waiting for before filming can start is the hiring of the rest of the cast members.

Ava comes with Mackenzie and me to speak with

the admissions officer at the preschool we want Tia to attend. The conversation is considerably easier thanks to Ava having already started the application process. We all agree that Tia should start attending after the Christmas holidays, giving Mackenzie and me time to find a permanent place to live in the area. That way, we can keep her with us as long as possible, and it gives her more time to bond with Mackenzie—not that I feel she needs it. Tia is besotted, although she still calls her M'kenzie. I can see Mackenzie itching for Tia to call her mom, but she never pushes the issue and lets Tia move at her own pace.

Just as we start the search for our ideal home, a five-bedroom property within walking distance of Grant and Ava's appears on the market. Mackenzie falls in love with it instantly. Ava loves that it's so close by, and Tia adores it because she finds a toadstool in the grass at the bottom of the garden and is convinced it's because a fairy lives there. It's a done deal. The sale goes through quickly although we decide to wait a while before moving in. Ava loves having us stay, and wants us all in one place over Christmas so she can be with Tia on the morning of the big day. It also gives Mackenzie and I time to redecorate our new place. Since I'm not great with furnishings, I send Ava back to the city with Mackenzie on a shopping spree with my credit card. I love the way they get on so well together. They stay at the apartment in Hollywood for a few days while Grant and I take care of the kids back in the bay.

Christmas itself is the best kind of bedlam, there are so many presents around Ava's tree, it's almost invisible. Tia and the boys are so excited Christmas eve, the last one doesn't fall asleep until gone eleven. In the run-up, we hid all the presents in one of the rooms at the new house, and it takes Grant and me a couple of hours to ferry them back as a surprise the following morning. It seems we have just finished and climbed into bed ourselves, when Tia wakes and runs around the house screaming, "Santa's been!" And the whole household has to get up again. We all go for a walk in the park and help Ava create an amazing feast in between opening presents together throughout the day. On Boxing Day, it's customary for us to encourage the children to sort through their wardrobes and used toys to find good quality items for charitable donations. Despite the mountain of gifts I donated in the run-up to the holidays, it's a practice Ava and I want to instill in our children. No matter how blessed we have become, we always remember the days when we weren't as fortunate and try to do our part in making someone else's life a little easier. Tia's favourite present this year is the letter Chloris leaves under the tree. With it is a map we all help her follow. It leads directly to the local dog shelter where I have it on good authority a litter of abandoned puppies are waiting to find their forever homes. I probably should have asked a few more questions before showing up with my daughter in tow. Instead of the cute and cuddly ball of white fluff I had in my mind, we are faced with six, black, stocky, and surly faced brutes. Of course, Tia doesn't want to wait to find anything more in keeping with what I had in mind, and it's love at first sight when one comes scampering over to lick her face. She decides against calling him Bob, favouring Mr. Josh instead, much to everyone's amusement. I'm disappointed further when his carers tell me that his predominant genetics appear to be those of a Cane Corso, a powerful breed that will develop into a strong and athletic dog. After being assured that they are loyal and affectionate with their families, and with good training, despite his formidable appearance, Mr. Josh will make the perfect companion for my little girl, he comes home with us and proceeds to wreak havoc. I decide to hire a professional dog trainer the following day, as his new best friend rigorously protects him from everyone's wrath, and I'm afraid that if I don't take charge quickly, he will grow up without any manners.

One weekend after the holidays, back in Hollywood, Josh makes Mackenzie an offer she can't refuse. As he gets ready for the official launch of his company, he still finds himself struggling to hire someone able to handle calls effectively. Even though she hasn't had to deal many while helping him to this point, Josh has been impressed by Mackenzie's aptitude and offers her the job full-time. I can see she is torn between wanting to be more self-sufficient, continuing to earn her own money in a job she enjoys, and the feeling she should be focusing solely on Tia's needs while she is transitioning into her new life. Josh and I convince her over dinner—one which he cooks, with the assistance of a diminutive, yet demanding sous-chef —that between us we can help her strike a balance between the two. He only asks that Mackenzie calls into the office periodically, and he travels with us to our new house to help install a state-of-the-art security system before setting up the office that Mackenzie and I will share, equipping it with the latest technology so she can fulfil the rest of her obligations remotely.

It's comical the way Tia takes to ordering him around—the six-foot-three giant is totally at the mercy of my four-year-old and the puppy that shares his name, who both seem to have taken a shine to him and follow him everywhere. As new friends go, Tia couldn't have chosen a better one. Despite his scary disposition, he is patient and kind, although he refuses point-blank to wear a sparkly pink crown while working. Of course, Tia smacks him with her wand and throws glitter over him to try and make him comply. Later that day, I'm sure I catch sight of him on the new CCTV wearing that very item, even though when teased about it, he is adamant it never happened and I was hallucinating.

We never see or hear anything more from Dan. It worries Josh no end. He hates pulling his men from watching the girls full-time, but with the launch of his new business and the sudden influx of job requests that accompany it, he needs all hands on deck. He is only appeased because Mackenzie agreed to continue working for him. With their daily contact, he knows where she and Tia will be at all times. The longer she works for him, the more crew members she becomes familiar with. I'm pretty sure that when she tells me she has 'bumped' into one of them while she is out and about, the meetings are not always quite as accidental as they are made out to be.

By the time Ava is ready to pop, we are settled into our new home and our new routine. The closer Ava gets to her due date and the more her belly grows, I see Mackinzie looking on enviously. With so much going on in our lives, our plans to expand our own family had been put on hold, but after life shows no sign of slowing down and concluding that no time would ever be the 'right time,' I drag her willingly to the doctors where we both have a medical before Mackenzie consents to having her contraceptive implant removed. Mackenzie seems much more at ease even with just the hope of a new baby in our future, and we are both so blissfully happy regardless that there is no pressure on her to conceive. We relax and decide to just let nature take its course, and it goes without saying I'm over the moon that she is receptive to our increasing our odds by consummating our relationship at every opportunity. With Ava living so near, it's easy to drop Tia off for a few hours so we can slip away to fornicate like rabbits. Of course we return the favour by having the twins over regularly, although I like to think Grant does little more than massage my sister's swollen ankles every time he is alone with her.

All in all, life couldn't have turned out more perfectly. Even the four-legged Mr. Josh wakes up one morning and decides to start behaving himself. Tia swears she knows nothing about the sparkles that coincidentally appear in his coat overnight.

The only problem with achieving perfection, is that it can draw out those lurking in the shadows—individuals driven by hatred or jealousy, determined to destroy everything you've built.

Chapter Twenty-Six

✧

"**J**ared!"

I try to prise my eyes open but I'm just too tired. It feels like I've only been asleep a couple of minutes. It's Friday and I'm in my trailer on location near the Santa Monica mountains. I've been here for four very long days, and have only recently climbed into bed following a night shoot. I asked my co-star, Tamara Teasdale to make sure I was awake by ten this morning as filming wrapped here last night, and I want to get back to my girls for the start of the weekend.

"JARED!"

Suddenly I'm struggling to breathe as a pair of fingers pinch my nostrils closed. My eyes fly open and I see Tam leaning over me, grinning. She was a model who transitioned into acting and is fast making a name for herself. She approached the producers for a chance to audition for the role of the evil goblin queen, and they were almost as shocked to hear from her as they were when I told them I was interested. She couldn't be naturally any further from her character if she tried; Tam is beautiful inside and out. As well as being devastatingly pretty, she has such a sweet personality that she embodies the girl-next-door archetype, and the roles she usually gets offered reflect this. She wanted to stretch her acting wings to portray a totally different persona and was prepared to spend hours in make-up each day to achieve her aim. Initially, I was worried about how Mackenzie might react to us being away together and in such close proximity for days at a time. However, after she got the part, I invited Tam round for dinner so Mackenzie could get to know her, and it soon became apparent that if anyone had cause to worry, it was me. A fact that I kept hidden from Josh when he popped over and his tongue fell out of his mouth at the sight of her. It was hilarious watching him fawn all over her when I knew no amount of effort would give him the kind of anatomy that she desired. I bat her hand away and gasp for air.

"It's nearly eleven, if you don't want to make you way back to your gorgeous fiancée, I don't mind going on ahead and keeping the sheets warm for you," she jokes.

"How would your current bed mate feel about that?" I quirk an eyebrow at her mischievously.

"How do you know I had company last night?" She looks down at me blushing furiously.

"If the trailer is a rockin', best not to come a knockin'," I laugh, and Tam grabs a pillow whacking me with it. Truth be known, Tam's trailer is nearby, and when I was back during a break in filming last night, I saw her sneaking someone in under the cover of darkness. The rest was pure supposition. "Who is she then?"

"It's really new. Just someone I met a couple of weeks ago, she wanted to drive down to see where I was working," she tells me excitedly. "I'd love for you to meet her before you leave, get your opinion."

"Why do you need my opinion?" I ask curiously.

Tam looks at her hands nervously and she suddenly reminds me of Tia when she is scared and unsure of herself. "I've made a lot of mistakes in the past. My friends say I'm too trusting and that the red flags were there, I just refused to see them. I really like this one Jared," she puts her hands on my shoulders and shakes them lightly to reenforce her point, "but I just want someone I trust to tell me if there's something glaringly obvious I'm not picking up on before I get in too deep."

"I'll tell you what," I smile reassuringly. "If you go an find me a pint of the strongest, drinkable coffee you can find, I'll swing by your trailer as soon as I'm up and dressed."

She squeals and hugs me, "Thank you."

When she disappears, I grab my mobile and see I have a voicemail, I hit play.

"SURPRISE!" A chorus of voices sing before Mackenzie takes charge, "Hey baby, we all decided to come and meet you at the apartment in Hollywood this weekend, save you having to drive out to the bay and back again. It was just going to be Me, Tia and Mr. Josh a bit later, but the boys' school had to close due to a burst pipe, Ava wanted to get out of the house for one last hurrah before four become five, and we didn't think pulling Tia out of preschool early for one day would affect her political career at a later date, so, here we are! We love you and can't want to see you. Anything you want to say to daddy darling?" The line goes silent for a few seconds then a little voice pipes up, "Mr. Josh broked one of your shoes, but it wasn't his fault."

If that dog has eaten another one of my trainers I might lose my shit. I wouldn't mind but he always favours the left one, I now have six trainers for my right foot with no counterpart, matching or otherwise. I smile and shake my head as I hit call on Mackenzie's number.

"Hi," she purrs.

"Well, if that isn't the sexiest voice in existence, I don't know what is." I murmur.

Mackenzie chuckles, "What time do you think you'll be home?"

"What time will you be naked on the bed with your legs spread waiting for me?"

"Jared, you know I might have you on speaker phone, right?"

"Do you?"

"No," she giggles, "But we do have a house full this weekend, so doing what you're suggesting might be a little difficult."

"I'll call you when I'm nearly home and you can make them all go out."

"I'm not ousting your heavily pregnant sister

because you want sexy time."

"Why? You said she wanted one last hurrah. Sitting on my couch, binging boxsets and stuffing her face with ice-cream isn't exactly wild."

"Jared, be serious. Grant got called into work, his flight doesn't hit the tarmac until after twelve. I'm supposed to be watching Ava until he gets back in case she goes into labour," she giggles.

"Fine!" I grumble teasingly, "If I get there before Grant's back to keep an eye on her, I'll message you when I'm in the parking lot and you can pop down and blow me. If you put your best effort into it, we can be back upstairs before she's finished her Ben & Jerry's."

Silence. Does that mean she's considering it?

"What time will you be back?" She finally laughs.

Definitely wasn't a no. I smile, "Depending on traffic, hopefully between one and two this afternoon."

"I can't wait." She whispers, then everything goes so quiet I think we may have been cut off.

"Mac?" I call.

"I'm here," she says after a couple of seconds.

"What happened? I thought I'd lost you."

"I just wanted to come into the bathroom so no one can hear me."

"That's my girl," I growl, wrapping my hand around my hardening length.

"Not for that," she laughs, "I have something to tell you and I don't want the others to hear me."

"What's wrong? If Mr. Josh has eaten one of my

new trainers, he won't need to be castrated by a vet, I'll use a melon baller."

"If you do that, he might sneak into the bedroom when you're sleeping and return the favour by biting *your* balls off," Mackenzie warns. She provokes some terrifying imagery in my mind and suddenly I'm not so hard anymore. "No, it's not about Mr. Josh. It's just that... I might be... you know?"

"Are you trying to tell me, what I think you're trying to tell me?" Suddenly I'm out of bed and wide awake.

"I'm not sure. I think so. I mean, I haven't seen a doctor or anything. I was looking at my calendar the other day and I realised I'm late, and not just by a couple of days. I got a test from the drug store and was going to keep it until you were back and we could do it together, but I don't know if I can wait that long."

"Do it now."

"Really?"

"Really."

"Ok, I'll call you back."

"No, don't hang up. I want to be with you. Do it while we're together, now."

"But you'll hear me pee."

"Babe, I've seen you pee before. What's the problem here?"

"I don't know. I'm just nervous I guess."

I roll my eyes. "Call me back after you pee. Make it a video call, I want to see your face when we check the results."

"OK." She hangs up just as Tam comes bursting through the door with my coffee.

"Why are you pacing?" Tam looks at me quizzically. "Are you sure you need this? You look pretty strung out already?"

"I do." I grab the cup she's proffering and take a swig without checking the temperature first. "Fuck!" I spew the hot liquid all over the wall with what feels like the charred remains of my mouth.

"Are you sure you're ok?" Tam looks at me concerned.

"I'm sure," I rasp, pushing her gently out of the door as my cell starts ringing. "I'll be over, soon." I tell her apologetically, as I slam the door and answer the call.

Mackenzie is sitting on the closed lid of the toilet and she swings the camera to show me the test she is holding in her other hand.

"How long?" I ask.

"Three minutes."

"We'll check it after two, I'm sure my sperms always been faster than a penguin on an ice slide," I tell her with a wink.

She gives me a bemused look.

Neither of us say a word. We both just sit there staring at our phones. I'm not sure if we are staring at each other or the clock. I sit on the edge of my bed until the way my leg is bouncing up and down in agitation wears thin. Then I resume pacing.

"Two minutes." I say as soon as the digits of my clock change. "Let's take a peek."

"Not yet, I don't want to get my hopes up for it to be a false positive or something."

The next sixty seconds are the longest of my life.

"Three minutes," Mac says nervously. "Shall we look together?"

I nod and she flips the camera of the phone so it is facing the back of the stick.

"Can you see it Ok?"

I nod.

"Jared, I can't see you," she giggles. "I bet you just nodded, now I know where Tia gets it from."

"Yes," I murmur. "Do it on three." I start counting. "One. Two. Three!"

She flips the test and we both look at the two pink lines.

"Oh my gosh!" Mac drops the stick and the phone. I don't see anything other than her feet until she has recovered enough to pick me up off the floor. Then I look at her beautiful face and of course, she's crying.

"Babe. You alright?" I ask lovingly.

She nods. "Drive safely, but hurry home."

"Try and stop me." We disconnect and I jump in the shower sporting a grin so big, I'm sure my face must look like one of Tia's drawings.

As soon as I'm dry, I phone the florists and arrange for three bouquets of flowers to be delivered to my address in Hollywood. One extra large for the woman who continues to make me the happiest man alive, one slightly smaller for the best sister a guy could wish for, and an even smaller, pink display for my mini-me. No lilies! Then I fire off a quick text letting Mackenzie know to expect a surprise delivery.

I rush around shoving my things into a holdall before loading up the car and saying my goodbyes to the rest of the cast and crew. I save Tam until last. I know her goodbye will take the longest since I promised to meet her friend, but I'm eager to be on the road the first chance I get. I walk over to her trailer and rap on the window.

There's a murmured, "Shit! Then she calls, "One sec." I wait impatiently for her to come to the door. When she does, she is tying the belt of her robe and looking distinctly dishevelled.

"Sorry, if I'm interrupting something..." I smirk and waggle my eyebrows, "...We can do this another time."

"Just get in here you jerk." She grabs me by the T-shirt, laughing as she yanks me inside.

There's a body lying in her bed, and whoever it is has their back to me.

"Honey," Tam calls. "I'd like you to meet Jared."

"Jared..." Tam presents me with a hand flourish just as her guest rolls over to face me, not seeming overly concerned that she is naked and her sheet is only barely covering her from the waist down, "...I'd like for you to meet Kendra."

Ice floods my veins as my eyes lock with the one woman I was hoping I'd never have to see again.

"Jared," Kendra purrs, "Long time no see. How is our daughter?"

Chapter Twenty-Seven

✴

"**M**y daughter. I've a legal document confirming you don't have one." I try to keep my voice level even though I feel like I'm about to explode any second.

"W... what?" Tam's hand flies to her mouth.

Kendra slides out of bed and walks over to face me. She's thinks her nakedness will impress me. I cross my arms and stare her down, completely unaffected. "Babe, can you give us a sec?" She asks Tam.

Tam nods and tries to leave, but I block her path.

"No way, you evil, conniving, bitch," I growl at Kendra. "I don't know what you have up your sleeve, but whatever it is, I want a witness and you need protection."

"You are well aware I'm not wearing sleeves, and as for protection," she giggles maliciously, "Didn't do you any favours, did it?"

"Is that a stretchmark I see?" Knowing Kendra, that remark will hit her harder than any profanity. I know I'm right when her face blanches slightly, and she screws her face up in disgust before grabbing a shirt off the floor, putting it on and wrapping it tightly around her body.

"What do you want Kendra?" I snarl.

"Visitation."

"Dream the fuck on." I can feel my temper rising.

"Now, now. I'm sure we can come to some arrangement. This little movie seems to be creating quite a stir. I bet you'll be making a pretty penny after it's release. I'm sure if you were to see your way to sending some of that profit my way, I could forget about ever dragging you through the courts for custody."

Custody!

I turn to Tam. "I'd say that was a pretty big, red fucking flag, wouldn't you?" It's taking every ounce of my restraint not to throttle the other woman in the room, but I force my eyes back to her. "If you want a fight Kendra, bring it on! Did you even read the papers you signed before sending them back? That contract was tighter than a jar of pickles on a supermarket shelf. It's going to cost you a bomb to try and drag me through the courts just to find out you can't win. And let's not forget the fact they also state that if you were to even try and contest them in any shape or form, whether you win or lose, you have to pay one million dollars for every year of Tia's life you missed, along with five million in punitive damages for causing her undue stress and mental anguish. I make that nine mill before I even step outside this trailer."

Kendra pales and withers in front of my eyes. "It's

fine, I have a backer, right babe?" Kendra and I both look to Tam.

"You're fucking delusional," she spits incredulously, rounding on Kendra and slapping her hard across the cheek. I don't know who's more surprised, Kendra or me. "When you said you needed a loan, I thought you meant a few hundred bucks to cover your rent or something. I didn't realise you were intending to try and bleed me dry if your pathetic attempts at blackmailing a good friend of mine didn't work. Not to mention the fact that you are trying to destroy a sweet little girl's life because you are a narcissistic whore."

Kendra rounds on Tam. Tam's handprint is still a visible outline on her pale skin. "I'm no whore."

"WHETHER THE MONEY'S LEFT ON THE NIGHTSTAND OR IT'S EXTORTED AFTER, IT BOILS DOWN TO THE SAME THING." Tam yells so loud Kendra flinches. "NOW GET THE FUCK OUT OF HERE BEFORE I CALL THE COPS AND HAVE YOU ARRESTED FOR BREAKING AND ENTERING!"

"Don't you mean trespass?" I whisper, shocked to discover the mild-mannered Tam I've grown to know and love has such a feisty streak.

Tam ignores me and storms out of the trailer. Seconds later, a brick is hurled through one of the windows, shattering it. It flies past Kendra, missing her by a hair's breadth. Tam comes angrily striding back in seconds later. "No, I mean fucking breaking and entering, stalking, blackmail, extortion, prostitution, trespass, and any other goddamn thing I can think of to get her charged with!"

"It'll never stick, there are no witnesses," Kendra shouts back half-heartedly.

I cough pretending to clear my throat as I raise my hand.

"ADD STUPIDY TO THE LIST," Tam shouts, before grabbing Kendra by the hair and physically removing her kicking and screaming from the trailer. "IF YOU ARE STILL THERE IN SIXTY SECONDS, I'M CALLING THE COPS!" She yells, before coming back inside and slamming the door.

"Wait! I need my clothes," Kendra's defeated whine echoes through the door.

"YOU DIDN'T SEEM THAT BOTHERED ABOUT THEM NOT SO LONG AGO," Tam yells. "FORTY-FIVE SECONDS OR INDECENT EXPOSURE WILL BE ADDED TO YOUR EVER-GROWING LIST OF FELONIES. AND IF I WERE YOU, I'D TAKE A VERY LONG VACATION, A VERY LONG WAY AWAY, BECAUSE IF I EVER SEE YOU AGAIN, OR HEAR ABOUT YOU BOTHERING ANY OF MY FRIENDS, THIS CASE OF AMNESIA I'VE SUDDEN DEVELOPED IS GOING TO RAPIDLY DISAPPEAR."

I open my mouth to speak but Tam holds up her hand to silence me. I snap my mouth closed more than a little terrified she might suddenly aim her wrath at me. She sets a thirty second timer on her mobile—allowing for the fifteen seconds that have passed since her last time check—and when the alarm sounds, she opens the door and peers outside.

We both do a quick search, but unsurprisingly, Kendra has gone.

I look at Tam to see she has reverted back to the sweet and placid girl I remember.

"Remind me never to get on your bad side." I whisper with raised eyebrows and a smile, before drawing her in for a hug.

"Did I ever tell you I get really bad PMS?" She answers with a smile of her own.

After making sure Tam is Ok, and taking some pictures of her trailer in case we ever need evidence of a random attack inflicted by a crazed, recognisable stalker who obviously managed to evade security. I hang around and help her find someone to repair the damage to the window before finally being able to set off for home. I'm about half an hour into my forty-minute journey when the radio cuts out, and the entertainment system notifies me of an incoming call. It's Josh and I accept it via hands free.

"Howdy neighbour," I sing, nothing can spoil my mood right now.

"Well, what's got you sounding so chipper? Kurt been in touch to declare his unwavering love and affection?" He laughs.

"Maybe," I grin, "Although I had to break the news I was already taken, so apologies if he is surly and irritable over the next few days. I shouldn't think you'd notice that much of a difference. What can I do for you? If you are just calling for a chat, I should be home in ten if you fancy a beer, or if you're worried because you can hear a commotion next door, that's due to me having a full house this weekend."

"I've not been home myself, I'm just on my way there now and a beer sounds great, but that isn't why I called. I actually saw the gang arrive on the CCTV earlier. Your brother-in-law turned up separately and took the kids out shortly after, so it should be pretty quiet when I get back."

"Probably gone to get ice cream, or pick up some pickles for Ava's cravings." I interject.

"Anyway, I just wanted to check to see if you'd ordered any flowers. The camera triggered the alert on my phone a couple of times, and when I checked the footage, I couldn't see a face because there was so much foliage."

"I'm glad they listened when I told them to go large. Yeah, it was me, I ordered three bunches so they probably needed to make more than one trip from the van."

"Three?"

"One for each of the ladies in my life."

"You're too smooth for your own good you. You're making the rest of us look bad. I wouldn't even know where to go to order any."

"That my friend, is why you are still single," I laugh. "What did they look like? I gave them free reign as long as the finished article was amazing. Only one exception, no lilies, Mac's allergic."

"Lilies?" Josh's tone turns grave and then I get it, that feeling. My skin starts to prickle and the hairs on the back of neck stand on end. As a chill sweeps down my spine, I start to accelerate without knowing why, even so, I don't get that much further ahead before I hit a dense patch of traffic.

"Josh?" He sounds like he is suddenly speeding and swerving around cars, I can hear horns blaring in the background. He must hear the panic in my voice because he tries to soothe me like a child.

"I'm sure everything's fine. I'm just pulling into the parking lot," I hear the screeching of tyres and the jerk of a handbrake. "I'll be upstairs in a second, I'll check everything's Ok and call you back." He hangs up but I can't wait for him to get back to me. Somethings wrong, I know it, and Josh could sense it too. I need to know my family is safe. At least Grant has taken the children out. The minute Josh disconnects I call Mackenzie's number. When the phones answered, I feel my body sag with relief. I speak before she does.

"Mac, thank goodness, is everything OK?"

"No, everything's not OK asshole," a male voice drawls, "Not for you. I however, have got the pleasure of being in the company of two beautiful women. I only came for one and now I'm spoilt for choice, so being the generous kind of guy that I am, I'll let you decide which one you want to keep. So, which is it to be, your pregnant sister or my wife?"

"STAY THE FUCK AWAY FROM MY FAMILY." I yell.

Without warning, even though I feel chilled to the bone, I start sweating. I can't cut through the traffic but I feel like I can't just sit and wait for it to clear either. Terror swamps me, making me heave. I want to get out into the air and run, run to my family, but if I do, I'm afraid of the call getting cut off. I sit, paralysed with fear and indecision, gripping the steering wheel so hard I'm surprised it doesn't snap from the pressure.

"Clock's ticking. Tick Tock. I can't hang around here all night waiting for you to make a decision. I guess it'll have to be a surprise when you get home."

"DAN!" I scream. "IF YOU HURT EITHER OF THEM, I SWEAR I WILL HUNT YOU DOWN..."

I'm interrupted by some kind of explosion, and then all hell breaks loose. Ava screams, "NOOOO!"

"AVA?" I yell, my heart is pounding so hard from fear and dread, I worry I'm about to pass out. It's impossible to comprehend what's going on. Everything happens simultaneously and it's over in the blink of an eye. I hear shouting, from two, maybe three, different voices. I can't make out what's being said as everyone is yelling and screaming over each other. There's a loud thud, a dog snarling, Mackenzie screaming, and then time stops as a gunshot rings through the air. "MAC?" I roar, just as the line goes dead.

Chapter Twenty-Eight

✦

"**M**AC? AVA?" I yell again, before I'm out of the car, abandoning it and all its contents in the middle of the road, with the door wide open. Then I'm running. My mind is blank. I can't let myself think of anything other getting home as fast as I can. I'm afraid that if I do, it'll break me. Mac, Ava, my unborn child, my unborn niece or nephew. I've never been overtly religious but I look up to the sky and give thanks that my peanut wasn't there. I know I need to phone Grant, to tell him to keep the kids out of the way until I get home and am able to assess the situation, but I can't, my mobile is still in the car. The thought of them walking into the shit fest I just listened to spurs me on. By the time I reach the end of my block, my lungs are burning and my legs are numb, they're on autopilot as they carry me home. The sight of the lights from the police cars and ambulance outside my building propels me forward. I charge ahead and when I reach the entrance to my building, I don't let anyone stop me from barging my way through and up to my apartment.

When I get there I find the door half hanging off its hinges, and it's not a small door, nor is it flimsy. I suspect that was the explosion I heard, and I scan the place frantically. People I don't recognise are wandering around the room. It's not them, but rather the large stain on the floor that draws my eye. The stain that looks suspiciously like blood, and a lot of it.

"Find him!" I hear a familiar voice growl in a low and dangerous voice. I look up and see Josh pacing furiously. He's a formidable figure, he's so pumped he looks like he is about to spontaneously combust. His face is red, his biceps swollen, every vein I can see looks engorged and angry. I'm so glad that I'm not the target of his rage right now. He has a paramedic virtually hanging off the arm he's using to hold his phone to his ear. She's stretching as she tries to patch up a wound on his shoulder, despite the fact he won't listen to her pleas to stop moving. He is striding around like he hasn't even noticed she's there. "And when you find him," he looks over to a policeman listening and watching his every move, "I want to be the one to bring him in." Josh spots me, hangs up immediately and strides over. Holding his hands up in front of himself to calm me down, he tells me, "They're fine."

Two words that almost make me want to weep with relief. I sink down onto the couch with my head in my hands.

"What happened?" I whisper, turning my head to glance at him as he sits beside me.

The paramedic trying to treat him sighs with relief, "Thank god, I was starting to get vertigo." It's then Josh seems to notice her for the first time, and like night turns to day, his whole demeanour softens when he offers up a smile.

"Well hello," he purrs, "You wouldn't be a darlin' and give us a couple of minutes would you?"

"No, I wouldn't," she snaps. "You've been shot and I need to stop this bleeding."

"Shot," I echo.

"If you give me two minutes now, I'll be a good boy and do whatever you ask after." He waggles his eyebrows at her.

"Not happening. Now sit still, I need to cut your T-shirt off so I can see what's going on."

Josh sighs, reaches behind himself to grab the neck of his top before dragging it off in one swift movement. "If you wanted to get me naked sweetheart, you only had to ask."

The paramedic takes in his chiselled abdomen, and blushes when she realises she's been caught checking him out. "Just searching for injuries," she murmurs before stuffing a load of wadding into the gaping hole in his shoulder. He doesn't even flinch, he merely smirks at her before getting serious and looking over at me.

"C'mon let's go to my place." We stand, much to the paramedic's frustration, and walk over to Josh's apartment with her hanging off him again. He opens his door, and once we are inside, he plucks her off of himself like a piece of lint from a jersey, depositing her outside before closing the door in her face.

"Sorry beautiful," he calls through the door as she bangs furiously on it from the other side. "When I'm done here, I'm all yours."

He leads me as far away from the door as we can get, before he speaks again.

"Where are they?" I ask.

"I don't know."

"What do you mean you don't know?" I can feel my temperature rising again.

"I need you to listen and not panic."

Easier said than done.

"It's unfortunate that you picked today of all days to send flowers. That's how he got in. He told the front desk his had to be signed for. Mac was already expecting a delivery and so didn't think anything of it and told the concierge to send him up. When you said there weren't supposed to be any lilies but I'd seen some on the camera, I thought something was up. That, coupled with the fact that there was no delivery van in sight when I got here, convinced me. So I didn't hesitate to bust in, where I found the dickwad we've been searching for on a cell talking to someone while holding the girls hostage."

"That was me he was talking to. What did you use to get through the door, C-4?"

"My body," Josh smirks briefly. "He must have been holding the girls at gunpoint, because as soon as I burst through the door, he swung his arm round and took a shot at me. I think he was expecting you, and when I turned out to be someone he didn't recognise, his aim drifted and he missed. I charged, and he was just about to take another shot at me when then this kid flew out from behind the sofa and whacked him hard on the back of his knees with a baseball bat."

"Kid? What Kid? I though you said Grant took the kids out."

"He did. One of them must have doubled back."

"Anyway, the ass went down as the shot went off. That kid may've saved my life. The bullet was aimed lower than my shoulder and could've ended up in a much worse place if it hadn't been deflected. In a nutshell, I ended up with a through-and-through that missed any major organs. He went to fire again and he pushed the kid out the way to do it. As soon as he did that, your dog ran out of nowhere and clamped onto his wrist. I lunged and yelled at everyone to make a run for it while I had him pinned so he couldn't fire. They got a good five-minute head start."

"Wait!" I start panicking, "You let him go, he is still after them?"

"No and yes. As soon as I was sure everyone was clear, I punched him. Hard. He went out like a light. While he was out, I called Kurt to ask him to trace Mac and the others so we could track where they were heading. I only turned around for a second, but when I turned back, the slippery fuck was gone. Someone in the building must have reported hearing shots and called the police, because as I was heading out the door after him, they arrived wanting to know what was going on."

"We need to get out there!" I half shout. "I need to find my family before Dan does."

"I've got my whole team on it. Trust me. We *will* find your family before he does. Is there anywhere you can think of they would go? Anywhere they know they'll be safe."

I think for a minute. "Mac always said other than when she's with me, the only other person that makes her feel safe is her brother. She says Dan's terrified of him."

"I'm offended," Josh actually looks does look affronted, "Where does he live?"

"I don't know." I rack my brains trying to think. We have been so busy she hadn't gotten around to visiting him, and I've never been to his place. "Santa Monica. He has a place on the beach."

"Name?"

"Jack." Josh quirks his eyebrow at me. "That's all I know. I've never met him. He married a few months ago if that helps. I don't know Mac's maiden name; she took the name Kingsley after she married, but she always used to work under the name 'Kenzie Kingsley'."

Josh gets on the phone and relays what little information I could give him.

"What now?" I ask impatiently, ready for action.

"You wait here until I get an address and can confirm that's where they are. I go deal and with the cops, then get my shoulder seen to by that feisty

EMT with the nice rack and come fuck me eyes. Do you think If I told her I think I might have bruised my dick when I fell, she'd kiss it better?"

"How can you think of that, at a time like this?" I growl.

"Relax," Josh smiles, "If there is one thing I'm sure of, panicking and going off half-cocked won't solve anything. Wait in here. I don't want the law snagging you so you can't make a quick getaway. The minute I get word on where your family are, I'll let you know, and you can go to them."

I drag my hand through my hair, "I abandoned my car a couple of blocks away. It's probably been towed and my sports car is back at the bay." Then, I have an epiphany. "I can use Grant's. Except, I don't know where he is or when he'll be back."

Josh hands me his car keys. "Here, take mine if you need to."

I accept them gratefully. "Thanks. What about Grant and the others?"

"They can follow on if they're not back before you have to leave. I've got a man downstairs watching out for them, I don't want my queen freaking out if she comes up here and sees the mess I've made. If you can, stay with the brother a couple of nights if that's where they turn up, and I'll get your place sorted while you're away."

"Your queen?" I smile, for a millisecond.

"I may, or may not have been upgraded, from Mr. Josh to King Josh when I was previously at your place sorting the security systems."

"I knew I saw you wearing that crown even after you denied it," I chortle.

Josh turns to leave but returns after only a few paces. "You know he shot me, right? That he was willing to murder me, or you, in cold blood. Christ knows what he would have done to the others if I hadn't arrived when I did."

"I know," I tell him gratefully, "I can't thank you enough, I know I owe you, I'm just not sure how I'm ever going to repay..."

Josh shakes his head. "Not what I'm asking. I can assure you I'll find him before the police, and when I do, things are going to get ugly. I'm asking how much ugly you can handle?"

I don't hesitate. "How ever much it takes to guarantee my girls' safety."

"That's what I was hoping you would say," he replies ominously, before clapping his hands together and changing his tone to a more jovial one, "Now where's that little firecracker."

Josh disappears, and I start pacing. It feels wrong to just hang around and wait. I trust Josh, I really do, but it doesn't stop me from feeling that I should be doing something.

Finally, Josh comes bursting back through the door. He is still topless, except for the bandage wrapped around his body to cover his shoulder. "Found them. You were right, Mac has taken them to her brother's, here's the address." I go to grab the piece of paper he is holding, but he jerks it back just out of reach. "Wait! Your brother-in-law has just pulled into the garage downstairs so you might want to take him with you. You better hurry, my guy Axel is trying to stop him from coming up here and things are starting to get a bit tense."

I nod, and toss Josh his keys back as I sprint out the door.

In the garage Grant is squaring off to a guy who looks like he wrestles grizzlies for fun. He spots me as soon as I appear. "Jared. What's going on?"

"Get in the car, I'll explain on the way." I don't give Grant the option of driving. I jump in behind the wheel, and he runs round the car to get in the other side. I glance over my shoulder to make sure Tia is secured in her car seat, "Tyler, buckle up."

"Daddy, that's Jacob." Tia giggles.

"Are you sure?" I ask confused, when Josh told me about the kid jumping out at Dan and hitting him with my old baseball bat, I naturally assumed it would have been Jacob.

Tia ignores me and continues flipping through the book on her lap. I look at Grant.

"Yeah, I was taking the kids out for ice-cream but we hadn't even got to the elevator before Tyler said he got this funny feeling and that he wanted to stay with his mom. He ran back and wouldn't come."

"What sort of funny feeling?" I ask, as I peel out of the lot and take off. I hand over the piece of paper Josh gave me. "Here type this address into the sat nav will you?"

"Said it was like his skin felt all prickly and the hairs on the back of his neck were standing on end. I thought he was coming down with a bug so let him stay put but told him to stay in your room as I didn't want Ava catching anything." Grant tells me as he fiddles with the navigation system. "Where are we going?"

I glance over at him and gesture to the back seat with my eyes, "While you were out Mac had to take the others to visit her brother. We are going to meet them there. I can't call her. Her mobile was *taken*." I put greater emphasis on the last word as a warning to Grant.

He can tell by the look I give him that I don't want to impart too much information in front of our young audience. "Is everyone OK?" He growls.

I nod, and he immediately tries to call Ava. His calls ring out to voicemail every time. We make the rest of the journey in silence. When we turn off the freeway, it becomes obvious we are being followed. I noticed the black Escalade as soon as we left Hollywood, although its tinted windows made it impossible to see who was inside. If it's Dan, there's no way I'm going to lead him straight to the others. I start taking detours to try and lose him. Grant looks over at me quizzically.

"Just checking out the neighbourhood," I tell him. It's like he reads my mind as he pulls his visor down and uses the mirror to try and see who is behind us. I keep bobbing and weaving through the traffic until I know we are in the clear, then I speed off before we can be tracked any further. Eventually we reach our destination and I pull off the road in front of a large pair of wrought iron gates. There's some kind of futuristic looking pole buried in the ground, off to one side, and I pull up beside it.

Nothing happens.

"Press the button," Grant prompts me.

"There is no button," I reply peering out of the window at the shiny dome on top of the pole.

"It's a Mayepole," Jacob announces from the back seat.

Grant and I look at each other, confused.

"Get out and dance around it," Grant chuckles.

"You get out and dance around it." I growl back.

"You both need to get out and dance around it." Jacob tells us scathingly, as if he shouldn't have to explain what we need to do, "It's the only way."

Grant and I reluctantly climb out of the car and awkwardly skip around the pole before getting back inside. Tia is laughing her little head off, slapping her hands on her lap.

"What next?" I ask Jacob.

"I don't know," he tells me laughing, "I just wanted to see if you'd both do it."

"Jacob that's not funny." Grant barks.

"It is from where we're sitting, right T," he chuckles, high fiving my daughter.

I roll down the window and stare directly at the dome, checking it for any indication of what we need to do to announce ourselves. As soon as I do, a red light skims across its surface before an electronic voice says, "Unrecognised. Calling main house."

"You've got to get me one of those for Christmas," Grant whispers in awe.

"You came. I knew you'd find us." Mackenzie's excited voice comes out of no-where, Grant and I start searching for any hidden cameras, "I'm opening the gate."

As soon as we are able, I drive through. Theres a long, winding drive that leads to a huge, palatial property. It's sleek and modern with a fountain out front. There's a triple garage to one side with what looks like an apartment overhead. As we approach, Grant points to the house and whispers in wonder, "I've changed my mind, you can get me one of those."

I snort. Then, as I pull up, the front door opens and Mackenzie comes hurtling out, closely followed by Tyler and Mr. Josh. She flings herself at me and I cling to her in relief. "I thought I'd lost you," I whisper, comforted by her familiar scent.

"Where's your mom?" Grant asks Tyler urgently.

"Inside, having a lie down."

"Show me where she is."

Jacob joins them as they dash off, having already helped Tia out of her seat. She is on her hands and knees petting her excited dog, as he leaps around licking her face.

I carefully take Mackenzie's head in my hands and stare at her beautiful face, "I love you," I murmur. "I always knew it; I just didn't realise how much until I almost lost you."

"I love you too, baby," she whispers, causing me to

instinctively remove one of my hands to cover her belly.

"Are you ok?" I ask, concerned.

"We're fine," she smiles softly as a walking thunderstorm charges toward me.

"Jack, I'd like you to meet..." Mackenzie starts.

When I realise it's her brother, I pull back from her so I can extend my hand for shaking. The next thing I know, I'm sprawled on the ground, clutching my jaw, and feeling like I've been clobbered by a wrecking ball.

"...the prick that knocked up my sister while she was married to another guy!" Jack finishes, as his giant, angry frame looms over me.

Chapter Twenty-Nine

✧

"Don't you hurt my Daddy!" Tia screams, launching herself at Jack's leg, pummelling it with her tiny fists. Mr Josh's protective instincts cut in and he is hot on her heels, latching himself onto his other calf, clamping down hard.

"Mr. Josh, NO!" Mackenzie shouts. The dog releases his hold, and goes to sit beside her looking suitable chastised. Jack hops around in pain while still trying to avoid Tia's blows.

"What the fuck!" He yells. "I'm calling animal control, that things a menace."

"Mr. Jack, you said a bad word." Tia stops her assault and holds her hand out for payment.

"You need to give her thirty bucks." Mackenzies glowers at him.

"Sue me." Jack gripes to Tia.

"Pay up!" Mackenzie growls, she puts her hands on her hips and Tia mimics her.

"I'm starting to regret asking you to visit." Jack tells her, as he pulls some notes out of his pocket and hands them off to my little girl. As soon as she has them, Tia grins up at him before running off.

"You told him about the baby?" I ask, from where I'm still lying on the floor.

"It just slipped out," Mackenzie tells me apologetically. "When we got here, I was in a bit of a state. I was babbling, trying to explain why I showed up unannounced with Ava and Tyler in tow, and it flew out before I had the chance to stop it."

"Is it safe to get up?" I ask Jack, who is stood with his arms crossed defensively, glaring at me.

He jerks his head in acknowledgment, and I pull myself to my feet just as the twins appear.

Jack does a double take. "Did you clone yourself while I wasn't looking?"

Tyler smirks, "I told you I had a brother." He looks at me, "Why were you on the floor?"

Jacob looks up at Mackenzie's brother in awe at his size and stature. He goes to stand in front of him, mirroring his pose by crossing his arms and standing with his feet slightly apart. "Who are you?" he asks in wonderment.

Tyler goes to introduce them, "Pebble," he deadpans, "Meet boulder." Jacob scowls at him while Jack furrows his brow in confusion.

"Are you Ok baby?" Mackenzie kisses my bruised jaw, just having her close again reminds me of what I could have lost. Despite our audience, I can't help myself as I pull her into a more passionate embrace.

"Seriously!" Jack snaps, "That's my sister!"

Mackenzie giggles and pulls back. "Jared," this is my brother, Jackson Longe. Jack, this is my fiancée,

Jared."

Suddenly Jacob isn't the only one starstruck.

"You can't have a fiancée, you're already married." Jackson barks at Mackenzie.

"Jackson Longe?" I murmur. "As in the actor?"

"Psychopaths don't count." Mackenzie rounds on Jackson, as he snaps back at me.

"Not anymore!"

"Shall we take this inside?" Mackenzie pulls on my arm. I hesitate not sure if I'm welcome. I look at Jackson who narrows his eyes in warning before nodding his head.

The inside of his house is as spectacular as the outside. Ava is sitting with her feet up on an enormous couch, cuddling and cooing over a newborn. Tia is squished between her and Grant on one side, and an attractive young woman, who I presume to be the baby's mother, is on Ava's other. The twins are sat huddled together in a corner talking in hushed voices.

I zoom in on my sister immediately, "Ava, are you alright?"

"I'm fine." She says dismissively before looking up from the baby and seeing the concern on my face. "Jared," she says seriously, "I'm fine, and it wasn't your fault."

"No, it was mine," Mackenzie mutters sheepishly.

"The hell it was." Jackson's anger resonates throughout the room. "When I find Dan, I'm going to fucking kill him with my bare hands."

"Get in line," I murmur, and receive the briefest

look of respect from the simmering volcano beside me.

"Jack," the only person in the room I don't know, speaks up. "What have I told you about swearing around the baby."

"She's barely a month old." He grumbles belligerently, before looking down to see who is tugging on his trouser leg.

"Mr. Jack, you said a bad word," Tia looks up at him and bats her eyelashes, hand extended.

"She's four and doesn't negotiate," I tell him with a smile.

He hands Tia another thirty dollars.

"Hi, I'm Jaime." The female I don't recognise comes over to shake my hand.

"I'm..."

"I know who you are," she giggles.

"How? How do you know who he is?" Jackson storms jealously.

Jaime ignores him, smiling at me brightly. "That over there is our daughter Harper Lucia. Who might this young lady be?"

"This is Tia," I tell her, as my daughter clings to my leg shyly.

Jaime crouches so she is at eye-level with my daughter, "I'm pleased to meet you Tia," she tells her, "Why did my husband just give you thirty dollars?"

"Um..." Tia looks up at me and I nod, "Coz he said a bad word."

"And what do you do with the money?" Jamie askes her.

"I give it to mommy and she keeps it for my school when I'm older."

"You're fucking married too?" Jackson snaps at me, his eyes go crazy and he steps forward. I brace myself, ready to take another hit.

"Jackson Richard Longe. Stay right where you are!" Jaime growls at him. He stops dead in his tracks and I laugh when it becomes apparent she owns his ass.

"I keep telling him not to say bad words and he doesn't listen," Jaime tells Tia, "So I think you should charge him double."

"What?" Jackson blusters.

I look at Mackenzie and she has tears streaking down her cheeks. Fuck! What have I done now? "Babe, what did I do?"

"Nothing. It's what she just said."

"About charging him double?" Jaime asks, "It's fine, he can afford it. Pay the lady Jack."

Jackson begrudgingly hands over another sixty bucks. Tia takes the money and runs over to hand it to Mackenzie. It's then the penny drops. "She called you mommy!"

Mackenzie nods, and I'm so happy I take her in my arms and kiss her.

"Not again!" Jackson grunts. "That's my f..." He looks at Tia's twitching fingers, "fantastic sister."

"You got that right," I laugh, and everyone else chuckles.

"You've succeeded where I've failed," Jaime tells Tia. She goes over to her husband and tucks herself under his arm before kissing him on the cheek. When he looks down at her, it's clear he's smitten. I think if she told Tia to charge him a million bucks, he would have found a way to raise it. That's if he didn't already have that much stashed. I recognised his name when Mackenzie introduced us. He used to be an extremely high-profile actor until a personal tragedy made him completely withdraw from the public eye. It never occurred to me that he could be related to Mackenzie.

"What's the plan now?" Grant asks from where he is sat on the sofa.

I look around the room. "Any chance we menfolk can have a chat somewhere more private?" I ask.

"We menfolk?" Ava bursts out laughing. "Who do you think you are? Wyatt Earp?"

I glare at her.

"I'll grab us a beer and we can head out onto the patio," Jackson says, throwing me a look of camaraderie, which I accept with a grateful nod.

"You do that, darling," Jaime joins in on the fun. "While we womenfolk stay here and start quilting. But just so you know, the next poopy diaper is yours, and you're not getting out of it unless it's Armageddon."

Five minutes later the 'menfolk' over the age of nine, are out on the patio, drinking beers and bonding over our hatred for one particular individual.

"I'd like to meet this Josh fellow and shake his hand," Jackson growls. "Even if he did let the fucker escape."

"I think you are about the only guy in the world that could do that hard enough to make him flinch," I rub my sore jaw and Jackson smirks.

"I'm not sure I know you well enough to be sorry about hitting you yet," he tells me, shaking his head solemnly. "I never liked Dan from the start, but by the time I first met him, he and Mac were already married. I always knew he was punching, but Mac seemed happy, and I never dreamed he'd go off the rails like this. Otherwise, I wouldn't have stopped until I got her out of there and away from him."

"YOU KNEW HE WAS HITTING HER AND DIDN'T DO ANYTHING ABOUT IT?" I bellow, standing, ready to attack. "SHE TOLD ME IT ONLY HAPPENED THE ONCE."

"WHAT DO YOU MEAN? HITTING HER? I MEANT PUNCHING ABOVE HIS WEIGHT." Jackson yells in my face, "IF HE FUCKING HIT HER, HE'S A DEAD MAN WALKING!"

I swallow, Grant gasps and stands, looking between us both as if he is about to step in the middle of a war zone.

"MACKENZIE! GET YOUR ASS OUT HERE NOW!" Jackson bellows so loud, he doesn't need to move before she comes running from inside.

"I'm sorry," I mouth as she approaches, "I thought he knew."

Can you give me and my sister a moment to talk?" Jackson focuses solely on Mackenzie, and he doesn't look at Grant or me as he dismisses us.

"I'm not sure..." I start.

"It's ok baby," Mackenzie gives me a weak smile. "Jack and I do need to speak."

I nod and reluctantly go back inside. Jaime pats the sofa beside her, and I go and sit down.

"I know my husband can be a bit intimidating at times, but his heart is in the right place. His family and friends are more important to him than anything. If you hurt them, you hurt him."

I huff in amusement, "Mackenzie said something similar once."

"Then you'll know what I mean. He'll blame himself for not being there, even if he wasn't meant to be." She smiles at me kindly, then glances over to Ava, who is still holding the baby while being surrounded by Grant and the others. "You have a lovely family."

"Thankyou," I tell her as I smile back. "You have a gorgeous daughter. It's been ages since I got to hold one that tiny."

"Well, it's time you were reminded what it's like. Since you are going to be my new brother-in-law, I suggest you start bonding with your new niece." She calls to my sister, "Ava, I'm cutting you off, your brother wants a cuddle."

I go and take Harper from Ava, settling back down on the sofa beside her mom. Harper is so tiny; I lay her on my chest, and she snuggles in, falling asleep instantly.

"Holy shit!" Jaime exclaims, "You're like a child whisperer. I've been begging her to take a nap for hours."

Tia taps Jaime on the knee, "Lady, you said a bad word."

Jaime gasps and her hand flies over her mouth. "If you promise not to tell Uncle Jack, I'll give you a hundred bucks!"

Tia's eyes go wide and she nods furiously.

"Phew," Jaime sighs to me, slumping back in her seat. "He'll never let me live it down if he finds out I slipped." She goes to find her purse and gives Tia the money. As she hands it over, she whispers, "You can call me Auntie Jaime."

"Kay," Tia skips off happily. She's back two minutes later, "I can't find M'kenzie."

Uh oh, we're back to Mackenzie. I summon up my serious dad voice, "Mackenzie or mommy, peanut? We don't want her getting confused, do we?"

Tia doesn't need to think for long, "Mommy. I just forgetted."

"Forgot," I correct her. "Here, let me hold the money for you until you find her."

Tia hands over her stash.

"I'm not sure how I feel about you bribing my four-year-old." I tell Jaime lightheartedly, as soon as Tia's gone.

She looks at me, crestfallen, "I'm sorry, I'm failing as a parent already, aren't I?"

"Ah, don't worry about it. I feel like I'm failing every damn day," I share to reassure her.

"Really? Because from where I'm sitting, you look like you have it all figured out."

"Thank you." I'm genuinely surprised considering the way my family and I descended on her home. "I'll take that as a compliment."

"You should." She smiles at me kindly before quirking an eyebrow at me, "So? Tell me how you and Mac met?"

"I'm sure you've heard the story from her already." I laugh.

"Not all of it," she grins, "She wasn't here long before you arrived, so now I want to hear the rest from you."

We sit chatting amiably until Jackson and Mackenzie reappear sometime later. Jackson has his arm draped over her shoulder and they are both smiling. They see me with Jackson's baby girl asleep across me and they both melt. As if she can sense she is being watched. Harper stirs, scrunches up her face and the room is suddenly filled with a foul stench.

"Want me to change her?" I ask.

"Yes," Jackson snaps at the same time Jaime snaps, "No."

I laugh. "Which is it?"

"You can take the next one. This one is all Jack's." Jaime grins. "He needs the practice."

"So does Mac," I wink at my girl, "You had better go with him."

Jackson and Mackenzie look at each other terrified.

Tia comes between them and takes Jackson's hand, "C'mon Uncle Jack, I help you."

I raise my eyebrows at a giggling Jaime, "What could go wrong?"

A lot apparently.

Chapter Thirty

A s soon as I tell Jackson about Josh suggesting we all stay away from my apartment for a few days, he offers us all a place to stay without hesitation. His home is certainly large enough to accommodate us all. He calls a guy named Tony and arranges for some essential supplies to be delivered. By essential supplies, I mean swimming costumes for everyone, since as soon as the twins spot the giant heated pool in his backyard, they threaten to either dive in fully clothed or go skinny dipping unless we comply. He also arranges new phones for myself, Ava and Mackenzie, as all the others were abandoned before we left Hollywood. I've barely charged mine before it starts ringing.

"Hello?" I answer cautiously, presuming it to be a wrong number.

"Just calling to check in." Josh's voice has me looking at the phone in disbelief.

"How did you get this number?" I ask.

"Ways and means," he chuckles, "Ways and means."

"Any news?"

"Not yet, but one of my guys is chasing down a lead as we speak. I just wanted to check you are ok for a bed for tonight, and to offer you a job."

"The bed, yes. Jackson has offered to put us all up for as long as we need. The job, why?"

"Because I have a vacancy. I asked one of my new guys to tail you when you left me earlier, and you shook him like a leaf from a tree in a blizzard. He was supposed to make sure you got to your destination safely and without being followed."

"Black Escalade?"

"That's the one."

"Jeez, I wish you'd said. I thought it was Dan, that's why I lost him. You didn't fire him because of me, did you?" I ask horrified.

"Course not, that would be unethical. Funniest thing happened though, I partnered him with Kurt, you know, for additional training, and he quit within the hour," he chortles. "I'll give you a call when I know more."

He's gone before I have the chance to say anything else.

Jackson's house is double-storey with all the bedrooms on the upper floor. Jaime helps us settle into various rooms before dinner. Grant is in a double room with Ava, the twins are in the bedroom next door, Mackenzie and I are in the room opposite, and Tia is bunking with us since she's in a strange environment and I know she won't settle if she's on her own.

Considering she has so many guests and a new

baby to contend with, Jaime couldn't be more hospitable. With so many faces to feed, she tells us that she has called one of her best friends to help prepare dinner. Her friend, an amazing cook apparently, lives next door with her husband. Jaime has also invited them to join us, along with some random guy who lives at the bottom of their garden. It sounds a bit of a weird set up and I can't help but wonder what we are letting ourselves in for.

After larking about in and around the swimming pool for most of the afternoon, we all go inside to get cleaned up before dinner. Thankfully, when he was picking up our swimwear, Tony thought to grab us all a few additional outfits. Nothing ostentatious, but at least we now have a change of clothes. Mac showers first, on the premise that she wants to help Jaime with the dinner preparations as much as she can, but I know she's really just looking for an excuse to fawn over Harper. Then I help Tia before leaving myself until last. By the time I'm ready to wander downstairs, I hear raucous laughter coming from the kitchen, where a lively party seems to be in full swing.

I round the corner to see everyone in hysterics at the antics of a man in the middle of the room. My eyes are drawn to the empathy belly he is wearing. He has one hand on his back as he waddles around pretending to be in pain, with Jackson the only one in the room looking on unimpressed.

As I appear, the source of all the entertainment looks up, as he does I clock his face.

"YOU!" We both shout in unison.

The whole room falls silent as we stare each other down. Tension fills the air, and Mackenzie gravitates to my side.

"What the fuck are you doing here?" He growls.

"Mr Mitchel, you said a bad word." Tia tugs on his trouser leg.

"Mitchel Dalton," I snarl. This is all I fucking need.

"What's he doing here?" Mitchel looks at Jackson who simply shrugs dismissively.

"He's Mac's new guy," he remarks casually.

"You never told me you knew this pr..." I look from Mackenzie to Tia as I correct myself, "person."

"Hell no!" Mitchel puts his hands on his hips and tries to look intimidating. Not an easy feat when you are wearing the curves of an expectant mother. "I forbid it." Mackenzie chuckles, as a beautiful woman goes to Mitchel's side and puts her hand on his arm. I hadn't noticed her before now, she looks familiar, and as I take in her swollen belly, it becomes obvious she is carrying his baby. It takes me a minute before I remember who she is.

"Jen?" I ask. "From the gala."

"You already know each other?" Jaime grins.

"We met briefly a few months ago," I say dryly, "We were sharing a dance before some possessive jerk came stomping over like a two-year-old wanting to steal back his favourite toy." I gesture to Jen's belly, "I take it you forgave him."

She smiles and nods, waving her ring finger in the air for me to see. "Afraid so, he actually persuaded me to marry him."

"Did you get a blood test to make sure you weren't drugged when you agreed?" I ask seriously.

"Mr. Mitchel," Tia tugs impatiently on his trouser leg again.

He tears his angry eyes from me and his gaze softens when he looks down at my daughter, "Yes sweetie."

Tia puts her hands on her hips and gives him a stern look. "You said a bad word."

"I'm sorry," he says, thinking that will be enough to absolve himself. When he returns his gaze to me, Tia tugs on his trouser leg again so he looks back at her. She holds out her hand with her palm upturned and then flexes her fingers. Everyone in the room giggles. No-one escapes.

"What do you want princess?" Mitchel looks down at her confused.

"Thirty." She tells him firmly, nodding her little head in emphasis.

"You want me to pay you?" He asks incredulously. "For what? Speaking?"

"For saying a bad word," Tia tells him authoritatively.

"And what if I don't want to pay?" Mitchel crosses his arms defiantly. It's surreal watching a grown man in an empathy belly arguing with a four-year-old.

"King Josh said to tell him if someone doesn't pay the queen and he will make them."

Mitchel bursts out laughing. "Who's King Josh?"

"Someone you really don't want to mess with," Mackenzie chuckles.

"I'm not scared of the king." Mitchel juts his chin in the air, before relenting, "but... I will pay the queen because she's cute." He reaches into his pocket and hands Tia some notes, "Here, go give these to your mom."

The look on his face when she runs over and hands them to Mackenzie is priceless. He obviously assumed she was Ava's child.

He glances at Jackson, Mackenzie, then Tia, before looking at his wife for some kind of explanation.

"Don't look at me," Jen tells him, before going to sit beside Ava.

"She's mine," I growl.

Mitchel's eyes snap back to me, and he suddenly seems to be even more furious with me than he was before.

"Outside," he grunts.

I frown, totally confused as to what has got him so riled up. "I'm not going to hit a pregnant man." I gesture to his belly.

"You won't get the chance," he growls. "Just like the last time."

"Fine," I snap, "Let's do this."

"No!" Several voices chorus.

Mitchel goes to rip off his pregnant belly.

"Don't you dare, Dalton!" Jen shouts from across the room. "You promised you'd wear it for twenty-four hours, and that's not up for at least another two."

He freezes. "But this is an emergency," he calls back, his eyes not leaving mine for a second.

"Do you think I can just not be pregnant every time I have an emergency?" She replies, her voice laced with a warning tone.

"No problem." Mitchel defiantly tightens the straps on his outfit. "I could beat this dude if I were eight months pregnant, with my eyes closed and one hand tied behind my back."

"Sure you could?" I sneer.

"It's fine, I'll go keep an eye on them," Jackson sighs at the inconvenience.

"If you're going, I'm going!" Grant stands. "I'm not letting Jared walk into an ambush."

"If you're going, I'm going." One of the twins stands. I think it's Jacob but I'm not totally sure until he speaks again in a low voice to his brother, "Did you bring the baseball bat Ty."

"No. But I have a deodorant in my room," Tyler whispers back.

"Stop it! All of you." Ava stands with Jen's help and shuffles into the centre of the room. It's a shrewd move, no one is about to argue with, or try to push past an angry, hormonal woman on the verge of labour. "We are not going to have a bloodbath; we are going to sort this out using our words." She looks at Tia, "The good ones."

Harper has been resting in a moses basket after a feed, she suddenly starts screaming. Ava points at Jackson, Grant, and Jacob in turn. "You, sort out your daughter, your wife needs a break. You, and you, sit back down."

"Yes ma'am," Jackson scurries off to do as he's told much to Jaime's amusement.

"Wimp!" Mitchel utters under his breath, inciting Ava's wrath.

"You." She points at him, "Be quiet."

"Yes ma'am." Mitchel mutters.

"Wimp," Jen giggles, earning herself a heated glare from her husband.

"Jared, What's this all about?" Ava asks me calmly.

"He's a sociopath," I tell her smoothly.

Mitchel opens his mouth to respond but Ava silences him with a look. He clamps his jaw closed.

"Jared?" Ava prompts.

I flap my arms in frustration, "I have absolutely no idea. I beat him in a poll for best ass once, I guess his ego never got over the trauma."

Michel snorts, as three of the four women in the room crane their necks to see if the title was correctly bestowed. I'm delighted when they look at each other appreciatively, and that my sister abstains from offering her opinion.

"Jen," Mitchel barks, just as Jackson snaps his wife's name when they catch their significant others checking out my rear. The two girls look at each other and burst out laughing.

"Let's get back to business, shall we?" Ava chuckles.

"Mitchel…" Ava looks to my nemesis.

"Call me Mitch," he shmoozes, and she immediately starts fangirling.

"AVA!" Grant and I bark at the same time, bringing her crashing back down to earth.

"Sorry," she mumbles at us, before smiling at Mitchel. "Can I ask why you have such a low opinion of my brother?"

Mitchel shuffles back and forth uncomfortably. He glances at his wife, then looks around at Ava and the rest of my family. "It may be best if we discuss this in private."

"Fine by me," I growl as the tension rises again.

"No," Ava snaps. "Unless *you* have something to hide, I suggest we settle this now. My brother and I have always been close, there's nothing you could say that I probably don't already know."

"Have you got something to hide, Mitch?" Jen frowns at him.

"No, of course not," he replies, although his face flushes slightly.

"Well then, spit it out. We're all getting hungry and the food's nearly cooked," she tells him authoritatively.

"Two words," he growls at me, "Kendra. Collins."

Jackson snorts derisively, as Jen looks at her husband and growls, "Who the hell is Kendra Collins?"

I feel the colour drain from my face as Ava looks between Tia and me.

"Boys," she addresses the twins. "Can you take Tia upstairs and wash your hands ready for dinner.

They both look at her as if she's insane.

"We've just showered, after spending the

afternoon in a swimming pool filled with salt water," Jacob moans, "I'm so clean the soap will fell dirty standing next to me."

"Jacob, please." I implore my nephew.

"Fine," he grumbles, standing and taking one of Tia's hands. "But if I start shrinking after being submerged in all this water, I'm not going to be happy. C'mon T," he tells my little girl. "Let's go and see if there are any fairies living in the bathroom upstairs. I thought I saw one earlier."

Tia squeals in excitement and they leave with Tyler following along behind.

As soon as they've left, Ava opens her mouth to speak and I silence her by holding my hand up. I cross my arms and stare Mitchel down. "Right let's have it," I growl. "What do you *think* you know?"

Mitchel narrows his eyes at me. "I know I found her in tears one night, mourning the loss of the baby she couldn't afford to keep after you kicked her to the curb. Mac deserves better than someone who hasn't got the balls to stick around to support the mother of his baby, whether it was planned or not."

There are a few startled gasps before Ava spits, "That fucking bitch! Let me guess, she got you to console her between the sheets."

Mitchel glances at his wife, "It was a long time ago babe, way before I even knew you existed." She nods in understanding. Before he met her, his list of conquests was undeniably extensive. He looks across at Ava and frowns. "I don't see how that has anything to do with what's going on here."

"Don't you?" Ava snaps. "Figure it out Einstein."

Mitchel's brow furrows in confusion as Jackson coughs to draw his attention. "I told you she was up to no good with those rubbers."

"Is she the one you said you caught tampering with the condoms that time?" Jen chips in.

"Well, that's what Jack seemed to think she'd been doing when I told him I walked in and found her playing around with them. I'd like to think that wasn't the case, but I couldn't come up with any other viable explanation. She made me cautious enough to be much more vigilant going forward," he tells her, before turning back to me and grunting, "Doesn't explain why you turned your back on her after she told you she was having your baby? She was devastated she couldn't afford to keep it. No woman should have to go through what she did alone."

"ARE YOU FUCKING STUPID?" I shout.

"Daddy, you said a bad word."

Of course she chose that moment to reappear. I hand her some cash, and she passes it straight to Mackenzie. Then, I pick her up and widen my eyes at Mitchel.

He looks between us, and I can see the cogs whirring in his mind until the penny finally drops.

"At last," Jackson murmurs when it does, "I thought we were never going to get any dinner."

Mitchel looks at me sheepishly. "I'm so sorry. I believe I may have greatly misjudged you." He slowly shakes his head in disbelief and remorse as he extends his hand for shaking, "I never thought she'd be capable of telling such a lie. Ready to call a truce?"

"Not yet," I tell him as I hand Tia over to Mackenzie. I don't hesitate before swinging round and punching him so hard on the jaw he staggers backwards. There's a ripple of gasps as Jackson and Grant leap between us.

Mitchel rubs his jaw as he rights himself.

"That was for the gala. Now we're even." I explain. "Still ready to call a truce?" This time, I extend my hand to him.

Mitchel grins and shakes it warmly. "I guess I deserved that."

"Yes, you did," his wife chuckles, coming to his side and tucking herself under his arm. "It's okay baby, I'll kiss it better for you later."

"Only reason I let him get away with it," he chortles, before they start making out in front of us.

"Good grief," Jacob moans, screwing up his face in disgust, "Again with the kissing."

Tyler puts his hand on his brother's shoulder, "One day," he tells him seriously, "You'll understand."

"What's that supposed to mean?" Ava asks her son. Tyler looks up at her cagily, shrugging dismissively. It's obvious he has a secret he's not willing to share.

"Grant." Ava snaps, much to her husband's amusement, "You *really* need to have that talk with your sons!"

Chapter Thirty-One

✦

D inner is a joyous occasion with everyone sitting around Jackson's huge dining table, laughing, joking, and generally get to know each other. We are joined by a gentleman called Clive, an amiable fellow with a dry sense of humour. Apparently, he used to own Mitchel's house before Mitchel did. He didn't want to sell, but he was too long in the tooth to keep up with the repairs and financial obligations that came with ownership. He and Mitchel negotiated, with it resulting in him retaining a small portion of the land and him renovating a more moderately sized property situated on it. Hence, why he was now 'living at the bottom of Mitchel's garden'."

Tia takes a shine to Mitchel much to Jackson's chagrin, as the 'official' uncle, he deems himself more worthy of her affection. Nevertheless, as soon as we have finished eating, she climbs up onto Mitchel's knee and proceeds to tell him all about her magic wand and fairy friends. He listens intently, nodding in all the right places, and I have to begrudgingly admit he seems a decent guy that will make a great dad.

"You know, I married a fairy," he tells Tia.

Tia looks at Jen wide-eyed. Jen rolls her eyes at Mitchel.

"It's true, she has a beautiful dress but she only wears it on very special occasions, and for very special people."

"And when she isn't seven months pregnant so able to squeeze into it," Jen adds.

"Oh, I forgot about that." Mitchel smiles adoringly at his wife. "Perhaps you could just show it to her instead?"

"Sure, I'll get it before we have dessert," Jen smiles at Tia.

"Do you have fairy dust too?" Tia asks totally smitten.

"Um… I don't think so." Jen tries to think.

Tia looks disappointed and Mitchel can't have that. "Course you do," he tells his wife, "What about all that sparkly sh…," he corrects himself, "Stuff you sprinkle over the fairy cakes you bake."

"Oh, my disco dust," she laughs, before looking at Tia and putting a finger to her lips. "Shhh, no-one is supposed to know about that," she whispers conspiratorially.

"Like daddy's magic wand," Tia whispers back, and everyone falls about laughing.

We chat for a while longer before Jaime announces she is going to fetch our pudding. Jen excuses herself to go next door and fetch her dress for Tia to see. While Tia is distracted, Jaime whispers that Jen bought it for a fancy dress party to celebrate one of their friend's birthdays. Apparently, the costume has wings with tiny LEDs that chase across the fabric when lit. From the description, I know Tia will believe Jen is the real deal when she sees it.

"Mind if I come with you?" Tyler asks suddenly when Jen stands, "I could do with stretching my legs."

"Sure," Jen smiles at him. "It's not far though, there is a hole in the fence and we use that rather than having to walk the long way round."

"No problem," Tyler gets up and they wander off together.

"I hope your brother isn't crushing on my friend's wife?" Jackson asks Jacob when the coast is clear.

"Nah," Jacob tells him, "He didn't want her going over there alone, said he was getting this funny feeling?"

"What sort of funny feeling?" I chuckle.

"He said his skin got all prickly and the hairs on the back of his neck were standing on end," Jacob laughs.

I'm out of my chair so fast it goes flying back behind me.

"What?" Grant says, immediately alarmed.

"The last time he said he had that feeling, he wouldn't go with you guys to get ice-cream because he wouldn't leave Ava, and look what happened."

"Relax," Jackson tells us, "Security here is top notch, no-one can get in without us knowing, and look at your dog." He points to Mr. Josh asleep by

Harpers moses basket in the corner of the room. "If by some miracle anyone did get in here without our knowledge, don't you think he would have let us know?"

Grant and I settle back in our seats, but I still feel uneasy. Somethings not right, I can feel it. Twenty minutes later, when Jen and Tyler still haven't returned, the others start to feel it too.

Mitchel stands first. "I'm just going to check and see what's taking my wife so long."

Grant, Jackson, and I all stand too.

"I'm coming, to see what Tyler's up to." Grant tries to sound blasé, but I can hear the concern in his voice.

"I'm coming," I say firmly.

"Me too!" Grunts Jackson.

"We can't all go. Someone needs to keep an eye on things here," I say, as we all look between us.

"I'll be here!" Jacob pipes up, standing and crossing his arms trying to look fierce.

The corner of Jackson's lip trembles as he struggles to keep a straight face. "I'll stay here with pebble," he says, as he tries not to laugh.

"Good idea," Mitchel replies. "The force of you two will probably equal the force of us three."

Grant, Mitchel and I wander out onto the patio at the back of the house.

"Follow me," Mitchel calls, as he starts strolling purposefully across the garden. He doesn't get far before a figure comes lurking out of the shadows.

"Looking for someone?" Dan growls.

"You fuck. Where's my wife?" Mitchel takes a warning step towards Dan, but is stopped in his tracks when eight burly men step out of the darkness, forming an impenetrable line of defence around the person he was aiming for.

"She's safe," Dan grins at the surprise on all of our faces. "Didn't think I'd step into the lion's den alone, did you? None of *you* scare me, per se, but I must admit my brother-in-law is a formidable guy."

"Why don't you step forward and face me like a man then?" Mitchel goads him.

"I would, but the odds aren't exactly stacked in my favour, right now."

He's right about that. I wouldn't have reckoned on his chances if he'd wandered into the line of fire alone.

"How did you get past our security systems?" Mitchel barks.

"Anything can be achieved for the right price," Dan sniggers, gesturing to the men lined up in front of him, "I must say these guys were extraordinarily cheap considering they're experts within their field. Getting in here was child's play for them."

"What do you want?" I growl.

"I came for my wife," he laughs in disbelief, as if I should have known. "So," he looks at Mitchel, "Your wife for mine. I tried to make a similar deal earlier but I underestimated the size of my opposition. As you can see," he sweeps his hand along the line of men before him, "I learnt from my mistakes."

"Where's my son?" Grant yells.

"Don't worry, you should be proud of him, he didn't go down without a fight. Little scrapper tried to take on three of my men while he was trying to defend his wife." Dan almost speaks in admiration of Tyler's courage, as he flicks his hand in Mitchel's direction when indicating whose wife he was talking about.

"If you've hurt him…" Grant storms.

"You'll what?" Dan yells. "I wouldn't say you were in a position to issue any threats right now. Would you?"

Suddenly, I feel an angry presence behind me, something so large and foreboding that the atmosphere around us seems to cower in fear.

Dan's eyes widen slightly before he has the chance to suppress his actions.

"Dan." Jackson's voice is so low and menacing, Dan recoils even though he is surrounded by muscle. "I hear you raised a hand to my sister."

Dan swallows and doesn't make a move to either confirm or refute the accusation.

"You know this is going to get settled here and now, with or without, your girlfriends." Jackson takes a step forward. He looks at Mitchel who gives him a small nod. We are heavily outnumbered but when Jackson looks across at Grant and I, we resign ourselves to what needs to be done, and give him a small nod in return.

"What's going on?" Jacob appears just before the fight is about to start.

Dan looks at him in surprise, "How did you

escape?" He blusters.

I look at Grant and smirk. He thinks he is Tyler. At least we now know Tyler hasn't been harmed.

"Looks like you underestimated us again," I tell Dan. "We have the girl and the kid, so I guess you've lost your bargaining chips. I suggest you get the hell out of here before things turn ugly."

Dan looks visibly worried for a second, but he narrows his eyes as he senses he is being played.

"Na ah. The kid may have got out but the girl is being watched. We would have heard if she had escaped." He points to the earwig one of his crew is wearing.

"Unless the kid managed to disable communications," Jackson says with a wry smile. He turns and goes down on one knee beside Jacob. "Pebble, I'm counting on you here," he tells him seriously. "I need you to go inside, tell the girls everything is fine, then sneak out of the room and go around the entire house making sure all the doors and windows are locked."

"That won't make a difference to these guys," Dan mocks him.

Jackson ignores his taunts and focuses solely on Jacob. "I need you to keep them all inside, no matter what happens out here. Put some music on, loud. You hear me?"

Jacob looks over at his dad and me. We both nod in confirmation. "I hear you," Jacob mutters.

Jackson offers him a fist, and Jacob bumps it with his own before running off. Jackson stands and waits until Jacob is safely back inside, flicking the door lock. Only then does he turn back to Dan. "Any last words, dipshit?"

The four of us brace ourselves for battle. It's not lost on me that Dan is the only one on our opposing team that does the same. Just as Jackson barrels forward to land the first punch, with Mitchel, Grant, and me hot on his heels, a voice booms out halting all action for a second time.

"STOP RIGHT THERE! HE'S MINE!"

Josh comes stalking out of the shadows like a panther. He grins at me as he walks over, totally disregarding Dan and his posse. "You're a feisty lot aren't you. Sorry it took so long for me to get here but I was across town when I got the call."

"Call? What call?" I ask, as everyone else on my side looks at him confused.

"The call to say one of my guys finally had eyes on that fella there." He jerks his head in Dan's direction.

If Dan was scared of seeing Jackson, it's nothing compared to the look he gives when he spots Josh. He huddles behind the largest of the men protecting him, curling up to try and make himself small enough to disappear and render himself invisible.

"If you don't mind, we're kind of in the middle of something right here," Jackson growls, impatient to unleash the fury bubbling up inside of him.

"Relax, it'd be a one-sided battle." Josh smirks at Jackson when he bristles. "I told my guys they weren't to lay a finger on you."

"Your guys?" I echo.

"Mmm, seems that when Daniel here decided to hire some mercenaries, he didn't do his homework very well. He was asking every Tom, Dick and Harry to help him out. It seems someone gave him my number, and Kurt 'happened' to get in touch to offer our services. Kurt can be pretty persuasive when he wants to be, you know what a pleasant telephone manner he has."

I snort.

"Since our request for financial compensation seemed to be an issue, Daniel was offered a large discount on our services to ensure we got the job. It seems he's never heard the saying, 'if it's too good to be true, it usually is,' and went along with everything we staged from the beginning to draw him out."

I look at Dan, he is so pale he looks like a ghost. I almost feel sorry for the guy. Almost. He takes a step back, turns and bolts. He doesn't get very far before Kurt steps out from behind a tree and slings an arm tightly around his neck. If it wasn't for the look of terror on Dan's face, you'd think they were old buddies the way Kurt greets him.

"Where do you think you're off to?" Kurt grins at him, "The boss wants to have a little chat with you."

"What about Jen and Ty?" I ask.

"They're next door with Axel. He is partial to a slice of chocolate cake and apparently your wife makes a decent one," he tells Mitchel.

"The best," Mitchel confirms. "I'm going to check on them, you got things here?"

I nod, and he disappears with Grant following to check on Tyler.

"Make yourselves known before you go storming in there, if he thinks you're a threat, Axel will lash out first and ask questions later," Josh calls. He turns to Jackson, "Sorry about your security systems, we had to disable them to prove we could get in before Daniel agreed to show. I'll make sure they are up and running before we leave."

"I shouldn't bother. If they were that easy to take down, they need replacing," Jackson growls.

"In that case, let me give you my card." Josh fishes around in his pockets but comes up empty. "Just call Mac, she'll arrange a time for us to come round if you want us to."

"Mac?" Jackson looks at me, and I realise I've never introduced the two men.

"This is Josh, my neighbour in Hollywood and the guy Mac works for."

"In that case, I want to shake your hand and thankyou for saving my sister earlier." Jackson extends his hand and Josh shakes it. When Josh goes to release his grip. Jackson doesn't let him go, instead he gives him a hard stare. "Dan hit my sister. I can't let you just wander off with him before I've had a chance to have a little chat with him about that."

"You can and you will," Josh tells him firmly. "While I commend your loyalty to your sister, you've a wife and a baby to take care of now. All I've got is a gunshot wound and a grudge. Trust me to have the chat on your behalf."

Jackson thinks for a second before releasing his grip.

I sidle up to Josh and whisper, "What exactly is going to happen to him?"

Josh claps me on the back. "Don't you worry your pretty little head about it. Daniel and I are going to have a little talk about the perils of playing with firearms," he looks at Jackson fleetingly, "and the consequences of hitting people's sisters. Then he'll have a few days to repent and recover, before I help him sell any remaining assets he might still own. Any money we raise will be transferred to his ex-wife, since he won't be needing it where he's heading. After that, I'm going to hand deliver him to the local police station where he will likely be charged with at least two counts of attempted first degree murder. As he'll barely have a cent to his name, I doubt that he'll make bail, but, on the off chance he does, one of my team will be waiting to put him up at their place until he comes to trial. Hopefully he'll get life. If he doesn't, or if he makes parole, Kurt and I will be at the gate, waiting to welcome him home and celebrate his release. Whatever happens, you can relax as you won't be seeing him again after today, I can promise you that."

"Can I ask for one more thing?"

"Shoot."

"You wouldn't be able to stop by Mac's mother's office and get him to sign the divorce papers since she doesn't know where to send them, would you? I'd like to start planning my wedding."

"Am I invited?"

"Guest of honour."

"Can I bring Kurt?" Josh smiles amiably.

"Don't push your luck." I grin back.

"Consider it done," Josh laughs. As we hear the voices of Mitchel, Grant, Jen and Tyler approaching, Josh claps his hands together. "Right, let's get this show on the road. We need to get out of here before the others come out to see what's going on. It wouldn't do for my queen to see me without my crown."

I huff out a laugh. Josh circles his index finger like a helicopter in the air, and seconds later everyone in his team has disappeared, taking Dan, who is still locked in Kurt's vice like grip, with them.

"I don't believe we got around to having our dessert." Mitchel announces as soon as he is in range.

Relieved that the ordeal is over, and that we all came through it unscathed, everyone tries to get back inside the house to relax. Unfortunately, Jacob has followed Jackson's instructions so well that we are left stranded outside for another two hours before someone finally hears our banging and manages to get past him to let us back in.

We couldn't have been more proud.

Chapter Thirty-Two

A fter dealing with the curveballs recently thrown in our direction, we quickly find our way back on track, allowing life to return to blissful normalcy.

I'm concerned about how Mackenzie, Ava, and Tyler will react to going back to the apartment in Hollywood after their ordeal. However, I soon realise my fears are unfounded when I suggest selling up and finding a new place in the area. Mackenzie insists she will feel safer staying across the hall from Josh rather than anywhere else in the city. I have to agree; having Josh living opposite is reassuring, even if the apartment won't be our main home. Whether we are there or not, I know he will keep an eye on the place for us, and despite recent events, I have to admit the building does have better security than most.

Josh proves true to his word, and after spending a couple more days at Jackson's place, when we return to the home we evacuated, we find it has been restored to its former glory, with no evidence of the devastation we left behind. He also manages to 'persuade' Dan to sign the divorce papers like I asked him to. I know it will be a few months before everything is finalised, but I'm ecstatic that we've managed to get the ball rolling. I want to marry Mackenzie as soon as she is free, although I'm terrified that she will need a lot of convincing before she is ready to take the plunge again. I get the reassurance that won't be the case when we go for our first ultrasound.

"I'm nervous," Mackenzie says, looking up from where she is lying on the bed. Her stomach is smeared with gel as we wait for the sonographer to return. She excused herself for a few minutes when she was called away unexpectedly, just seconds before she was about to start.

I turn the hand I'm holding and raise it to my mouth, kissing the inside of Mackenzie's wrist. "Why are you nervous?"

"Well, nervous-excited," Mackenzie smiles at me. "I wish Tia were here. I feel bad that she's not."

"You know we agreed to keep things quiet until after this scan. We'll tell her tonight."

"Tell who? What?" Jan, the sonographer, returns with a broad grin. She is a petite woman with a larger-than-life personality. "Forget that. I'm too nosey for my own good. Sorry for the delay."

"It's fine." Mackenzie smiles back at her. "On both counts. We were talking about my other daughter. She'll be so excited to know she is about to become a big sister. I wanted to bring her today but she's at pre-school and we agreed not to say anything until we had the results of this scan."

Jan furrows her brow and looks through her notes, "I'm sorry," she says flicking through some papers, "I thought this was your first baby."

"It is," Mackenzie giggles. "Sort of."

Jan looks to me for help. "I just need to check if your wife is on any medication at the moment?"

I laugh at her confused face. "We're not married."

"But we will be," Mackenzie chips in, "As soon as my divorce comes through."

Jan blinks and looks at me suspiciously. "Are you the father?"

"I am. To both children." I grin like an idiot, and Jan's expression clearly shows she thinks we're both slightly unhinged.

"It's not what you think," Mackenzie pushes herself up on her forearms to see Jan more clearly. "We're not crazy."

"Honey, I'm not paid to think, just to take the pictures," Jan replies, sounding sceptical, as she plonks herself on a stool and rolls it over to sit beside Mackenzie on the opposite side of the bed. She picks up the transducer, but Mackenzie grabs her wrist before Jan is able to place it on her abdomen.

"The CliffsNotes, I married young and he didn't turn out to be a very nice man. So, we parted ways and I only recently filed for divorce so I could marry the love of my life..."

Love of her life? I beam like the sun.

Jan jerks her head in my direction and Mackenzie nods before continuing, "Jared already had a beautiful little girl when I met him. She didn't have a mom and after she got to know me, and I fell in love with her, she asked me if I would like the job. Of course I said yes, and now we are hoping to expand our family."

"Wow," Jan sighs, "That's kind of romantic. Are you hoping for a boy or girl this time round?"

"Either." Mackenzie and I both say at the same time.

"As long as the baby is healthy, we don't mind," Mackenzie finishes.

Jan sniggers as she starts gliding the wand she is holding over Mackenzies body.

"What?" Mackenzie looks at her quizzically.

"Everyone says that, and for the most part, it's true. Parents will fall in love with whatever little bundle of joy happens their way. But deep down, they usually have some kind of preference. "For example, if I told you that you had the choice, if nature wasn't at play, and you got to decide right here and now what you wanted the gender of your baby to be, which would you pick?" Jan looks between the two of us. We both grin and nod at each other.

"After three," I say before I start counting. "Three. Two. One."

"Boy." Mackenzie says.

"Girl." I parrot at the same time.

"Really?" Mackenzie raises an eyebrow. "I thought you'd like a boy since we already have a girl."

"Is that why you'd like a boy?" I ask, and she nods.

"I think it would be nice to have one of each."

"Well, I love the thought of having another little girl who is as sweet as her big sister and looks just like her gorgeous mom. Besides, have you met the twins? They can be a bit of a handful."

Mackenzie laughs.

The sound of a periodic whooshing fills the room and all eyes are instantly drawn to the monitor beside the bed. Mackenzie's eyes fill with tears and one hand covers her mouth as the other points to the centre of the screen. "Is that our baby?"

Jan smiles at her kindly. "It is."

I squint at the screen and point to the left slightly. "Is that?"

Jan looks at me smiling. "It is."

We both look at Mackenzie who is staring at the screen mystified.

"Do you want to tell her or shall I?" I joke.

"Looks like you could both get your wish," Jan tells her.

Mackenzie frowns. "What do you mean?"

"Twins, baby," I smile. "Look."

Jan coughs and looks away as I point to the shadow to the left of the main feature. Suddenly, the colour drains from Mackenzie's face.

"Twins?" She murmurs, a little stricken. "I always thought you were joking when you said it was a possibility."

"Even when I presented Tyler and Jacob as evidence?" I chuckle. I rub her hand soothingly, and stand briefly to lean across and kiss her on the forehead. "Babe, we got this."

She looks straight at me and gives a weak smile. "I thought that was the placenta or something."

"No," Jan points to the screen and waves her hand a bit. "This is the placenta."

"Well, what's that then?" Mackenzie points to the right of the screen.

I follow her finger and frown. Whatever she is seeing is lost on me.

Mackenzie looks at Jan and they have some kind of telepathic conversation, where Jan smiles and Mackenzie's eyes widen like saucers.

"What?" I ask them bemused.

"Do you want to tell him or shall I?" Jan jokes, mirroring my words from earlier.

"Triplets?" Is the last thing I hear Mackenzie whisper, before everything goes dark.

∞∞∞

"I did not faint!" I exclaim incredulously to Ava and Grant while sitting in their kitchen. Mackenzie and I have just returned from our scan to give them the good news. Olivia, the newest addition to the family, is snuggled against my chest. Thankfully, Tia agreed to the name change for Grant and Ava's daughter after clitoris—sorry, Chloris—left a note pinned to her door one night. The note explained that while she was flattered, it could get confusing to have a child running around named after her.

After all, if Ava needed the fairy's help, how would she know if Ava was calling for her or the baby if they had the same name and lived in the same house? "I slipped. Some of that gel she was using must have dropped on the floor."

"You slipped while you were sitting down?" Mackenzie teases. "One minute you were fine and telling me we got this, the next you had toppled off the stool and were lying on the floor unconscious."

I narrow my eyes at her as everyone else laughs.

"It's got me worried." Mackenzie tells me seriously.

"What do you mean? I slipped. It was an accident and it won't happen again. We'll be fine." I tell her panicked. "We're in this together babe."

"Are we?" There's a teasing tone to her voice and she smirks at me, "I think I'd feel happier if I got you locked down before the birth. I've a feeling things are going to get pretty hectic for a while after."

"Really?" I'm overjoyed she is as desperate to get hitched as I am.

"Really."

"What about your divorce?"

"My mom called, she's pushing it through as fast as she can, it should be finalised within the next few weeks. I want to start planning now so we can go ahead as soon as possible," she grins. "While you were resting on the floor after you *slipped*, I found out there's a good chance I could deliver prematurely. So..." Mackenzie bats her eyelashes as she looks at me coyly, "Mr Jones, will you marry me, even though I'm likely to be as large as a house by the time I walk down the aisle?"

"Try and stop me." I lean forward and kiss her, being careful not to crush my new niece in the process. "This wasn't exactly what I had planned, I wanted to surprise you with a big romantic proposal?"

"I think you've given me enough surprises for the time being, don't you?" She smiles and pats her tummy affectionately.

"What sort of wedding would you like?" Ava asks excitedly, "I'd love to help with the arrangements."

"Small. Friends and family only," Mackenzie replies. "I don't want to feel like I'm putting on a show for a load of strangers I barely see. If it's ok…" She looks at me, "I'd like to ask Jack if we can have the wedding at his place, down on the beach."

"Sounds perfect." We gaze at each other tenderly.

Grant pretends to clear his throat, and when I look over, he taps his watch. "Time to pick up the queen. Want me to go get her while you two steel yourselves to break the news?"

"No, it's fine," I hand Olivia off to Grant. "We'll go. We can stop for ice cream on the way home."

"Be careful," Ava draws my attention to her, "Check there's none on the floor when you go in, we wouldn't want you *slipping* over again."

I ignore her and stalk off haughtily to find my keys as everyone else bursts out laughing.

Chapter Thirty-Three

F inally, it's the day of my wedding. It's taken longer than we planned to reach this moment, but every challenge that caused a delay, we faced and conquered, making it even more special. Mackenzie has blossomed and with less than two months left until her due date, she radiates a calm, maternal warmth, her serene presence lighting up every room she enters.

The kids are all off school for the summer vacation, and the whole family has descended back on Jackson. It's handy having Mitchel living right next door. All the men moved into his place last night while the women stayed at Jackson's. I gaze out the window at the weather; the sun is already high in the sky, and there's little breeze even though we are by the sea. I'm wearing grey trousers with a matching waistcoat over a short-sleeved white shirt, and I just know I'm going to melt the second I step out of the air conditioning. With Mackenzie so far along, I'm worried the heat will be too much for her, even though I insisted a temporary pavilion be erected on the beach to protect her during our nuptials. My phone starts ringing and I grab it off the bed, smiling as I answer. I was expecting this call.

"Jerry. How's it going?"

"Fucking fabulous, that's how it's going! I'm sorry I can't be there for the wedding but the phones been ringing off the hook. I don't know how you knew that film was going to be such a hit, but I'm calling to apologize for ever doubting you. Do you know how much money we are raking in?"

"I've a pretty good idea," I chuckle. Even I was shocked when I saw how much my bank balance had increased over the last month.

"They've already started penning the sequel, but the writers are desperate to know if you are willing to get involved. Tamara has only agreed to reprise her role if you do the same."

There's a knock on the door, and Mitchel bursts in. He is wearing a baby carrier strapped to his chest, and his son is screaming his lungs out as Mitchel leaps around like a kangaroo on steroids. I'm not sure if he is trying to soothe him, or if he's auditioning for the role of 'World's Most Hyperactive Dad'." Jackson and Grant follow him into the room.

"One minute Jerry," I say, as I look at Mitchel. "What the hell are you doing?"

Grant sniggers.

Jackson rubs his temple, "Couldn't you have got a louder one?" He deadpans.

"Trying to get him to sleep," Mitchel tells me, before he casts Jackson an unimpressed glare.

"And you think jumping up and down like a jackhammer is conducive to making that happen?" I roll my eyes and when Mitchel stops bouncing, I balance my phone between my cheek and shoulder as I gently lift the baby out of the carrier. He snuggles to my chest and stops crying instantly.

"See, I told you," Jackson tells Mitchel. What he told him I have no idea.

"Wait until he has three to juggle, I bet he'll lose his superpowers then," Mitchel pouts.

I look at Grant who just smirks, and shrugs.

"Sorry Jerry." As peace reigns, I resume my call, "What was that about a sequel?"

"Sequel?" Mitchel's ears perk up. "Is there a part for me?"

"You'd make a good fairy," Jackson smirks at him.

"And you'd make a good troll," Mitchel banters back. "They'd save a fortune on make up since you wouldn't need any."

"Who's that?" Jerry shouts in my ear, "I can hear voices in the background."

"Mitchel Dalton and Jackson Longe," I tell him.

"Crap on a cracker!" Jerry squeals suddenly. It sounds like he is having an aneurism on the other end of the line.

"Jerry? You Ok?" I ask concerned.

"Will they, do it?" Jerry starts screaming excitedly, "Do you know what this would mean? The publicity would be off the charts. We wouldn't need to see a script to know the film would be a sensation. Everyone thinks you and Mitchel hate each other.

Jackson has been out of the business for years, if he were to make a comeback..."

"Jerry, calm down," I try not to laugh. "I'm not making any decisions until I've seen the script, but you can tell them if it's good enough, and the timings right, I'd be interested. I'll have to run it by Mac first, I can't just up and leave for filming when she is about to have three newborns, a toddler and a dog the size of a small pony on her hands." I glance at Mitchel and Jackson, joking, "As for the other two, I'm not sure I could work with either of them."

Jackson smirks again, while Mitchel is obviously affronted, crossing his arms and grumbling, "What? I'm a pleasure to work with."

"Who told you that?" Jackson quips, widening his eyes as he pretends to look surprised.

Grant taps his watch and I nod.

"Jerry, I have to go," I chuckle. "We'll pick this conversation up another time."

"Break a leg. Or whatever one says in this kind of situation," Jerry replies jovially, before he hangs up.

I hand the baby back to Mitchel and clap my hands together as he starts screaming again. "Right let's get this show on the road."

"Give him here." I watch as Jackson takes the baby from Mitchel, and as he starts screaming louder. Jackson holds him at arm's length as he addresses him like an adult. "Tell uncle Jack what you need Zach, but please use your inside voice."

Zach screws his face up and lets out a wail so high-pitched, I'm surprised a window doesn't shatter.

Mitchel and Jackson wince.

"May I?" Grant holds out his arms and Jackson willingly hands the child over. Grant cuddles him close, rubbing his back. Zach quietens immediately.

Jackson and Mitchel look at each other dumbfounded.

"There's two of them," Mitchel murmurs.

"Two of us?" I quirk an eyebrow.

"Baby whisperers," Jackson answers in awe.

"C'mon," I laugh. "Let's not keep your sister waiting."

The beach is idyllic.

The sun-drenched golden sands have clear blue waves rhythmically lapping against the shore. Rows of white chairs are situated beneath a giant open-sided awning, put up to provide the children some shelter from the sun. There's a gap down the centre to provide an aisle which is lined with pink and white flowers. I take my position in the pavilion up front, under an arch trimmed with the same type of flowers decorating the floor, watching as our guests take their seats, impatient for Mackenzie to appear.

As best man, Grant stands beside me. The wedding celebrant joins us and gives a small nod, a string quartet strikes the first chords of 'Make You Feel My Love.' I watch as Tia appears at the end of the aisle. I look at Grant, and we both smile. She is wearing the cutest little pink bridesmaids dress, her hair has been professionally curled, and a garland of pink and white flowers rests on her head. She grins broadly as she walks toward me. She has a small wicker basket draped over her arm, and as she reaches in, I expect her to toss flower petals in her wake. She doesn't. Instead, she covers the path with thousands of tiny, shimmering particles that catch and reflect the light as they fall, creating a sparkling, ethereal effect as they float through the air before landing at her feet.

"Don't worry," Grant whispers. "Ava made sure Chloris provided biodegradable fairy dust for the occasion."

"Of course she did," I chuckle. When Tia reaches me, I crouch down, kiss her on the cheek and whisper, "Good job, peanut."

Before I can stop her, she throws a handful of glitter all over me. "I wish you happy ever after," she squeals joyfully. Our audience giggles, and as I look up, I see Mackenzie approaching on her father's arm. Our eyes lock, and I stand mesmerized as she walks towards me. Mackenzie's dress is simple: two swathes of ivory material cross over her chest to form a V-neck, before gathering under her bust and falling loosely to the floor. It's impossible to hide her enormous bump, but I wouldn't want her to. She's exquisite, even more so because she is carrying my babies. Instead of a bouquet she is carrying the magic wand Tia brought her. It's been decorated with the same white and pink flowers Tia is wearing in her hair. As she stands before me, I can't help but notice the bottom half of her dress is shimmering.

"I see you've been wished a happy ever after too," I whisper.

"I have," she giggles as she takes in my sparkling outfit.

"Like the bridal bouquet," I grin. "It's very... unique."

"Isn't it?" Mackenzie beams at me, "Tia designed it."

We both chuckle as I instinctively place my hand over her swollen belly. "How're you doing?"

"Ok." She looks tired, but glowing with happiness. "I didn't sleep well last night; I had terrible gas pains and my back was killing me. I needed you there to rub it."

I frown subtly as the music stops and the ceremony begins. Tia was supposed to go and sit with Ava after she'd played her part, but she steals the show by standing between Ava and me, holding one of our hands in each of hers. Neither of us mind, it feels right having her with us.

We are about half way through when Mackenzie groans and doubles over in pain.

"Fuck! Babe, are you ok?" I hand Tia over to Grant so I can help the celebrant support Mackenzie.

"I'm fine," she gasps, struggling to stand upright.

"Daddy, you said a bad word." Tia doesn't miss a beat.

I look at Grant who pats his pocket to indicate it's empty.

"Go and see Uncle Jack while Daddy makes sure Mommy is ok." Tia nods and skips off.

"Why me?" I hear Jackson growl.

"Pay the queen," a deep voice threatens. I look up from caring for Mackenzie to see the guest sitting behind Jackson, leaning forward with his arms crossed and his head bent over Jackson's shoulder. Even though I can't quite see his face, I know it's Josh because of his size and the fact that he is the only man wearing a hat for the occasion. He is sporting a bright golden crown made of cardboard wrapped in foil, but he looks rather regal all the same. I can't help but smile. Only Tia could convince him it's a good look.

"You're not fine," I growl at Mackenzie. "What's going on?"

"Nothing." Mackenzie takes a deep breath and forces herself vertical. She looks at the celebrant, "Could we move things along?"

"Babe…" She's as white as a sheet. I want her to sit down for a few minutes to compose herself, and look around for a vacant chair.

"Jared!" She snaps. "Focus. We are getting married."

"What?" Jackson's terse voice sails over to where we are. We automatically look in his direction. "I've given you thirty bucks."

"Price went up." Tia tells him without flinching.

"Since when?" Jackson folds his arms across his chest and looks at her as if he is facing off with an assassin.

"Since I have brothers and sisters in mommy's tummy." Tia tells him, wiggling her fingers in his general direction.

"Don't forget I told you to charge him double," Jaime whispers, as she smirks at her husband.

Jackson glares at his wife and hands Tia another sixty dollars. Tia grins, but Jaime stops her from running off.

"And the rest," Jamie giggles to Jackson.

He harrumphs and hands Tia another thirty. Tia looks at Jaime who nods, before running back to hand the money to Mackenzie.

With nowhere to put it, Mackenzie hands the money to me. I shove it in my pocket and can't resist throwing Jackson a wink. He throws his wife a look that would turn most grown men to stone, but she simply kisses his cheek and whispers something in his ear, which turns his unamused look into a warm, reluctant smile.

"My legs are sleepy; can I go sit with Uncle Jack now?" Tia asks.

"Yes peanut." I tell her affectionately.

She runs off and climbs onto Jackson's knee, making him beam like the cat that has got the cream, proud to be the chosen one. Mitchel and Josh both glare at him.

"Haven't got a crown though, have you?" Josh grumbles in his ear.

I take each of Mackenzie's hands in my own as we stand before each other. The celebrant has just resumed the service when there is a loud pop, and I look down to see a puddle of clear liquid pooling at my feet.

"Mac? Have your waters just broken?"

"No," She barks, as she doubles over in pain again.

"We need to get you to a hospital." I try not to yell, but I'm unsuccessful in my panic.

People rise out of their chairs and start to rush over to help me make Mackenzie more comfortable.

"STOP!" Mackenzie shouts so forcefully, everyone freezes on the spot. "These babies are not coming out until I am married." It looks from her stance she is squeezing her legs tightly closed.

"But..." I start to argue.

"But, nothing!" She pants. "Everyone! Sit. Back. Down!"

People look at each other before they do as they're told.

Mackenzie grabs the celebrant's shirt. "GET ON WITH IT!" She shouts so aggressively his eyes go wide and he immediately starts speaking at speed.

I look at Ava who is on the phone. "Ambulance is on the way," she mouths to me.

"Arghhhhh." Mackenzie screams, and grips my hands so tightly her fingernails embed into my skin. I open my mouth to speak and she silences me with a glare.

"MAC!" Jackson bellows from his seat making Tia jump.

"SHUT THE FUCK UP!" She yells back, breathing in short sharp bursts.

"Mommy..." Tia starts.

Mackenzie's voice softens instantly as she looks over to Tia still sat on Jackson's lap. "I know baby, I slipped, I'm sorry, uncle Jack will pay you."

"He won't," Jackson barks. There's a chorus of gasps, and he looks around apologetically, "I'm out of cash." He looks to Mitchel for help.

"How did I know that was coming?" Mitchel sighs and shakes his head before handing a wadge of notes straight to Tia.

"Continue," Mackenzie orders the poor man tasked with officiating our wedding.

I didn't think the celebrant would be able to speak any faster. I'm proved wrong when he ups the ante and increases his pace further.

We rattle through the rest of our vows and as soon as we are declared as husband and wife, I give Mackenzie a quick peck, before Grant and I each put one of Mackenzie's arms around our necks, and haul her back up from the beach into Jackson's house where we get her as comfortable as we can in one of the bedrooms.

"Where's the fucking ambulance?" I yell at Grant, as I run my fingers through my hair in agitation. Mackenzie is alternating between writhing in pain and stints of controlled breathing exercises.

"I'll go check." He dashes out of the room as Mitchel and Jackson enter.

Mitchel's rolling up his sleeves, "We need to take a look to see how far along she is, as the most qualified here I think I should take a peek."

"Most qualified?" Jackson snorts. "You played a

doctor in a movie... Once!"

"Well, you can't look. It's your sister." Mitchel scrunches his face up in disgust. "That'd be wrong."

"She's my wife. I'll look." I shove them both out of the way, even though I don't relish the responsibility. When Tia was born, I stayed well away from the business end of operations. I haven't a clue what I'm supposed to be looking for, but pride won't let me admit that.

I grab the hem of Mackenzie's dress.

"We don't need an audience!" I bark nervously, stalling for time.

They leave, as Ava arrives, and Grant reappears.

"Where's Tia?" Mackenzie mumbles.

"With King Josh," Ava reassures her. It's then I notice Ava has a mobile phone in her hand. "The ambulance is five minutes away. Mac is it Ok if I take a look so I can relay what's going on?"

Mackenzie nods.

I sit beside my wife and hold her hand, while Grant waits just outside the door in case he is needed. Ava peels back Mackenzie's dress, pulls down her underwear and gasps.

"I can see a head." She calmly tells whoever is on the other end of the phone.

"Babe, how long were you in labour?" I ask, as Mackenzie pants and grunts her way through another contraction. "Why didn't you say?"

"I wasn't sure at first," she whimpers. "And I really wanted to marry you."

I kiss her and she kisses me back before her face

scrunches up in pain once more.

"Ok, got it." Ava puts the phone on speaker and lays it on the bed.

"Mac." Ava looks up at my wife. "The first baby's coming, the professionals will be here any second but until they get here, we're all you've got. Are you with us?"

Mackenzie looks at me, then Ava. She takes a deep breath, squeezes my hand and nods resolutely. "Let's do this!"

Two and a half hours later, our family of three has doubled in size.

And even though I've had to postpone my honeymoon, I feel like I'm permanently covered in glitter, my toddler has forgotten about the letter Chloris left her and wants to name one of the babies after a woman's certain lady part, sleep is about to become a distant memory once more, and I'm stuck at my brother-in-law's house since my car isn't big enough to transport my new family—yep, I ordered the new car seats but forgot that with Tia's, I needed room for four—everything's perfect and I wouldn't change a thing. I'm finally lucky enough to be living my dream life with the woman I adore by my side, someone who shares my passions and brings joy to every moment we spend together.

I guess magic and miracles do exist, and I'm excited to see what wonders the future holds.

Epilogue

✳

"**R**ight." Jacob paces in front of us with his finger hovering over the button on a stopwatch. "I'm looking for speed and efficiency, accuracy, technical proficiency and your ability to adapt whilst using your problem-solving skills should the unexpected occur."

As his words sink in, I can tell Jackson and Mitchel feel the weight of the challenge ahead.

I hear a snigger from the gallery. Mackenzie, Ava, Jaime and Jen are all sat in a line on the couch ready to watch the show as they cheer us on.

Jackson, Mitchel, Grant, Tyler and me are all kneeling before a plethora of giggling babies on changing mats. We are surrounded by everything necessary to facilitate the changing of a dirty diaper. Mitchel has a snorkel and mask resting on the top of his head.

"It's not a fair contest," I moan at Jacob. "You should be down here with us in the trenches. Instead, you've left me with two."

"You should know by now, that one doesn't like getting his hands dirty if he can help it," Grant chuckles.

Jacob doesn't deny it, ignoring his dad as he answers me with raised eyebrows, "If you had one baby at a time like a normal person it wouldn't be an issue, would it?"

"Says the twin! I hope you have quads one day," I grumble. "I can't help it if my wand's packing the extra potent jizz. You'd better hope it's not a trait that runs in the family or else you're screwed."

"Daddy..."

Tia is kneeling in front of us men, right in the centre behind the line of babies. She's the second judge and jury of the whole competition.

"Sorry peanut," I tell her, "I'll pay you after the event."

"Suck it up princess." Grant nudges me with his shoulder as he chips in, "You used to help with the twins, really you've got an unfair advantage the amount of practice you've had over the years."

"As have you," I growl back. "Maybe you should take the extra one."

"Ready Tia," she looks up as Jacob speaks and nods, before leaning forward on her knees and concentrating. Jacob shouts, "On your marks..."

We all adopt the same position as Tia, ready to get started as soon as Jacob gives us the word.

"You know my jizz is pretty potent," Mitchel suddenly pipes up.

"Here we go..." Jackson groans, and we all relax back from our starting positions.

"I'm just saying," Mitchel states matter of factly.

"If my wife wanted triplets, I'd have given them to her. We just decided we'd start off easy."

"We did, did we?" Jen laughs.

I grab the baby powder and squeeze the bottle so a puff of white talc blows all over Mitchel.

"You know, he'll use that as an excuse when he loses," Jackson gripes before imitating Mitchel in a whiny voice. "I had powder in my eye. I couldn't see properly."

We're interrupted by the intercom announcing a visitor at the gate.

"One sec." Jackson gets up to see who it is. He kicks Mitchel lightly with his foot as he stands. "Go and wash your face while I'm gone. I want to win this fair and square with no excuses from you."

"Shall we just takeover?" Ava calls, "The poor things will have developed nappy rash in the time it's taken for you lot to get organised."

"No." Everyone shouts in unison.

"It's Josh." Jackson calls as he re-enters the room a few seconds later. "He has come to upgrade our security systems."

"That's what he thinks," I state forcefully. "Move over a bit Grant, he can take one of mine."

Grant sniggers, "Good luck with that."

I go to meet Josh at the door and clap him on the back. "Hey buddy."

Josh eyes me warily. "I hate it when you use that tone. What do you want?"

We walk back into the living room just as Mitchel is using a baby wipe to clean his face, and Jackson is resuming his position on the floor.

He looks at the two empty spaces and doesn't need to be told what I'm about to ask him to do.

"No way," he starts backing out of the room with his eyes wide. "I've never changed one of those in my life."

Then it's about time you learned," I joke, grabbing his jacket from the back and using it to propel him forward.

"Na ah, not doing it. It's not fair on the kid," Josh squirms out of my grip.

It seems I'm going to have to employ some dirty tactics to get Josh to help. With a mischievous grin and an overzealous pout, I call out, "Tia, King Josh doesn't want to play our game."

One distraught look from my eldest makes Josh fold like a pack of cards, even if I get a death stare while it happens.

"Just copy everything I do," I whisper when we are in position.

"I can't believe I took a gunshot for this family," he whispers back dramatically.

"Ready Mitch," Jacob calls. Mitchel puts his snorkel in his mouth and pulls the mask that has been resting on the top of his head down to cover his face. Once it is in a comfortable position, he gives Jacob a thumbs up.

"Why is Mitchel wearing a snorkel? Do I need one?" Josh asks in a panic tone.

"No," I laugh, "Apparently, he wasn't quick enough changing his son once and he got a bit of pee in his eye. Caused quite the drama from what I understand. You're in charge of Lexi, she doesn't have Zachs aim. You'd only have to worry if you were changing Ben, but Tyler's taken him, and because he's far tougher and braver than Mitchel, he's adamant he doesn't need to wear any armour."

"I heard that," Mitchel mumbles around his mouthpiece.

"You were meant to," I call back.

Josh nods but still doesn't look happy. In fact he looks terrified.

"Finally!" Jacob groans. "Everyone ready?"

"No!" Josh grunts.

"King Josh!" Tia addresses him sternly.

"Yes." He reluctantly changes his answer.

Tia gives Jacob a firm nod and he starts the event. "On your marks... Set... Go."

The next five minutes would give a chart-topping comedy a run for its money at the box office.

We hadn't bargained on Jacob mixing up the diaper sizes, or substituting two full bottles of baby powder with empties. That was without Zach deciding to set off his sprinkler midway through the proceedings, Tia's dog running away with the baby wipes, and the triplet in my care, Charlotte, taking a noxious dump right after her old nappy had been removed, and before her new one was in play. The stench stuns everyone.

"What are you feeding her?" Josh's bulging eyeballs look like they're about to shoot out of his skull as he tries to hold his breath for an extended length of time.

"Toxic waste. I reckon." Jackson looks just as green as he replies.

"You can't help it, can you baby?" I coo at my daughter, who blows bubbles at me affectionately.

"If that shit burns a hole in my floor, you're paying." I look up to see Jackson is talking to Tia not me. "It's coming out of that college fund I've been financing, and yes, I'm well aware that I now owe you for saying 'shit'. Twice!"

Tia just giggles, even though I'm pretty sure he is being serious.

"I told you I needed the mask," Mitchel tells his wife after the activity finishes. He comes in a solid fifth place behind, Tyler, Grant and me—joint second—and Jackson in that order. Poor Josh comes last since his diaper doesn't stay on for more than a second after his baby is lifted from the mat. I think it was to be expected from us all.

With the children back in the care of their mothers, the twins and Tia. The 'menfolk' head outside for a post-match analysis and to reward our efforts with a beer.

"So, how's things going?" I ask Josh, while Mitchel and Jackson are off to one side, squabbling over whose diaper-changing technique is more effective. I haven't seen him since the wedding a few weeks ago.

"Good." He takes a slug from the bottle of beer he is holding. "Although Kurt wants to know when Mac will be back at work. So do I for that matter, he is scaring off half my new clients."

"I don't know," I chuckle. "You'll have to ask her. She might want to leave completely now she's had the babies. They're a round the clock job in themselves at the minute."

"Please tell me you're joking," Josh looks mortified. "Do you think she would reconsider jacking it in if I paid her double."

"Probably."

"I'll have a chat with her before I leave. Although, just so we're clear, there's no pressure for her to rush back, and I've made sure she's all set to work from home. She can do as little or as much as she wants. Even if she only agrees to stop Kurt from bitching in my ear an hour a day, and a year from now, I'll be happy."

"I appreciate that." We tap our bottles in understanding.

"There is one more thing though." Josh side eyes me.

"Go on."

"It's nothing really," I watch as he squirms uncomfortably on the spot, picking at the label on his beer bottle. "I'm getting married."

"What?" I splutter, trying not to choke on my drink.

"Cool your jets, it's a marriage of convenience for a few months at best. She's so not my type and the sister of one of my buddies."

"I'm not sure I understand."

"I can't really tell you much, but a buddy I know

has got himself into a spot of bother and I've agreed to help him out. His sister will be moving into my apartment for a while. The marriage thing," Josh gives a deep sigh and shakes his head in amazement, "I'm still not really sure how that came about. Anyway, I won't be home a lot over the next few months, so she'll have the place to herself most of the time. I was wondering if you could keep an eye on her when you're around. She doesn't know anyone from this neck of the woods, and you'd be doing me a solid if you or Mac could stop by once in a while to check she's alright. She's the total opposite to Jimmy, the quiet sort—from what I remember she buries her head in a book most of the time. I'm pretty sure if I didn't tell you she was there, you would have never noticed."

"This trouble your buddy is in. Any chance it could find it's way to my door? I won't put my family at risk."

"If I thought there was even the slightest chance of it, I wouldn't ask, I swear."

"This woman, is she better than you at changing diapers?" I joke.

"Dude, everyone is better than me at changing diapers," he laughs.

"I can't argue with that."

"If she's not from around here, where's she from?"

"Vermont, initially. But I haven't seen her since she was thirteen. She was always hanging around, crushing on Kurt, until we left to join the SEAL training programme at eighteen."

"I didn't realise you'd known Kurt that long."

"Yeah, Kurt, Jimmy, and I go way back. It's the only reason I've agreed to help Jimmy out. We all grew up in the same neighbourhood, and the plan was for Jimmy to join the SEALs too. They declined his application on medical grounds and he didn't take the news well. His life took on a different trajectory after that. Maeve is the only family he has left. She washed her hands of him long ago, but he's still scared someone might go after her to get to him. He thinks if she marries me, it will make anyone think twice about messing with her."

"I can see that logic, but you're not reassuring me here. What if someone does come after her? I can't have my family getting caught in the crossfire."

"No-one will. I promise you. This is all purely precautionary. Kurt and I have done some checks and we can't see any imminent threat to Jimmy, let alone Maeve. He won't tell us what's got him in such a tizzy until we see him in person. If I think there's any cause for concern after that, I'll get her a new identity and set her up somewhere else."

I raise my hand to cut him off. "I don't think I need to know any more. If your certain it's going to be safe, of course I'll help out."

"Cheers." We both take a draw from our bottles then clink the necks again.

"Just promise me if there is even the slightest whiff of any trouble headed in my direction, you'll let me know immediately."

Josh nods.

"So, when's this wedding taking place?"

"Next week, and she'll be moving in straight after."

"And how does your bride-to-be feel about suddenly having to move across the country to marry the friend of someone she used to crush on, someone she hasn't seen in thirteen years, and in order to protect the brother she wants nothing to do with?"

"I don't know," Josh sighs heavily again. "I'll tell you after I've dropped the bomb, and she's had the chance to find out."

If you skipped the dedication at the
beginning as many people do:
Thankyou for choosing this book to
read.
I hope it made you smile, please
pass it along for someone else to
enjoy.
If you're able, please share a
review on Amazon, a fun pic on
your socials:
#anovelchallenge,
or simply try one of the other
books
in the series.
Any one helps more than you
know!

Thankyou.
D

P.s. Keep 'em peeled for Kurt's story
landing with a bang 2026!

Books In This Series

Healing Hearts Series

If you enjoyed reading Jared and Mackenzie's story, find out how Jaime first crossed paths with Jackson in Healing Hollywood Hearts, or why not take a peek into Meeting Mitchel's Match for Jen and Mitch's story?

Like Lovin' 2 Leading Ladies, both books can be read as a standalone and are also available from Amazon.

Healing Hollywood Hearts

Single, charismatic and hot enough to melt your flame-retardant panties with a single smile. Hollywood's latest export is in the UK to promote his new movie.

Mitchel James Dalton! I never expected to meet him, let alone become the envy of millions when live on national television, he proved he was every inch the hero his adoring fans expected him to be by rescuing me from the most humiliating experience of my life. I should be thrilled when he tracks me back to my hotel room desperate to see me again. But a searing encounter with a stranger more scorching than the coffee he ended up wearing, means Mitchel has competition. One man has a hidden agenda, the other is hiding a dark secret. Both have been burned by betrayal.

Can I save them both from the ghost that is haunting them? If they can help me survive going on the run with a fairy, a boss that's probably looking to fire me, two pint-size mischief makers and the snakes that are lurking all around, I owe it to them to try. I'm determined to find them their happy ever after, I just hope I don't have to sacrifice my own in the process.

Meeting Mitchel's Match

I never thought my best friend would open his heart to love again after a getting burned by a betrayal that scarred us both. Yet here I am in Las Vegas, all set to cheer him on from the sidelines as he prepares to walk down the aisle. Agreeing to be his best man was the easiest decision I've ever had to make, especially since it brings with it the added bonus of 'accidently' being able to bump into the bride's best friend.

I'm rich, charming, popular and handsome. If you don't believe me, just ask one of the millions of fans that flock to see my movies as soon as they are released. You'd think Jen would be pleased to see me, and may have even been a little grateful, especially after I swooped in to rescue her from a cheating ex hell bent on humiliating her in public.

OK, so it didn't all exactly go to plan, which is probably why I now find myself naked and stranded outside of her hotel room in sin city. She isn't like the usual women I leave in bed the morning after a single tryst. Life would be so much easier if I could keep my distance. But then again, easy is boring and overrated, not to mention the fact that right now, that girl has got to pay!

A standalone romance featuring a guarded playboy, a broken-hearted heroine and the twist of fate that puts them back on the path to finding love again.

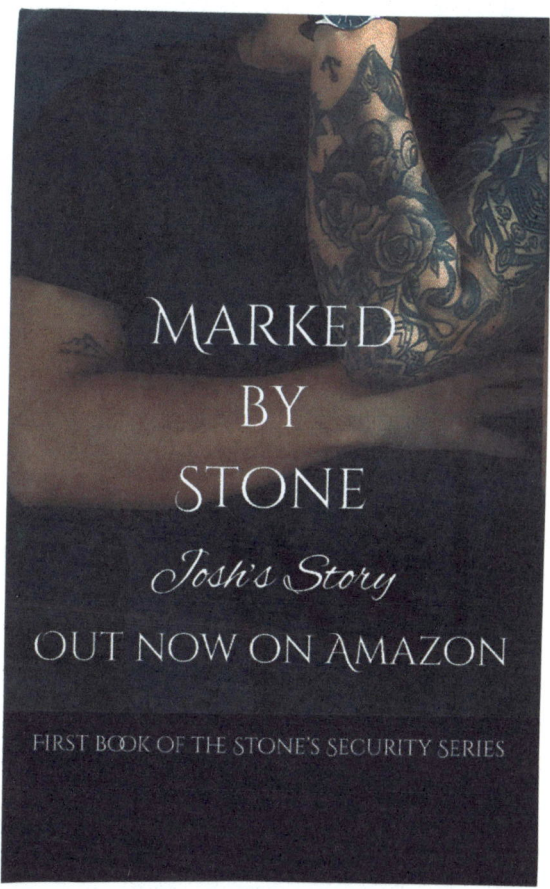

MARKED BY STONE

Josh's Story

OUT NOW ON AMAZON

FIRST BOOK OF THE STONE'S SECURITY SERIES

Printed in Great Britain
by Amazon